Evangelynn Stratton

# Lady Knight

# Lady Knight

Book one of

## The Lady Trilogy

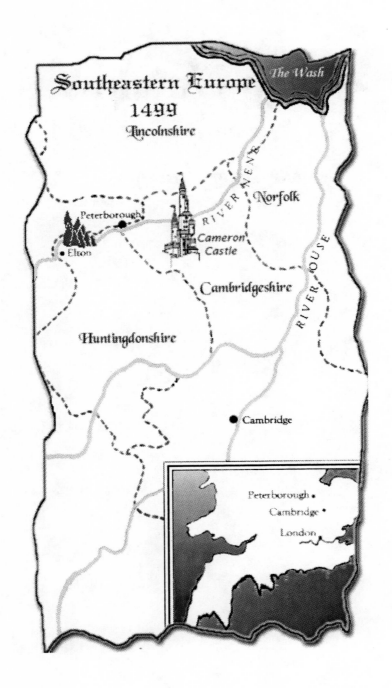

# Lady Knight

## Evangelynn Stratton

## Writers Club Press

San Jose New York Lincoln Shanghai

# Lady Knight

Writers Club Press
an imprint of iUniverse.com, Inc.

For information address:
iUniverse.com, Inc.
5220 S 16th, Ste. 200
Lincoln, NE 68512
www.iuniverse.com

evangelynn@knightimes.com

Cover art and editing by StormKatt Productions©
StormKatt.com
PO Box 88799 Seattle, WA 98138

ISBN: 0-595-09838-X

Printed in the United States of America

*To my daughter Mélanie, who believed in me and convinced me never to give up.*

# Acknowledgments

I wish to thank:

All my friends who offered to read the unfinished projects (one chapter at a time); my horse, Charger, who was my sounding board and captive audience; my daughter Mélanie for all her help and support in editing and creating the cover graphics; and my Lord and Savior Jesus Christ for giving me hope, strength, and talent.

# Some terminology used

*Aquamanile*: A water pitcher of bronze, gold, or silver used for washing.

*Demesne*: Land held in possession for one's own use.

*Destrier*: "Great horse" used for jousting.

*Girdle*: An ornamental belt for emphasizing the waistline or hip curve.

*Great Sword*: Two-handed sword, also known as the broad sword.

*Manor*: Estate consisting of lord's demesne and tenant's holdings.

*Palfrey*: A well-bred, easy paced mount used for travel.

*Prioress*: A nun at the head of a priory or nunnery.

*Solar:* Noble's bedchamber.

*Steward*: Chief official of an estate.

*Sumpter horse:* Horses that carried baggage for travel.

*Tourney*: Short for tournament, mock battles for entertainment value.

*Villein:* English term for serf.

# A little background history

Henry VII (of England), often called Henry Tudor (1457-1509) king of England (1485-1509) and first ruler of the house of Tudor, fits predominately in this story. In 1485, at Bosworth Field in England, he met and defeated Yorkist king Richard IV, who had seized the throne from the Lancastrian Henry VI in 1471. Henry Tudor was subsequently crowned Henry VII in London. In the following year he married the Yorkist heiress, Elizabeth, eldest daughter of Edward IV, uniting the houses of York and Lancaster and ending the Wars of the Roses.

After his accession, Henry had to contend with several Yorkist uprisings, notably one led by the English impostor Lambert Simnel. My character Gideon believes that he works for this man. Who he really works for will be revealed in the next book in this series, LADY SEER.

I hope you enjoy LADY KNIGHT, both for its story, and for the history of this tumultuous era. I incorporated facts into the story to make it more realistic for the reader.

Elton was a real medieval village, and the story of Dacus and Aetheric is true.

# Prologue

White Tower, London
July, 1499

King Henry Tudor carefully looked over his royal guard, his next decision a crucial one. His gaze fell to one man, Matthew Cameron—son of his longtime friend Baron Lander Cameron. Henry had to inwardly admit he had a soft spot for this handsome young knight, whom he had personally knighted on the battlefield during the fight for the crown.

"Sir Matthew! Step forth!"

Matthew knelt before his king. "I am here for your bidding, your majesty."

"I wish to speak to Sir Matthew alone." He dismissed the other disappointed knights, whom had all harbored hopes of being chosen for this important mission.

"Arise, Matthew." The knight stood up and grinned at his king, the two being close friends through his father's relationship.

"Matthew, I am putting you in charge of finding these renegades, and stopping them. I trust you shall not disappoint me."

"I shall do my best, Sire, although I fear your over-confidence in me is unfounded. Perhaps an older, more experienced knight…"

The king waved off his comment. "Now, Matthew, spare me your modesty, we both know your bravery has been proven."

Matthew turned his gaze downward with a sheepish grimace. "Aye, Sire."

"You shall take a regiment to the last known position of these raids, I believe upper Lincolnshire. Notice has been sent to all lords in the vicinity to gather their men and join you. I want these raids stopped."

"Do we know why this is happening, Sire?"

Henry shook his head, his mouth pinched into a tight frown. "Who knows? They strike unmercifully, killing even women and children whom happen in their path. Then they disappear like ghosts."

"And their leader?"

"No one has come forward with a name. We only know he rides a white horse and is ruthless." His tone dropped to one almost pleading. "Please, Matthew. They must be stopped. I am counting on you."

The roguish blond knight nodded complacently; it would not do to argue with the king. "Aye, Sire."

"Excellent, you will leave first thing tomorrow." The king paused, then in a more solemn tone added, "and, Matthew…please attempt not to get distracted this time. I expect you to report back, in person, within the month. Do I have your word?"

Matthew's smile faded. "Aye, Your Majesty." He bowed and took his leave.

As Matthew turned, he was thankful the king couldn't see the look of trepidation on his face. What the hell had he gotten himself into this time? He quickly headed back to his room, where a willing chambermaid lay waiting. It might be a long time before he would have access to the favors of another woman.

# ❧Chapter One❧

### England, summer of 1499

et smelled the smoke before she saw it. She urged her mare to a gallop, maneuvering through the narrow forest trail until she crested the hill overlooking her village. Reining her horse into an abrupt stop, her heart pounded with dread as she beheld the horrible sight. Flames rose from several burning huts, and she heard the screams of terror and clanks of steel against steel. Terrified villagers ran for their lives; a few stood to defend their homes. She drew her sword and kicked the horse down the hill to protect her town, even if resulting in her own death.

A townsman with a bleeding gash across his face staggered up to her. "Pet! Praise the saints you are here!"

"Where is Robert?" She leapt off her horse as the man collapsed to his knees.

His breaths came in short, shallow gasps. "I know not...too many...there are too many..."

She helped him to his feet. "Take my horse and flee. I must find Robert."

"But..."

"Do it!" She pushed him up on the horse and slapped it on the flank. The injured man clung to the mane as the animal lunged forward and headed back to the forest out of danger.

An arrow whizzed past her head as she raised her sword for battle. A formidable foe, she killed two renegades before they even realized she was there.

She silently wished she had chosen to go with her father.

The irony of the situation was cruel. The king had ordered all faithful followers to take up arms against the renegades, and Pet's father had

1

complied. He took her two older brothers and most of their men to hunt the outlaws. Now Pet's village was suffering for that decision. The renegades had never struck this far south before, so the village was not prepared. Now Pet fought for her life and those of the townsfolk.

Another arrow barely missed her. She swung her sword around in time to parry an attack from behind. Within two maneuvers, her sword pierced the man's heart. Before he died, the man's eyes expressed astonishment he was about to meet his fate at the hands of a girl.

The village fought gallantly, but the renegades fought without mercy or compassion. Pet heard the hopelessness in her people's cries, and strengthened her efforts. She yelled for her people to get inside the manor walls to safety. Many obeyed, but the strong stayed to fight. A wayward arrow grazed her shoulder, and she winced in pain. Two more fell by her sword.

The renegades were unrelenting. One on horseback rode too close, and she reached up and pulled him off. On horseback she would be able to spot Robert easier. After mounting, she searched frantically. She brought down two more before she finally saw him.

He fought three at once. Pet urged the frightened horse toward him, reaching him just as an outlaw was about to plunge a knife in his back. She kicked the man in the face, effectively stopping him. Robert looked up at Pet and smiled widely.

"Hello, baby sister!"

She smiled back at her twin; she was a whole minute younger. "Thought you could use the help."

He nodded, and then their exchange was cut short as she let out a scream from an arrow piercing her upper left arm.

He shouted out her name in alarm. She brought her right hand up and grabbed the shaft of the arrow, snapped it short, and threw the rest on the ground. "I am all right," she winced.

"No, ride! Get out of here!"

"I cannot leave you!" She leaned forward and reached out with her uninjured arm. "Get on behind me." As she spoke, a man came up behind Robert with his sword raised. "Robert, behind you!"

Robert spun around and stopped the thrust barely in time. Two more men approached, heading toward Pet. "God forbid, Pet! You are no good dead. Get out of here!"

She saw the men at the same time she felt the weakness wash over her from the pain. Robert was right; if she passed out and fell off the horse a sword would surely strike her down. "I will get our men!" She reluctantly reined the horse around and turned toward the manor.

"The wench!" a man yelled. "Get the wench!" Two men on horses started after her.

"No!" Robert screamed, and plunged his sword into the man who gave the order. He didn't see another man on horseback come up behind him.

Pet heard him scream, and reined up only to see Robert get struck down by a silver-haired man on a white horse. Her outcry of horror rang over all the fighting. The silver-haired man turned his gaze on her; a look of controlled hate consumed his smug face. Pet committed his image to her memory.

The two riders bore down on her. Not knowing if Robert was dead or alive, she hastened her horse away at a full gallop. The men reached her side in minutes and tried to grab her reins, but she maneuvered skillfully out of their grasp. They blocked her entrance to the manor, leaving the forest her only retreat. The horse's hooves pounded the soft ground as she pushed the weary animal to its limit. Suddenly her horse lunged forward and dropped to its front knees. Pet went tumbling over the horse's head as she realized the bastards had shot the horse out from under her. The arrow had pierced the horse's shoulder—the animal would live—but didn't hinder the fact that the two men had dismounted and were heading straight to her. No time to worry about a horse, she quickly grabbed her sword and readied herself for battle. She would not die without a fight.

Their biggest mistake was only two men were sent to stop her. They quickly realized they were no match for her fighting skills. Her first thrust disarmed one man, and while he scrambled for his weapon she turned on the second. He was ugly and dirty, with black rotting teeth and the stench of a dead animal. She grimaced in abhorrence.

"You cannot beat me," she stated flatly. "Put down your sword and I will spare your life."

The man sneered lewdly at her. "Now, you art a right pretty lil' thing. A whit too vicious forasmuch my likin', but others like their woman with a whit 'o spunk. That body of 'ous looks like t'was made for beddin' a man."

Her lips curled into a hateful sneer. "Then, die." In two moves she disarmed him and drove her sword in his heart.

The other man had recovered his weapon, but was now reluctant to use it. When she turned to face him, he dropped to his knees and threw his sword at her feet.

"I don wan'to die! You would'na kill an unarmed man, would you?"

Pet rolled her eyes; she hated it when a man suddenly turned to cowardice to save his life. "Pick up your weapon and fight like a man!"

"No, just go away." The man lowered his head and refused to look at her. Disgusted, she shook her head, and began to leave.

The minute she turned, the man grabbed his sword and descended on her. Expecting this, she spun, brought her right leg up and kicked him in the chest. He stumbled backwards as she knocked his sword from his hand with another kick. They stood eye to eye, her with a cold, vacant expression, him with total fright.

"You-you cannot kill me," he stuttered. "I am unarmed."

"We have already been through that." She drove her sword into his abdomen; he fell to the ground with a loud cry of anguish. Gazing without compassion at the bleeding man—lying, thieving, murderers deserved to die—she watched as he clutched his belly in despair. "Now bleed to death like the dog you are." She ambled away, satisfied he would never help burn another village.

The horses had scattered except for the wounded one. It was on its feet and shaking with fear and pain. Pet approached the mare and calmed the injured animal in her low, soft, mesmerizing voice. "'Tis all right, girl, you shall be fine." The horse responded to her gentle touch.

Her only thought now was Robert. Her gaze fell to the village, by now just small wisps of gray smoke on the horizon. She had no choice but to walk back. When she got closer, it was clear the renegades had departed, leaving behind a fear-ridden, smoldering remnant of the once peaceful town. Scattered bodies of the murdering outlaws lie everywhere; human debris Pet would later order tossed in a pile and burned. She learned from a townsman that her father's men had finally made their way down from the manor, and were chasing the renegades toward the west. Sir Raymond the giant, the estate steward and master at arms, led them.

Her eyes blinked with irritation from the smoke as she searched for Robert. People cried in dismay around her; she pushed through them in her hunt for her brother. She finally found him, surrounded by four townsfolk trying desperately to tend to his wounds. He drifted in and out of consciousness as the life drained from his battered, bleeding body. A pretty young villein girl sat beside him gently stroking his hair; his head was in her lap. She looked up at Pet with huge tears streaking down her ash-covered face.

"He saved my life," she sobbed. "He was wounded, and still he saved my life."

Then they all relayed stories of how a man on a white horse left Robert for dead, and how he had killed several more before finally succumbing to his injuries. The loyal townsfolk surrounded him and didn't allow anyone through. Sir Raymond had arrived just minutes later, driving the renegades away.

Pet knelt and looked lovingly at the face so mirroring her own; deep brown eyes, straight nose, and fair skin framed by ebony hair. Robert was considered remarkably handsome. He had his pick of women, but so far had refused to take one as his bride. But he was only twenty, and there was plenty of time to marry.

His eyes flickered open for a few seconds. "Baby…sister," he gasped. "You are safe."

"Aye, thanks to you." She choked back her tears; Robert would not see her cry.

His eyes slowly closed again, and Pet scanned the area around her. A small hut nearby had escaped the torch. She put one hand under Robert's head, and the other under his knees. Even though he outweighed her by fifty pounds, her powerful legs enabled her to lift him up. The people parted as she carried him to the hut. The pain in her heart dwarfed the pain in her arm.

Two children huddled in the corner as Pet kicked the door open. She laid him gently on the bed, and turned to the small children. "Lord Robert is injured."

They came forward and stood beside her, watching Robert's face as she helplessly tore off his doublet to check his wounds. The boy tapped Pet on the arm.

"I can get some water," he offered.

Pet allowed herself a small, brave smile for the child's benefit. "That would be good. Take your sister with you." The children left her alone to tend to her brother.

"Robert, you will be all right, 'tis but a small wound." She kept comforting him as she finished removing the clothing around his wounds. Some were small, survivable, but the wound the man on the white horse inflicted was mortal—he had thrust his sword through Robert's back, piercing the liver. Pet's heart fell to her stomach when she realized the inevitable.

He opened his eyes and saw her expression. "Pet," he whispered, "I am not going to make it."

She again produced the brave smile. "Hush, what kind of talk is that?" The boy returned carrying a bucket half-full of water. She tore a piece of the bedding cover and dipped it into the water, then wiped Robert's face with the cool liquid.

"Pet, you know 'tis true." His voice broke as he writhed in pain. "Listen…I want you to have Goliath."

She vigorously shook her head. "Goliath will only let *you* ride him. Besides, you are going to be fine. You just need…"

"Pet, do not shake your head so," Robert gasped. "It will only make your brains rattle." His eyes closed, and his face contorted in pain.

She managed to cough a small laugh. Even in death, he teased her.

"That's my girl. You are going to be in charge, now." He wheezed as blood trickled from his mouth.

In desperation, Pet threw her arms around her dying brother. "You cannot die, Robert. I cannot live without you." She buried her head in his shoulder.

"Aye, you can," was the weak reply, "…and you shall. The people need you. Take," his voice broke. "Take care of them." His breathing was getting shallower. His eyes opened again. "Do not cry for me, Pet. Death cannot separate us. I shall always be with you." He grabbed her arm with a surprising amount of strength. "As long as you are alive, I will be also." It was practically a command.

She raised her head from his shoulder, and kissed him gently on the cheek. "I love you, Robert."

"I love you too, my beautiful Rose. Some day someone will find you, someone who shall love you as much as I do." His hand let go, and he heaved one last breath. His eyes closed forever as his body gave up its life.

"No!" she screamed. "No, no, no, no, no!" She threw herself across his body and pounded the bed with her fists.

Outside the hut, the villagers heard her cries, and exchanged looks. The men lowered their heads, and the women and children began to cry. Their beloved twins were no more. It was if every one of them had a piece of their lives stolen from them.

Within minutes, Sir Raymond rode back into town and saw the villeins gathered around one small hut. He reined up and jumped off the huffing animal. A man looked at the giant with tears welling in his eyes.

"'Tis lord Robert," he uttered. "He took a sword in the back."

Raymond's face went white, and he stumbled backward from the shock. "Pet?"

The man motioned to the hut, and Raymond nodded. "Let them be alone," he ordered, and sat down on the ground. The rest of the waiting villagers sat also, staring at the hut entrance as if in a trance.

She stayed with him for over an hour, during which she experienced a gamut of emotions. At first there was denial, then anger, then she bargained with God to take her instead. Finally she began to relive their entire life in her numb, grief-filled mind.

They had been inseparable from the beginning. They were born small, their health further compounded by the death of their mother from the complicated births. A wet nurse was finally found, and they began to thrive. As toddlers, they preferred each other to all other company. It was Robert who gave her the nickname Pet—from the age of six, she refused to be called Rose. One day Robert called her Pet, and the name stuck. She wanted to be exactly like her twin. If they put her in a dress, she became distraught and tore it off. Her father obliged her because he loved his twins with all his heart; besides, the twins looked so adorable dressed alike as little pages.

When Pet was eight, an incident involving her older brother Geoffrey resulted in the smaller Robert getting beaten in a feeble attempt to defend her. The incident caused the twins to turn to Raymond for help, and he became their self-appointed guardian. He suggested they learn to fight to defend themselves, and they took up the challenge like a personal vendetta.

Being somewhat diminutive, they were determined their smallness would not defeat them. Together they worked hard to build muscle; they ate voraciously to gain weight and grow. By the time they reached ten Robert had passed her on weight and height, so she worked harder and ate even more. Sword training began at twelve. At first it was all Pet could do to lift the heavy weapon, but through her stubbornness she prevailed. Her muscles grew with the intense exercise, but she filled out in other ways Robert didn't. She became quite a beauty, but denied that aspect of her being. Her hair was cut short, and she dressed only in men's clothing. Romance didn't interest her; fighting and getting stronger seemed to be her only passions. By the time she was sixteen she had already broken many hearts with her cold indifference.

The twins decided early in life not to exhibit the terrible tempers they saw on their brothers—especially Geoffrey—and learned to control their anger, along with other emotions. They were considered quiet and chose their words carefully, sometimes going whole days speaking only to each other. The twins trained hard together; they became skilled fighters while their siblings seemed interested only in women and drink.

At fifteen Robert decided to dress entirely in black, and Pet readily agreed. They preferred soft leather pants to the tight hose well-dressed Lords wore. Their entire wardrobe—boots, coats, pants, tunics—were made especially for them. With their black hair, short on Robert, shoulder-length on Pet, they bestowed quite an image. They were The Twins; they would always be together.

Now she was alone.

She had always denied her womanhood, so it was curious why Robert in his dying breath had acknowledged it. *My beautiful Rose,* he had said. She gazed down at his face, leaned over and kissed him for the last time. "Goodbye, Robert," she whispered. One tear threatened to run down her cheek, and she quickly brushed away its existence. Robert had asked her not to cry, crying was weak, and she was strong. Controlling her emotions was important to Pet, and right now she was experiencing the biggest test of that ability. She clenched her jaw and exited the hut.

The waiting villagers, what was left of them, stood up as she came through the door. In a tone totally lacking in emotion, Pet lifted her chin to keep it from trembling.

"Robert is dead."

Everyone averted their eyes to the ground, the sky, each other, anywhere but on her, for although her voice hid her pain, her eyes could not. They all felt her grief. Raymond approached her and looked her over warily. Robert's blood—as well as her own—spattered her body. She refused his comfort and just motioned toward the hut. "Bring him to the manor. He will be buried in the family plot. Gather the townsfolk and find digging tools; we have work to do."

He started to speak, and decided against it. Grief overcame her to the point he doubted she would hear him.

Pet's emptiness consumed her. She was driven forward only by the need to bury her agonizing heartache. She knew the village now looked to her for guidance. The dead outlaws were separated from the townsfolk. They took the bodies of the villagers to the church cemetery and the renegades were tossed into a pit outside the town. The numbers of the dead overwhelmed the town priest, Father Samson, but he made himself busy conducting simple blessings on the bodies and consoling the survivors. By the time night drew near the villagers were exhausted, but Pet still pushed them on. Since many of the villeins were burned out of their homes, Pet ordered everyone inside the large stone manor house since it had escaped any damage. Gardens and stables surrounded the manor, and a high wall protected it. The great hall was large enough to accommodate the weary people, and anyone with an ounce of energy left set to work in the kitchen preparing food for the hungry throng. While they were eating, Pet and a few men searched the smoldering village for pallets, cots, blankets, or anything suitable to sleep on. Pet's endless drive wore out everyone. Finally things started to settle down. Except Pet.

She sat at her family's table surrounded by at least a hundred people, feeling more alone than she thought humanly possible. It was as if she were violently ripped in half. She and Robert were a unit; together they made a whole. Now Robert was buried in the family plot with old ancestors. As she sat lost in her grief a hand tapped her on the shoulder.

"Lady Rose?" Only one person got away with calling her that, her old nursemaid Agatha, who had cared for the twins since the day they were born. She was the closest thing to a mother Pet had.

Pet turned her head wearily and looked into Agatha's tear-filled eyes. Robert had been like a son to Agatha, and Pet knew her grief was almost as deep as her own. "I am all right, Aggie, go to bed."

Agatha held out her arms. "You art not 'all right' any more 'an I am." Pet stood up and fell into her arms. They hugged for a long moment, and then Pet pulled away. Agatha wiped her tears, noticing Pet had none. "There's a matter 'at needs your attention, Rose."

Pet sat back down and stared straight ahead, too numb to think. "And what matter would that be?"

"The orphans."

Pet raised her head. "Orphans?"

"Seventeen of 'em to be exact. We dinna want ta further burden you, henceforth I hast been watchin' after 'em. What do you propose we do with 'em?"

Pet sighed deeply. Orphans. Another burden to address. The village would have to be rebuilt; long hard work was ahead of everyone. It would be all they could do to look after their own children, let alone watch after seventeen orphans. If only her father was back—he would know what to do.

She rose slowly; her strength felt drained. "Show me." Agatha led her to a corner of the huge room where two rows of children were sleeping. They ranged in ages from one to ten. A few coughed, no doubt from inhaling the smoke, but otherwise seemed undamaged. Their faces were as dirty as their clothes. Pet's first thought was a bath was in order.

"See that clean clothes are found for them." Pet turned to leave when a small, deep cough caught her attention. Pet squinted to make out the small face of the baby who made it. Her face fell in recognition. "Oh, no, not Mary."

"'Fraid so," confirmed Agatha. "Her mother took an arrow in the back. Poor lil' thing's by 'erself now."

Pet closed her eyes. One more death to personally contend with. Mary was the baby of Robert's best friend, Lewis, who had died in an accident soon after Mary's birth. Robert and Pet took Lewis' wife, Jenny, into the manor, giving her a job and somewhere to stay. Now Jenny was dead and little Mary was just another orphan. So much death. So much waste.

She climbed the stairs, stopping once to look down on the scene below. People lay shoulder to shoulder; some cried, some soothed, but all were in a confusion of loss. As she made her way down the hall, Pet stopped in front of Robert's room. She pushed the door open and grim reality struck her as she realized he would never be back. She entered and shut the door behind her, and was instantly overwhelmed by the solitude. His bed still sat unmade from that morning when they had discussed who was going to set the fur traps and who would dig the new well. Robert wanted the well job, and Pet capitulated, even though she hated trap duty. If she had stayed instead of him, maybe she would be in that cold grave and he would be mourning her. She lay down on his bed. His scent still lingered. Her eyes burned with hot tears, and she blinked them back.

"I shall not cry, Robert," she whispered. "I will make you proud of me." She closed her eyes and in moments fell into an exhausted sleep, her clothes still stained with Robert's blood.

## ❧Chapter Two❧

et awakened before dawn; her muddled mind fought awareness as she recalled the day before. She glanced around and remembered she was in Robert's room. At least here she still felt his presence.

As she sat up, she realized every muscle in her body hurt. There were several gashes needing attending; she barely remembered receiving them. She desperately needed a bath, but right now a clean change of clothes would do.

She crossed the hall to her room and took off her torn and bloody clothes. The arrow quickly made known that it still pierced her arm. She ripped off her sleeve to expose the arrow, and inspected the wound. She'd had worse. It missed the bone, and her muscles would heal.

With her hand firmly against the broken shaft, she gave one strong push and the arrow came out. A grimace was the only emotion she allowed herself. She washed the wound with some cold water still sitting in yesterday's aquamanile, and wrapped her arm with a strip of cloth. Then she put on a sleeveless tunic and clean pants. Her bare, muscled arms would shock a stranger, but to her people it was a common sight.

Pet washed her face and hands as well as she could, and hazarded a look in the mirror. She looked terrible. Downstairs people were stirring, babies were crying, and others prepared food. Pet went directly to the kitchen and told the overwhelmed cooks to do what was necessary to feed the townspeople. The storerooms were full, so there was no reason for anyone to go hungry.

Next she went outside to check the building supplies. There were some planks, some mortar, and lots of tools, but not enough to rebuild a town. Trees would have to be felled and dragged in from the forest. So much work for such a disheartened people.

As she stood there surveying the supplies, a strong arm grabbed her from behind and swung her around.

"Hark child! What is this?" It was Raymond the Giant, as he was affectionately known, and he was frowning at her crudely bandaged arm. He was a burly fellow, barrel-chested, rugged and thickset, with flaming long red hair and beard. He had once been a Royal knight, was a bit old-fashioned, and still spoke the King's English. "Didst thou take an arrow?"

Pet simply looked at him without answering. Raymond was almost a second father to her, nearly twice her size, and didn't take kindly to her putting herself in danger. When she didn't answer, he frowned even deeper and insisted on unwrapping the bandage to take a look at the wound.

"This is not good. Why did I not see this yesterday?"

She shrugged. "I was covered in blood."

"Hmmm. Who removed the arrow?"

She pursed her lips and remained silent. A look of exasperation washed over his face.

"Thee?" He rolled his eyes in frustration. "I swear Pet, thou and Robert are…"

He stopped when he realized what he had inadvertently blurted from habit. He pulled her into his large arms. "Ah, Pet, life is intolerable sometimes. Thou art not alone in thy grief. I loved him too, thou knows that. The whole village mourns with thee."

"I know."

He pulled away and again looked at her arm. "Come on, I am going to tend to that."

"'Tis fine."

"Do I hast to pick thee up and throw thee o'er my shoulders?" She simply stared defiantly back at him, or as defiant as one could be knowing full well he could do it. "I thought not. Now, come hither." He took her by her good arm and led her to the kitchen, where he grabbed a bottle of clear hard liquor and poured it over the injury. She winced when the alcohol hit the open wound.

"Had a medicine man tell me once that spirits help heal a cut. Did it myself once on the battlefield. It healed up quite nicely." He re-wrapped the arm and gave the results a satisfactory nod.

"There are orphans, Raymond."

That comment didn't seem to faze him. "There are always orphans after a raid."

Pet was silent for a moment as she stared at the floor. "We have ne'er had orphans here."

"We have ne'er had a raid here."

She nodded, deep in thought.

"What dost thee plan to do?"

She raised her head in surprise. "Me?"

"Thou art in charge here until thy father returns."

She rubbed her eyes. "I do not want to be in charge."

He didn't answer as he gazed on the child he had known since birth. He and Agatha had taken the small twins under their wings and helped them grow into the strong, brave fighters he had witnessed yesterday. Helping to bury Robert was the hardest thing he had ever had to do; his tears had flowed freely last night for his young master. Now he worried about Pet. He knew she would be lost without Robert, so keeping her mind active seemed the logical thing to do.

"Maybe some of the families will take a few," he offered. She raised her eyebrows and nodded. It was worth a try.

She entered the dining hall where people tried to eat the food the cooks had lain out for them. There was a bit of pushing, but for the most part the people were being cooperative. The room grew silent when she stood up on a chair and cleared her throat. She spoke calmly in a low, soft voice, saying more than most people had ever heard her say in their lifetime.

"The town must be rebuilt. You will all stay here until 'tis done. I shall see to it you are all are fed and have somewhere warm to sleep. 'Tis not going to be easy. Everyone will have a job, and I expect they will do it.

Now, we have a problem. There are many orphans. Are any of you willing to assume an extra child? I expect you to be kind to them, and in exchange I promise to give you extra coin."

There was a murmur among the townsfolk, and a young woman stepped up.

"Milady?"

Pet clenched her jaw but held her tongue. She hated being called that, but the woman meant only respect.

"We lost our son last year." She glanced at her husband. "We would be willing to take a boy."

Pet pointed to the corner. "The children are o'er there. Take your pick. Anyone else?"

A few more families came forward, all wanting boys. Pet couldn't blame them; boys were always desirable over girls. It was one of the reasons she hated being a girl. Boys were stronger and could help parents later in life, while girls were a burden and were only good for marrying and producing children. At the end nine children were left, six girls and three small boys. One boy, Andrew, was a cripple, so he was useless to a poor family. When no one else came forward, Pet thanked the families that did and got down from the chair. She made her way to the corner where nine sad, dirty little faces stared up at her. Realizing she probably cast a frightening sight to small children, she kneeled down and produced a small smile.

"Hi, I am Pet."

The children cowered together, bonded by loss and fear.

"Do not be afraid." She observed a small girl who stared at her, and held out her arms. The girl paused, then willingly pressed into Pet's arms.

Andrew, the crippled boy, limped up to her and put a hand on her shoulder. She turned and smiled at him. He stared at her bare arms and timidly ran a thin finger over her well-developed muscles.

"You are strong," he avowed with awe.

Pet smiled. "Aye, I am. I have worked hard to become that way." The boy's face fell with dejection, and she quickly added, "You will be too, someday."

He shook his head. "No, I will not."

"You shall 'ere I train you."

His face lit up. "Oh, would you?" Then, almost as quickly as it lit up, his face fell. "It would help none."

"Certainly it would. I got help from Sir Raymond, and look how big he is." She pointed to the huge knight standing by the food tables. Andrew's eyes grew large as she continued. "And I was small and weak…think of what he could do with you."

Another small girl stepped up. "I want to be strong like you."

Pet shrugged. "You can be, 'ere you want to." All the children started talking at once. Sir Raymond watched this scene with interest. Pet had the children wrapped around her finger within seconds. He smiled as he watched her; his pride in her knew no bounds. She was a survivor.

In a few minutes Pet left the children and ordered a servant to feed them. She strolled up to Raymond and realized she hadn't eaten since yesterday morning. Grabbing a piece of bread, she bit off a piece and nodded to the children. "They will be fine," she assured herself more than him.

"What art thou going to do with the urchins?" He rubbed his beard as he watched the nine children. Little Mary was lost among the bigger children; she sat on the floor looking up at them with frightened eyes.

"First I am going to give them a bath. Then I am going to keep them."

Raymond jerked his head around with his jaw dropped in astonishment. "Thou art going to do *what*?"

"There is nowhere for them to go. I am going to keep them here." She casually ambled away, leaving Raymond sputtering behind her.

"Now, just a minute! I think not…I really cannot believe…"

She abruptly turned around. "What would you have me do, Raymond? Leave them to starve in the streets? I knew each of their parents. Some were friends, some I wish were. Can I just let them all die?" Even when the words she spoke were argumentative, her tone never rose above the usual soft, low timbre.

"Alas, nay, although I think…"

"Good. 'Tis settled." She again turned and headed for the servant's quarters. Raymond's argument was swallowed in the din of the crowd. He stood helplessly by as Pet ordered two tubs filled with warm water—one for the boys and the other for the girls. The servants gave each other puzzled looks. Why would Pet, a Lord's daughter, bother to bathe villein children?

Poor Raymond somehow ended up in charge of the boy's bath, and he swore he finished wetter than them. Pet watched the girls frolic, splash and laugh in delight, supposedly getting clean in the process. It was probably the first hot bath any of the children ever had. Servants helped dry them off, and they gathered clean clothes. In a short time the children stood before her, lined up like a small army except for little Mary, whom Pet held. They were a curious bunch, of all shapes and sizes and colors; some had blond hair, some had freckles; all had rosy cheeks. Pet had memorized all their names by now; Stuart, four years old; Rosie, six years old and named after Pet; Andrew, seven years old; Georgie, four years old; Constance and Cassandra, sisters five and eight years old respectively; Anna, nine years old who adored Mary, and Julie, a very pretty but quiet seven year old.

"What a fine sight you make, "Pet gushed with admiration. They all beamed with pride. Building their spirits was important to her; it helped keep her mind off Robert. "Now, all of you go outside and keep out of everybody's way. Here Anna, you take Mary." She handed the baby to the oldest girl, and then the children ran outside. Raymond came up behind Pet with a deep scowl on his face.

"I still think thou art making a big mistake. Oh, do not give me *that* look."

Pet stared at him with 'that' look, a cold, blank gaze he had grown very familiar with over the years. "'Tis your right to think so." She left to inspect the village, and he shook his head as he watched her go. She carried too much pain and burden for such a short life.

The village was a mess of smoldering shops, but the mill was untouched and all but one field was in good condition. There was still time to plant another crop in the torched west field, so maybe the damage was not as bad as first thought. Once the shops were rebuilt people could almost return to a normal routine.

Pet ordered the women and children to salvage whatever items they found from the burned huts and bring them to the manor's courtyard. The men had the heavier job of tearing down barely standing houses and building new ones. Pet, of course, helped the men. They had learned not to question her ability; she was as strong as most of them and worked harder than them all, even with an injured arm.

The church was also spared, for which Pet was thankful. The people needed something consistent to rely on, and she would insist the Sabbath be observed as usual. Father Samson was sweeping the walk when he saw Pet walking past the church on her way to the manor, located next door.

"Pet! A word!" He hollered after her and ran as fast as his ample figure and short legs would carry him. When he finally caught up, huffing and gasping, he put his hand on his heart and rolled his eyes to the sky. "I must watch the sweets. Terrible for the girth, you know." She waited patiently while he caught his breath. "In my storeroom...I have a nice slab of marble. I was thinking maybe a marker for Lord Robert?"

Pet felt the pain surface again. She hadn't expected to have to deal with Robert's gravestone so soon. "'Tis a good color?"

"Oh, beautiful, beautiful! Come see!" She followed the little priest to his small supply room, where he lifted a cloth that covered a rose-colored piece of shiny polished marble. Pet nodded acceptance and turned to get away before her emotions took over. Father Samson covered the stone and followed her.

"I hear there are orphans."

She stopped, and then nodded. "Aye. Nine of them."

"I heard Mary..."

"Aye." She again tried to walk away.

"I might be able to help with the orphans."

She stopped again. "Howbeit? You are no nursemaid."

"Oh, no, no, not me," he chuckled, "Lord knows I am no good with children. No, I meant I know someplace they can go and be cared for."

Pet shook her head. "I am keeping them."

"But…" His voice trailed off as she approached the gates to the manor. Without warning, a panicked chicken suddenly flew up in her face, almost knocking her backward to the ground. She stood in unnerved silence at the sight before her.

Chaos reined throughout the courtyard. Chickens ran everywhere, laundry lay scattered on the ground, and the children ran with wild abandon while barking dogs and harried servants chased after them. When Agatha saw Pet, she stomped up to her as fast as her old legs could carry her.

"You 'ave got to do somethin' 'bout these urchins of yours," she exclaimed with exasperation. "They've been terrorizin' the whole courtyard all mornin'!"

Pet didn't alter her expression. "I see."

"First they let all the cows out in the field. Whilst we were gatherin' all them, they broke into the hen house and let all the chickens loose. We are still roundin' 'em up."

Pet raised an eyebrow.

"And as 'ere that wa'ent enough, they tore down all the linen from the clothes lines and ran around pretendin' they could fly."

Pet raised the other eyebrow.

"They are wild, I tell you! The servants are run ragged, they are, they 'aven't had time to make the beds!"

Pet watched the children running around without a care in the world, not having to attend to chores, just being children having fun. She sighed. This would never do—she had to help rebuild the village; she couldn't be nursemaid all day to nine children. Maybe in a few months, when things settled down…

She looked back at Father Samson, still standing in the road. She hurried back to him.

"Where?"

He took up the conversation as if it had never stopped. "There's a nunnery in a town not far from here. My sister, the Prioress, has started an orphanage for the children left alone from these terrible raids." He shook his head. "Awful thing, these raids. I pray they catch them."

"They shall." Pet began considering her options. This might be perfect; somewhere to store the children while the town got rebuilt. The little priest babbled on, describing the orphanage in great detail while Pet worked out details in her detached mind. She could take them there, come back, get things settled here, and by then her father and brothers would most likely be back and she would no longer be in charge. Then her father could deal with them. Aye, this was perfect. She interrupted the priest in mid-sentence.

"Would you write me a letter in your own hand to present to your sister, as an introduction?"

Father Samson was actually silent for a few seconds. "Why, certainly, certainly. That would not be a problem." He chuckled again. "My sister is a Sister. I find that so amusing."

"Very funny."

"Aye, well, I shall get busy on that letter. Whom are you going to get to take them?"

"Me."

"You? Milady, do you think that wise? The people here need you."

"The children need me more." Without a further comment, she turned back to the manor.

She rounded the children up, and upon discovering they were all filthy again ordered another bath. It would be their last one for quite a while. That kept the servants and the children busy while she gathered provisions for a journey. She needed to bring horses capable of carrying small children, so a trip to the stable was necessary.

She wanted to keep the livestock to a minimum. She would ride alone, and a sumpter horse would carry supplies and extra weapons. If the children rode tripled up, she would only need three gentle horses. Suddenly she had a shrewd idea as she viewed her nephew William, her oldest brother's bastard, who was brought to live with them in the manor when his mother abandoned him. He had plans to be a great knight, and could always be found with the horses. He was twelve, old enough to help her with nine unruly children.

"William, would you like to accompany me on a great adventure?"

He turned away from the horse he was currying, and smiled widely when he saw Pet. He adored her, as most did, because she was always kind to him when his father sometimes was not.

"What kind of adventure?"

Within minutes she convinced him into going with her. He didn't hear much past the fact he got to ride his own horse and carry his own sword. Robert had been training him to be his squire, and Pet promised she would carry on in his honor. Now there was the small task of picking a horse for herself.

Her favorite palfrey was in foal, so a long trip would not be advisable. Her father and brothers had taken all the other really worthwhile horses. She examined the wounded mare that took the arrow, and was confident she would survive. One by one, she visited each stall and checked out each horse for the journey. She avoided one stall. Goliath, Robert's huge warhorse, stood nervously pawing the ground. Pet finally resigned herself to the inevitable. She strolled up to the stall and reached out her hand, petting the giant brandy-colored horse on the neck. He was a magnificent animal; presented to Robert by the Baron of Avebury himself.

"You miss him too, do you not?" she professed to the fidgety animal. He immediately calmed down. "He told me to ride you. What do you think?"

The horse nickered, and Pet smiled affectionately. "Well, we shall see." She untied his rope and backed him out of the stall. His size instantly overwhelmed her. "By the saints, you are big," she muttered. She slipped his bridle over his head and led him outside to the courtyard. A groom saw her, and turned white when he realized what she was about to do.

"Milady! I meant, Pet, uh…you do not mean to ride Lord Robert's…"

"He is mine now," was her soft reply. "Robert told me to ride him."
She patted the huge animal. "He will not hurt me."

"But…"

"Help me up."

The groom's eyes grew wide. "Bareback?"

She gave him an icy glare, and he knew better than to argue. He
made a step with his hands, and Pet skillfully hoisted herself up on
Goliath's back.

The horse pranced forward, nipping at the bit. His long, flaxen mane
blew softly upwards; his tail swished in nervous anticipation. "So you
want to run, do you?" She led him to the gates. "Let us see what you can
do." She let up on the reins, and the large animal instantly went into a
gallop. They rode through a meadow at a full run; she felt the horse
relax as he became used to her skill. She was one with the animal as she
maneuvered him into circles, changing the leads of his feet, testing his
readiness. Robert had trained him well.

She rode back to the courtyard and dismounted. The incredulous
groom took Goliath away for a rubdown. As Pet watched him prance
away, she barely controlled the urge to smile with the knowledge she
was able to ride him. Until that day, Goliath would only let Robert on
his back. Her inner smile faded with the realization she had never *tried*
to ride him before. Could it be she always had that capability?

She sat down with Sir Raymond and plotted the trip. The town of
Peterborough, where the nunnery was located, was about thirty miles
away, a day's ride for one man on horseback traveling fast. Taking nine
orphans, William, five horses and a sumpter horse would be much
slower, and that was if no unforeseen problems arose. The trip by the
road would take almost three days; through the forest trail following the
river, however, would only take two. Pet opted for the forest.

The children were excited about their 'adventure'. Andrew was a little
afraid, as he had never ridden a horse, but Pet assured him he would be
fine. She even promised he could be the one up front and hold the reins.

Pet sent the children to bed early. She stayed up late preparing for the
trip, as they would leave early the next morning. Sir Raymond would

take over the building duties until she returned, or her father and brothers arrived.

Father Samson came over that night with the note introducing Pet to the nunnery, and a messenger was sent ahead to make ready their arrival. Pet again slept in Robert's room, but this time after a long, warm bath. She convinced herself to fall asleep, not knowing what fate had in store for her the next day.

# ❧Chapter Three❧

ir Matthew Cameron, eldest son of Baron and Lady Cameron of Cambridgeshire, shifted his weight in the saddle, weary from riding almost six days straight. The knowledge he was near the river crossing where he would be able to wash and rest drove him forward. Almost there, he told himself. The trail through the thick forest was the shortest route to the main road leading to London. Taking the forest trail had enabled him to take two days off his long trip.

As he rounded a turn, he heard the *whooshing* of the river, and urged his tired horse on just a little faster. He patted his horse's neck, imagining it wanted to rest as much as he did. His mission for the king had taken too long, and was not successful; the renegades he sought after had escaped his grasp. The little side trip in Lincolnshire to visit an uncle hadn't helped his timeliness, but the bath, clean clothes, and fresh horse certainly helped his spirits. A few more days and he would be in front of the king, who awaited his presence.

He saw the riverbank and could almost feel the clean, cool water engulfing his body. He would camp for the night, letting the rush of the river lull his tired body to sleep. His horse could eat grass by the river banks, he would perhaps kill a rabbit or quail for dinner, cook it over a nice fire…

Suddenly he drew his horse up short; the sight greeting him caused his eyebrows to narrow and a frown to cross his face. A young lad, dressed entirely in black leather, blocked his path. He stood with his legs apart and arms folded, ready for a confrontation. Matthew sized the adolescent up quickly. He was undoubtedly the son of a noble—possibly a squire—judging by his clothes, and stood about five foot seven inches. Thigh-high boots and custom made leather tunics were not prevalent attire for a common lad his age. Multiple weapons adorned his body. A great broadsword was sheathed behind his back; a lighter sword adorned his side. Each booted leg held several daggers. The lad had raven-black hair draping over his shoulders, a bit long for Matthew's liking, and an unnerving gaze. His dark brown eyes stared with no fear; Matthew couldn't detect any emotion whatsoever in the expression. He was a handsome boy, however, with a fair face Matthew had no desire of bloodying. If fact, the lad was extremely comely.

Matthew winced at the broadsword. If the lad could use it, he might be in trouble. Then, with a chuckle, he had to remind himself that *he* was a king's knight, not some young whelp out to impress people with an array of weapons he most likely couldn't use, and conjured up his most authoritative voice.

"Step aside lad, I have no wish to pummel you!"

The boy stood firm but didn't draw his weapon.

"I said, step aside, boy! I am Sir Matthew Cameron of the King's Royal Guard." He hoped that would impress this insolent pup. It didn't.

"It would not matter 'ere you were the king himself." The lad's voice made Matthew pause; it was soft and steady with the same unnerving lack of emotion as his expression. Perhaps a little high for a lad that had passed puberty.

Matthew began to dismount. "Now see here, lad…" The great sword was drawn so quickly if Matthew had blinked he would have missed it. He put his sword hand up in submission as he finished his dismount.

"Look, son, I am hot, tired, hungry, thirsty, and badly in need of a bath. I have no desire to run you through." When the lad didn't answer, Matthew let out a sigh of annoyance. "I simply want to camp here for the night. Certainly that is not too much to implore?"

"You cannot stay. Mount your horse and leave, Sir Knight."

Matthew decided a re-evaluation was in order; he studied the impertinent lad a little more carefully. The young man held the heavy broad sword with calm, steady hands. He obviously was well muscled for his age and size, and had already exhibited agility and speed.

Matthew wondered if he might have misjudged the lad's ability, and perhaps was in for more of a fight than he had bargained for. Perhaps some diplomacy was in order.

"There is plenty of room for us both, boy. Let us set up camp together; I would welcome the company."

"I would not." The stony gaze didn't waiver.

Matthew heard a snicker, and noticed for the first time a young boy standing behind and to the right of the lad, looking entirely amused. Matthew failed to see what was so funny.

"Very well, so there are two of you. I would still welcome your company."

"Mount your horse and leave Sir Knight." The broad sword lifted a little higher.

"Surely you do not mean to fight me, lad. I am older, bigger and stronger; you stand no chance against me." There was another giggle from the younger boy, but this time Matthew ignored him. "I do not wish to strike you down."

"Nor I, you." The lad in black gripped the sword tighter and crouched in a fighting stance.

"By God's bones boy, is this worth your life?" Stony silence was his answer. He decided he would have to teach this young whelp a lesson. "Very well, you leave me no choice but to draw my weapon." He still hesitated, half expecting the lad to stand down, but he didn't yield.

"Draw your sword, Sir Knight. I will not strike an unarmed man."

Matthew carefully drew his great sword from the sheath across his back. A great, or broad sword was a heavy weapon, and it took much skill to use it. It delivered a more powerful blow to your opponent and caused considerable damage when it connected. That is, if you could use it skillfully. Matthew had never really mastered it. He wondered why the lad had chosen it; he didn't think it would be the weapon of choice for a young man his size.

He readied himself for the fight, figuring he wouldn't hurt the boy, just disarm him and let a little wind out of his sails. Confronting a knight was not a smart thing to do, and he aimed to teach him that. He took a deep breath. "I will not strike the first blow."

"Very well." The lad charged at him with adept speed. Matthew barely blocked the blow, and was shocked at the amount of strength behind the strike. He had not been up against a formidable opponent in months, and he quickly realized this lad would put his somewhat limited skill to the test. A second blow was delivered, then a third, and Matthew marveled at the swiftness and expertise the lad exhibited. When Matthew finally delivered his first offensive strike, the youth parried and returned it with unsurpassed speed.

"You fight well, lad." Matthew liked to exchange banter during his encounters; sometimes it threw his enemy off his concentration. That was not the case this time.

"I expected more from a king's knight."

Matthew felt his pride crumbling. "I shall try not to disappoint you further." All right, inasmuch as this boy wanted a fight, he was going to get one. He struck a forceful blow and it was deflected expertly, as expected. Matthew barely jumped out of the way of the riposte.

The youth swung around and executed a hit, catching Matthew on the arm. A rip appeared in his shirt, and blood eased out the gash underneath, contrasting boldly against the white shirt.

"I draw first blood," the lad baited, with a slight hint of satisfaction in his voice.

Matthew glanced down at his arm, and a flush of anger washed over him. "By the devil's arse boy, 'tis not a fight to the death!" He ducked again as a powerful thrust missed him by inches, taking a four-inch gash from the tree beside him. He did a double take at the tree, then at the lad who was readying for another strike. The reality suddenly hit him. The boy meant to kill him, and he just might succeed! He dropped to the ground as the sword came down, rolled away and leapt back to his feet.

"Are we here to chop trees, or to fight?" he taunted. His limited experiences had taught him an angry opponent was usually one out of control. Now, if he could make this lad lose his temper...

"Do you yield, Sir Knight?"

Matthew laughed. "Yield? You jest, son. I have only been toying with you." The lie sounded convincing enough; surely that would make him angry.

"Then I suggest you start fighting."

Matthew wished he had never opened his mouth. He fought for his life as he defended himself against the fiercest rally of blows he had ever had the misfortune to experience. Never had he been forced to fight so hard; this lad was not good, he was incredible. Matthew prayed to live through the fight so he could befriend the youth.

Somehow he was maneuvered so his back was to the river. Realizing he was not in control of the fight, he simply defended himself. A strike ripped his pants, but didn't draw blood; so far not one of his blows had touched the lad.

Suddenly an undercut struck his sword, and he lost his grip for just a few seconds. It was all the time the skilled lad needed. With one strong upward hit, Matthew's sword flew straight up, paused for a millisecond in midair, and then plopped in the water directly behind him. He swung around and gazed in astonished silence at his sword lying on the river's floor. Then he felt the point of cold, hard steel on his back. He raised both hands in complete surrender, and slowly turned to face the lad.

"Surely you would not kill an unarmed man o'er a campsite?" Funny how the only thought he had at that moment was how fetching the lad was. No man should be that pretty.

The lad lowered his sword, but kept his controlled, steady gaze. "I suppose not." They stared at each other for a moment, and then the boy glanced behind Matthew at the river below. The corners of his mouth turned up slightly. "I do recall you saying you needed a bath?" With one quick move he brought his leg up and kicked Matthew backwards, knocking him off balance.

Matthew let out a whoop, and tried to steady himself from falling. He felt himself start to give way, and reached out for anything to stop his fall. The only thing he found was the front of the lad's tunic.

"Let go," the boy demanded, and pushed him again. Matthew was not about to let go. If he was going in, the lad was going with him.

There was a loud ripping sound, and Matthew felt himself fall abruptly backwards over the edge. He plunged into the river, landing with a large splash that accompanied his yelp. As he sat sputtering in the waist-high water, he glanced at his hand to find the ripped tunic still in his grasp. He raised his eyes slowly to see the 'lad' standing on the bank, dripping wet from the splash, with the most exquisite pair of perfect, firm breasts he had ever laid eyes on.

"You are…you are a…a *girl!*"

Pet jumped down to the water and grabbed her torn garment out of the stunned knight's hands. She covered her nakedness with the ripped tunic. "I should have run you through when I had the chance." She left Matthew sitting in the river, mouth agape, his pride totally shattered and his manliness destroyed.

The younger boy laughed heartily and jumped into the river, offering the fallen knight his hand.

"My name is William. Are you hurt, Sir Matthew?"

Matthew let the boy help him to his feet. "Only my pride, boy." They tromped up the bank, where Matthew sat on a fallen log and proceeded to take off his boots and pour out the water.

The clearing was suddenly alive with what seemed like a hundred children; they surrounded the bewildered knight with a barrage of questions.

"Are you a *real* knight?".

"Have you met the King?"

"May I ride your horse?"

"Where is your armor?"

"Can I touch your sword?"

"Did Lady Rose beat you?"

"Are you going to marry her?"

As the children continued their bombardment, Matthew couldn't take his eyes off the naked back walking toward a packhorse. Lord, it was a beautiful, muscular back that tapered into a small, firm waist without an ounce of fat. Not soft and flabby, like most ladies he had pleasured. Her hips were small yet well shaped. And those legs! Her thighs rippled as she walked, and Matthew realized he had too much to covet at once. She opened a pack and pulled out some sort of garment; it looked like a vest. She slipped on the sleeveless tunic, tied the front, and finally turned around. He then noticed the reason behind her surprising strength—firm developed arms many men would envy but find undesirable—women were supposed to be rounded with plump bellies for childbearing. Matthew found her uniquely exciting. The mere fact that she could strike him down with one blow made him desire her. One arm had a bandage wrapped around it. He frowned to think she had fought him with an injury. His curiosity could no longer stand the suspense, and he turned to William.

"Who is she?"

"You have been bested by the Lady Rose Boulton," answered William, with a large smile. He lowered his voice to almost a whisper. "Although I would not call her that, 'ere I were you."

Matthew remained fascinated as he watched her remove a short bow and a quiver of arrows from the packhorse. *Boulton.* Why did that name sound familiar?

"I think you made her mad," William continued, "but with her 'tis hard to tell. Do you always end fights by ripping your opponent's clothes off?"

Matthew felt his face flush. "That was an accident."

Pet then sauntered up to rescue him from the children. "Leave the knight alone. Go gather firewood for our supper." She turned to Matthew as the children scrambled off. "I trust you will live, Sir Knight?"

"My name is…"

"It does not matter what your name is. You shall not be here long enough for us to become acquainted." She glared at her nephew. "William, what are you smiling at?"

William quickly straightened his face. "Nothing."

Matthew stood, and bowed. "Whether or not you want to know, my name is Sir Matthew Cameron. By what name should I address you?"

"None, since you will not be here to call me anything."

A child ran by and nearly knocked Matthew over. "Are all these children yours?"

Pet glowered at him with a look that could cut stone. "Absolutely. I started breeding when I was five."

Matthew felt his blood rush to his face and turn burning red. "I meant, are all these children in your care?"

She tested her bow and nodded.

"Are they villein children?"

"They are children. 'Tis all that is important." She started to walk away.

Matthew started after her. "I meant no offense! Where are you going?"

"To get dinner."

Matthew grabbed her arm. That is a man's job, let me…" He quickly let go as her icy glare fell upon him. "Er, I mean, why do you not let me help?" He smiled charmingly; at least he hoped it was charming.

Pet looked him over. From the moment she laid eyes on him, she knew he would be trouble. He was handsome enough, she supposed, if you cared for wavy dark blond hair, deep blue eyes, high cheekbones, straight white teeth, and an adequate muscular build. Not that she had noticed. She had not had to use one-fourth of her skill to beat him, and was shocked when he ripped her tunic off so abruptly. No man had ever laid eyes on her naked body. She knew her body was not feminine; this ill-mannered knight was probably laughing to himself of how ugly she was. No matter. He would soon be gone, and her embarrassment with him.

"I need no man's help. William, see that the knight is safely on his way." She turned and swaggered off.

Matthew was in no hurry to go; he had to know more about this enthralling woman. He lifted up his barely bleeding arm. "But I am wounded!"

She paused without turning. "The cut is not deep."

"How do you know?" Matthew argued. "You are not the one bleeding to death!"

She sighed loudly with exasperation, turned around and ambled back. "Let me see." He held up his arm and she ripped the shirt open to expose the small cut. He looked at her with a large smile; he liked having her tend to him. He had a feeling not many men had that privilege. Her hair caught in a soft breeze, and errant tendrils blew freely about her face. The urge to reach out and run his fingers through the thick, soft mane was almost unbearable.

"'Tis as I said; the wound is shallow. Had I had wanted to cut you deeply, I would have."

He frowned with the revelation. "You mean you did this on purpose?"

She shrugged as she ripped a piece of his shirt to make a bandage. "You kept dropping your left shoulder. I wanted to get your attention."

Matthew opened, then closed his mouth and glowered. She had certainly done that, all right. The whole time they were fighting she had been analyzing his moves? *Amazing.*

"You are an incredible woman."

"If you say so."

"Again I beseech how to address you."

She simply stared and refused to answer.

"Very well, I shall call you Lady Knight."

She pulled the bandage tight and stood up. "I am not a knight."

"You fight as well as one."

"Better, apparently."

As his face dropped in embarrassment, she felt a tinge of pity. "Very well, since you are mortally wounded you may share our camp. William, keep the children on their task; I want a roaring fire when I get back."

He watched as she took her bow and arrows and disappeared into the woods. Never had he been so fascinated by a woman. William had remained quiet throughout the whole exchange, to the point Matthew had forgotten he was still there.

"She will capture your heart, Sir Matthew."

He sighed deeply. "She has already done so." He stood up and grimaced. "I am soaking wet; I must change clothes. Whilst your lady is gone I shall take my bath."

William chuckled. "I would hurry. It will not take her long to bring down dinner."

Matthew didn't doubt that. She probably hunted as well as she fought. William followed him to the knight's horse, which had found a nice clump of grass and was chewing enthusiastically. Matthew took a clean change of clothes from the bundle tied behind his saddle.

"I was saving these for when I arrived before the king."

"Aunt Pet has a way of altering plans," William explained.

Matthew turned his head around. "Pet?"

"'Tis her, um…nickname." William suddenly changed the subject. "May I attend to your horse, Sire? I am very good with horses."

The knight smiled at the eager boy. "I would consider it an honor." He left William with his horse and went upstream a bit to allow some privacy for his long awaited bath.

A while later, clean, shaven, and wearing fresh clothes, Matthew felt better. Smelled better, too. He hated being dirty, unlike the filthy peasants who seldom bathed and smelled like their goats.

He helped the children build an exceptional fire. They all seemed eager to help him, and even though he had no experience with children he found himself delighting in their innocence and energy.

A while later Pet returned with four rabbits and five quails. She paused when she saw the logs arranged around the fire with everyone sitting around, telling stories and having a great time. The knight was wearing fresh clothes and had shaved. He was laughing with William, who obviously was quite taken with him. She ambled over to the two and plopped the kill at their feet.

"Here. I killed it, you cook it." Before Matthew could protest, she marched off to put away her bow.

William let out a small snicker. "She hates skinning animals."

Matthew picked up his dagger and grabbed a rabbit from the pile at his feet as he muttered under his breath. "All she would have to do is glare at them, and they would gladly jump out of their skins."

As the two skinned, Matthew sought all the information he could about Pet, as William seemed to be a wealth of information. He told Matthew about Robert, the raid on the village, what a brave fighter Pet was, and how she was taking the orphans to the nunnery to be cared for while she rebuilt the village. He learned about Pet's sense of justice, and her loyalty to her tenants. By the time the animals were ready to cook, Matthew understood a little more about the Lady Boulton. As the dinner cooked, Pet's absence was explained as she appeared from her own river bath with her wet hair hanging in streamlets around her face. Matthew drew a breath when he saw her run her fingers through the soggy mop to get the tangles out. She was out of her leather, and was wearing tight hose, a soft wool tunic, and sandals. Her long muscular legs made Matthew roll his eyes; women's legs were his weakness and hers were incredible

An hour later everyone had eaten their fill, and William and Pet laid the smallest children down on bedrolls. It was a warm, star-filled night; therefore heavy blankets were not necessary. Pet held little Mary, who had a deep, croupy cough, until the baby fell asleep. Matthew watched her with extreme admiration.

After the last child had been laid down, Pet sat down on a log by the now-glowing embers of the fire and grabbed her eating dagger. She picked up a stick and began to sharpen it into a point. Matthew approached and watched from behind as she finished one stick, tossed it in the embers, then picked up another stick and started the process again.

He cleared his throat. "May I join you?"

"If you wish." She never looked up from her self-appointed task. Another point went into the fire.

"Those would make good tent spikes," Matthew joked, and only received deathly silence. He sat down beside her, careful not to crowd her as he had a feeling she required her own space. He joined her in the useless pastime, grabbing his dagger and a stick. She paused and cast him a sideways glance when she noticed what he was doing, then continued without speaking. Matthew desperately thought of anything to say to break the ice encasing her.

"William told me about your brother. I am sorry."

She stopped for a few seconds and glanced up at him. Then she lowered her gaze and Matthew felt drawn when he saw a flicker of the pain she held so deeply within her. Then, in a flash, she was back to her task of sharpening points. After they both indulged themselves with the meaningless activity for a while, Matthew finally found the courage to speak.

"May I ask what we are doing?"

"We are making points."

Matthew cringed; well, that certainly cleared things up. He plunged onward. "May I beseech for what purpose?"

"For no purpose, we are simply making points." He couldn't comment to that, so he didn't. She, however, stopped whittling and gazed up at the stars. "Robert always said we needed to do some things in life that had no purpose, so the things we did do on purpose would have more meaning."

Matthew was taken back for a moment. "Robert sounds like he was very insightful."

Pet nodded, and dropped her gaze from the stars. "He was." She paused, and then continued. "Robert and I were always together. He was the only one I really talked to. We would sit around for hours every night, making points, or playing chess, when everyone else had gone to bed. We would talk about everything; no subject was sacred." She tossed a point in the fire, and let out a frustrated sigh. "I know naught why I am even telling you this."

"Perhaps because you need to tell it," he offered, "and I am here to listen."

She threw another point. "Perhaps."

"You miss him terribly, do you not?"

She turned and her gaze penetrated his being. "More than anyone could ever imagine."

He didn't answer or comment. They made a few more points in silence, when Matthew decided a subject change was in order.

"Today, when you met me on the trail, why did you not tell me you were a woman?"

He swore he detected a slight hint of a smile cross her face. "And risk not seeing your expression when you ripped off my clothes?"

"That was an accident; I am sorry. Although, I will *not* say I am sorry for the view you so graciously blessed me with."

The icy stare returned with a vengeance. "You do not have to lie, Sir Knight. I am well aware my body does not possess feminine attributes."

He drew himself up in astonishment. "I would not say that. You have a magnificent body."

"Maybe for a man."

"I find you an enigma, stimulating. You put all other women to shame with your distinctive beauty."

"Pretty words from such a pretty knight. I am not just a simple maiden you can awe."

"I am only too appreciative of that, Lady Knight. To the contrary, I am the one who is in awe." He saw his words pleased her. She was such a contrast from the silly, selfish, giggling females who threw themselves at him over the years. She utterly intrigued him. "William referred to you as 'Aunt Pet.' Is he your nephew?"

"He is my oldest brother's bastard."

"And the name 'Pet'?"

She shifted uneasily. "'Tis a sort of...a nickname."

"Come, Lady Knight, you kill me with curiosity. Howe'er did one arrive with a name like *Pet*?"

There was a long pause. Finally, without looking at him, she answered, "If I tell you, you will laugh."

"I give you my knight's honor, I shall not make merriment at your expense."

She suspiciously studied his face. "Very well, since you are a knight, I will hold you to that." She threw another point in the fire. "When Robert and I were born, my mother died, leaving my father and two brothers to care for two infants. My father gave the task of naming us to my eldest brother William. He decided upon Robert for the boy, and as for me, he thought it would be *cute* to name their baby sister after a rose." She looked up and found him listening intently. "My mother loved roses. She planted a huge garden on our manor. There are roses from all o'er the country in all colors and…"

"You are off the subject."

She glowered and continued. "To shorten a long story, they named me after the petals of the rose. My name is," she rolled her eyes and grimaced, "Rose Petal." She swiftly brought her dagger to his throat. "If you laugh, I will kill you."

Matthew choked back the laughter threatening to erupt from him and shorten his life. He somehow even managed to suppress a smile.

She threw another point into the fire with added force. "I beseech you, do I look *cute*?"

"Oh, no, Lady Knight," he managed to gasp between convulsions of suppressed laughter. "Certainly not cute."

"Robert started calling me Pet, and the name stuck. You may call me that."

"Thank you my lady…er, I mean Pet. At last I have a name to go with your lovely face."

She put away her dagger and stood up. "A long day awaits us. I am going to retire. Good night, Sir Matthew."

A wave of excitement rolled over him at her use of his name. Her soft, controlled voice had such a mesmerizing quality to it; he could have listened to her all night. He stood up and bowed.

"Good night, Lady Pet."

She winced. "Just Pet. I am no lady." She turned and sauntered away.

"Oh, you are wrong, my lady knight," Matthew muttered to himself. "You are more woman than I could ever pray to conquer." He lay on his bedroll and looked up to the stars, his arms behind his head in contemplation. "But I certainly can try." He fell to sleep harboring a smile.

# ❧Chapter Four❧

**S**ir Matthew opened one eye to a pair of smaller eyes staring at him. The child smiled, and he smiled back.

"Hello," he sleepily greeted the small girl.

The little girl giggled and ran away, whereupon Matthew heard another giggle off to his right. He turned his head to see a boy looking him over with vast interest.

"We have been waiting for you to wake up."

Matthew grinned. "Why is that?"

"You are a real king's knight. We might not ever see one again."

"Because you are going to live at the orphanage?" Matthew rubbed his eyes. He was not used to getting so rudely awakened so early in the morning.

"Oh, that is only for a little while. After that, Pet is going to be our new mother."

"What?" He didn't have a chance to recover from that piece of news, as the leaping body of another small child suddenly walloped him in the belly. He let out a loud "*oomph*," and looked to see the little boy who had just landed on his stomach. The child started bouncing up and down, laughing uncontrollably, and Matthew let out loud grunts for the boy's benefit. Another child, a girl with large blue eyes, stood at his feet with a shy smile.

"I pet your horse," she murmured in a soft voice. "He is very nice. I gave him an apple."

"Thank you, *oomph*…he likes apples, *oomph*," Matthew wheezed back between jumps. The older boy began talking again.

"I want to be a knight someday, but I cannot."

"Why not? *Oomph*."

"Because I am crippled." The boy lowered his head in shame. The jumping child leapt off Matthew's stomach and ran away, and Matthew sat up in gratitude until another child crawled into his arms. He looked at her, a beautiful girl with long golden hair, and smiled.

"You are pretty," she said sweetly.

Matthew frowned in mock disapproval. "Knights are not *pretty*. Knights are handsome."

"Lady Pet is pretty."

Matthew laughed sincerely. "Lady Pet is gorgeous."

"Why, thank you."

He jerked his head up to see Pet standing there, a droll look on her usually emotionless face. She was again wearing her leather in ready for the ride, and was holding the baby girl she had rocked to sleep the night before.

Matthew scrambled to his feet. "Howe'er long have you been standing there?"

"Long enough to know you have been sufficiently pummeled for one day. Children, leave the knight alone. He has a long journey to complete." The children all expressed extreme disappointment, but finally did what they were told.

"Thank you," he laughed. "I thought I had met my match with them."

Her eyes sparked for just a second. "I believe you met your match yesterday."

His smile disappeared and was replaced with a sour grimace. "You are ne'er going to let me forget that, are you?"

She didn't answer, just smiled faintly and strolled off. The camp was bustling with activity. The children were eating, William was leading the horses out for some morning grass, and the fire was crackling with a pot of something boiling. Matthew followed after Pet like a lost pup.

"About my long journey," he began. She sat the baby down by an older girl, and handed her a piece of bread and jam. "I would like to accompany you to your destination…to assure your arriving safely."

Pet turned to him and folded her arms; her want of expression made it impossible for him to read her thoughts. "I see."

"I have given it much thought. It would make me feel better; these woods are not safe." He tried to sound commanding and strong. He watched her eyes for any hint of emotion, but her face was blank. Finally she nodded.

"Aye, mayhap you would be safer with me." She strolled away, leaving his pride wounded once again.

"That is not what I meant!" He followed after her, and proceeded to trip over a running child. As he fell forward, a firm hand grabbed him.

"Are you sure?" Her eyes locked with his.

Her face was just inches away, and as she held his gaze he felt his heart pound harder. Her touch made him shudder. She had long, black eyelashes sweeping over incredible almond-shaped brown eyes flecked with gold. He became immersed in her deep stare; it was as if she was reaching inside of him and tearing his heart out through his throat. When she finally released him he felt out of breath and light-headed.

Pet proceeded to her packhorse and began putting on her weapons. As she strapped on her swords, she looked down at her trembling hands. She closed her eyes and clenched her fists. No blue-eyed knight would make her lose control, even if his eyes reached inside her soul and felt her innermost thoughts. What was wrong with her? She was not some silly maiden who swooned over every handsome man who called her beautiful. She hadn't eaten yet; that was it, she was hungry. Control, she must keep control. She sauntered back to the children, grabbed a large piece of bread and began chewing it eagerly. Lack of food in her stomach was not going to make her weak and vulnerable.

They were all packed and ready for travel in an hour. All except for Andrew. Matthew saw Pet kneeling by the boy, attempting to comfort him, and not having much success. As he wandered over to offer assistance, he saw the boy was sniffing back tears and rubbing his foot.

"What is the problem?"

Pet sighed in frustration. "A horse stepped on Andrew, and now he is afraid to ride."

Matthew faced the boy and feigned anger. "What is this? A future knight afraid to mount?"

"It stepped on me," Andrew sniffed.

Matthew laughed heartily. "Lad, if I had a gold piece for every time a horse stepped on me, I would be a far richer man." The boy found no humor in that, so Matthew switched tactics. "Stepped on you, huh? Here, point out this murderous beast to me!"

Andrew pointed to a gentle mare serenely chewing grass as a small girl held its lead rope.

Matthew nodded knowingly. "Well now, there is the problem...the mare obviously knows you are far too brave and noble to be riding an unfit creature such as her, and she attacked you in sheer jealousy. You need a mount more fit for your standing." His eyes twinkled. "How would you like to ride with me?"

Andrew's eyes grew large. "Oh, could I? Oh yes, Sir Matthew, I would like that very much!" He gave the knight a huge hug. Matthew stood up and put his hand on the boy's shoulder. Pet had watched this scene with her usual droll composure, but Matthew thought he detected a glint of gratitude in her eyes.

"Shame on you, Pet, putting this future knight on such a substandard beast!" He winked at her and she slowly smiled, melting him clear down to his toes.

William helped all the children mount, and handed little Mary to Pet. Andrew proudly took his place behind the knight, and finally they were on their way. Matthew soon learned why traveling with ten children could be so time-consuming. Someone had to relieve himself or herself every half hour, or was thirsty, or got bit by a bug and was surely going to die. In two hours they had only gone four miles. Pet noticed Matthew's expression as they rode side by side.

"Starting to change your mind, Sir Knight?"

He managed a glib smile. "I am having the time of my life. After this experience, I can face the fieriest enemy with nerves of steel!" She granted him another small smile.

His eyes fell to the huge horse she rode, a fine animal the color of brandy with a flaxen mane and tail. "That is a magnificent animal. Where did you get him?"

Pet reached down and petted the great horse's neck. "He belonged to Robert."

"I have searched my whole life for a destrier such as that. Howe'er is he in jousting?"

"I know not," she shrugged. "Robert was not a knight. He ne'er had time for useless activities such as jousting."

Matthew ignored her insult. "Pity, he is perfect for it. Might I ride him sometime?"

"He is a one-man horse. He would not let you on his back."

"Did you not say he was Robert's?"

"Aye."

"And yet you ride him?"

"Robert was my twin; we were like one. 'Tis not surprising Goliath lets me ride him."

Matthew felt a trace of envy for the man who so shared Pet's life. He silently wished he could have met Robert before his death; perhaps they could have been friends.

Finally it was time for lunch, and while the children ate and ran out some pent-up energy, Matthew had a chance to talk alone with Pet. She was sitting on a log, holding little Mary, who still had a bad cough and was feverish. Pet dabbed cool water on the child's forehead and held her close, comforting her. She caught Matthew's concerned look as he sat down beside her.

"I am worried about her." He stroked the child's forehead.

"As am I. She does not seem to be getting any better."

"The nuns shall heal her."

Pet laid the sleeping child down. "Let us hope."

Matthew watched as she tenderly stroked the child's head. "You will make a good mother to these children. Andrew told me you intend to come back for them." She nodded. "May I beseech what you intend to do about a father for them?"

"They will not need a father."

Matthew laughed at her impertinence. "So a husband is not in your plans."

"No."

"And what is your objection to marriage, Lady Pet?"

"Nothing, if you happen to be a man. A woman's plight is a different story." She leaned forward on her elbows. "I could ne'er lead the life of a 'Lady', mewed up in a solar all day in a flowing gown, doing needlepoint and gossiping, with a curst and shrewd husband to make demands of me."

"Ah, but marriage offers more than that."

"Such as?"

He shifted nervously at suddenly being put on the spot. "Well, such as children."

She glanced around her at the mob of youngsters laughing and playing games in the small clearing. "Do I look like I have a shortage of children?"

He cleared his throat. "A husband offers protection."

"Am I in need of protection?" She cocked her head and raised her eyebrows, anxiously awaiting the answer.

"Ah…" He racked his brain for another example. "Very well, how about companionship?"

"My horse offers me all the companionship I need. He is there when I need him, does not argue with me, and leaves me alone when I so desire."

He was running out of options. There was only one thing he hadn't mentioned. "Marriage brings other…uh…pleasures." He waited for the inevitable reaction.

"I suppose you are referring to the marriage bed."

He nodded and grinned enthusiastically.

"I have a feeling that brings more pleasure to the man than to the woman."

"It does not have to be that way, if two people are in love…"

"Love?" she jeered. "Love is for fairy tales."

Matthew sobered his smile. "You do not believe in love, Pet?"

"Love is for the weak and stupid. I am neither." Before he could offer his brilliant argument extolling the virtues of love, she stood up and yelled for the children to make ready for departure. In minutes they all were on their way again.

Pet again rode with little Mary in front of her, and Matthew with Andrew behind him. There was not much chance of a conversation until the first relief break. William, harboring a discontented face, joined Matthew sitting in a clump of grass.

"'Tis not much fun riding at the end," he complained, "but Pet says 'its necessary."

"She is right," Matthew agreed. "Someone responsible must always bring up the rear. 'Tis a very honorable position." He watched the lad draw up tall and proud. "Besides, 'tis just for a short while; we should arrive at our destination ere nightfall."

William shrugged, and made a sour face. "I do not care, really. I am in no hurry to get back to Elton. Lord Boulton is going to be enraged upon hearing about Robert's death."

Matthew's face suddenly contorted into shock. "Did you say Lord Boulton...of Elton?"

"Aye...what is wrong, Sir Matthew?"

Matthew put his head in his hands in despair, and then raised his gaze slowly to rest his eyes on Pet. She was wiping the tears from a child with a skinned knee. *Mother of God, would fortune ever smile on her?* A rush of fear for this young woman bolted through him as he watched her. Why had he not connected the name before? A vivid flashback ran through his mind.

The king himself had asked Matthew to help organize a small army to stamp out the outlaws that seemed to strike without warning. Messages were sent to all resident lords to gather their men and meet at a specified location. When the assembly was complete they sought out the renegades, but always seemed to be one step behind them. Frustration began to set in, so it was decided to break up into small scouting parties. Lord Boulton and his sons were in one of them; they were all to report back within four days with any information. Matthew's party received news the renegades were heading further south, and they returned to the base camp to wait for all parties to return. Lord Boulton's party never did. Two days later when the army moved south, the bodies were discovered in a small clearing. The entire scouting party had been savagely butchered; they must have stumbled upon the larger renegade band and stood no chance. They put up a skillful fight, evident by several renegades lay slain among them. The other lords feared for their own lives, and fled back to their manors in panic. The mission was aborted, and Matthew ordered his remaining men to take the slain bodies back to Elton. From what he could gather, the renegades then hit Pet's village, probably in retaliation for joining the king's men against them. Now Matthew had the dire duty of reporting the failure to the king.

So now she was entirely alone. He watched her with the children, so confident, so strong...but was she strong enough to withstand this? She would need help, and Matthew knew he wanted to be the one to help her.

"Sir Matthew?" He looked over to see William's concerned face. And what of him? Should he tell him his father is dead? Matthew had never felt such a rash of indecision before. Pet was putting all the children back on their horses, admonishing them that there couldn't be so many breaks or they would never reach their destination and would have to live as wood nymphs the rest of their lives. No, now was not the time. He needed to tell her when they could be alone, whereupon she would have to tell William.

"Sir Matthew?" William couldn't understand the despairing look on the knight's face.

"Er, nothing is wrong, William. I...I am just worried about those storm clouds." William looked up at a single white fluffy cloud, and back to Matthew, but the knight had already left for his horse. William looked up at the cloud again, and shook his head.

Matthew automatically lifted Mary up to Pet, and then wordlessly mounted his own horse. Pet eyed him suspiciously.

"You are too quiet, Sir Matthew. Is something wrong?"

Matthew glanced at her then lowered his gaze. "No—nothing." He kicked his horse and trotted away from her.

He was noticeably quiet for the rest of the trip. Pet was acutely aware of his change of mood, and wondered why she cared. She finally convinced herself his mood didn't matter; they would be parting company the next day and he would be out of her life forever.

With only four more relief breaks, a bee sting, and one fall off a horse, they arrived at Peterborough relatively intact. Dinnertime approached, and the children were restless on top of hungry, tired, and crabby. Matthew had never been so glad a trip was over in his life. His own mood was not that pleasant; he had snapped at William a few times and so tried to keep to himself. He was not looking forward to the task before him.

The orphanage was ready for them. The messenger Pet had sent with the letter from Father Samson arrived the day before, and the nuns had been very busy awaiting their arrival. A hot meal was prepared, and the nuns took over the children's care from the weary adults. Pet was mostly concerned for Mary, and talked about her in great length to the nuns. She was assured the baby would be fine. After what seemed like hours, Matthew saw Pet head for the front door for some fresh air, and he followed her. Suddenly a plump, green-eyed nun stopped her.

"Lady Rose? I am Samson's sister, the Prioress."

Pet smiled politely. "Aye, he spoke of you."

The Prioress looked extremely concerned, and nervously wrung her hands. "We were so sorry to hear about your loss." Pet nodded in response, knowing the messenger must have told them about Robert.

The nun continued. "We were wondering, under the circumstances, would you still be returning for these children?"

Pet cocked her head in confusion. "Circumstances?"

"We only heard this morning about your father. We thought mayhap…"

Matthew loudly cleared his throat, stopping the nun mid-sentence. She looked at him, and he shook his head with a look of alarm. Her eyes grew wide when she realized what he was implying.

Pet glanced at the nun, and back at Matthew. "What about my father?"

"Would you excuse us, sister? Come, Pet, we need to talk." He threw open the door and nudged her outside. Once there he proceeded to pace like a caged hound while she watched him solemnly. He had never felt so helpless in his life.

Pet folded her arms and watched him intently, wondering what had caused this silent rage. "'Tis something you want to say, Sir Matthew?"

He stopped pacing, stared helplessly at her face, and then pointed to the stoop. "Sit down," he ordered.

"I shall stand." Her chin lifted in defiance.

"Damn it, Pet!" he yelled, and then quickly lowered his voice. "I am sorry...I am not very good at this sort of thing."

"Just tell me." Her expression was set in stone, and she clenched her fists so tightly her fingernails dug into her palms.

He let out a breath he didn't realize he was holding. "Pet, I..." he hesitated.

"Just tell me, Matthew."

His eyes met hers. "Pet, your father and brothers are dead." He immediately hated himself for being so insensitive. Lord almighty, how could he be so stupid? This was not how he'd planned on telling her. He should have softened the blow a little; build up to it, let it out gently. Now she would go into hysterics and it would be all his fault. He was an idiot, a stupid, blundering...He stopped berating himself when he realized she hadn't uttered a word. There was no change in her at all. Nothing.

"Pet? Say something."

Her gaze remained steady. "You knew, and told me not?"

That was it? That was all she was going to say? He searched her face for any sign of emotion and found none. "I only realized it today when I finally recognized the name. I...I knew not how to tell you. Besides, there was William to consider."

She took a deep breath, let it out, and closed her eyes. "William," she barely whispered. He watched as she buried her pain and fought for control. It was so amazing to watch her do that; he envied her that ability.

"Would you like me to tell him?" Matthew flinched at his offer, not knowing how to tell a child his father was dead.

"No." She opened her eyes. "He is my nephew, I will tell him." She turned toward the barn where William was tending to the horses. Matthew reached out and spun her around.

"Do you not even want to know how they died?"

She looked at the ground, then back at him. "No."

"Damn it, this is not natural, Pet!" he shouted. "Do something! Get mad, cry, yell, but do something!"

"I cannot." She left him in stunned silence.

He sat on the stoop and waited. In a short while William came out of the barn alone, desperately blinking back tears. Matthew went to him and held out his arms.

"I am here, William."

The boy pressed into his arms, and cried against Matthew's chest. "I am weak," the boy sobbed. "I am a man, and I shed tears. Pet is a woman, and she sheds none." He pushed away in embarrassment. Matthew put a comforting hand on the boy's shoulder.

"Pet has to deal with her pain in her own way. I am twenty-eight. If I lost my father, I would cry."

"You…you would?" the boy sniffed.

"Gladly. 'Tis not unmanly to shed tears for a great loss such as yours."

William nodded, and produced a brave smile.

"William, will you ready my horse? I need to say good-bye to Pet." The boy nodded, and left while Matthew went in search of Pet. She was standing behind the barn, looking up at the full moon. She said nothing when he approached and timidly put a hand on her shoulder.

"There is an inn on the outskirts of town. I shall stay there tonight and take my leave tomorrow."

She simply nodded.

"What will you do now?"

"I know not. Everything has changed, now."

"Pet?"

She slowly turned and their eyes locked. "Aye?"

"After I see the king, would it be all right if I come by and see you?"

"If you wish." She lifted her head and looked back at the moon. The moonlight turned her raven hair into various hues of shining silk. "'Tis beautiful, is it not?"

He never took his eyes off her. "Aye, beautiful." There was a long uncomfortable pause, and he finally said, "Good-bye, my Lady Knight."

"Good-bye, Sir Knight…and thank you."

"For what?"

"For telling me."

He nodded, and left. She turned and watched him leave; she admitted to herself that she would miss him. But he probably thought she was cold and callous, even heartless. No matter, he was out of her life now. Her family's deaths cut her to the core, but she had to deal with the pain the only way she knew how. And she would have to do it alone.

# ⇝Chapter Five⇜

he next morning an urgent knocking awoke Matthew from a self-induced comatose state. After he left Pet and secured a room at the inn, he proceeded to lie awake and think of her. When he discovered sleep was impossible, he wandered downstairs to the tavern and drank himself into a besotted stupor. Would he ever be the same after meeting the beautiful black-haired warrior? She invaded his thoughts by day, and controlled his dreams by night.

He fell out of bed and staggered to the door to halt the pounding assaulting his throbbing head. The sun was just barely up; who the hell could be disturbing him this early?

It was William. As soon as Matthew opened the door, the lad shot into the room and began shouting.

"You have got to stop her, Sir Matthew! She will get herself killed, and then I will have no one!"

Matthew winced as he put one hand up to silence the boy, and the other hand on his head. "What are you talking about, William?"

"Pet! She is going after them!"

Matthew stumbled back to the bed, and wearily sat down. "I pity whoever *they* are."

"Please, Sir Matthew! You must stop her!" William was frantic, and Matthew tried to awaken his liquor-befuddled mind enough to focus on his words.

"Very well, start at the beginning. Where did she go?"

William took a deep breath. "She woke me up ere dawn, and had me help her get Goliath ready. Then she told me she would always make sure I was cared for, and if I never saw her again to remember her."

Matthew snapped to attention. This didn't sound good.

"And then she told me she had to go after the outlaws, by herself. She is going to get killed, just like Robert, and I do not want her to die!"

"Will anyone at her manor stop her?"

"Well, there is Sir Raymond, but she is now his lord, er lady. I know not if he can…"

"I do not want her to die either, William. Hand me my boots." He had slept in his clothes, but had somehow managed to get his boots off before he passed out. "Howe'er long ago did she leave?"

"About an hour, maybe two. The nuns would not let me go, I had to sneak out to find you."

Matthew desperately fought to gather his thoughts. "Very well, all right, help me get my horse."

It was half an hour later by the time Matthew paid his bill and readied his horse. He disregarded breakfast in lieu of expediency. He leapt on his horse and looked down at William. "I promise to send someone back for you as soon as I can, lad."

"Please, Sir Matthew! Take me with you…I do not want to stay here." Tears began welling up in the boy's eyes, and Matthew let out a large sigh.

"Very well, get on." He extended his hand and lifted the boy up behind him.

He felt a quick trip to the nunnery to tell them he had William was in order, then he galloped off with William holding on for dear life.

William told him Pet was going back to her manor to collect weapons before embarking on her vengeful vendetta. Matthew pushed his horse hard, stopping only when absolutely necessary to rest. Halfway there William discovered that Matthew's pack fell off somewhere, so now the knight was without clothes and money. A gnawing in his gut told Matthew that meeting Pet was the beginning of a turn in his life, but where that turn was taking him the good Lord only knew.

There was only one incident, of sorts. As they rounded a bend, a long over-hanging branch caught William unawares, and he refused to let go of Matthew when he lost balance. They both tumbled off the horse, landing in briars that tore their clothes and scratched all exposed skin. Matthew properly reprimanded William, telling him if he was going to fall, he was to fall alone. They were back on their way in minutes, determined not to let their bruised bodies hinder them.

Thirty miles never seemed so expansive to Matthew. The closer he got to Elton, the more he imagined Pet's body lying bloody and battered like her father and brothers. By the time they exited the forest he had pictured her dead in so many ways he was crazy with delusion.

William pointed excitedly when the manor loomed up before them. Matthew didn't even bother to slow his dripping wet horse through the streets, inducing him to dodge peasants and workers carrying various building supplies. They passed the church and galloped through the manor's open gates, causing servants to jump aside before he reined up the exhausted animal. Matthew dismounted, yelling for William to cool his hot, tired horse, and he sprang to the manor's large double doors.

Not bothering to knock, he simply threw open the doors and burst in. A servant girl was just passing by, and she leaped back in shock at the sight that greeted her. He was completely disheveled; his hair was uncombed, his face was unshaven, his clothes hung in torn disarray and he had bloody scratches all over him. The poor girl thought he was a raving madman.

"Where's Pet?" he demanded. The hapless servant pointed a shaking finger to a doorway, and he tramped over, slamming the door against the wall as he rushed in.

"Pet!" She was standing at a table looking down at a map, and looked up in complete surprise to see him. He didn't bother with pleasantries; he just started shouting at her.

"What do you think you are doing? Are you crazy? William is mad with worry, and you go running off…"

The largest man he had ever seen, who picked him up off the floor as if he weighed nothing, stopped him. One hand lifted him up by his pants; the other hand was wrapped around his throat. The giant sneered in Matthew's face with distrust.

"What would you have me do with this rabble, Pet?"

Matthew gasped for air and beseeched Pet for help. "Tell him you know me, Pet! Please!"

By now she had strolled up to them, while observing Matthew's unkempt condition. He obviously had ridden all day to find her, and she hated to admit she had a trace of pleasure in seeing him. "'Tis all right, Raymond, I know this unruly knight. He is relatively harmless, unless you count his penchant for ripping off people's clothes."

The giant dropped Matthew, and he fell to the floor with a loud 'ugh'.

Pet waved Sir Raymond off. "I will talk to him alone, Raymond."

The huge steward gave Matthew a disapproving glance, then strutted out the door. "I shall be just outside," he cautioned, and shut the door.

Pet folded her arms and looked him over. "You look like hell."

"As well I should!" Matthew felt every emotion surface at once, and could no longer hold his anger. "I am awakened by a panicked boy who begs me to take him home, I ride all day without food, I am knocked down into bramble bushes, and finally arrive here to be attacked by your giant! Of course I look like hell!"

She simply looked at him with her usual droll expression. "What are you doing here, Matthew?"

"What do you *think* I am doing here? Trying to stop you from killing yourself!"

"William should not have bothered you. I have no intention of committing suicide."

He paced in front of her, trying to think of words that would bring her to her senses. "What else would you call it, if you go after these men by yourself?

"Justice."

"Ha!" he yelled, and then upon seeing his argument was not getting him anywhere, he stopped and implored her eyes. "I had visions of you dead. Do you know what that did to me?"

"No, why not enlighten me?"

"I...it...oh, why am I even bothering!" He leaned back against the wall and closed his eyes in submission.

Pet's smile disappeared as she stared at him. "Matthew, they killed my entire family. There are four fresh graves in my family plot. I have to go after them."

He opened his eyes and straightened up. "Howe'er do you know? I told you not how they died."

"You did not have to."

"So, nothing I say will stop you?"

"Nothing comes to mind."

"By God's bones, you are so exasperating!" He hit the wall with his fist.

"And you are so emotional."

"Well, somebody around here has to be! You certainly have no emotions!"

"I think you have enough for both of us."

He took a few deep breaths to calm himself. She was never going to listen to him if he was ranting like a madman. "Very well, I am calm and rational," he spoke in slow, precise words. "Now, listen to me, Pet. I know what these outlaws are like. They will strike you down without so much as a thought. You are the only one left in your family. You have to stay alive."

"I have full intentions of staying alive."

"You are being stubborn!"

"And you are yelling again."

"Augh!" He turned his face to conceal his rage. Why was she so obstinate? He set his jaw and faced her; he could be just as stubborn as her. "Very well, fine. I am going with you."

"You?" She smiled and then quickly straightened her face. "Matthew, you would be more a hindrance than a help. These men are not going to stand still whilst you joust them off their horses."

Whatever pride he had walked in with just died with a pathetic whimper. "Do you think so low of me?"

"I know not what I think of you. I only know you have not the skill I need."

"Then teach me."

Her eyebrows lifted in surprise, then she smiled widely; it was a genuine smile he had a feeling she didn't display very often. "You would take orders from a mere *girl*?"

"When the girl is you, yes. And there is nothing *mere* about you."

"I admit you have potential." She circled around him and studied him intently, while stroking her chin. "Take off your shirt."

"Excuse me?"

"Take off your shirt. Raymond, get in here." The giant instantly appeared at the door. Pet nodded to Matthew, who had meekly taken off his shirt as instructed and stood at attention the moment the giant was called. "What do you think, Raymond? Sir Matthew has valiantly volunteered to accompany me." They strolled around him like he was a hunk of meat being inspected for the evening meal. Pet was not disappointed; he had a wonderfully muscled body. A few areas could be improved upon, but for the most part he was a perfect specimen. Raymond couldn't keep himself from ribbing the embarrassed knight.

"Hmmm. A whit puny, maybe, but aye, I suppose we could work with him."

Matthew stood there and seethed. *Puny?* He prided himself on his body. He certainly had never been called *puny*. What was it about this girl that would cause him to forgo all sense of pride?

"Very well, Sir Matthew," she said. "I accept your offer and your challenge. You may accompany me, and I will train you until you are good enough to be of some use." She rubbed a hand over one of his arms and examined his muscle. "Definite potential." As she stepped around Matthew she looked askance at Sir Raymond. "Raymond, feed him and see if you can find him some clothes. A bath might be in order, too. I must find William." She turned and left.

Matthew rotated slowly and lifted his gaze to meet the giant's eyes. He must have stood seven feet tall and easily outweighed him by twice as much. And Pet had just sauntered out and left him alone with him.

Raymond laughed and slapped Matthew on the back, causing him to lunge forward and practically fall over. "She likes thee, Lad. Never hast I heard her argue like that!"

Matthew started to relax a little. Maybe this huge man wasn't going to kill him, after all. "You call that arguing? She ne'er even raised her voice."

"Believe me, for her that was almost an out and out fight! But we tarry; come with me and we shall get thee some food." He led Matthew down a long hall, and into a huge dining area overcome with peasants. Matthew had never seen so many villeins crowded in a manor hall, and stopped to gawk before Raymond grabbed him and assisted him into a small room. It was a private dining area, away from the grand banquet room.

"Why are all those people out there?" Matthew asked incredulously.

"They are Pet's tenants that got burned out by the renegades. She is letting them all stay here whilst the village is getting rebuilt. Thou knew not?"

Matthew shook his head. "I have ne'er met anyone like Pet. She has an overdeveloped sense of justice."

A huge belly laugh erupted from Raymond. "And beautiful to boot!" He sat down and motioned Matthew to sit beside him. "Tell me son, thou likes her, dost thou not?"

Matthew nodded complacently. "Aye, too much. I know not why I am even here. She does not like me at all; she thinks I am a bumbling idiot."

The giant suddenly got very serious. "Now, listen, son. I practically raised Pet, henceforth I think I know her better than thee. If she liked thee not, dost thou think she would bother to argue with thee? No, thou would hast been thrown out like a piece of rubbish. She likes thee, lad. Trust me."

"If you say so." His tone conveyed he seriously doubted it.

"Good! Now let me see to some food."

A short time later, Matthew ate voraciously while lending an ear to Raymond. He told him about the manor, how many acres were used for crops, and general information about the operation of Elton. Matthew listened intently. The manor was not as large as his home in Cambridgeshire, but it was run with great fairness and competence. After a respectful avoidance, the subject finally got back to Pet. Matthew told Raymond everything from the first moment they met to the last night when he had to tell her about her family.

"What bothered me," Matthew divulged, "is that she did not cry, not a single tear."

"That is not surprising," Raymond soberly offered. "Pet doth not cry. She cried not even for Robert."

"Yet she tells me she loved him."

Raymond leaned back and studied Matthew intently. "Love him? It went way beyond love." He paused as if making a hard decision. "Come boy, I hast something to show thee." He led him away from the crowded eating area, down another hall to an end room. As Raymond opened the door, he explained how this was Lord Boulton's private study. Books lined shelves, a desk occupied the center, and a large fireplace loomed in the corner with an enormous painting over it. Raymond didn't have to say a word. Matthew crossed the room and looked up at the portrait.

"Oh, my God," he whispered. "I had no idea."

The painting showed two young people dressed entirely in black leather, outfitted with weapons grand enough to serve the king. The artist had captured Pet expertly, so Matthew could only assume he had done likewise for Robert. They were eerily identical, with the same eyes, nose, lips, hair, and expression. Robert stood taller, was more muscled, but other than that they were exactly alike except for hair length. Matthew suddenly felt a hint of the loss she must be experiencing. He couldn't keep his eyes off the painting, being especially drawn to Robert, a specter of the past reaching out to him.

"What was he like?" he asked the giant.

"Robert? Thou 'ave met his sister, thou 'ave met Robert. Although, Pet hast an inner strength Robert was ne'er able to master. I know not how he could hast dealt with her death the way she is coping with his." Raymond paused as he studied the painting. "Thou ask me if she loved him? Son, she cherished him. I dare say thee would not miss thy right arm as much as she misses him."

Matthew swallowed the lump in his throat. "I believe you."

"Lord Boulton adored his twins. This painting was commissioned last year. The artist did a good rendering, think thee not?"

Matthew nodded. The lump in his throat had traveled down to his belly.

Raymond gave him another slap on the back and let out a laugh. "Enough sadness, I believe my lady mentioned a bath and clothes. Come, lad, we do not want to keep our lady waiting!"

Later, Matthew sat in a warm tub in the middle of his room and closed his eyes, contemplating his plight. What the hell was he doing here? He was supposed to be on his way to the king. He winced upon thinking about the king; he was going to be as mad as a hornet's nest when he found out Matthew had purposely taken a detour. William said Pet had a way of altering plans, which was certainly an understatement.

He heard the door open behind him, and assumed it was Raymond returning with something to wear. He had to tell him why he was penniless and without clothes, thanks to the lost pack. He felt helpless and at the mercy of strangers who didn't even know him. Ah, but the bath felt good, he could fall asleep right there in the tub…

"I brought you some clothes."

His eyes opened wide and he swung his head around. Pet stood by the bed, a respectable distance away, but still in his room while he was naked in a tub. As a noble, he was used to servant girls helping him with a bath, and he certainly was not a modest man, but having Pet stand there so nonchalantly completely unnerved him. She was dressed casually in a gray tunic, which fit her like a second skin, and tight hose. She was barefoot. And devastatingly beautiful. "Pet! Wha…what are you doing here?"

"I just told you, I brought you some clothes."

"Could not a male servant have brought me them just as well?"

Pet casually waved him off. "Spare me your modesty, Sir Knight. We have to talk."

"Right *now*?"

She sat down on the bed and casually crossed her legs. "Does my presence make you nervous?"

"Your presence always makes me nervous."

That news seemed to please her, as she let go with a small smile that made Matthew's bath water seem warmer. She had such a wonderful smile, it was a pity she didn't do it more often.

"We start training tomorrow at dawn. I will have a hearty breakfast brought up to you; make sure you eat well else you shall ne'er make it through the day."

Matthew smiled at that. "I trained at the king's castle. What bethink you I cannot endure training?"

"You will not be training to impress ladies at a tourney with your jousting skills, complete with pretty flags and shiny armor. This is not a game."

Matthew straightened his face. "I ne'er said t'was."

"Good." She glanced at the clothes. "I pray these fit. I only brought soft lounging clothes, I have something else in mind for tomorrow." She stood up and strolled to the door, never taking her eyes off him. "You can still change your mind, Sir Matthew. You can be on your way tomorrow and make your appointment with the king."

She was daring him to quit, and Matthew refused to play her game. He set his jaw and looked as impressively manly as he could, sitting in a tub. "The king can go to hell."

"Good." She smiled and left him wondering what horrible things she had planned for him.

The following morning while Matthew attempted to eat all of the food sent up to him, a knock came on his door. It was Pet.

"Matthew, are you decent?"

"More decent than I was last night," he called.

She entered, holding a pile of black clothing. "I brought you fighting clothes." She laid them out on the bed while he thankfully pushed the food aside and made his way to her. It was a leather outfit just like she wore—doublet, pants, sleeveless tunic, and boots. "I pray they will fit. They were Robert's."

Matthew looked at her in disbelief. "Oh, Pet, I cannot wear Robert's…"

"If you are going to train with me, you must be properly outfitted. You are about his size."

"Aye, but…wearing his clothes? I pray not that he…"

"You are a king's knight. Robert would be honored."

"But…"

"Matthew, we can stand here all day and argue, else you can get dressed. Which is it going to be?"

He picked up the boots. They were excellently made, with numerous buckles running down the outside for custom fitting. "They look unworn."

"They are. We received them last week, and did not have a chance to break them in. Now, get ready, while I do the same." She left the room.

Matthew stared at the clothes, and felt an unexplained nuance of sadness. These were Robert's clothes, and Pet had just handed them over as if they meant nothing. He had never worn all leather. Especially curious was the sleeveless tunic leaving the arms exposed. The soft leather pants stretched over his muscular thighs; the doublet felt like it was made for him. The boots were a bit snug, but he knew they would stretch. When he was all dressed, he looked in the mirror and hardly recognized himself. Robert and Pet had fine taste in clothes.

He opened the door, and found Pet leaving the room directly across from his, dressed identically in her leathers. They observed each other for a few seconds, and then she faintly smiled.

"You look different."

"I *feel* different." It was true. For some reason the outfit made him feel confident, ominous, *dangerous.*

"Follow me." She led him down the stairs and into an armory room. Numerous weapons hung on the walls, or stood in corners. There were many different size swords, daggers, short axes, flanged maces, pole axes, halberds, falchions, war hammers, long bows and arrows, plus shields and bucklers. He raised his eyebrows in contemplation—this room could supply half the king's men; she kept her armorer busy.

She took a two-handed great sword and tossed it to him; he caught it deftly and looked it over with admiration.

"This is a fine weapon."

"T'was Robert's. You are his size, you should be able to handle the weight of all his weapons. Here." She threw a smaller one-handed diamond edged sword he also fancied. "We shall start with the smaller sword and work up to the great sword. My experience with you tells me you need practice."

He immediately grew defensive. "I am better with the smaller sword."

"That is good to know. So am I."

His hopes sagged. "Is there anything in here you know not how to use?"

She glanced around the room, studying each item. "No."

He sighed. "That is what I thought."

"Sheathe your weapons and follow me." She led him down several halls and through a door to a private inner courtyard. Sir Raymond was already there, and cast an approving look at Matthew.

"The leather looks good on you, Sir Matthew. Pet, shall you be needing me today?"

"No Raymond, we are starting with the swords. Go see to the building, and make sure the people are being well-fed."

He rendered a short bow, and turned to leave. "My prayers are with thee," he murmured to Matthew as he ambled past him. Matthew had the sudden urge to flee while he still could.

"Sir Matthew!"

He turned only to have his arms pulled behind him and her sword drawn across his neck, stopping just short of cutting his throat. She leaned her face close to his. "The first rule is to ne'er let down your guard."

"I was not ready!" he protested through clenched teeth.

"Pleas of a dead man…you must always be ready! Now raise your sword." She struck out at him.

He fought well, at least he thought so, except she always deflected his blows and countered with her own.

"Concentrate!" she demanded. "You are not planning your strikes!"

"Howe'er can I when you come at me too fast?"

"Stop!" She stood watching him heave deep breaths, while she was hardly breathing hard. "Matthew, you must have control, else you have naught. You are using too much energy to move. Plan a pattern of strikes, first to test your opponent, then to best him. Come forth, let me show you."

So she did, again and again, until Matthew had the pattern down. The next time they sparred, he was able to parry her blows.

"Aye!" she exclaimed with satisfaction. "You are learning. Remember your breathing, slow, steady, deep, controlled."

She worked him with few breaks. They both stripped to their sleeveless tunics, when at last he understood the reason for the extra coolness on the arms. Finally he stripped off everything above his waist. His body glistened with sweat; he had never worked so hard in his life. Pet was not even perspiring. Her toned muscles were used to the workouts she and Robert performed daily. During breaks she drank water and calmly talked to him, giving him pointers on his hand positions, his stance, anything she observed he could do better. She missed nothing. Matthew was exhausted by noon, when Raymond came by to see how things were going. Pet left for a few minutes, giving Matthew a much-needed reprieve from the grueling workout. He sat on a stool, leaning forward with his elbows on his knees, and wiped his face with a damp cloth.

"Howe'er goes it, son?" the giant asked, as he sat beside him.

"She is trying to kill me."

"She is trying to keep you alive," Raymond retorted, and let go with a chuckle. "She is teaching you what thou needs to know to survive, not howe'er to impress nobles at a fancy tourney."

"You have not a fine opinion of king's knights, do you?"

Raymond just chortled.

"Was Robert as good as her?"

Raymond's smile disappeared. "Robert was good, but no, he had not her control."

"Ah yes, control. She uses that word often."

"As well she should. She has more than any other pupil of mine."

Matthew lifted his head in surprise. "*You* taught her?"

"I taught the twins all I knew by the time they turned fifteen. The rest they did by themselves." He shook his head. "She long ago passed me up. I hast ne'er known a fighter like her."

"Nor have I. The first time we met she bashed me into a river."

Raymond bellowed a booming laugh. "Thou art lucky she didst not skewer thee and have you for supper."

Matthew nodded with a dejected look. *Especially after what happened next*, he thought.

After much too short a lunch, Pet was ready to work with the great sword. He was puzzled when she handed him wristbands.

"Here. These will help the strength in your wrists."

Matthew put them on. "Do I have a problem with my wrists?"

"How do you think I disarmed you so easily that day at the river?"

He shrugged. "Luck?"

"I make my own luck. Pick up your sword."

The heavy great sword was not Matthew's favorite weapon. He grasped it with both hands and readied himself. Pet patiently gave him pointers as she taught him another pattern, utilizing the weight to strike a more powerful blow. Occasionally she stopped to show him a better hand position, and would put her hands over his for demonstration. When she touched him, he had problems concentrating, and his heart pounded a little harder. Sometimes he couldn't help staring at her. She caught him a few times, and promptly reminded him to keep his mind on the sword. He realized she had no idea the effect she had on him.

Within minutes he was a sweaty mess again, and off came the shirt and doublet. She made him practice a move he had trouble with, and started to lose patience. As an example, she whipped her sword tip across his belly and left a thin scratch in its trail. "I could have just gutted you like a deer! You left your belly undefended! Matthew, you must concentrate."

After that he started to pay better attention. She showed him the maneuver she used to knock the sword out of his grasp. They practiced it over and over, until his muscle began to burn, and still she pushed until the dinner hour was upon them. Matthew was ready to drop, but she simply told him to eat and order himself a bath, and turned away from the kitchen. Matthew watched her leave with great disappointment.

"Where are you going?"

"I must check on the village. I will see you tomorrow. By the way, how are you at the bow?"

"I would say I was adequate, but I know that would not be good enough for you."

She smiled slightly, and turned to walk away. He started for the kitchen; he was starving.

"Matthew." He spun around to see her standing at the end of the hallway. She nodded slowly. "You are learning well."

He felt a stroke of encouragement shoot through him. Before he could respond, she disappeared into a doorway.

After dinner, the servants filled the tub for his bath. As he stripped off his clothes, he remembered Pet's surprise visit the night before and moved a dresser in front of the door. No black-haired vixen would be walking in on him tonight. He soaked until the water turned cold, then he wearily crawled into bed, naked and exhausted.

# ⊸Chapter Six⊸

et surprised Matthew the next morning by suggesting they ride out to the meadow for target practice. Raymond had preceded them and set up the butts—targets set up on earthen mounds. It was a sunny day, so Pet also suggested they not wear their leather. She had donned her hose and a loose blue soft wool tunic. Matthew wondered if she knew she was driving him mad with her long, hard legs. Knowing her, he doubted it.

They let their horses graze while they took their bows and arrows and paced off a reasonable distance from the targets. Matthew was amazed Pet could handle a war bow, the strength required to pull one meant the archer needed constant practice to keep in condition. Matthew was a skilled archer, but he had no doubt she was better. So it came as a surprise when her first shot was not a bulls-eye.

He took his shot, and hit the center. She flashed him a sideways glance, but shrugged it off. Her next arrow came closer to the center, but his hit dead on. She again shrugged.

"You shoot well. As you can see, I am not as proficient with the bow. Perhaps this will be a short session."

Matthew felt a little of his manhood was restored. After the whopping he took the day before with the swords, he was beginning to wonder if Pet could be beat at anything. They shot a few more rounds, her arrows never reached the bull's eye.

It was Matthew's turn. As he took aim, a startled pheasant suddenly flew up about twenty feet away and took to the air.

"Shoot it!" she yelled. "We can eat it for dinner."

Matthew took aim, fired, and missed. "Damn! Sorry…"

As soon as he spoke, Pet grabbed an arrow, loaded it, and shot instantly. The pheasant came down and hit the ground in front of them, the arrow planted firmly through it.

Matthew turned slowly and cast her a disappointed mixed with angry look. "Why did you do that?"

"Because you missed," she stated matter-of-factly.

He let out a breath of aggravation. "I am not talking about that…why did you pretend you could not shoot?"

She avoided his gaze and hurried to the bird with him following close behind. He grabbed her by the arm and firmly turned her around.

"Why, Pet?"

She tried her best to look innocent. "Raymond indicated that I may have been a whit intense yesterday, and suggested I should build your self-esteem."

Matthew swallowed his anger. "Pet, I ne'er want you to pretend to be something you are not, just to appeal to my false pride. I can accept the fact of who you are, and what you can do. Hell, that is what I love about you. Promise me you will ne'er do that again!"

"Very well, I promise. Thank you, Matthew; you are a man of honor."

His eyes softened as her comment melted his heart. "And you are the most incredible woman I have ever met."

Their eyes locked in a gaze neither could break. Matthew brought his face closer. "Pet," he whispered, as his lips descended on hers. For one brief second he tasted her essence before she pushed him away with a force of desperation.

"I pray we have had enough practice for one day." She turned abruptly before he grabbed her and turned her back.

"What are you afraid of, Pet?"

She swallowed hard; her hands wouldn't stop trembling. "I am not afraid of anything."

"Except how you feel about me?"

She shook her head and backed up from him. "I told you, I know not how I feel about you." She turned and ran to her horse.

Matthew smiled as he watched her go. He touched a finger to his lips, remembering what her lips felt like just for that brief period.

Pet tightened the cinch on Goliath's saddle as she fought the narrowing in her throat. Tears stung her eyes and her hands were still shaking. How could he make her feel like this? It was just a kiss, a small kiss, but somehow Matthew made her feel emotions she didn't think herself capable of feeling. She closed her eyes and fought for her blessed control, her massive inner strength she had spent so much time mastering. Deep breaths accompanied mental discipline. By the time Matthew led his horse up to hers she was back to normal.

"Pet?" he started, before she turned on him with the glare he had grown so used to.

"Do not do that again," she angrily warned, her eyes stormy with rage. "I am not interested in your passion or feelings. I have but one purpose in life right now—vengeance for the men who murdered my family. I can not let you—or anyone—get in the way."

He reached out a hand and stroked her cheek; she responded by taking a deep breath and closing her eyes. "Why do you fight me so, Pet? Why can you not let yourself care for me as much as I care for you?"

She quickly opened her eyes and stepped back out of his reach. "I cannot." She mounted Goliath and galloped away.

Matthew watched her go, feeling both elated and guilty. He knew after experiencing that brief kiss no other woman would do. He wanted her desperately, but it would take time. And time was the one thing he was willing to invest, if it meant winning her heart.

Later, he ate lunch with Sir Raymond and extolled the morning's events. Raymond expressed extreme surprise Pet had feigned incompetence.

"I simply said she was being too hard on thee, I did not say to lie for thy benefit. I hast only seen her do that a few other times, and that was with Robert."

"Robert?"

"Aye, the lad was not as good as her. She is a natural and he had to work hard to keep up with her. She even beat him at chess, always calling his checkmate. But he ne'er resented her; he loved her greatly."

"I know the feeling," Matthew muttered under his breath.

"Alas…I know that look—methinks thou art in trouble."

Matthew jerked his head around to see what Raymond was talking about. Pet stood in the doorway wearing her leather; a look of stony determination sent chills down Matthew's spine.

"She looks angry," Raymond observed. "What did thou do to her?"

"I kissed her," he answered, in a tone assuring he knew he would pay the price for his foul deed.

Raymond raised his eyebrows. "*Kissed* her? Oh, lad, thou art in more trouble than I thought!"

Pet reached them at that point, and, ignoring Raymond, glared down at Matthew.

"If you are done filling your face and gossiping like an old woman, do you think you could spare the time to put on your leather and meet me in the courtyard?" She sauntered off, taking long strides avowing she meant business.

Raymond shook his head. "I was right…thou art in trouble."

Matthew sighed, and then stood up. "Well, I best not keep the lady waiting."

Raymond grabbed Matthew's arm and pulled him downward. "She respects strength, Lad. Thou has it, do not let her back thee down." With that said, he let go and sat back, satisfied he had espoused useful knowledge.

Matthew nodded, not really in a mood to argue with the giant. He left the dining hall and leapt up the staircase to his room. In a few minutes he was dressed and ready to accept what his beautiful hellcat was willing to offer.

He entered the courtyard and closed the heavy wooden door behind him. In an instant, a dagger came whooshing past his head, missing his right ear by only inches, and imbedded itself in the door behind him.

"I missed on purpose…I am a dead shot."

Matthew gave the dagger a sideways glance. "I believe you."

Pet strolled up and pulled the dagger from the door. "If you were my enemy, you would be dead."

He stepped carefully away from the door. "Remind me ne'er to be your enemy." He followed her to a table where at least twenty daggers were laid out.

"These are special throwing daggers. I have my armorer making as many as he can before we leave."

"Why so many?" he wondered.

"Because once they are thrown, they usually get left behind. Now, take off your doublet."

Matthew complied, and she turned the leather jacket to the inner lining. "These notches are here to hold these daggers. We can each carry ten at a time. Let me show you how to load them." He watched intently. *This was ingenious, this hidden method of carrying deadly little knifes inside a doublet, which one by one could be brought out and used to kill.*

"Who thought of this?" he asked.

"I did."

"Why do I not find that surprising? "

"There—now put your doublet on." She handed him the now-heavy coat laden with knifes. He took it, felt the weight, and made a disapproving face. "You shall get used to it," she stated. "That doublet will save your life."

"If you say so."

"I do. Now, take a knife and throw it at the wall—like this." She expertly threw a dagger, sticking it in the wall across the court. "Now you."

Matthew had never seriously thrown a knife before; he'd played around as a boy, but never tried to actually hit anything. He picked one up gingerly by the blade and gave it a feeble toss. The handle hit the wall and the knife fell to the stone floor with a dull clank.

Pet rolled her eyes. "Let me wager a guess…you have ne'er done this before." Matthew simply looked sheepish and shrugged. She sighed loudly, and picked up a dagger. "Come forth," she ordered, and he happily complied. "Look," she showed him, "the wrist supplies the snap, like this." As she demonstrated the movement he stared at her face. She pretended not to notice. "With the force supplied by your arm, you should be able to do this very well." She handed him a knife and stood beside him, holding her hand over his so he could feel the movement. He was being driven crazy by her closeness, and could only stare at her. She snarled with exasperation, and looked at him.

"Matthew, you are not being serious."

"On the contrary, I am being very serious."

"Matthew…" She could see she was getting nowhere. "Please understand. I intend to slit every man's throat or else run every man through who murdered my family. 'Tis the only thing I can think of. I know you want more from me, but I am not capable of being any more than what I am."

"I do not want you to be any more than what you are."

"Then help me. Matthew, I need you. Please try to concentrate and learn this."

He nodded, and reluctantly took his eyes off her. "All right, I am sorry. I will try."

And try he did. Pet was right; within an hour he was sticking every throw. She was pleased, and showed it by granting him a large smile. He decided to impress her with an especially powerful throw. Instead of hitting the wall, however, the wayward knife hit a bench where it grazed the tail of a sleeping cat. The poor feline howled, and shot off running erratically, knocking over some quarterstaffs leaning against a wall. The staffs fell on a hapless dog, who took off barking frantically after the cat, chasing it up a tree onto the roof where it frizzed out its tail and hissed. Pet watched this entire scene silently, while Matthew winced at the commotion he caused. She slowly turned to him and raised one eyebrow.

"Now let us work on your aim."

He heartily agreed.

A few hours later his arm was sore, but his aim was true. Raymond came out to check on his progress, and Pet was anxious to show him off.

"Raymond, you must see this—Matthew is a natural thrower. His arm is strong, and his aim…" she paused, and looked at Matthew with a gleam in her eye, "…has improved greatly."

Raymond relished in the change he was seeing in Pet. He loved her so dearly, just like he had loved Robert. She was all he had, since he had never married or had children. Matthew seemed to bring new life to her, which Raymond found encouraging, but he was not going to bring that to her attention.

Pet had tacked a red scarf on the wall. "All right, Sir Knight, hit the scarf—and remember, 'tis your enemy."

Matthew took aim carefully; he certainly didn't want to miss in front of Pet's steward. He tried to remember everything she told him: breathing, control, aim, release. After a few seconds, just when he was just about ready to release the throw, Pet leaned into to him.

Matthew," she practically whispered.

"What?"

"The enemy would have reached you and cut your head off by now."

Raymond guffawed, and waved Pet off. "Let him make his throw, Pet. We can work on speed later."

Matthew threw, and hit the scarf.

"Well done, lad!" Raymond bellowed. Matthew feigned indifference, while inside beaming with pride.

Pet nodded with satisfaction. "Rest a minute, I have something to attend to." She left the men alone in the courtyard.

Matthew headed for the drinking bucket and dipped the ladle. "She is a slave driver," he muttered half-seriously as he took a drink.

"Ah, that she is, boy, and a pretty one at that." He suddenly grew serious. "If I may beseech thee, what are thy intentions toward her?"

Matthew grinned as he sat down on the bench. "I would think that was painfully obvious."

"Thou likes her, then?"

"Like her?" He let out a small snort. "I am totally taken with her. I mean to make her mine."

Raymond bellowed his infectious laugh, and stood up. "She shall ne'er belong to anyone but herself, but I wish thee luck." His smile abruptly disappeared. "Go slow, boy. She is not like common girls. Her pain is heavy and deep."

"As well I know."

After Raymond left the courtyard, Matthew sat on the stool and waited for Pet to return. He checked the position of the sun; it would be dinnertime soon. Good, he was hungry. He passed the time wistfully, taking deep breaths, listening to birds sing, just being lazy.

Suddenly his hair was grabbed and his head was jerked back. A cold edge of a dagger rested across his throat. Pet put her mouth down to his ear.

"Your throat is now cut, and you are laying on the ground bleeding to death." She let go of his hair and stepped over the bench to chastise him. "You did not even hear me coming!"

He rubbed his head with one hand, and his throat with the other. "I expected not to be attacked sitting here in the courtyard!"

"You must always be alert, Matthew!" she admonished. "I just killed you! What good are you to me dead?"

"I am sorry…I will try harder, Pet." He hung his head and stared at the ground, more angry with himself than she was.

Pet swallowed the temptation to apologize for losing her temper. He could be a great fighter, better than her, if he could somehow control his emotions and pay attention. If that meant she had to be brutally hard with him, then so be it.

"Very well…let us finish and go for dinner." She worked with him for a few more hours, and then let him go. He didn't see her for the rest of the evening.

The next three days were intensive for Matthew. Pet worked with him from dawn to sunset, training him on every weapon imaginable, but concentrating on the sword and dagger. Matthew felt his muscles grow stronger and his skill increase. Pet always disappeared in the evenings, so Matthew spent his time with William, who dearly loved the attention. Matthew couldn't shake the feeling Pet was avoiding him.

Finally, on the fourth day, Pet dismissed him after an extremely grueling sword practice.

"You have learned all I have to teach," she disclosed with complacency. "Tomorrow is the Sabbath, and we should rest. We leave the next day."

He was stripped to the waist and gleaming with sweat; she hated to admit she liked looking at his body. She was confused about her unusual feelings toward him, so had carefully avoided him the last three days. So she was caught off-guard by his blunt question.

"May I spend some time with you tomorrow?"

"Why? We have spent every day this week together."

"No, not training. I mean, take a walk, a ride—you know."

She gave him her infamous blank stare. "No, I do not."

"Pet, I want to be alone with you." His face grew serious.

"No."

"Still scared of me, huh?" His wide mocking grin returned.

"I am not afraid of anyone…especially *you*." She turned quickly and took long strides away from him.

"You fool yourself, Pet, if you do not admit you care for me."

She stopped. "You fool yourself if you think it matters." She opened the door left without looking back.

Matthew shook his head with a half smirk. Damn, she was the most obstinate, stubborn, maddening…beautiful, magnificent creature alive. He had played her little game of avoidance, simply because he wanted her to know he could. It drove him wild to be so close to her every day. He went to the table and began gathering the weapons to put away, a task she assigned to him days before. He thought about all he had learned from her; she had made him into a superior fighter where before he had been only adequate. She had brought out all his faults and pounded them to oblivion. Now he felt ready for anything.

Suddenly it felt like the hairs on his neck were standing on end. He raised his sword and swung around quickly, just in time to parry the blade descending on his back.

Pet nodded approvingly. "You heard me. Excellent."

"No, I felt you."

"Even better. You have made great gains, Sir Matthew. When this is o'er, the king will have a better knight."

"I suppose so." As she left, Matthew felt a sense of loss. He was not sure he still wanted to be a knight. His world had been turned upside down by a gorgeous black-haired warrior who didn't want him, and whom he wanted desperately. If Pet taught him anything, it was how to plan an attack. Well, he was planning.

Later that night Pet sat in the kitchen with a sullen expression, chewing on some chicken. Raymond entered and upon seeing her, went and sat down across from her.

"Matthew tells me his training is complete and thou shall leave after the Sabbath."

She took a bite of a drumstick. "Aye."

"He also tells me thou hast been avoiding him as much as possible."

"Aye." She took another bite and washed it down with some ale.

"Very talkative tonight, are thee not?"

She swallowed. "No."

Raymond sat back and contemplated her mood. "What bothers thee, child?"

"Nothing."

"He shall make a great fighter. He is already better than Robert."

She paused mid-bite. "I know."

"Certainly thou realize he adores thee, Pet."

She sighed and turned to him. "I am just another conquest, a notch to add to his bedpost. He is a highborn knight, and probably has bastards scattered all o'er the countryside. I do not plan to provide him with another one." She stood up to leave.

"Pet, the lad does not appear that way to me. He is honorable, from a good family, and he seems to be quite ta'en with thee. Why dost thee not give him a little encouragement?"

"He does not need encouragement. And I do not need romance." She left before Raymond could argue with her.

He shook his head; she would soften, she just needed more time to heal.

# ᵔᴥChapter Seven᷾

atthew began his pursuit the next day. Pet couldn't do anything without running into him. When she checked on the horses, he was there. He was in every hallway she walked down. He was determined to be a pest until she relented and went for a walk with him. She finally agreed just to shut him up. It was another hot, humid day, so she decided he could accompany her to check the vineyards. The grapes were just becoming ripe, and she needed to estimate a harvest date. Matthew grinned with victory as they began walking between rows of vines, brimming with plump purple grapes. The vines were high enough to effectively block them from anyone's view, which Matthew planned on fully using to his advantage. She tried to avoid him, but he would not be ignored. If he put a hand on her shoulder, she would shrug it off. If he reached out to touch her hair she would move her head. He was enjoying their little game when he finally put his arm out against the surrounding stone wall, effectively blocking her path. She stared at him impassively as he smiled down on her.

"Pet, what do you think of me?"

"I think you are standing in my way."

"That is not what I meant."

"Very well, I think you have trained well. You still need some work on…"

"I am not talking about fighting."

"Then what *are* you talking about?"

He rolled his eyes. "Me, Pet, what do you think about *me*?"

She studied him for a few seconds, as always carefully choosing her words. "You are pleasant enough to look at." She tried to push past him. His arm didn't budge, and he brought his other hand up to touch her cheek. She jerked her head away to avoid his touch, but she couldn't go anywhere and his hand gently stroked her soft skin.

"Is my touch so loathsome?"

"No, 'tis just not wanted." She turned and strutted the other direction, ending his advantage over her. He stumbled after her.

"Why are you so difficult?"

"I am not difficult, I am just sensible."

He grabbed her arm and turned her around. "Lord knows, Pet…this is sensible." He drew her to him and brought his lips down on hers.

At first she didn't fight him. It was too fast, too unexpected for her to know what was happening. The kiss was deep, probing, and she felt an urge in the pit of her stomach like a burning she needed to quench. Suddenly she couldn't catch her breath as the kiss assaulted her senses and excited her traitorous body. She finally put her hands on his chest and pushed him away. She gasped for air as if she had run a mile.

"Do…not…do…that!"

He grinned openly as he saw the effect his kiss had made on her; he didn't even have to think about the effect it had on his own body.

"Tell me you did not enjoy it."

She backed up from him. "Matthew, if you need to…satisfy your manly urges, there are many women around the manor who would be happy to share your bed. I could send one to you, if you wish."

Matthew stared at her in disbelief. Good heavens, could he have been more misunderstood? He was only trying to soften her, not bed her. Is this what she thought of him?

"Satisfy my…" he stuttered incongruously. "Pet, is that what you think this is all about?"

"What else? Men such as you do not kiss a woman with honorable intentions. I will not be another of your notches. I have told you, I have one mission—to kill the men who murdered my family."

Matthew frowned. "Notches? What are you talking about?"

She turned and briskly strutted off, and he ran to catch up. "There is more to life than killing, Pet!"

"Not whilst the outlaws are still living."

"You take life too seriously."

She spun around. "And you take it not seriously enough!" Her voice lowered to her usual softness. "Matthew, I have lost my entire family. Right now I need your fighting skills, your friendship, and nothing else." She met his gaze with a pleading look. "Please, Matthew…I am not ready for what you want from me. I simply do not have it to give." She lowered her eyes and pursed her lips.

Matthew felt about as low as the caterpillar crawling by his feet. He put a hand on her shoulder. "I am sorry, Pet. You are right, I am a man, and you are so damned, well, you drive me to distraction. But I ne'er wanted to hurt you. Sometimes I am a fool. Please forgive me."

She nodded and produced a small smile.

"I want to be your friend, Pet. Can I still be that?"

"Aye, Matthew. I would like that."

He smiled back, and they strolled back to the manor together.

They left early the next morning. Pet gave Raymond final instructions, as he would be in charge in her absence. Matthew felt like a private arsenal with so many weapons attached to either his horse or his person, but Pet didn't want to take the chance of running out of options. They carried only bedrolls and weapons, plus water flasks. For food they would live off the land or eat at an occasional inn. They made quite a sight, two people in black on huge horses loaded with arms. Matthew felt exhilarated to finally be leaving, after sitting up most the night berating himself on what an idiot he was. He had moved much too fast with Pet, and frightened her. He was determined to make it up to her, and had made a vow to himself he would not accost her during this mission. They would find these renegades and make them rue the day they attacked anyone with the name Boulton.

They rode all morning, asking everyone they met if they had heard any word about the outlaw band. They ate their mid-day meal at an inn, causing quite a stir among the surrounding farmers and townsfolk. Everyone wanted to meet the two warriors in black. No one suspected Pet was a girl, which Matthew thought inconceivable because it was so obvious to him a boy couldn't have her face, let alone her body. Then he had to painfully remind himself he had thought her a lad when they first met. A comely lad. A *very* comely lad. How could he have been so blind?

They passed the time telling stories about their childhood. Matthew told about his two younger brothers, Paul and Luke, and how he had tormented them most of their lives until they got old enough to gang up on him. He talked about his mother, and how she raised her boys to be gentleman and how they all at some time failed her high expectations. Someday he wanted Pet to meet his family, and she agreed they sounded like a lively bunch.

Pet talked mostly about Robert. It became so excruciatingly apparent to Matthew her entire life had revolved around him. How she was coping with his death was beyond him. He often found himself wondering how he would feel at the loss of one of his brothers. First he supposed he would scream in anguish, get angry, and then cry, but there was no way he could hold it all in like Pet. He took some comfort in the fact he was probably the closest thing to Robert that Pet had. She needed him—and he was not about to let her down.

They stayed the first night at an inn, at Pet's insistence. It might be the last night's sleep in a bed, she explained, before they took to the forest. Matthew didn't argue, just lay awake at night wishing he were by her side.

The next day they got a lead from a traveler at the inn who had heard the outlaws had attacked another village about a day's ride away. They headed off, stopping only to eat and perform necessary bodily functions. By nightfall they reached the blood bath the renegades left behind. Pet was brutally reminded of her own village as she treaded among the smoldering ashes, talking to anyone who could coherently give her information. Matthew did the same, asking questions until someone could at least give him a direction to go in.

They camped nearby for the night. Matthew made a roaring fire that they cooked a rabbit over, and later sat talking while they made points. Pet was becoming more relaxed around him as she realized he was taking the mission as seriously as her. He secretly congratulated himself on his remarkable restraint. There were so many times when he wanted to hold her, or kiss her, but he held himself back. He was convinced she would come to him in her own time, and he could wait.

The third night out they got their first break. They entered a town and ate at an inn where the keeper was still cleaning up a mess made by a group of rowdy men who wanted liquor and whores. One young whore was beaten, and told the keeper the man had bragged about being in an outlaw band no one could catch, not even the king's own men. The enterprising girl saw an opportunity to perhaps sell the information to a willing party, and asked the man too many questions before he got suspicious and began beating her. Before the men were thrown out, they managed to make quite a mess of the place, breaking chairs and tables, and tossing ale and food all over. Pet and Matthew asked to question the poor girl, who couldn't have been more than fifteen. Pet asked most the questions, and the girl answered her as "Sire" or "Milord." Matthew had to restrain himself from laughing; the poor young girl seemed taken with Pet, thinking her a good-looking young warrior riding to her rescue. Pet gave the girl some coins for her trouble, more than Matthew thought appropriate. As they mounted their horses, Matthew gave Pet a wide smile and couldn't resist teasing her in a mocking sad voice.

"Methinks you broke the poor girl's heart."

"You are cruel, Sir Matthew. She is just a young girl…and a pretty one at that. I saw the way you looked at her."

He was immediately indignant. "Me? She is a whore, Pet. I do not succumb to whores."

"And why is that?"

"No challenge," he answered, and wiggled his eyebrows.

She thought about that for a few seconds, and then smiled mischievously. "Ah, I understand. Whores willingly remove their clothes whereas you prefer to rip them off." She kicked her horse and started galloping away. He became flustered and yelled after her as he kicked his horse to follow.

"That was…" he started.

"I know—an accident."

The information the girl had provided was accurate; they picked up the outlaws' trail within the hour. They followed it through the forest until mid-day, when Pet suddenly put up her hand and halted Matthew. She dismounted and told Matthew to stay with the horses while she explored up the trail. He reluctantly agreed, not wanting her out of his sight, so sat cross-legged and waited while the horses took the opportunity to graze. Looking down, he spotted a piece of leather with long laces attached to it, and he picked it up. A sling! He hadn't used one of those in years, when he and his brothers used to knock down old crockery they set up as targets in their courtyard at home. He picked up a stone and inserted it in the sling, then swung it around with a smile on his face. If memory served, he used to be quite good at throwing; he wondered if he still was. He stood up and was twirling the sling just as Pet came back. She watched as the rock went flying, adeptly hitting his chosen target, a small limb on a tree about fifteen yards away. He nodded with satisfaction that he hadn't lost his touch.

"If you are done playing with your toy, we have planning to do."

He turned around and frowned at her, disappointed that she obviously was unimpressed with his slinging skills. "I would not exactly call it a *toy*," he countered. "After all, David slew Goliath with a sling."

At the mention of his name, Goliath shook his great head and nickered. Matthew reached out and patted him on the nose.

"Sorry, boy...I did not mean you."

Pet rolled her eyes at his childish antics. "I found them," she stated. "They are just setting up camp."

"How many?"

"I would say there are forty or fifty of them."

Matthew grimaced in dismay. "Forty or fifty? Pet, there are only two of us! Howe'er are we supposed to overtake that many by ourselves?"

"One at a time," she answered. "Help me get the horses out of sight." They led the horses off the trail until they found a small clearing where the horses could eat and they could set up camp. They took all the gear off the horses and staked them out to eat. Then, equipped only with their daggers, Pet led Matthew to where the renegade camp was.

They watched undetected from a small bluff as the men drank, told lewd stories, and ate some horribly smelling concoction from a large stew pot. The men proudly showed each other their spoils, and talked of the maidens they raped in the last raid. One man in particular could be heard from their vantage point.

"Got me a young'un, I did!" he bragged in a thick cockney accent. "Could'n'a been more'n ten! She was tight and sweet, she was. Bled like a litl' pig. Pity to 'ave ta kill 'er after she gave me such a satisfyin' ride!" He then provided more graphic details while his comrades listened with interest.

Matthew clenched his fists and leaned into Pet. "He is first," he whispered.

Pet nodded, as bile crept up her throat. She closed her eyes tightly, and lowered her head. Matthew glanced at her, and instantly felt alarmed.

"Are you all right, Pet?"

She raised her head with her composure returned. "Aye. Let us return."

They slid away backwards, and went back to the horses. Matthew was still upset by the lewd renegade, and was unusually silent. Pet noticed his sudden want of humor, and secretly respected him for being upset from the rape of a villein girl. She never let on, but he was starting to sway her, since he stopped trying to woo her. His presence with her was comforting. Raymond liked him, William liked him, and damn it all, she liked him. But now was not the time, she had some throats to slit.

They waited until nightfall, talking quietly around a very small fire to avoid detection. The horses were packed up for a speedy departure if necessary. Matthew hadn't been told what she was planning yet although he certainly had some ideas of his own. If Pet didn't kill that bloody bastard, he would.

Finally she stood up. "'Tis time. Tonight we need only our daggers."

"Do you mind telling me what we are going to do?"

"We are going to crawl 'twixt them, cut some throats, and plant our daggers on some of the others. We will get them to eliminate some of their own. Then we ride ahead and wait for them."

"I get the child rapist."

"All right, he is all yours. Let us go."

When they got there, a few last men were still sitting around, so drunk they were about to fall over. Matthew groaned impatiently; Pet simply waited with the diligence of a saint. His respect grew for her every waking moment.

Finally every man was passed out and snoring. In the morning, finding dead among them would create suspicion, which would cause unrest. If they could induce enough mistrust, the men might start killing each other, and that would be less for them to have to kill. The idea appeared sound to Matthew.

It was time. Pet took one side, Matthew the other. He watched as she crawled silently along the ground into the camp. He made his way to the other side, where he could do his handiwork. Matthew had been on missions and killed men before, but never had he slithered like a snake into a camp and slit somebody's throat.

True to his word, he made his way to the bragging child rapist. The unconscious man awoke only enough to see Matthew's face before his windpipe was cut off from making any sound but a dying gurgle. "That is for every child you tortured," Matthew seethed. "Now burn in hell with the devil." Extreme satisfaction flowed through him knowing no other child would suffer by this scum's hands. He made his way to another man, finished the deed, and then looked for a good person to plant the dagger on. *Oh well, anyone will do*, he thought, and placed the bloody dagger in a sleeping man's hands. He then made a hasty retreat.

Pet was not back yet, so Matthew waited impatiently. He just wanted to finish and get the hell out of there. From his vantage point he could see the whole camp, but for the life of him he couldn't make out Pet anywhere. He strained his eyes searching, but she couldn't be found. Suddenly he jumped when someone touched his arm from behind.

"God bless me, Pet! Do not startle me like that," he loudly whispered.

"Come on," she motioned, and they quickly departed.

Back at the horses, they tightened the cinches on the saddles and walked the horses around the camp out of earshot. When they were a good distance away, they felt safe to speak. Pet mounted Goliath and turned to Matthew with an inquiring expression.

"Did you...?" she started.

"Aye, I got the dirty heathen. And another one."

"Good. I got seven."

He grimaced. "Seven? Hell, why stop there? You might as well have killed them all."

"I thought about it." She caught his concerned look, and shrugged. "They kept waking up. I could not let them see me, could I?"

A chuckle burst from him, and he quickly sobered his face. "I suppose not."

They rode in darkness, thankful for a bright moon, until early morning when sheer exhaustion set in. A suitable spot off the trail supplied them with a resting place, and it was not long before they were both fast asleep.

Matthew awoke to water dripping in his face; his muddled mind finally deciphered it as rain. While they slept, storm clouds had moved in and were now threatening a large cloudburst. A clap of thunder awakened Pet before he could. By the time they gathered up the bedrolls and moved the horses and themselves into the trees, their doublets and pants were soaked clean through. A large low-hanging evergreen provided shelter, and they sat on the bedrolls and shivered.

Pet was shaking so badly from the wet chill Matthew feared she would fall ill. He watched her for a few minutes before taking matters into his own hands.

"Pet, come here," he ordered, and held out his arms. She obliged by scooting over so he could wrap his arms around her. "Take off your wet doublet," he shouted over the sound of the downpour. Their linen undershirts were fairly dry, and Matthew rubbed her bare arms to help warm her. He took the driest blanket and threw it over them, then held her tightly to help preserve their body heat. Within minutes, he was extremely warm, as his tormented body responded to her closeness with all its virility. She simply seemed to accept the circumstances as something any two people would do to keep warm. For Matthew it was much more; holding her close was like heaven. He secretly hoped the storm would last for hours so he could just sit there and hold her. Her hair beckoned him, and he buried his face in the wet, silky stuff and nuzzled her. Lord, she felt so…*right*. He told himself this didn't *really* go against his vow not to touch her. After all, she was cold, was she not? Was it a sin to use this convenient opportunity to hold her close? He never vowed to be a saint.

"Talk to me, Pet. It will help pass the time."

"What is there to talk about?"

"Anything you wish."

"Very well. Tell me about your numerous conquests. I believe that subject might be amusing."

"Conquests?"

"As in love affairs. I avow you have had many, that have produced several bastards."

He laughed at her frankness. "I have no bastards, Pet."

"Are you so sure?"

"I am fairly positive. I am rather chaste, compared to other men's standards."

"Most men have no standards."

"Most men have not my mother."

She was quiet for a while. The storm continued to rage, and he happily continued to hold her.

"So, there has been no one special? No one to…share your bed?"

He laughed again. "Well, I would not say that. There was Elenora."

Pet stiffened, and he felt a trace of comfort that she seemed a little jealous. "And who was Elenora?"

"A vixen who just showed up one day, shared my bed, and left me without so much as a good-bye."

Pet was silent for a long minute. "What was she like?"

He feigned a dreamy look, and sighed. "She had the softest hair. I could not stop stroking it. And large green eyes."

"And she shared your bed?"

"Oh, every night. She kept my feet quite warm."

Pet drew back and looked at him incredulously. "Your feet?"

"Oh, I am sorry…did I fail to mention that Elenora was a cat?"

Pet actually laughed. It was a small snicker, but a laugh, nevertheless.

"Why, Pet…I do believe that is the first time I have heard you laugh."

With that, she fell quiet, and there was no more conversation.

The storm subsided, and he silently cursed the sun. When Pet finally pulled away from him, he felt a desperate need to pull her back. He fought the urge as they draped things out to dry. Pet left him with the horses and said she was going to check the trail to see if the outlaws were on the move. Actually, she just needed to get away from Matthew.

She had allowed herself to be held long after she had stopped shivering. His body felt so…*right* holding her. As she stomped through the underbrush, she found a log and sat down. Why did she stay in his arms? She kept telling herself to pull away, get up, do *anything*, but she didn't. What the hell was wrong with her? She hadn't been *that* cold, and she warmed up fairly fast. Why did she let him hold her like that? And why did he bury his head in her hair while he was holding her? *All right*, she told herself, *she needed to rationalize the situation.* Matthew was just a companion on a mission, that is all. They were cold, and they helped each other warm up. *Get in control.* She was way past marrying age, indeed, her father had granted her leave to never marry. A man couldn't be a part of her life; she had known that for a long time. Deep breaths accompanied her self-lecture, and she finally regained her precious control. It was then she noticed the sounds of horses.

She ducked down behind the log and watched the renegades ride by. They all harbored a frightened look and seemed to be in a hurry. Two men had their hands tied up behind them, and Pet inwardly smiled knowing the two falsely accused men would most likely die. After they passed, Pet hurried back to Matthew, who had been holding his own private conversation with himself.

While she was gone, he paced and thought. When in blazes did he fall in love with her? Loving this girl was insane, if not hopeless. She was now the head of her household, the Lady of Elton, and a warrior who yielded to no one. She didn't need or want him, for that matter. She was brave, courageous, intelligent, and independent; she didn't need a man who could only offer her love, which she had no use for. He angrily kicked a non-budging rock, and hopped around on one foot after emitting a loud curse. Of course her timing, as always, was impeccable, as she picked that moment to return to him.

"Your dance is amusing, but they are on the move again." She headed for Goliath.

He mounted his horse without speaking, being flustered with the knowledge she once more had seen him make a fool of himself.

The renegades headed deeper into the forest. Matthew and Pet followed them for hours until it appeared the outlaws had reached their destination. Matthew hid the horses while she went ahead to investigate, and joined her a short time later as she crouched watching and listening behind some bushes. As they watched, it was apparent the outlaws were waiting for someone. Matthew was chagrined to discover even more men joining the main band they were following.

"Pet, 'tis hopeless," he complained in her ear. "There's no way we can defeat so many!"

She disagreed by shaking her head. "One by one," she muttered. "One by one."

# ❧Chapter Eight❧

s Matthew and Pet watched the renegades, it became more and more apparent this was some sort of pre-arranged meeting. There was so much noise and commotion it was difficult to understand just one conversation from where they watched. The outlaws were definitely waiting for someone—someone important. Matthew watched intently as a small group of men rode into the clearing leading a packhorse. The leader rode a great white horse, and was not like the rest of the motley men; he had fine clothes and weapons. His silver hair was cropped short like a noble. Matthew suddenly became aware Pet had drawn her sword and was starting to stand up.

"Pet…wha…what are you doing?" He reached out and grabbed her arm, but she shook him off and continued to rise. Her face was contorted into uncontrolled rage, and Matthew realized immediately all logic and reasoning had left her. He tackled her to the ground, and was resisted with more strength he thought possible from a girl her size. She hit and fought him, muttering, "'Tis him…'tis him." It was as if she didn't know who Matthew was. If she had been a man, he would have slapped her in the face to bring her back to her senses, but he couldn't bring himself to hit her. They struggled for a few seconds as they rolled over each other until they finally came to rest against a large tree, with Matthew on top of her. She fought him erratically, lashing out with her hands until he was able to grasp her arms and hold her down.

"Pet, stop it! 'Tis me, Matthew! What are you trying to do, get us both killed?"

"Let…me…go!" She managed to get one hand free and answered him with a fist to his face. Her rage made her powerful, and Matthew was having the fight of his life trying to control her. Damn, she was strong! It was only because of his greater weight holding her down that he was able to grab her arm and contain her. He dropped all his 200 pounds on her and held her arms, then brought his face down to hers.

"Pet, stop it." He couldn't yell in fear of being heard; all he could do was try to talk her out of the senseless behavior. He had been witness several times to Pet gaining control of herself; it was always an amazing thing to watch. It seemed to be a self-talk sort of thing, something she didn't seem quite capable of at the moment, for God-only-knew the reason. He would have to do it for her. He kept his voice low and soft, like hers.

"Pet, listen…you are out of control." She further squirmed, but he held her tight. "Come on, Pet, do not fight me." He impulsively kissed her on the cheek. "'Tis me, Pet, pray, get control." He kissed her on the forehead; God she smelled good. "Deep breaths, 'tis right, you can do it." He kissed her face all over; it seemed to be calming her. She closed her eyes, and he saw the self-control start to take affect. "Good, you can do it, Pet, I could not have bear it if you got yourself killed." He kept kissing her forehead, nose, cheeks, then finally relented to his impulse and gently kissed her lips. To his ultimate surprise, and delight, her eyes opened and she kissed him back. The gentle kiss turned into one spawned of passion, and he forgot he was still holding her down even though she was no longer fighting. His tongue implored her mouth to open, and he groaned when she granted him access. Within seconds his tortured hormones responded, and he became fully aroused, compounded by the fact he was lying on top of her. Time began to stand still, and his rational mind fought with his greedy body as to the next course of action. With a reluctant moan, he finally relinquished her lips, then slowly let go of her wrists and raised his head to look into her fully open and under-control gaze.

"If you are quite done crushing me, Sir Matthew, I believe I would like to breath again."

He reluctantly rolled off her and lay by her side, taking deep gulps of air. Lord, what she did to him!

She sat up and rubbed her wrists where he had held her so tightly. "You have an interesting way of getting someone's attention."

"Sorry...t'was all that came to mind at the time," he answered between gasps. "You were a whit hard to control." He sat up also, and frowned when he saw she was rubbing the soreness on her wrists. "May I beseech what happened to you? Why did you go crazy like that?"

"The man with the silver hair."

"What of him?"

She lowered her head and closed her eyes. "He killed Robert."

"Robert?" He reached out and touched her shoulder. "Well, no wonder...I am surprised I could even hold you back."

"I am too." She looked at him with determination born of hate. "He is *mine*, Matthew." She took a few deep breaths, and noticed his concerned look. "I am all right. Let us go back and see what we can hear."

By this time the silver-haired man had dismounted and was giving some sort of speech. Pet and Matthew listened intently.

"We have gotten the king's attention," he was saying. "He sent valiant knights, and we struck them down! Entire families of nobles have been wiped out!" The crowd cheered enthusiastically.

Matthew leaned into Pet's ear. "He probably means you...he might not know you are alive." She nodded pensively.

"The King must know we mean business," the outlaw continued. "Tomorrow we strike again. This time I want no survivors."

Pet turned to Matthew. "We must stop them," she stressed.

"When the king learns of this latest raid, he will send all his army to answer the people's demands for justice. You will be hiding by then, whilst I shall strike! King Henry shall die, and will pay for the battle of Bosworth Field!" The crowd yelled and cheered.

"Good Lord," Matthew uttered. "He is a Richard Loyalist."

Pet showed a look of disbelief. "Richard is dead."

"But Pet, do you not see? There are many Yorkists still incensed Richard was defeated and Henry became king. This whole thing was organized to catch the king off guard. Henry will send every last available knight away from the castle to catch the outlaws, while the silver-haired man will sneak in and kill the king. People are dying for this crazed man's personal vendetta."

She shrugged. "I am not interested in why, only that he killed Robert, and I mean to kill him."

Matthew was rapidly turning events over in his head. "He is most likely a Yorkist. There are impostors still trying to take o'er the throne. Pet, I must warn the King."

She watched him for a long moment, and then turned away. "Do what you must do. I only know I must kill the man who killed Robert."

"Pet, there are larger things at stake, here!" Her determined expression didn't change, and Matthew let out a huge sigh. "I will not leave you, Pet." He caught a flicker of relief in her face. " We will think of something. We have got to come up with a plan."

"I am thinking."

The renegade leader continued. "You know I am your friend. I let you keep your spoils. I let you have the women. Tonight, I bring you ale!" One of the horses he had brought was unloaded of a large cask. The men cheered some more.

"When this is o'er, you shall all live as nobles, in fine houses with comely whores who will spread their legs at the mere wiggle of a finger! You will be rich and have many servants as a reward for overthrowing the Tudor king!"

Matthew shook his head. "He is lying, and the poor bastards believe him."

"Do not feel too sorry for those 'poor bastards'. I intend to kill every one."

He raised his eyebrows and looked at her. "You have a plan?"

"I think so. Follow me." They prowled silently around to the other side where a man with a long cloak and hood was leaning against a tree watching the proceeding. Pet and Matthew stopped just at the other side of the tree.

"We need his cloak," she whispered. She drew a dagger from her coat and Matthew suddenly understood what she was going to do. He caught her attention and shook his head. The man was much bigger than her, and Matthew would be able to handle him easier. He crept up behind the man, putting one hand over the unsuspecting man's mouth and the other around his neck. In one quick motion he snapped his neck, then dragged the limp body to the awaiting Pet. She took one look at the man, then at Matthew, and nodded in approval. After grabbing the cloak they quietly went back to the horses, where she produced a small pouch from a saddlebag, and wagged it in the air at Matthew.

"I know not 'ere 'tis enough to kill them, but it certainly will make them ill."

Matthew took the pouch, and smelled the contents. "What is it?"

"Something my father kept in his study in case he ever needed to drug someone. 'Tis an odorless and tasteless herb that will kill in the right proportions. I mean to pour the whole thing in that ale. The cloak will conceal my identity."

"No, Pet, I will do it."

She raised her chin in defiance, not used to her orders being counteracted. "But…"

"The cloak is more my size, I am most definitely a man, whereas if you are seen there is some doubt. It would be safer for me to go out there amongst them."

She glared at his logic, and then slowly nodded. "Perhaps."

Matthew smiled inwardly. He liked it when he could take a little control from her; it made him feel more like the knight he was, not an inadequate moron like he usually felt around her.

He put on the cloak and dropped the hood over his head. His shorter styled hair would stand out among the filthy shaggy-haired outlaws. The crowd was rowdy and loud, and no one gave him any notice. Pet watched nervously as he blended in, slapping men on the back, laughing loudly and acting drunk. Finally he made it to the center where the cask was.

The men lined up, fighting for position to be next in line for the ale. Matthew stood by the cask, pretending to be simply trying to keep peace. He even broke up a fight. Pet thought his acting was going too far; let the damned outlaws kill themselves. He opened the pouch under his cloak and slowly raised his hand to rest at the top of the cask, all the time carrying on a conversation with someone. His large hands hid the pouch, something Pet would not have been able to do. The powder dropped unsuspectingly into the airflow hole, then Matthew casually strolled away.

As he made his way back through the crowd, Pet caught her breath when a man yelled at him and summoned him over. She drew her sword, not knowing what she would be able to do against so many men. It turned out Matthew was simply needed to help move a large log to a better position by a fire. The silver-haired man was standing close by, and Pet held her breath when Matthew lingered to listen to a conversation. Finally, he entered the woods, and she circled around to meet him. He was surprised and flattered by her reaction when they came face-to-face.

"You take too many chances! Was it necessary to come so close to the leader? What if you had been recognized as a noble? You could have been killed!"

Matthew was removing the cloak the whole time she was scolding him. He tossed it on the ground and grinned widely. "Why Pet...I knew not that you cared."

She paused and answered in a more calm, controlled tone. "Certainly I care. I need you for the mission; what good are you to me dead?" She pivoted away and began making her way back to their horses. He followed close behind with his silly wide grin growing wider by the second.

"Why do you not admit it, Pet! You care for me."

She turned around sharply. "I care about this mission. You are simply necessary."

"And was it necessary for you to kiss me back whilst I held you?"

"I was...confused. I knew not who you were."

"Oh, you would kiss any strange man like that?"

"No, I...you...oh, ne'er mind!" She stomped off indignantly while Matthew praised himself for getting her rattled.

She killed time with her bow and arrows as he sat on a stump and watched her. Damn, he loved it when she was angry, which was most of the time, lately. Breaking through her cool facade was a challenge he gladly accepted. And that kiss! Any woman who could kiss like that would have to be a wildcat in bed. He fully intended to find out for himself, in time.

He watched as she made herself busy, testing the bowstring for the hundredth time, checking each arrow for non-existent flaws, just generally ignoring him. He wondered if he should tell her he was in love with her. No, she would think him stupid and weak, if memory served, and her opinion of him was not high enough to risk any further erosion of his status. The bold approach—that is what he would do. He would simply not give her a choice in the matter.

"Our silver-haired man has a name," he offered.

She looked up. "Oh?"

"Aye, he was referred to as Gideon. He is working for someone named Lambert Simnel. Apparently he is a professional revolutionary hired to overthrow King Henry."

She didn't answer, just went back to playing with her bow.

"You are awfully silent, Pet."

"I am readying my bow. I suggest you do the same."

He got up, went to his horse, unloaded his bow and arrows, went back to the stump, and sat down. "Very well, I am ready."

She glowered in irritation at him. "I would appreciate a more serious attitude."

He produced his ever-charming smile, which unfortunately never seemed to have much effect on her. "Why? We could be dead in a few hours, 'ere whatever you are planning does not work. I might as well be happy until then."

"I have no intentions of dying."

"Actually, neither do I. That would not go good with my plans of making you my wife."

She showed no reaction. "That is not funny, Matthew."

"I did not intend it to be."

Aware at the solemnity in his voice, she was first shocked, then angry, then amused. She shook her head, and hid her laughter. "And might I dare beseech if *I* have any say in the matter?"

"Very well. When this is all o'er, will you take my hand in marriage?"

"No." She started tending to a crucial matter on her saddle.

"Why not?" He stood up and went to her side. "You like me, and in time could learn to love me. You just will not admit it."

She looked at him in disbelief. "I shall assume delusional behavior is normal for knights. And what of you?"

He paused in uncertainty. Should he admit he loved her? His smoldering eyes beseeched hers, attempting to find one hint of a spark. "I want you."

"That is all?" She folded her arms and waited.

*Damn it, tell her you love her.* He cleared his throat. "Sometimes that is enough…at least in the beginning."

Her whimsical smile returned and she tossed her head, causing black hair to fly over her face. "You are amusing company, Matthew. And I might even say I am somewhat flattered. But please choose another victim for your affections and marriage prospects. I am not, nor ere will be, interested in marriage."

He felt thunderstruck. *Victim?* Never before had he asked a girl to marry him, even thought he certainly had many opportunities. Young maidens were always making themselves available to him at the king's castle, dropping hints and acting coy. All those women seemed like silly little superficial flirts, now. Any of them would have jumped at the chance to marry the first-born son of a rich noble, and a knight at that. Yet Pet had just soundly rejected him without so much as a second thought. He was not going to drop the subject without at least an argument.

"Why not, Pet? Does marriage to me make you reel in revulsion?"

"Marriage to any man does."

"Why?"

She lowered her head, pursed her lips, and made him wait for the answer. "I have my reasons. Matthew, we are wasting our time on this conversation. We have much work to do. Are you ready?" She stuffed all her arrows in her quiver and threw it over her back. He did the same, and was damned if he was going to drop the conversation.

"What reasons?"

"None I have to qualify with you."

He winced at her sharp tone; apparently the subject was not a popular one with her. "I pray you do. I bade for your hand in marriage, and you practically slapped me in the face. Do I not at least deserve a reason why?"

Her demeanor changed slightly; he detected a stiffness and perhaps a hint of...fear? "There is none that I am willing to give." She left him standing in perplexed silence; the smile wiped off his face.

He followed her back to the outlaw camp, where the rowdy men were still drinking the drugged ale and carrying on. He kneeled beside her and they watched as the men started to pass out in varying positions, some still sitting up, others on the bare ground. Pet smirked at Matthew. Their prior conversation was forgotten and done with as far as she was concerned.

"The powder is starting to work. We must wait until dusk, when they are bedding down, then we begin."

Matthew's head was still reeling with a shattered ego and shackled desire. He didn't answer, as his mind was not really on the mission. The Lord knew he loved this girl...how was he going to win her over? What didn't she like about him? Perhaps his physical attributes were not appealing. Was he too big, or too small? Or could it be she just plain hated him? No, she couldn't kiss him the way she did and not at least *like* him. Never had a girl been so frustrating to him.

"Matthew, are you listening?"

He turned to her with a blank face. "Huh? Oh...yes, I am listening."

"Really? Then what did I say?"

"Uh...we are going to wait until dusk, then begin."

"I said that five minutes ago."

"Sorry. I am listening now. Go ahead." He felt the total fool.

An agitated look crossed her face. "Do I really have to tell you what we are going to do? You are not stupid, Matthew. You are a knight, after all."

Right now that didn't seem to mean too much. "No, Pet, I know what we are doing." He knew the minute she showed him the powder what her plan was. Extremely clever, actually.

"Matthew?"

Her deep brown eyes caught his blue ones. "Aye?"

"Why do you allow me to give you orders?"

He shrugged. "Why not?"

"Because I am a woman."

"Aye, you are. A very beautiful woman who can best any man with any weapon and is a brilliant strategist. I would say that qualifies you to give me orders."

She nodded, and hid her reaction. It wouldn't do to let him know how pleased she was with that answer. "Let us get the arrows ready."

They spent the next half-hour setting their arrows in groups of five in a circle around the camp. They would fire alternately to make it appear the camp was surrounded. A skilled archer could shoot approximately ten arrows a minute. With them both shooting, they hoped to create enough chaos and kill so many that the gang would be whittled down to just a few. Then close fighting might be in order, but nothing they couldn't handle. He shook his head in admiration as he thought about her plan. With God's help, it just might work. And the sooner, the better, because he was nowhere near dropping the subject of marriage. She was going to be his wife; he had made up his mind. She just didn't know it yet.

They waited for most of the men to fall asleep or pass out. Gideon and his group didn't drink the ale; instead they sat talking around a small campfire apart from the others. Matthew found it characteristic they would distance themselves from the peasant outlaws. Hired mercenaries were usually paid well to stir up common folk, but that didn't mean they had to associate with them. They didn't even seem to realize the gang was drugged. Pet finally motioned to Matthew to get ready. He nodded in return, and circled the camp to the first cache. He loaded his first arrow, and waited for Pet's signal. The sleeping, snoring men were oblivious to anything. Poor bastards, getting shot as they slept. Not a very honorable way to die—but then, these men weren't honorable to begin with.

All too soon the signal came—a flaming arrow fired straight up—and Matthew began shooting into the crowd of unaware men. It was more or less a slaughter. A few moans were heard, but for the most part the men simply twitched when an arrow hit them, and then went motionless. Pet was faster than he was; he noticed she was getting to her positions faster and shooting many more arrows. Then again, he didn't have a personal vendetta like she did to encourage his speed.

All at once Gideon and his men jumped to their feet and began a confused inspection of the clearing. Since they were completely on the other side away from the main group, the arrows had gone unnoticed until then. Matthew realized the reason for their sudden awareness—Pet was aiming at them. Matthew uttered a curse, and watched in fright as the men drew their swords and headed into the woods. They were going to try to find the archer or archers; they didn't know how many there were. *Damn*, he lamented. Why did she have to try to kill the only men who weren't drugged? If they found her…

The hell with the sleeping renegades, they were all most likely dead anyway. He dropped his bow and began running to where he had last seen Pet's arrows fly. Before he got there, however, he heard Gideon's men yelling and he heard the clank of steel. Matthew's heart began racing as he made his way toward the sounds. He weaved through the trees in desperation, and instinctively reached inside his doublet and grabbed a few daggers. The clank of steel grew louder, and he burst upon the scene, running head on into one of Gideon's men. The startled man only had a chance to widen his eyes before Matthew planted a dagger in his heart. Then Matthew quickly assessed the scene. Two men, not including the one Matthew just killed, lay dead on the ground. Four more men, who now hesitated to attack her having realized she was a formidable fighter, surrounded Pet. Gideon,

the bloody coward, was standing off to one side with two others
barking orders to kill her. Matthew took a dagger and threw it at the
closest man. It stuck nicely in his back and the bewildered man fell
on the ground in agony. Pet used the distraction to strike out with the
sword she had confiscated from one of her opponents and attacked
the remaining three men. The three were not even close to having her
skills. She countered every blow, and took little gashes of skin every
time she struck. Matthew folded his arms and watched impassively as
she toyed with the beleaguered men. It wasn't really even a contest. At
this point, Matthew could have just stood by and watched, but
thought he might as well narrow it down to two. He threw another
dagger at one of the reluctant men, planting it soundly in the
abdomen. Pet finally acknowledged his presence.

"T'was good of you to join me, Sir Knight!"

"I could not let you have all the fun!"

The other two men backed up, then with white faces turned and ran.
It was then Matthew and Pet noticed Gideon and his other companions
had taken off as soon as Matthew joined her. Perhaps the ratio of two
to five wasn't good enough for them.

Pet started to run after them, but Matthew grabbed her. "No, Pet, let
them go."

She turned, wild-eyed, to face him. "No! He killed Robert. I *shall*
avenge his death!" She shook off his arm and ran.

Matthew groaned; why did she have to be so tenacious? "Pet," he
called. "You are not going to be able to catch them!" He cursed when she
ignored him, and reluctantly followed after her.

Before they could reach the clearing, they heard the sound of
galloping horses pounding the trail. Pet started to mount one of the
renegade's nags, but Matthew was able to grab her and hold her arms.
Her eyes were wild with determination, if only he could talk some sense
into her.

"Pet, listen to me! 'Tis almost dark. We cannot just jump on these
horses and go after them! We need our own horses, and weapons. We
can not track them tonight."

She practically shook with frustration. "But he is getting away!"

"We will find him again, Pet, I swear it. But not tonight."

She shook herself loose from his grasp, and angrily threw her sword on the ground. A chagrined cry was uttered as she dropped down to her knees, her hands creating tight fists as they beat the ground. She closed her eyes, and again Matthew stood by powerless as she gathered her self-discipline. It was always a wonder to watch. He knew to remain still until she opened her eyes, and did so until she stood up. Her face was back to the usual controlled emotionless stare.

"You are right. It would be meaningless to try to pursue them tonight." She noted his concerned look, and softened her voice. "I am fine, Matthew. Thank you."

He shook his head. "I did nothing."

"Aye you did." She lowered her gaze for just a second. "More than you know."

"What do you mean?"

"I have ne'er lost myself as much as I have on this mission. You have saved my life twice. I must tell you that is most unnerving."

He chuckled. "Perhaps you have allowed yourself more emotion because you know I am here to stop you from killing yourself. Not an unpleasant task, which I accept most whole-heartily, since I still intend to make you my wife."

She glowered back at his smug, grinning face, and wanted to punch him where he would remember it for a while. She fought the impulse. "We have work to do. Any man still living must be killed. Gather all the spoils so we can return them to the villages. We will also need one of these horses as a pack animal; the rest can all be set free. Let us get to work."

They spent the next hour fulfilling her orders. The renegade gang was no more, effectively whittled down to Gideon and his four remaining men. No village would fall prey to further raids.

Matthew found a worthy packhorse and loaded the beast with everything of value they found on the dead men; coin, weapons, silver cruets and chalices, even a magnificent silver processional cross that was partly gilded and decorated with enamel. They led the heavy-laden animal the small distance to where their own horses were staked out. It was now totally dark, and Matthew made himself busy getting a fire going. In his haste to escape, Gideon left a pack of fine food behind, so they sat before the fire and ate sweet bread, pheasant, pork and cakes. They washed it all down with wine from a flask he found.

Pet was exceedingly quiet. Matthew knew why; she was incensed Gideon got away.

"We will find him, Pet."

"I will find him. You must report to the king."

He sighed with reluctance; she was right. The king must be informed that the outlaw gang was wiped out, but a threat was still present to the throne.

"You are right, I shall accompany you back to Elton, then take my leave." A vast feeling of dread swept through him. He didn't want to leave her, ever.

A light mist began to envelope them, adding to his depressed mood. Neither spoke for a long time. The mist turned into a light rain, and Matthew decided he didn't relish the thought of sleeping wet again. Thinking ahead for such an eventuality, he had taken several blankets from the renegade camp. He went to work setting up a makeshift tent large enough for the two of them. Pet watched with reserved interest.

"May I inquire as to what you are doing?"

"Making us somewhere dry to sleep." He stood up and examined his handiwork. "There. What do you think?"

*T'was actually a nice little tent.* "We are going to sleep in that?"

He nodded.

"Together?"

Another nod.

"I think not."

"Honestly Pet, we are past worrying whether I intend to ravage your virtue. You know me well enough by now. Get in."

She glared at him for a few seconds, then dropped to her knees and crawled inside. It was very cozy; he had even managed to make pillows out of something. He crawled in behind her, and they lay down back to back. He pulled some covers over them, and wordlessly they both tried to ignore each other and doze off. After a reasonable amount of time, in which he was quite positive she had fallen in a sound sleep, he rolled over carefully and cuddled up to her back. He left no space between them as he molded himself to her contours. One large arm encircled her, as he settled in comfortably and almost immediately fell in a slumber holding her, a smile upon his face.

He didn't know Pet was wide-awake during his repositioning. She remained still as his arm draped around her and his warmth penetrated through her clothes, and then closed her eyes when his breathing became steady, joining him in restful sleep.

# ❧Chapter Nine❧

atthew awoke to the sound of the horses being saddled and prepared for departure. He frowned at the empty space beside him with a foreboding feeling that Pet knew he had slept with her last night. He exited the tent, and noted the depressing rain had given way to the promise of sun. Stretching his arms, he smiled at Pet, who gave no indication of being upset at his final sleeping position.

"You let me sleep. Why?"

"I thought some extra rest would be helpful, considering the long journey still in store for you."

His face fell as he remembered his planned trip to the king. Why didn't that seem important anymore?

"Besides," she continued, "men seem to need more sleep than women. I believe because they expend so much more energy whilst sleeping."

He froze. "Energy?"

"Aye. All their moving about."

He winced; she *did* know. She turned to hide her smile.

They finished packing up the remaining bedding, and nibbled on some of Gideon's leftovers. Then, with the packhorse deftly in tow, they proceeded on to the trail. They ignored the deathly silence of the renegade camp, which would soon be foul with stench from the bloated, rotting bodies. Neither felt the slightest remorse for the murderous band; Pet only felt regret Gideon still lived.

It took the better part of the day to exit the woods and find a main road. They stopped at an inn to eat—again causing many stares—then had to make a decision to stay the night or try for the next village. Pet got her way, as usual, for going to the next village, as there was still plenty of light left for traveling. Matthew wanted a bath and to sleep in a real bed, although he had to admit he slept rather sound the night before. Now he couldn't imagine not holding her while he slept.

It was just becoming dusk when they approached the next town. As they rode up to the inn, Matthew suddenly bolted upright and reined in his horse. There were two riders just dismounting in front of the inn, one resembling Matthew in coloring but much larger, the other younger, smaller with darker features. Pet looked at Matthew with alarm.

"What is it?"

A wide smile encompassed Matthew's face. "It cannot be so!" he yelled, and kicked his horse into a trot. Pet had no idea what could not be so, so cautiously followed him. Matthew was already off his horse and hugging the larger man by the time she rode up beside him. She stayed mounted as she watched the men embrace each other.

"Luke! Paul! What are you doing here?"

"Father sent us into London for a business deal! What are you doing here?"

The older one seemed to do all the talking while the younger one simply looked up at Pet. Their eyes locked, and he nodded with acknowledgment. He then slowly smiled, as he looked her over with appreciation. Matthew and the other man finally turned and noticed her.

"And who is your fine young traveling companion who wears these same formidable clothes? Have you finally taken on a squire? Introduce us to this lad, Matthew!"

The younger one rolled his eyes. "Luke, you idiot…'tis obvious she is a girl." He turned his gaze back on her. "And a mighty pretty one, at that."

"What? Why, Paul, I do believe you to be correct! My apologies for being dull witted and blind, Milady."

Matthew gave a sheepish look and gazed up at Pet. "Forgive me my rudeness, Pet, where are my manners? These are my brothers—the massive one here with the big mouth is Luke, and this one who stares at you with his mouth agape is Paul. This is the Lady Ro…" He stopped dead as her glower made him shiver. "I mean to say, this is…uh…"

"My name is Pet."

Luke smiled widely, and held out his hands to assist her off her horse. "Allow me, my fair beauty!" The glower was transferred to him, and he dropped his hands. "Perhaps not."

Pet dismounted as Matthew hid his smile behind his hand.

Paul continued a thorough inspection of her in a dumbfounded state. Pet raised an eyebrow, and inspected back. He wasn't much older than her, and appeared to be in fair physical shape for his age. He was smaller than his brothers, with darker hair and deeper blue eyes, and conveyed a slight mysterious aura. She contemplated the differences from his brothers—a bastard perhaps?

Matthew had not missed their silent interchange. He grabbed her arm possessively, and led her away. She was finding the whole situation amusing. Brothers? This could prove to be entertaining.

He spoke to her briskly as he escorted her in the door.

"He is too young for you."

"Who?"

"My young pup of a brother."

"Too young for what?"

"You know what."

"No, I do not."

"Never mind, I will book you a room."

"I will book my own room."

"Fine." He let go of her arm in frustration.

She watched with a straight face as he stalked off to his brothers, who were just entering the front door. Luke was either ignoring the situation, or hadn't noticed Matthew's demeanor.

"'Tis a lucky chance to meet you here, Matt! Surely you and your lady shall dine with us!"

"She is not my lady."

"Then may I beg to inquire as to what she is?"

"She is his equal." Paul had remained quiet until that moment, and both brothers turned at the same time to look at him.

"She is more than my equal," Matthew corrected with a shake of his head.

Paul couldn't take his eyes off her, as she talked to the innkeeper several feet away. "She is fabulous. Is she…?"

"Aye!" Matthew quickly answered.

Luke nodded, and gave his big brother a wide grin. "I believe you have finally met your match, brother. I hope she leads you a merry chase."

"She has already done so."

Pet sauntered up to Matthew and nodded up the stairs. "I booked us two rooms. I am going to unload the horses and see to their comfort, then I will join you for dinner."

"I will come with you," Matthew offered.

"No. Stay and visit with your brothers. I shall not tarry long." She smiled at Paul and Luke. "'Tis a pleasure to meet you."

Paul took her hand and bowed as he kissed it. "I avow the pleasure will be all ours, Milady."

She flashed Matthew a sideways smirk, while Luke laughed wholeheartedly.

"Worry not, Pet. We shall douse him in cold water during your absence."

At that she smiled, and left.

The brothers sat and ordered ale. Luke gave Matthew a little jab in the arm.

"So, howe'er is the fearless knight? Was the mission a success?"

"At first, no. Then I met Pet."

Paul stared at the wall with a dreamy faraway look in his eyes. "She is a mission in herself."

"I must warn you brother, she is mine. At least, I plan for her to be."

Luke raised his eyebrows, and gave a chuckle. "And have you informed the lady of that?"

"Aye."

"And she rejected you soundly, did she not?" Paul added hopefully.

Matthew took a large swig and cleared his throat. "Enough of me. Howe'er are mother and father?"

Luke nodded. "Fine, he has gained more land holdings, and I believe he said something about buying another ship—or was it a shipping company?"

"And mother is mother." Paul added. "Sassy as ever and in charge of everything."

"And still anxious for grandchildren, I suppose," moaned Matthew.

"She gave up on you, and is now badgering me to marry," Luke lamented. "Please hurry with your lady Pet. I fear Mother will drive me mad."

"There will be no hurrying her. She is…different."

"I will second that," Paul agreed.

"I mean, she is on a sort of personal mission. Until she accomplishes that, there will be no marriage."

"Mission?" asked Luke.

"She is set on avenging her brother's death."

"Can she use those swords she carries?" Paul asked.

Matthew gave a stony stare and took a swig of ale. "Only too well, I fear."

"A lady warrior?" Paul smiled. "She seems not the type you usually woo, big brother."

"There is no wooing her."

"Matthew," Luke implored, "do you forget the lady Christine Bollings? Mother is still harboring hopes for a union, there."

Matthew leaned back with a lazy smile. "I do not forget her, I simply do not want her. She is a brainless bore who offers me naught, save for a warm body. Besides, she was far too willing to let me test her favors."

"And your lady Pet is not?"

"You have no idea."

Paul frowned while listening to his brothers' exchange. "So is she to be tossed aside like the others after you make your conquest and grow bored?"

"Brother, you condemn me falsely. I have never 'tossed' anyone aside. 'Tis not my fault all women think only of marriage and come to premature conclusions. I made no promises to anyone, least of all Christine, whose arrant drivel could drop the leaves off a tree."

Luke practically choked on his ale. "So, what do we tell mother?"

"Tell her naught, for now."

"Aha, I was right," Paul quipped with a satisfied grin. "You are nowhere close to winning this girl's heart."

"No, but I shall. I have to."

Paul and Luke exchanged a skeptical look at his serious tone, something they didn't hear often from their eldest brother.

"Matthew," Luke proclaimed, "if I did not know you better, I'd say you are in love with this girl."

Matthew's sober look could have burned a hole through a castle wall. "I am, totally and completely."

Paul held a dubious expression as he leaned forward and rested his arms on the table. "Brother, are you certain she is not but another challenge? You have had many chances to give a girl your name, but a last minute flaw in the girl's character always stopped you. What of this warrior's flaws?"

"Pet has none. She is strong, capable, intelligent…"

"Beautiful," Paul added.

"Aye, although her beauty is not her greatest asset."

"So," said Luke, "are we to assume you are finally going to become serious about something? Father could still use you in his business, considering your way with numbers."

Matthew shook his head. "No, my only desire is to become Lord of Elton and father of nine children."

"Only nine?" Luke chided. "The activity required producing that many is a job in itself."

"No, these children are already born. They are orphans, and Pet is going to raise them as her own."

"Good heavens, why?" asked Luke.

"Because that is the kind of person she is. When she sees an injustice, she seeks to right it." He sighed heavily. "She is the kind of person I need to be. I have ne'er known anyone like her."

Luke and Paul exchanged another look. Their brother was indeed smitten like never before.

As if on cue, Pet entered the inn and approached the table. All three men stood up, and Luke relinquished his chair by Matthew so she had no other choice but to sit by him. She caught the action, and looked suspiciously at Matthew. He smiled back innocently, and motioned to the chair. He knew better than to try to seat her.

"The horses are unburdened, and I paid extra for a rubdown." She took off her broad sword and leaned it against the wall by Matthew's, then sat down. All three men sat down after her. Food was ordered and the men turned their attentions to her. Paul was first to ask a question.

"So, you lower yourself to ride with our worthless and reckless brother?" It was meant as a teasing jab, but she didn't smile.

"Reckless, yes. Worthless, no. He has proved himself useful—at times."

Matthew folded his arms and frowned. "Thank you."

The food came at that moment, and she reached for a piece of bread. "You are most welcome."

There was silence as they loaded their plates, until Luke cleared his throat. "Lady Pet, please enlighten us as to howe'er you came to be in the company of our brother." Matthew grew nervous when her stony gaze changed into her droll smile.

"He challenged me for a campsite."

"My pardons, but 'tis *you* who challenged *me*."

"Very well...I challenged *him* for a campsite."

Luke laughed, and shook his head. "T'was not known to me that Matthew has taken to engaging young ladies in combat. He is usually more chivalrous."

"He thought me to be a lad, and speaking in his defense, he did attempt to avoid it."

"Therefore you fought?" Paul asked.

"Aye."

"Well, do not torment us! Pray, howe'er did it end?"

Pet pursed her lips and glowered.

Matthew took a large gulp of ale and stared at the wall.

Paul and Luke watched this silent communication with great amusement. Never had they seen their unworried, carefree brother so struck dumb.

"Well?" Luke finally asked. "Will not either of you release us from our suspense?"

"I won," Matthew said.

Pet almost spit out her food. "You? Pray, my memory is not as weak as yours! I had you disarmed, and could have run you through!"

"A mistake I avow you have regretted many times o'er."

"So many I have lost count."

"Excuse me," Luke interceded, "But would one of you please enlighten us? Howe'er did the fight end, exactly?"

"He…"

"Pet!"

"…Ripped off my tunic when I pushed him into the river."

"Argh," Matthew groaned, and sprawled down in his chair.

Paul suppressed a chuckle, but Luke made no attempt to conceal his amusement. "So! First you force her to fight you, and then when she wins fair and square you attempt to skew the result by disrobing her! Not exactly knightly behavior, brother!"

"T'was an accident!"

"Has Matthew ever told you howe'er he became to be a king's knight?" Paul asked the question, causing Matthew's eyes to widen in terror.

"Paul! I…I do not think Pet is interested in…"

"I would be delighted in knowing," Pet answered.

"Mayhap my brothers would like to know how you came about your unusual name?"

Pet turned to Matthew and shot daggers with her piercing eyes. "You would not dare."

They stared at each other for a short moment, and then Matthew slowly smiled.

"Checkmate." He wiggled his eyebrows at her.

Pet's look could have straightened horseshoes at that moment. In a few seconds she produced an evil smile, and turned to Luke and Paul.

"My given name is Rose Petal. My twin brother shortened it to Pet. 'Tis a name that brings me much embarrassment, and I thank you in advance for not laughing at my misfortune."

Matthew groaned, and sank lower in his chair.

"'Tis not such a bad name," Paul lied with a straight face. "So am I now free to divulge how Matthew met his fate as a knight?"

"By all means."

"Our father, Baron Cameron of Cambridgeshire, is a personal friend of King Henry. During the War of the Roses, father thought Matthew, at the tender age of fifteen, needed a direction to follow."

"Actually, he still thinks so, but that is another story," added Luke.

"Father took Matthew with him to the battlefield. Henry himself was there, so t'was most important for Matthew to impress the future king. He made himself constantly underfoot."

"Indeed," Pet said.

"So," Luke continued the story, "it seemed the army had been given wrong information as to the location of the enemy. All of Henry's top generals were there, all quite flustered that their strategy was off.

"Matthew was trying hard to impress the future king, and father feared Henry grew weary of Matthew's constant badgering. In desperation, father sent his over-eager son on an away mission for something—he forgets what—just to get rid of him. On the way, Matthew had to relieve himself, and took to a clump of woods."

By now Luke laughed hysterically, while Matthew hid his face behind his hands. "Unbeknownst to him, he came upon a man who was in a small ravine, squatting with his pants down around his ankles. Matthew began to...uh...relieve himself, hitting the poor twit on the head." He began laughing so hard Paul had to take up the story.

"The man was so startled, he drew his dagger to defend himself from the rude attack. He tried to get up and run, but became so entangled in his pants he fell forward on his own dagger, killing himself instantly. Matthew felt horrible, and brought the man's body back to the army encampment.

"It turned out the man was an advance spy for the Yorkist army, and held plans for the enemy's position. Because of this information, the battle was won, and Matthew was declared a hero for apprehending and killing an enemy spy. He received the accolade right there on the battlefield by Henry himself.

"Henry promised father he would make Matthew one of his royal knights after his accession. Of a surety, the king was never told the actual story, which Matthew was unquestionably reluctant to tell, and did so only after much interrogation by our mother. She knew something was wrong with the concept of Matthew being a hero."

Matthew cowered in embarrassment, as Pet fought laughter harder than she ever had before in her life.

"Therefore," Luke concluded, "Matthew is a favored knight of the king, and is held in high esteem, all without raising his sword, so to speak."

"That explains a lot," said Pet. She cast a look at poor Matthew, who was afraid to show his face. She felt an inkling of pity for him, and decided to take mercy and raise his standing a bit to his chortling, hysterical brothers.

"Although, Matthew has the makings of a fine warrior—if he can ever keep his mind on what he is doing."

"He has always had a problem that way," Luke offered.

"Very much so," Paul agreed.

Just then a loud noise was heard from behind, and all eyes turned to see what the commotion was. Two men stood pushing each other over a disputed debt, one yelling obscenities and waving a sword. The other man had no weapon. Pet quietly reached inside her doublet and brought out a dagger.

"I owe you naught!" the unarmed man was saying. "My debt 'tis paid!"

"Show me your proof!" the angry man demanded.

"You know I have none, you two-faced clod! I trusted you for your word!"

"Then perhaps I should teach you a lesson, you worthless arse!" He brought his sword up for a strike as everyone looked on wordlessly.

Suddenly the sword-yielding man's arm was pierced with a flying dagger, and he yelped in pain as he dropped his sword. Matthew and his brothers watched as Pet slowly sauntered up to the screaming man, and in one swift pull withdrew her dagger from the man's arm. Matthew winced; why could his Pet not stay out of things?

"I believe this is mine," she said impassively. "So sorry. It must have slipped."

Everyone in the inn started cheering; it turned out this man was a hated merchant who loaned money to desperate people, then collected many times over the borrowed amount. Pet swaggered back to her table and sat down. Paul and Luke were speechless; Matthew just shook his head. She picked up a piece of pastry and gnawed as if nothing had happened.

The excitement died down, and things settled back to normal. The injured man removed himself, vowing vengeance. Finally Paul and Luke found their tongues.

"Well," said Luke, "that was a skillful throw."

"Not especially. Matthew could have done as well."

Matthew squirmed in his chair; he wasn't used to having her defend him.

"So, you have managed to make a warrior out of our brother," Luke continued. "'Tis about time someone made something out of him."

"At least I did not try to ride a green-broke colt at the age of seven, and get bucked off into a nest of hornets," Matthew shot back.

"Ah, I can still feel every sting," Luke added with a grimace. "Mother stayed up all night and soothed my skin with vinegar. I smelled like a pickle for a week!"

"Remember when little Paul let all the rabbits from their hutches and partridges from their coops right before that big banquet? Never have I seen father so furious! He had been gathering them for weeks, and the guests were stuck with only venison and fish."

"I did not want them to die," said Paul.

"Better them than you," Matthew chuckled. "If mother had not come to your defense, I fear you would have been the main dish!"

Paul gave a dry expression to his brother. "At least I did not fall out of a tree trying to impress a fair maiden with my climbing prowess."

"Ah, yes," Luke chimed in, "Matthew, what was it you broke that time? An arm? Leg? My memory fails, help me here."

"I believe that was the leg," Matthew said with a sheepish grin. "I broke my arm falling through the ice on the lake chasing after a puppy."

Pet listened with interest as the brothers told stories on each other. It was obvious the brothers were very close. She suddenly felt an aching for Robert as she listened to them exchange jokes and jabs. Emptiness swept over her with the realization that she no longer had a family.

As she listened, Pet was able to draw some conclusions about the Cameron family. The sons fiercely loved their parents, with a special fondness for their mother, Lady Ellen Cameron. When they spoke of her there was a sense of respect and reverence that made Pet feel a pang of envy. She never had a mother, so listening to them reminisce about their childhood was painful.

Paul, the youngest at age twenty-one, was the sensitive hopeless romantic. He was extremely handsome, with straight dark hair and deep blue eyes. Pet learned his darker coloring was from his father; Matthew and Luke both favored their mother. She was relieved to know he wasn't a bastard. He was a poet, loved animals, didn't believe in violence and avoided it at all costs. He also possessed strong analytical skills and a strong power of observance. He was quiet, serious, a lover of women, and highly looking forward to taking a wife. Despite his demeanor he was vastly loyal to his brothers, but believed in justice to the fairer sex.

Luke was more like Matthew, only with distinct differences. Bigger, stronger, with boyish good looks, he was insecure around women, who often found him too shy, and was an excessive joker. In truth, his jokes usually excluded him from engaging in a serious conversation. A lover of horses, he ardently engaged in buying and selling the animals. He liked to make money and was always scouting for new businesses for their father to purchase. If there was a doubt of obtaining a new venture, his father always sent Luke, knowing full well that he would come back with the advantage in his favor.

Then there was Matthew, impulsive, happy-go-lucky, with no focus, who even stumbled upon knighthood falsely. A bit on the selfish side, he went after what he wanted with great fervor, then usually tossed it—or her—aside as a new project caught his interest. Women swooned for the overly handsome knight, who would flit from maiden to maiden, never settling on one and breaking many hearts, earning him the dubious reputation of a rake. Paul and Luke expressed total shock no woman had yet come forth to declare him father of her bastard. Matthew declared, while looking quite chagrined, that his reputation was totally unearned and was the result of malicious and jealous gossip.

As dinner drew to a close, Matthew and Luke both reached for the last piece of bread. While they agreed to share it, Pet noticed they both wore an identical ring on their little finger of their right hand. When she asked about them, Paul held up his hand, showing one, also. Matthew offered the explanation.

"'Tis our family crest—see, a green dragon on a red background. It has been our crest for generations, started by a great, great someone. Mother had one made for each of us on our tenth birthday. As we grew older, we each took to wearing it on our little finger."

"Mine's so bloody tight I cannot get it off," Luke said, as he tugged on his ring.

"I can remove mine quite nicely, seeing as I have not grown to the size of an ox," Paul said.

"Oh, an ox now, am I?"

"If the shoe fits."

Matthew put a hand up in front of each brother. "Silence, both of you, or I shall sic Pet on you." They both shut up.

Hours later and after many more chronicles of the brothers Cameron, Pet stood up and announced her retirement. Matthew accompanied her to the stairs, where she insisted he return to his brothers, and thanked him for sharing his family with her.

Later in her room, Pet thought about the Cameron family, and how different they were from the family she once had. She craved their closeness, something she had had only with Robert, but recently was starting to feel with Matthew. By this time tomorrow he would be on his way to the king, and she would be home, alone. Why did her heart feel so empty? Could it be she had actually fallen…? No, she told herself, it was not possible. Her life had purpose, his had none. If anything, she must distance herself from the reckless knight who had somehow wormed his way into her heart.

# ❧Chapter Ten❧

atthew and his brothers talked well into the night, when fatigue finally overtook them and they retired. But not before Luke volunteered to ride along with Matthew and Pet to Elton. He heard about the village, and how it was burned, and wanted to help Pet. Besides, he needed to find out more about this young warrior whom his brother seemed so determined to win over. Paul was going home to Cambridgeshire castle to take the information he and Luke had obtained for their father. Cambridgeshire was still about two day's ride away, whereas Elton would be reached that evening, so Paul could not help thinking Luke was getting the better deal. But then, he always did.

Pet already had Goliath saddled and ready when Matthew and Luke finally made their appearance in the stable. As Pet led the massive horse out, Luke gave a low whistle.

"Where ever did you find such a magnificent animal? Here, I must take a look at him!" He circled around the horse, inspecting every muscle, so it seemed, muttering comments to himself. Matthew was used to this behavior; Luke could never pass up a look at a beautiful horse much like Matthew never could a beautiful woman.

"Could I perchance ride him?" Luke asked eagerly. "I would love to test his gaits."

Pet shook her head. "That would not be advisable." With no further explanation, she led Goliath away.

Luke trudged dejectedly to Matthew, who was saddling up his own horse. "She does not like me," he said in a hurt tone.

121

"It has naught to do with liking you," Matthew answered. "Goliath belonged to her brother, and was a one-man horse. You probably would not last a few seconds on him."

Luke raised his eyebrows and nodded. "Oh, well, that is a different story. I have become rather fond of my bones, I would not want to lose any." He went to prepare his own horse.

The dry weather had held, although clouds threatened some light rain. Out in front of the inn, Pet waited for Matthew and met Paul preparing to leave. He smiled at her as he led his horse over, which looked rather diminutive beside Goliath.

"Do you think your steed is large enough?"

She smiled, and didn't answer. Goliath always did have that effect on people.

Paul suddenly got serious, and looked around quickly to make sure his brothers weren't within earshot. "Pet, if I may have a word?"

"Aye, Paul?"

"Luke has decided to ride with you and Matthew."

She raised an eyebrow. "Oh?"

"He is strong, as you can see, and is quite handy. He can help you build your village. He is a good man, with a big heart, but…" He shuffled his feet nervously.

"But, what?"

"Luke is harmless, but Matthew is not. Do not misunderstand, I love my brother, I just do not approve of his treatment of women."

"And just howe'er *does* he treat women?"

"Oh, he is wonderful at first, all flowery words and all, but he grows bored quickly, and soon he is off to another. Women fall in love easily with him, but he has never given his love. I cannot tell you how many hearts I have had to soothe. I do not want that to happen to you." He shifted his gaze to the ground.

Pet smiled, touched at his concern. "Paul, 'tis sweet of you to care, but worry not. Your roguish brother has no effect on me." As she spoke the words, she knew they weren't true. But no one would ever know, least of all Matthew.

"Good, because I have the feeling you are special. Actually, you are…" He lowered his gaze again.

"I am what?"

"You are incredible." He quickly mounted his horse, and looked down at her. "I wish I were the type of man who could win your heart, but I do not flatter myself into thinking I am. Matthew shall not stop until he gets what he wants. He has made it clear he wants you. Be careful, Pet."

"I will. Have a safe journey, Paul."

"And you. Tell my brothers farewell for me; I am already late in my departure." He reined around, and galloped away. As she watched him, his words strengthened her resolve to be rid of Matthew as quickly as possible.

Matthew and Luke led their horses around the corner, laughing at some joke Luke had told, but sobered up when they saw Paul riding away in the distance. Luke scratched his head in puzzlement.

"What, he did not even say goodbye?"

"He expressed his farewells for me to relay. He could not tarry longer." She cast Matthew a sour glare, and mounted Goliath.

Matthew frowned as he mounted his horse. What did he do now?

The three rode down the road side by side with Matthew in the center, leading the packhorse with the loot they obtained from the outlaws. Pet was going to turn it all over to Father Samson once back in Elton. Luke and Matthew exchanged brotherly banter, while Pet remained quiet. Paul's words still echoed in her mind. She was actually grateful Matthew had someone else to talk to so she could avoid him. It would make their final goodbye easier. And it *would* be final—she had made up her mind to tell him never to seek her out again. Elton would be rebuilt, the children would be returned, and life would settle into some kind of normalcy. Matthew did not fit into the life she had planned.

Matthew was listening to Luke ramble about some horse deal he closed, but his mind was on Pet. Hell, he might as well admit it; his mind was *always* on her. Usually a conquest had given in by now, but she was different. He was willing to do whatever it took to win her. Right now she seemed angry with him, and he had no idea why. She talked to Paul, perhaps he said something? Paul was always criticizing him for his treatment of women, even though he was not totally to blame. Women took one look at him, and immediately thought marriage was eminent. Was that his fault? If he so much as kissed a girl, she was all starry-eyed with love. He was not the relentless paramour everyone made him out to be. He had made every effort to be a friend, and indeed more, to her. So why was she angry?

"So," Luke was saying, "he finally had to admit the horse was lame! I got it for half its worth, and sold it the next month for twice what I paid!"

"You always were the ruthless deal maker, Luke," Matthew answered absent-mindedly as he stared at Pet.

"Well, I knew t'was only a stone bruise, but the poor chap had no idea. Father was most pleased with that deal."

"I think we have trouble."

Both men reined up their horses at Pet's observation. The road was blocked ahead of them by a man, whom they all recognized as the man from the inn—the one Pet had keenly planted her dagger into. The one who had vowed vengeance.

Pet drew her sword at the same time Matthew did. They glanced at each other, and Pet nodded. As they began to dismount, the man started to laugh.

"Thought you were going to get away with wingin' me, and losin' me what was owed me? Who's laughin' now, wench? Oh, I would think twice about usin' them swords, ere I was you. Thomas! Get out here!"

At his command, a younger man appeared from behind a tree, holding a small child around the neck. Pet brought her hand up, and Matthew lowered his sword at the same time she did.

"See, the way I figure it, you got a blinkin' bleedin' heart, what don't like to see some poor little underlin's get hurt. Now this waif, I don't care about her, but you do, don't you? See, if I don't get what's owed me, I'll have Thomas kill her— it is that simple. Well? Do I get my money, or not?"

Pet stared at the man with contempt. "It takes a brave man indeed to hide behind a small child."

The man chortled with great gusto. "Oh, spare me your preachin', I have no need for it. Either you give me all your coin, or she dies."

Pet was silent, then smiled as she leaned into Matthew. "Do nothing," she ordered, and then turned to the waiting man. "Sir, as you see, my partner and I are hired mercenaries. We do not carry many valuables, unless you count these worthless trinkets." She pointed to the packhorse, hoping the man was as greedy as she thought. "You are welcome to them. As for me, my greatest possession is my horse, which you can see, is quite a fabulous animal that would fetch quite a price. Other than him, I have naught to give you."

Luke about fell off his horse in aggravation. "Surely she does not mean to hand over that animal to this—this scum!"

Matthew cast his brother a stern look. "Quiet, Luke," he said softly. "She knows what she is doing."

The man rubbed his chin as he looked Goliath over. "Well, now, he does appear to be quite a specimen, don't he? Hmmm." As he thought, Pet again leaned toward Matthew, speaking low.

"Do you still have that sling?"

"Oh, you mean my *toy*?"

"Spare me your indignation, just be ready."

"Very well!" the man announced, "I will take your horse and everything on that packhorse in exchange for this worthless child's life. Throw down your swords! Thomas, collect them."

Pet and Matthew laid down both sets of their swords and Thomas cautiously picked them up and carried them over to his father.

"We are weaponless," Pet called. "Hand me the child, and I will hand you my horse."

"Thomas—give her the waif!"

The man named Thomas roughly picked up the small girl and threw her at Pet's feet. The child immediately started crying, and Pet dropped to her knees to comfort her.

"The horse!" the man yelled.

Pet stood up, assured the child was scared, but unhurt. "I will bring him." She sauntered past Matthew and grabbed his hand, dropping a good-sized rock in it. "As soon as he begins to mount, hit Goliath in the flank with your sling." She grabbed Goliath's reins and strolled up to the man, handed him the reins, and stepped back—way back.

"He is a wonderful horse to ride, very large as you can see. Any man who rides him appears very important to others."

Matthew reached very slowly in his pocket and retrieved the sling. He put the rock in the leather triangle and waited.

"Well now, is that right?" the man was saying. He drew himself up tall. "I just might ride him into town; let the people know they cannot mess with me." He looked up at the huge animal and frowned. "Thomas, come 'ere and help me on this great beast!"

"Aye, father," Thomas answered, and ran to his father's side.

Matthew was ready. He went unnoticed as the son shoved his ill-fated father up on the horse. He swung the sling around three times, and let the rock fly. It connected very soundly right on Goliath's flank.

If hell itself had been revealed to the world, it would not have compared with the power of the furious horse. He lunged forward, reared, twisted, and bucked, all with the hapless man holding on for dear life. He cried for Thomas to hold the animal, but Thomas couldn't get close enough to grab him. In one more twisting buck, the man went flying over Goliath's head, landing hard in front of the frenzied horse. Goliath once again reared, and when he came down, his front hooves landed on the fallen man's leg. He screamed in agony as his bone snapped. Pet finally was able to grab Goliath, who calmed down immediately. Matthew had already grabbed the swords, and Luke had dismounted and grabbed the child.

"My leg!" the man wailed, "he broke my leg!"

Pet led the horse up to the man and stopped. "Do not worry. Someone will come along eventually and rescue you." She took another step, and then turned with a smile. "Oh, for your knowledge, there's no such thing as a worthless child." She led Goliath up to Matthew and Luke, and knelt down by the crying girl.

"Shh, 'tis fine now, you can go home. Do you know your way home?" The child shook her head.

"We have to return the girl. Matthew, hand her up to me after I get on Goliath. Oh…good throw."

She tossed the compliment out as if it was meaningless, but Matthew knew it was difficult for her to say. As he handed the girl up to Pet, now sitting on a totally calm Goliath, he half smiled and posed a question.

"Thank you, but I am curious. Why did you have me hit him? Would he not have bucked anyway?"

She seated the little girl in front of her. "Most likely, but I was not leaving it to chance. That is the way Robert trained him; he put volunteers on his back and hit him in the flank. Goliath began to relate strange riders to being hit, and would go wild." She paused and rewarded him with a small smile. "I mean it, Matthew. You did well." She reined the horse back toward town, leaving Matthew feeling extremely pleased with himself.

Luke, meanwhile, had found some rope, and was tying Thomas to a tree. The screaming, wailing man still lay in the road lamenting his leg. Luke was glad to be leaving him so he wouldn't have to listen to him any longer. He mounted and rode up to Matthew, and they followed behind Pet, who was a few steps ahead.

"Your lady is certainly unique," Luke commented. "I would never let her go."

Matthew acknowledged with a solemn nod. "I do not plan to."

Within minutes of reaching the town, a hysterical woman saw Pet, and came running up holding out her hands. Pet handed the child down to her, while the mother thanked Pet profusely. Her mission accomplished, Pet reined around and the three again rode out of town.

When they came back to Thomas and his father, a small unsympathetic crowd had gathered. Townsfolk were jeering and kicking the lame man, who was attempting to crawl away while screaming for them to have mercy. The three could only assume the crowd had all been victims of the man's business practices. Thomas, still tied to a tree, could only offer insults.

They made up for lost time by galloping for a while. Pet forever had to stop and wait, as Goliath was the fastest horse. They eventually slowed to a walk to rest the horses. Luke and Matthew talked on a wide range of subjects, until the topic came around to the renegades.

"'Tis terrible," Luke was saying. "The king is most anxious to have this gang caught. They stir up resentment of nobles."

"There is no more gang," Matthew answered. "The mission the king sent me on is complete, but not without casualties." He cast Pet a downhearted look.

"Oh? So, you did find them? Well done, Matthew...you make us proud!"

"Hold your pride, brother, t'was not me, but Pet who found and killed them."

At that, Pet turned her head, proving she had been listening after all, and not ignoring them like Matthew thought. "Do not be so modest, Sir Knight, if memory serves, you were there also."

Luke was incredulous. "You, Pet? You accomplished what a small army could not do?"

"I told you, Matthew was with me. T'was not that difficult."

"I did naught, Pet. You were the one who had the ideas."

"You helped carry them out. Give yourself some credit."

"I am honorable, if naught else. I will not take credit where none is due."

"Then why not tell the king how you apprehended and overtook the spy from the Yorkist army? I avow he would find the story most interesting."

Matthew turned red with embarrassment. "Henceforth I will never hear the end of that. Have you no pity, Milady?"

"Not when it comes to you."

"Enough, you two!" Luke shouted. They both turned to look at him. "You fight like an old married couple. My ears shall sting if you do not cease."

Pet frowned, but Matthew appeared very pleased with Luke's analogy.

They reached Elton by nightfall. Raymond was delighted to see Pet unhurt, and surprised to see Matthew still with her. Luke was also a surprise, but a nice one, since he had come to help. Raymond explained the progress after the horses were taken care of, and supplies unpacked.

"'The town itself has been rebuilt. Now we are working on the tenants. The townsfolk are reluctant to help with the free landholders, therefore progress has been slow. Even so, all but four homes have been rebuilt."

"We will have those homes built in a few days," confirmed Luke.

Pet was mostly concerned about the crops, and if there would be enough manpower to harvest everything. The staple crops at Elton were those of most English manors: barley, wheat, oats, rye, peas and beans. Raymond assured her everything was under control, but Luke seemed concerned, and decided to talk to Raymond by himself later. The opportunity came after dinner, as the men enjoyed a brandy in the study by the fireplace. Pet had made herself scarce, which annoyed Matthew to no end, as he wanted to spend time with her alone.

"So, what is your yield, Sir Raymond?" Luke began.

"Four to one for barley, four to one for wheat, a whit o'er two to one for oats, and four to one for beans and peas."

"Ah, but have you considered the price fluctuations for wheat? Two bushels plants an acre. Even without drought or flood, your labor costs and price uncertainty could make a lord's profit on crops precarious, at the least."

"Aye, yes, but I also take into account our butter and cheese production."

Matthew rolled his eyes and yawned. He was sure this was all just fascinating, but he didn't have the slightest idea what they were talking about, and really didn't care to. He just wanted to find Pet. He wandered through the large manor, looking into unlocked rooms, until he found her in her father's library—the one with the picture of her and Robert over the mantle. She was reading the last quarterly report of the manor's profits, and looked as lost as Matthew had felt listening to Luke and Raymond. She didn't notice him standing at the door, until he purposely made a noise and she glanced up.

"Oh, Matthew. I was just reading these, um, figures. I am the master of Elton, now, hence I suppose I must learn how to run it."

Matthew sat down at a chair by the desk. "Raymond seems most capable. Why not let him handle it?"

"Because that would not be right. 'Tis my responsibility."

Matthew leaned forward. "Does it have to be, Pet? Have you not just wanted to give it all up at times?"

"Give it up? No, ne'er. 'Tis my home."

"But, it does not have to be." He reached out and took her hand. "Pet, I could offer you so much. My father is lord of all Cambridgeshire. As eldest son, I stand to inherit a great deal. Pet, marry me. You would never have to work again."

She withdrew her hand, and stared at him with incredulity. "You are nothing if not persistent, but the answer is still no, and shall always be. I want not to be lazy, and sit around all day whilst servants do my bidding. Do you really think so low of me?"

"Very well, I will let you work all you want. Now will you marry me?"

"No."

He hit the desk with his fist. "Why? Do you care naught for me?"

She leaned back in her chair, and folded her arms. "I care about you, Matthew, but that is all."

"That is enough, for now. More will come later."

She looked up at the portrait of her and Robert, and her face took on a saddened quality, mixed with what seemed to be apprehension. "Matthew, I..." She stopped and seemed not able to continue.

He reached out and grabbed her hand again. "What, Pet?"

Her expression was like one he had never seen on her before. For a moment she withdrew within herself, and her eyes stared straight through him.

"Pet? Are you all right?"

She slowly focused on him, and blinked. "Aye. I am fine." She closed her eyes, and he saw her inner control sweep over her, and in a moment she was herself again. Matthew couldn't help think she had been on the verge of telling him something, but had stopped herself. She jerked her hand away.

"Matthew, there are plenty of maidens willing to take your hand. If you are so anxious to be married..."

"I am not so anxious to be married, I am anxious to keep you."

"You cannot keep what you do not possess."

"Damn it woman!" He clenched his fists and took a deep breath. There was no avoiding it; he had to tell her how he felt. "Pet, I—I have to tell you something."

"Tell me, or yell at me?"

He ignored her sarcasm. "There is a major reason I want to marry you."

"I am sure, and 'tis probably why I am not interested."

"Would you let me speak?" She fell silent, and he tried to continue. "You see Pet, I...you..." *Just tell her you love her, you imbecile!* "First of all, I do not consider it weak to..."

Luke and Raymond burst into the room at that moment, cutting his words off mid-sentence. Matthew sat back in his chair with a groan.

"So this is where you two went off to!" Raymond bellowed. "I was about to relay the story to Luke how Elton changed lords so abruptly in the 1100's. Luke thought Sir Matthew would also like to hear it."

"Thank you, Luke," said Matthew, as he slumped down in his chair.

Pet appeared extremely relieved to have company, and gladly pushed her ledger book aside. "Aye, Raymond, please tell the story—I never tire of it."

Raymond cleared his throat dramatically, and began. "In the eleventh century, Elton was a flourishing village with an Anglo-Saxon lord. When he died, his widow married a Danish noble named Dacus."

Pet took up the story. "The bishop of Dorchester, a man named Aetheric, joined an escort traveling with King Cnut to the ends of the kingdom. When the party stopped to spend the night in Nassington, that was a town close to Elton back then, Aetheric and four of the king's secretaries were lodged in Elton in Dacus's manor house."

Even though Matthew was upset at the intrusion, he found himself listening intently. Pet knew more about the history of her town than he knew, or ever cared to know, about Cambridgeshire. It obviously meant a lot to her. And he had just stupidly asked her to give it up. Could he make any more blunders in winning her?

Raymond let out a big belly laugh. "Dacus could not help brag about the cattle and sheep that grazed his meadows, the plows that cultivated his fields, and the rents the village paid him. Aetheric remarked that he would like to buy such a manor."

"The stupid and vain Dacus had no intention of selling," Pet continued, "but told his guest that he would turn the village o'er if Aetheric gave him fifty golden marks the next morning at dawn. The bishop called on the king's secretaries to witness the offer and asked if Dacus's wife agreed to it. She agreed, knowing it was impossible. When everyone went to sleep, Aetheric mounted a horse and rode to Nassington, where he found the king playing chess because of boredom. Cnut ordered a quantity of gold to be sent to Elton, and at dawn Aetheric wakened Dacus and triumphantly presented him with the money."

"Oh, did he wail!" continued Raymond. "He tried to renege, but his arguments would not be heard. The outwitted couple packed up their furniture and belongings, and departed with their household and their animals, leaving bare walls for the new lord. Aetheric was not sure what to do with his new acquisition, but ended up assigning the village of Elton to Ramsey Abbey as one of its conventual manors, designed for the monk's support."

"So," Matthew asked, "howe'er did Pet's family end up with Elton?"

"My great, great grandfather was a Norman knight," she answered. "Ramsey Abbey endowed loyal knights with estates in return for military services. My ancestor was given Elton, and all the land and tenants. It has taken care of my family very well for generations."

Luke nodded with a smile. "I thought you had a whit of Norman blood in you! Anyone who can throw a dagger like you, well, I should have known. You have a right to be proud. Elton is a fine village."

Matthew agreed. He wished he'd never opened his big mouth and asked her to get rid of it just to marry him. What could he have been thinking?

They all talked some more, then the festivities wound down, and Luke and Raymond excused themselves. Pet was making an attempt to follow behind Raymond, when Matthew grabbed her arm.

"I still wish to talk with you," he said.

"I do *not* want to talk with you."

"So, you now plan to ignore me, because I wish to marry you?"

"No, I plan to tell you goodbye."

He drew himself up. "Goodbye?"

"Matthew, it is time to sever our relationship. You must return to the king; I must retrieve the children and help them begin their lives here. I have a lot to learn, and I fear you are in the way." She turned to leave.

"Just like that, you plan to toss me out of your life! I think not, Pet!" He grabbed her before she could protest, and brought his lips down on hers.

She was so taken by surprise it took her a few seconds to respond. But during that few seconds the passionate kiss stirred Matthew down to the depths of his soul. Holding, kissing, being this close to her just strengthened his resolve to make Pet his own. He pulled her tighter, until her body molded into his. She began to kiss him in return, her hands fondling his back as he raked his hands through her soft, shaggy mane. The kiss deepened, becoming a means for two people desperately seeking ultimate closeness. Matthew groaned from the passion she exhibited. She suddenly pulled away, out of breath and weak, her breaths coming in jagged gasps much like his. Their eyes locked in mutual longing. She took a few backward steps, then turned and ran down the hall to escape him.

"Pet," he gasped, but she left him there, leaning against the wall with closed eyes, trying to regain his composure.

She ran to her room, slammed the door, and curled up in a ball on her bed. Her breathing was labored and sporadic. Blinking back the stinging tears, she closed her eyes in desperation. "Oh, Robert," she whispered. "Help me. I fear I am in love with him." Her fists clenched as she fought the memory of his kiss. "What am I going to do? Oh Robert, what am I going to do?"

# ❧Chapter Eleven❧

atthew opened his eyes and realized the sun was already up. He didn't remember what time he finally fell into a fitful sleep. He lay awake the night before wondering why Pet fought him so relentlessly, and what he could do to win her over. His heart was lost to her. He could still taste the kiss, and how she felt pressed against him. Oh Lord, give him strength…she had done unwittingly what many had tried—she had captured his heart. Stupid and weak, be damned, she had to know he loved her.

When he entered the dining room, Raymond and Luke were already deep in discussion planning the felling of trees to make planks. Matthew sat down, poured some tea, grabbed a biscuit, and listened in total boredom. He was finally able to work a question in when Luke paused for a drink.

"Where is Pet?"

The two men looked at each other, then at Matthew, with confusion clouding their faces.

"Thou knowest not?" Raymond asked after a short hesitation.

"Know what?" Matthew felt a panic building again, something he felt often ever since he met her.

"She departed early this morning to get the children. She said thee would be leaving today, and she could not delay her departure to say goodbye."

Matthew felt devastated. She just left, like that, leaving a passionate kiss, and no farewell between them? Did he mean so little to her?

"I am going after her." He leapt to his feet, determined she wasn't going to discharge him that easy. "Raymond, I need a fast, fresh horse."

"Thou are in luck, lad. She did not take Goliath, fearing he needed rest. I will let thee take my own horse; he is fast and strong, and should be able to catch up to the mare she took."

Luke concealed his amusement as he watched his brother storm out. The man was in love; there was no getting around it. And Luke was extremely pleased that it was Pet who held his brother's heart. It was time someone led him a merry chase, and she certainly seemed to be doing just that.

The horse Raymond supplied was indeed a good one. Matthew rode hard, pushing the animal to its limits before stopping to rest. He painfully remembered the last time he rode all day to go after the raven-haired warrior who seemed to have a penchant for taking off on him. Only, this time he didn't have a small passenger riding behind him, ready to pull him off at the first tree branch.

A light rain was falling by the time he reached the orphanage. He dismounted with a jump, leaving the horse to fend for itself, and ran to the front doors of the large nunnery. Before he could knock, the door opened and the Prioress greeted him with a solemn face.

"Lord Matthew...I was hoping you were on your way. We—we know not what to do."

"What are you talking about? Where's Pet?"

"She needs you, Sire. Maybe you can reach her. She will not respond to any of us."

His sense of concern reached its height. "Is she hurt? Where is she?"

"Follow me." The Prioress led him down a long hallway, then turned onto a corridor, and stopped in front of a door where several other nuns sat praying on wooden benches. The stark walls matched the alarming silence.

"We did all we could, lord Matthew. Pet arrived right before she died."

Matthew felt a tremor shake through him. "Died?"

"The child, Mary. She fell gravely ill soon after you brought her. Breathing became labored, and she possessed the fever. We did everything but she was so small, and did not have the strength to fight. Pet arrived hours ago, and held the child until death claimed her. We have tried to take the child away to prepare her for burial, but Pet will not let us take her. She is in this room." She quietly opened the door.

Matthew swallowed as he blinked back tears. He stepped inside the room, and shut the door behind him.

Pet sat cross-legged on the floor, holding the precious bundle close to her chest. She stared at the floor with no expression. There were no tears. He took a deep breath and knelt down in front of her. Pet didn't recognize his presence; he doubted if she even knew he was there. His love for her increased at that moment as he watched her desperately clutch the dead baby, not willing to let her go.

"Pet?" He looked into her eyes, and saw nothing. "Sweetheart, it is I, Matthew. Look at me." He had never dared use an endearing name for her before, but it just came out, and he realized he meant it. She still didn't acknowledge him. Her shocked blank stare broke his heart. Would there be no end of suffering for this brave, young woman?

"Pet, give me the child." He reached for the bundle, but she jerked away. "Pet, the nuns want to prepare her. Come on, give her to me."

She slowly lifted her eyes and focused on his face. The pain in her eyes filled the room as well as his soul. "Matthew?" The word was barely audible.

"Aye, I am here, Pet. Let me have Mary." He held out his hands.

"No—no, she needs me!" She clutched the baby even tighter.

"Pet, sweetheart, she is gone. There is naught you can do. Please, give her to me." He reached out for the bundle, and this time she weakly gave it up. He carried the lifeless bundle to the door, and handed the child to the waiting nuns. Then he went back to Pet.

She stared ahead at nothing. Helplessness engulfed him, and he drew her into his arms and just held her. He stroked her hair as she laid her head on his shoulder, and he tried to console her the best he could. Why was this brave, proud girl made to suffer so?

"'Tis all right to cry, Pet," he said, as his own tears ran down his cheeks. She looked up and brought a finger to his face, wiping away the moisture. She looked at her finger, wet with his tears, then back at him.

"I cannot cry, Matthew. Cry for me." She sounded so heartbroken, so defeated; he drew her to him and let his own tears feel her sorrow. Finally she pulled away and he saw a bit of control had returned to her face.

"She had no chance to live. Her short life held no meaning."

"No, Pet—you are wrong. You loved her. Love, no matter how short, is never meaningless."

She stared at him for a long moment, and then nodded slowly. He helped her to her feet, and they left the room. The Prioress stood waiting, and when she saw Pet, she put out her arms and welcomed Pet into her grasp. Pet allowed herself to be hugged, then pulled away. She asked the Prioress if Mary could be buried in the nunnery cemetery, and she readily obliged. A small wooden coffin would be obtained, and there would be a graveside funeral as soon as possible at Pet's request. With that matter taken care of, Pet turned to the nun with a determined look.

"I need to see my children."

"Aye, of course. They are in the north wing, where the other children are. Follow me."

She led them to another section of the large nunnery, to the orphanage wing, where dozens of children were cared for. They entered a large room, where a fire was crackling and cheerful pictures hung on the walls. Children were everywhere, playing, reading, even napping. Pet's children were all sitting in a little circle while Anna, the oldest, attempted to read a nursery rhyme.

"They are always together," the Prioress said to Pet. They have not made any other friends while they have been here. Go to them, I shall let you know when we are ready for the burial."

Suddenly Andrew looked up and saw Matthew. He jumped up and threw his arms around the overwhelmed knight, as did Georgie and Stuart.

"You did not forget us!" Andrew cried.

"Howe'er could I forget a future knight?" Matthew teased back, as he hugged the boys.

The rest exploded with glee. Anna ran into Pet's arms, and other children hugged whomever they reached first. "Pet! You came back!"

"Of a surety I came back, did you think I forgot you?"

The children jumped around excitingly, until Pet calmed them down. "Children, I have something to tell you." The tone of her voice indicated the severity of the message.

Anna instantly began crying. "'Tis Mary!" she cried, and sought the refuge of Matthew's arms. He held her while Pet looked on helplessly. She had no idea how attached the children had become to Matthew, and he to them. A sensation of regret ran through her. How would she explain his imminent departure? Of course, Matthew was thinking no such thoughts; he had no intentions of leaving.

The other children were all aware Mary had been very sick, so the news of her death was almost expected. They all cried, and Matthew and Pet did the best they could to console them. As Pet watched Matthew talk and try to cheer up the children, she realized for the first time that she didn't question his presence. It was as if she almost expected him to be there when she needed him, like Robert used to be. Had she used him to replace Robert? Confusion ran rampant through her mind.

They explained to the children they were all leaving for home on the morrow. This time would be different, however, as they were traveling on the road in a wagon the nuns were loaning them. They would get to stay at an inn, and reach home the next day. Pet had prearranged this when she first brought the children there, and they were excited for what was sure to be a grand adventure.

But first, there was a child to bury.

A young nun tapped Pet on the shoulder and informed her they were ready for the burial. They all followed the sister to the gated cemetery located to one side of the nunnery.

The little casket containing Mary's body sat beside a small hole in the ground. Many nuns stood around the grave, their heads bowed in reverence. The children and Pet got on their knees, while Matthew stood with his head bowed. He wished he had known the child better.

The Prioress said a few short words about God's love and heaven, but Pet didn't hear much of what she said. The children all cried, and she wished she could release her pain in the same way. Words became a blur as she heard the Prioress say her message.

"God have mercy on her, and bring her into his bliss that shall last forever, wherefore each man and woman that is wise, make him ready thereto; for we all shall die, and we know not how soon. Amen"

Pet rose, took one last look at the small casket, then turned and lumbered silently away. The prioress looked at Matthew, and shook her head.

"'Tis a strange girl that cannot cry. She buries her pain so deep, I pray someday it does not surface all at once."

Matthew handed the Prioress a piece of paper. "Buy the child a stone. Send the bill and this note to the Cameron estate in Cambridgeshire. My signature is my bond."

The Prioress nodded, and thanked him. He gathered the children, and followed Pet back into the nunnery to ready the children for bed.

Pet was given a room, and Matthew volunteered to sleep in the stable. There was a good straw pile that would make a soft bed. He threw a blanket on top, and settled down for what restless sleep he could muster.

He dozed on and off, waking up at every little sound, when deep in the night he was sure someone had spoken his name. It was pitch black in the barn; the only light was through a small window casting gray shadows on the wall. He sat up and tried to focus on anything around him.

"Matthew?" The voice was so low he barely heard it.

"Pet? Is that you?" His heart soared at the same time his mind flashed concern.

"Aye." She stepped closer and he could make out her fully clothed figure.

"What is wrong, Pet?"

"I—I do not think I can be alone tonight. I keep thinking of Mary." She paused, and her voice lowered to almost a whisper. "I need Robert."

He reached out and grabbed her hand. "No, you need me. Come here, Pet. Lay beside me, and use my arm as your pillow." He pulled her down and she lay down beside him, rolling over on her side facing away. He made no pretense this time, and curled up behind her with his arm wrapped around her. "You should know by now, Pet, you never have to be alone." She closed her eyes and let him hold her, and soon her breathing was steady and soft.

He had mixed feelings. She had, for the first time, come to him for comfort, but it had taken the death of a child. No matter. Regardless of the circumstances, she had come to him, and sought his arms. This was encouraging. He fell asleep holding her close, a smile on his face, and contentment in his heart.

Pet awakened with a jolt. It took a few seconds to remember where she was. She rolled over to discover she was alone, and it was already daylight. She called Matthew's name; her reply was a horse's nicker.

She got up and stumbled outside. It proved to be a sunny day, and she squinted at the brightness after leaving the dark barn. Matthew and the children were all busy packing up the wagon. When the children saw her, they all ran to greet her, laughing and jumping excitingly.

"Pet! Sir Matthew said to let you sleep, so we did!"

"Constance wanted to wake you up, but I stopped her."

"Did not!" "Did too!"

"I stayed up all night."

"I do not want to ride in the wagon, I want to ride a horse."

"I am hungry!" "Me too."

"I am thirsty!" "Me too."

"When do I get my own horse?"

"Why did you sleep in the barn?"

The barrage was endless, and Pet looked helplessly at Matthew with a small grimace. He just smiled back, and continued to hitch the horses to the wagon.

"Very well, children, everyone be quiet," she finally commanded. "Have you all eaten yet?" Most nodded, except little Stuart, the quiet four-year-old.

"Stuart? You did not eat?"

He shook his head.

"Fine, you all stay here and help Sir Matthew hitch up the horses. Stuart and I are going to find something to eat." She took the little boy's hand and began to walk to the door. As she strolled past Matthew, he leaned into her ear.

"You snore," he said in a low voice.

She stopped and glared at him, then formed a small smile. "Children, to help you pass the time, why not beseech *Sir* Matthew how 'tis he came to be a knight? You might find the story amusing. I know I did." She strutted off feeling smug, leaving him flinching.

When everyone was fed and everything was ready for the trip, Matthew tied their riding horses behind the wagon since he would have to rein the wagon horses. *Pity she hadn't brought Goliath*, he thought. *He could pull this wagon by himself.* Pet approached just as he was finishing.

"What are you doing?" she asked.

"Tying the horses behind. Why?"

She let out a short laugh. "I am not riding in the wagon. I will ride my horse. You may ride in the wagon."

Matthew produced an I-don't-think-so smile, and shook his head. "Oh, no, sweet Pet, not this time. You are riding in the wagon with me."

"I think not." She started to turn when he caught her arm.

"May I remind you I was not even invited along on this expedition? That you left me back at Elton without so much as a goodbye? Pray tell, Pet, who would be reining these horses if I were not here?" He folded his arms and gave her a cocky grin.

Her look could have boiled water. "Very well, mayhap you have a point. But you are here now, and I see no reason why we should both suffer."

"Would you be suffering so to ride with me? Is my company so horrid?"

No, I—oh very well, I will ride in front with you. But I warn you, I am not pleased with riding in wagons." She frowned, and added, "I must say, for a knight you certainly do not act very chivalrous."

"On the contrary, I believe I am behaving quite gallant. I rode all day to reach you after being rudely abandoned, and am accompanying you back without complaint. All I beseech for my reward is to again hold you at night. Fully clothed, naturally," he quickly added.

She grinned back through her teeth. "Naturally."

He suddenly got serious. "You knew I would come, did you not?"

"Wh-what is your meaning?"

"Yesterday, when you left me at Elton, you knew I could not go to London, not after…"

She backed up, her face white. "After what?"

"Come Pet, do you think I could forget a kiss such as that? It stirred me down to my toes. And if I am not mistaken, it had the same effect on you."

"You are mistaken. T'was just…a temporary lapse in judgment. It shall not happen again."

"I fear you are the one who is mistaken." He strode toward her as she backed up.

"Stay away! The children—"

"Are not watching. I wish to test your judgment again."

"No!" She ran quickly to the children, who were playing on the nunnery's front lawn. Matthew watched her with a large grin.

"Temporary lapse. Who does she think she is fooling?"

The trip was finally under way. Matthew was hoping by having her up in front with him there would be opportunity for small talk. However, the children had other ideas. If one wasn't asking a question, one was telling some long, elaborate story. Even though it was not what Matthew had planned, he still found he rather enjoyed getting to know the children better. One exchange was particularly memorable.

Julie, the pretty little blond with the huge blue eyes, especially liked Matthew. She was a quiet child, who preferred to just sit and be close, as other children monopolized the conversation. Finally, when there was a rare pause, she tapped Matthew on the shoulder.

"Sir Matthew, are you going to marry Pet and be our father?"

"Aye," he said without hesitation.

"No!" Pet corrected quickly. "Matthew, do not feed these children's heads so. Lies are not becoming for a knight."

The little girl giggled, and gave a Matthew a hug.

"She will marry me," Matthew said softly in Julie's ear, "she just does not know it yet." Julie giggled again.

The sisters, Constance and Cassandra, entered in the rally.

"Who *will* be our father, Pet?" Constance asked.

"Aye, Pet, who?" Cassandra added.

Pet squirmed in her seat. "Where is it written that a child must have a father? I believe we will all be just fine without one. Men are messy, and domineering, and not enjoyable to have around anyway. Who needs them?"

"Oh, so now I am messy and domineering, is it? Have you nothing good to say about me at all?"

"I think Sir Matthew is very handsome, do you not, Pet?" Constance asked innocently.

Pet frowned. "He is pleasant enough to look at."

"And very brave," Julie added. "I pray he would make a fine father."

The other children joined in.

"He lets me ride his horse," Andrew said.

"I have plenty of horses for you to ride," Pet countered.

"He is a knight, and can protect us!" Rosie offered.

"I can protect us all just fine," Pet said back.

"He likes you very much," Anna said with a smile. "He would make a fine husband."

"It matters not that he likes me. Enough of this! Have you all joined together against me? Go to the back, and hush." They all moaned and groaned, but did as they were told.

Matthew had kept quiet and let the children state his case for him, but now could not keep still. "It *does* matter."

Pet turned and gave him a perplexed look. "That you like me? No, it does not. I have had many men like me, and I did not rush to the altar with them."

"But did you like them as well? As much as you like me?"

"I never said I liked you."

"Come on, Pet, admit it. You rather like having me around."

"Very well. Sometimes you are tolerable."

He chuckled. "Is that up from insufferable?"

"No, you are still that."

He laughed, and shook his head. She was a stubborn woman.

Their planned night's lodging was full, for which Matthew was thankful, as it did not look like the kind of place for children to stay at. Besides, it was a cloudless night with lots of stars, and the children wanted to sleep outdoors anyway.

The girls stayed in the wagon, but the boys wanted to rough it on the ground. The nuns had supplied them with plenty of bedrolls for just this happenstance, so no one would get cold. They all made themselves busy making their beds. After dinner, Anna approached Pet with two younger ones in tow.

"Pet? The nuns taught us a prayer. Would you like to hear it?"

Pet stopped what she was doing. "A prayer?" She suddenly realized she had been a bit lax practicing her own faith. She hadn't even thought of a bedtime prayer. "Aye, Anna, that would be nice."

The children all gathered in a circle, and joined hands. Anna took Pet's hand, and forced her to join. Matthew stood by alone, until Andrew reached out and included him in the group, also. Anna cleared her throat.

"Very well, just like the nuns taught us." They all started reciting together.

"Day by day, O dear Lord, three things I pray: To see thee more clearly, to love thee more dearly, to follow thee more nearly, day by day by day. Amen."

Pet kissed them all goodnight, and tucked everyone in. While she was busy with that, Matthew took some bedrolls and blankets, and made a cozy mattress for him and Pet. He pointed to the bed, and smiled at her, motioning for her to lie down.

"You are not serious," she seethed.

"I may be messy, and domineering, but I am always serious. I said my reward for this misadventure is to hold you at night, and I intend to collect. Now, lay down."

She cast him a sideways look, and slowly lay on the inviting blankets. As usual, she rolled over on her side, and, as usual, he cuddled up behind her with his arm draped around her. "I know not how I ever slept before," he teased, as he nuzzled her neck and she fought to pull away.

"Do not get used to this," she simmered. "In one more night you shall be gone, and my company will not keep you warm."

"Quiet, woman. Soon you will be my wife, and I will keep you warm and naked under covers."

She stiffened, and he laughed at her reaction. He most likely would not have laughed if he could have seen the stricken look on her face.

Soon the whole camp was asleep.

The next day went without incident, making good time on the road, and they arrived in Elton by nightfall the next evening. Pet was busy with servants and children, showing everyone their rooms she had ordered made ready. The house was busy with noise and activity. Matthew was helping Luke unhitch the horses from the wagon when Raymond approached him.

"Sir Matthew? May I have a word with thee?"

"Aye, Raymond, what is it?"

The huge man looked very grim, and took a parchment from his pocket. "This arrived yesterday. 'Tis from the king."

Matthew's first thought was that the king was extremely angry with him for his absence, and was ordering him back. "Alas, let me see."

"'Tis not for you, 'tis for Pet."

"For Pet? What does it say?"

"Nothing I fear she wants to know. The king is ordering a reduction of her land-holdings to one third, since there is no male heir. He does not feel a young girl can manage a township this large. The land is to be relinquished to the Ramsey Abbey."

"That is unfair," Luke shouted. "She is more than capable of running Elton!"

"What!" Matthew frowned, and held out his hand. "Give me that." He read it all himself, with a grim expression matching Raymond's. Obviously the king had been informed of Pet's father and brothers' deaths. It was common for a widow, or single daughter to have their land reduced in the case of the lack of a male heir, unless…He suddenly smiled, and handed the parchment back to Raymond. A fiendishly clever idea was starting to form.

"Give this to her later tonight, when the children are all settled. Do not tell her you showed this to me. It might upset her."

"Aye, Milord. I hope this can be prevented."

"You can count on it." Matthew's smile perplexed Raymond. What on earth did he have to smile about? Raymond returned to his duties, leaving the brothers alone.

Luke stared at Matthew, a quiet stare with unnerving intensity he used when he was unhappy with something.

Matthew turned at looked innocently at him. "What?"

"I know that look. What are you up to, now?"

"Brother, I am wounded by your low opinion of me. I am up to naught, I assure you."

"Why do I not believe you?"

"I simply plan on taking her with me to the king, and speaking in her behalf. I avow once he meets her, he will see that she is capable and smart."

Luke still harbored the doubting glare, but knew he wouldn't get anything else out of his older brother. He hated confrontations with Matthew, so dropped the subject and moved on to unfair land-holding laws. Finally they went in for dinner.

Matthew purposely avoided Pet after eating. He saw Raymond approach her, and that was his cue to leave. If Pet needed him, he wanted her to come to him. He sought out William and took a late night stroll in the gardens with the boy, talking about horses, of course, and anything else but Pet. It was a clear night with bright moonlight, so it

was fairly easy for Pet to find them. Not to mention the fact that
Matthew made sure he talked loudly and laughed often. William was
laughing at one of Matthew's stories, when they both became aware of
her presence. They both twirled around to see her standing behind
them with a drawn and near-panicked expression.

"Matthew? May I have a moment?"

William took the overwhelming hint to leave, and simply said
good night.

"You may have all the moments you want, fair lady; the rest of your
life, if you so desire."

"Matthew, this is no time for jokes. Something terrible has happened."

Matthew forced himself to straighten his face. "I am sorry, Pet—what
is wrong?"

"The king has…" Her voice broke, and he reached out and touched
her shoulder.

"What? What has the king done?"

Her bewildered eyes rose to meet his. "He—he is taking Elton away
from me. Not all, but almost. He says I am not capable of running such
a large township. Matthew…what am I going to do?"

He frowned grimly, and appeared deep in thought. He had to
muster up all the acting ability he had. "Hmmm," he thought out
loud. His face suddenly brightened. "I just had a thought…why do
you not come with me to the king? I shall speak in your behalf, and I
am certain he will, um…come up with a way to help you." *It just
might not be the way you want.*

"Oh, Matthew. Is there no other way? I just got the children back."

"The villeins have all been returned to new homes. Your staff is no
longer overwhelmed, and the children will be in their care. Besides, they
will understand. You must do what you can to save your land."

She looked discouraged. "I suppose. Do you think he would see me?"

"Of a surety, Pet. I am one of his favorite knights, and my father is a
personal friend. He knighted me himself, remember."

"Aye, I know. On the battlefield. For bravery."

"I will ignore your sarcasm, for you are under duress. But I assure you, the king likes and respects me, and he shall listen to what I have to say. Come with me Pet, 'tis the only way."

She was placid as she stared at the ground. "I suppose," she said in a quiet tone.

He reached out, and lifted her chin to meet his gaze. "It will take us three days to reach the king. Three days, three nights." He stared at her silently and seriously. His heart was racing harder just from looking at her, and the anticipation she could soon be his was driving him mad. He wanted her so intensely, could he wait much longer?

Her eyes locked with his. His turned to liquid as his desire showed through and he reached out for her. She took a step backward and ran up against the hedge wall, stopping with a jerk. "P—please, Matthew…do not."

He kept coming closer. "Do not what?"

She moved along the wall as he followed her. "I have to go in, now. Good night, Sir Matthew." She turned just as he grabbed her by the arm, and pulled her into him.

"Not so fast, pretty Pet. I need you to have another temporary lapse in judgment."

"Matthew, please, I…"

He brought his face down to hers. "Just hush, and kiss me." His lips descended onto hers softly, gently, taking his time before building pressure. She at first succumbed, then suddenly stiffened and recoiled backwards, gasping for air as she pushed him away.

"No. I—I cannot do this, Matthew."

"On the contrary. You do this very well." He reached out for her as she backed up.

"No. Please Matthew, let me go." Her eyes seemed to fear him, which was not the emotion he wanted from her.

"Go, Pet, I will make no further attempt to seduce you, hard as that may be."

"Good night, Matthew." She ran back through the garden trail leaving him frustrated as ever. But this time he didn't mind. Kissing her was just a taste of what was in store for him. He desired her above anything else, and if everything went as planned, she would soon be his. He strolled back to the manor house, whistling.

# ❧Chapter Twelve❧

atthew was up early the next morning, his whole outlook on life buoyant. He whistled as he got dressed, and bounced down the stairs two at a time. The smells from the kitchen told him the cooks were hard at work. Good, a hearty breakfast would start the day off right. He found Luke already eating in the small dining room, and as he sat down across from him he flashed a large grin.

"Greetings, brother! I hope there is plenty to eat. I could eat an ox!" He poured some tea as Luke looked on with consternation.

"My, we are certainly chipper today. Would there be a reason for your o'er-enthusiastic mood?"

"The sun is shining, the birds are singing, and the future proves promising."

Luke frowned, and shook his head in disgust. "You are in love."

"Is it so obvious?" Matthew asked, as he piled food on his plate.

"Painfully so. Tell me brother, would it not be preferable if the lady shared your sentiments?"

"She fights me now, but only because she is stubborn. Soon she will be more than happy to take my hand in marriage." He began eating voraciously.

Luke leaned back and studied his brother's face. "Matthew, from what I have seen of Pet, she has definite ideas of where she intends her life to go. I do not believe those plans include you."

Matthew just smiled, and chewed his food as Luke continued his opinion.

"Perhaps—just this once—could it be your lust has overshadowed your reasoning? Maybe she is better left alone, without you confusing the matter?"

Matthew's grin just got wider. "There is no confusion. She loves me, I know it. No one could kiss me the way she does…" His voice trailed off as he became deep in thought, the smile still intact.

Luke shook his head, and resumed eating. When Matthew wanted something, he was relentless, even if someone got hurt. Still, that didn't mean Luke couldn't at least try to talk some sense into his brother. "Matthew, you know you can be a mite overbearing. The girl probably kisses you because you give her no choice. Subtlety is not one of your virtues."

"You worry too much, Luke, You are beginning to sound like Paul."

"As well I should. He has had to comfort many maidens whose hearts you crushed."

"Oh, bah!" Matthew scoffed. "I hardly even talked to most of those girls, let alone crush them. They all went running to Paul because they wanted him, not me. I was an easy person to blame for injured feelings."

"Perhaps," Luke answered, "but I feel you are attracted to this girl simply because she resists you. 'Tis always a game with you, Matt. The chase is what you crave, and when you nab your prey, another comes along."

Matthew's face suddenly sobered. "Not this time, Luke. Not Pet. You know not of her as I do; she needs me. Twice now I have had to bring her back to reality, once from anger, once from grief. She buries her feelings, and she has simply buried her love for me. I love her, Luke, and I mean to have her."

The ardent tone of his voice made Luke consider the possibility this time his brother might be serious. "Then I wish you well, Matt. I hope the lady…"

He stopped mid-sentence as he looked over Matthew's shoulder, his eyes widened in stupefaction. "Good Lord!"

Matthew spun around to see what had stopped Luke dead. His eyes also widened at the sight that greeted him.

Pet stood in the doorway, dressed entirely in black leather, but this outfit was like none Matthew had ever seen. The boots were shorter, below the knee, with twice as many buckles holding five daggers on each boot. A long linen-lined jacket with puffed shoulders hung over a smaller form-fitting doublet. Leather gloves covered her hands. A sword with a diamond-profile blade and copper-gilt crossguard hung from a sheath in her wide belt, and a short ax hung from the other side. A great sword with a fishtail pommel hung on her back, along with a quiver of arrows. She held a long bow. Luke's mouth hung open, but Matthew simply stood up and looked at her as if she had lost her mind.

"Pet, dear, you look ready to take on the entire French army. Do you not think a visit to the king would call for perhaps a, uh, *softer* look?"

"No," was her instant reply. Her face was cold and determined, no doubt a response to the previous night's meeting with Matthew in the garden. "And I am not your *dear*. If you are done dallying, I would like to get on the road. I want to get this meeting with the king o'er and done with."

Matthew folded his arms and circled slowly around her, inspecting her as if he was judging an animal at a fair. Her eyes followed him with forced indifference.

"You would not happen to have a duplicate of this outfit, perhaps in my size?" He knew the answer was most likely yes, as Robert always wore matching clothes.

"And if I do?"

"I would be honored to wear it." This was perfect. They would appear before the king wearing completely matching, extremely formidable clothes showing strength and unity, sort of a two-man/woman army. No one would doubt they were together, which was exactly the impression he wanted to make.

"Very well. You may have Robert's outfit, and use his weapons—on one condition."

"And that would be?"

"I do not have to lay with you at night."

Luke laughed, quickly changed it to a cough, and began concentrating intently on his food. Matthew ignored him, and frowned at Pet.

"This shall take some thought. That is a lot to give up for just an outfit."

Her eyes didn't waiver. "'Tis your decision."

Matthew knew she had countered his move and forced him into a dilemma. He really wanted the outfit, but he also really wanted to hold her at night. Maybe he could instill some guilt and she would back down...

"I am hurt, Pet. I was under the impression you enjoyed lying with me."

"You were under the wrong impression."

"Was I?" He could mention the night she came to him at the nunnery, but decided not to bring up painful memories. The last thing he wanted to do was hurt her. Well, they would have the rest of their lives together, if all went as planned, so he supposed he could give up three nights.

"Very well. You will lay alone the next three nights, and I hope you freeze."

She slowly formed a victorious smile. "In August? That would be highly unlikely." She let him absorb his predicament, and then went back to a stone face. "That is for the clothes, the weapons will cost you extra."

Luke coughed up another laugh, and downed some tea to disguise it. Matthew again ignored him.

"So what is the price for the weapons? My arm? Perhaps my leg?"

"Nothing so severe. You simply have to promise never to kiss me again."

Luke began a coughing fit, and this time Matthew could not ignore him. "Luke, I believe you need to attend to that cough!"

"I believe you are correct, brother. I will just step into the kitchen for a moment." He left the two alone, and broke into a belly laugh the second he closed the door. He had never seen anyone, let alone a woman, beat Matthew at his own game.

Matthew stared at her in disbelief, then amusement. "Pet, no weapon is worth your kiss."

"Suit yourself." She shrugged, and stared at the ceiling.

"Are we forgetting my payment for talking to the king in your behalf? Is that not worth something?"

"I thought you were doing that out of friendship."

"I was, but then you started putting conditions on things. 'Tis only fair I am compensated also."

She folded her arms and glowered. "Very well, what is your price?"

"Hmmm. I would say at least one night, and one kiss—at my discretion."

"What!" She blew out a large sigh. "That totally defeats my purpose."

He started to feel more in control of the situation. "And what purpose is that?"

"Never mind. Very well, you get to hold me one night, but no kiss."

"I will not bargain the kiss."

"Augh! You are impossible! Very well, two nights."

He rubbed his chin. "Make it three, and I might consider the kiss."

"Then you get the clothes for naught!"

"That is my price."

"You are not bargaining fair. What kind of knight are you?"

"The kind who wants to hold you, and kiss you."

"No! That must not happen again." She set her jaw and raised her head defiantly. "Fine, I will lay with you at nights. No kiss."

He was laughing so hard inside it was all he could do to keep a straight face. She fought so hard to keep him away from her, but it was a losing battle. He would have her, all of her, and soon. If postponing kissing her made her at ease, so be it.

"Very well, I agree. No kiss, but for the trip only; I am making no promises after."

"That is fine, as I intend to leave you in London and return to Elton as soon as the king grants me my land."

"What if I do not want to stay in London?"

"You are a king's knight. You have no choice."

"Do I get my clothes or not?"

She sighed, and pointed out the door. "Everything is waiting for you in the armory."

"You were going to give them to me anyway, were you not?" He smiled with confidence.

"Certainly not." She tossed her head, and left the room. As soon as she left, Matthew tossed back his head and laughed.

Luke stuck his head out of the kitchen. "Is it safe?"

"Aye, brother, would you like to help me arm myself? My lady and I have an appointment with the king."

About an hour later Matthew felt like a one-man army. The clothes fit him expertly, in fact, a little too expertly. When he commented to Raymond, who was helping him pick weapons, the huge knight grinned knowingly.

"The clothes fit because they were made for thee, Sir Matthew. Pet has a staff of manor tailors, and she ordered these outfits whilst thou were here training that week. They took thy measurements without thy knowledge." He looked around him in apprehension. "If she knows I told thee, she would have my head."

Matthew was stunned. His cockiness and arrogance were replaced by admiration and respect, for a generous girl who always gave of herself. Love grew ten-fold in his heart at that moment. Would it be possible to truly win her?

Raymond handed Matthew a war sword, with a diamond shaped profile. The cross guard was gilt in copper, and seemed a bit lighter, and more well-balanced than what he was used to. He gave it a few swings, and laughed with delight. "This sword is excellent! 'Tis almost as if it were made for me. The weight is perfect, and still delivers a powerful blow." He lowered the weapon and looked at Raymond's trying-to-be-innocent face. "Raymond, do not tell me she also had this sword made?"

Raymond cleared his throat. "Very well, I shall not. It is much more than that, Matthew. Thou hast an entire array of weapons, that I am cleverly supposed to guide thee to."

Matthew looked at the daggers, swords, axes, and other weapons Pet had her armorer make for him. Each weapon was perfectly balanced, flawlessly made. He stared in disbelief at the display, finding it hard to choose just a few.

"Why are you telling me these things, Raymond? 'Tis obvious Pet does not want me to know she did this."

"Because, Sir Matthew, to be blunt, the lass likes thee, I daresay she might even be in love with thee. And I know thou loves her, unless I have lost my wits in my old age."

Matthew nodded with a sheepish smile. "Raymond, I love her more every moment. I shall make her mine."

Raymond cleared his throat, and lowered his voice. "Matthew, thou know not everything about Pet."

"I plan to find out."

"No, I mean...go slow, Matthew. She is hurting badly."

Matthew strapped on his great sword, the most beautiful weapon he had ever held. "Losing your entire family will do that."

"It is more than that. She has deep, deep pain, that I fear shall kill her if it surfaces."

"What kind of pain could hurt that much?"

"Matthew, I—I need to tell thee..."

"Are you ready yet?" Pet's voice drew both men to attention. "Goliath is saddled, do I have to wait for you all day? Raymond, did he find suitable weapons?"

"Aye, Pet, he found a few he liked."

"Good." She looked him over, and hid a smile. The clothes she had made for him were superb, and he looked as ominous as her. "I have something for you, Matthew. Would you come with me?"

He looked at Raymond, but the giant just shrugged with an I-don't-know look. He followed Pet silently out to the front, where Goliath stood waiting, packed as before, with every conceivable weapon strapped to him. Beside him was a sight that made Matthew draw up short. Another horse, Goliath's size and just as spectacular, stood pawing the ground with impatience. He had the same coloring as Goliath, except his mane and tail were black. The animal tossed his head as Matthew circled around him, in awe of the size and perfection of the huge horse. Luke was holding him, answering the question of where he had disappeared to so abruptly.

"He is too fine for you, brother. What say you of this animal?"

"He is…well, words escape me!"

Pet stroked the horse's neck in admiration. "He was offered to me at the same time Goliath was offered to Robert. At the time I thought him too large. When you admired Goliath so much, I sent a messenger to the Baron asking if the horse was still available. Fortunately, he was. He is yours." She turned and started to walk away, when Matthew reached out and grabbed her, an amazed look on his face.

"Why Pet?"

She shrugged nonchalantly. "Truly selfish motives, I assure you. I grew weary of having to wait for you to catch up to me. Now we will make better time. Now, unhand me, so we can ready for our trip."

He let go, wanting instead to grab her and test her judgment again, but resisted the impulse. "Pet, I fear I may have bargained too harshly. I accept your original terms, you do not have to lay with me at nights—unless you want to."

She whipped around in surprise. "Truly?"

He nodded. "Truly."

"Fine. Now ready your horse." He watched her walk away as if she had done nothing, making him feel small and petty. He readied his horse in record time.

Saying goodbye to the children was difficult, but they all seemed to understand the necessity of the trip. Little Julie hugged Matthew and fought back tears.

"'Tis fine, Julie, we will soon be back." He lowered his voice to a whisper. "Pet and I will be married soon, and I will be your father."

That got a giggle from Julie, and a suspicious glance from Pet.

Luke watched the scene from close by, and then approached Matthew when the children had been sent back inside. Matthew was tightening the cinch on his saddle as he strolled up.

"I shall be leaving for home on the morrow, Matt. My work here is done, and I know father is anxious to see me. Do you have any words for our parents?"

"Aye, I do. Tell them I will be bringing my bride home in a few days to meet them. That should make mother happy."

Luke's frown was as intense as Matthew's smile. "So certain are you? The girl fights to keep you away, what makes you think she will agree to your hand?"

Matthew just smiled his cocky grin, and offered no further comment. Pet yelled from across the courtyard at that point, insisting he stop talking and get working.

"See? Already I am henpecked!" He laughed loudly, as Luke shook his head in skepticism.

Finally they were under way. Matthew mounted his new steed, and tested the reining. The animal responded beautifully, showing excellent training. Pet watched him with mirth, as he was like a little boy with a new toy. She was glad the Baron still held the horse for her, and that she had requested it brought to her manor. Matthew had so admired Goliath that she saw no reason not to give her horse to him. It was intended for him to keep his mind off other things—like her.

"What is this animal's name?"

She realized he was speaking to her, and came out of her daze.

"He is unnamed. That is for you to decide."

"Pet, my delight knows no bounds. Howe'er can I ever repay you for such a gift?"

"Gifts are not given to receive one in return. Consider him a birthday present."

He froze, and then frowned. "My brother's mouth flaps too much."

"Do not blame Luke; it just slipped out in ordinary conversation. So, next week you become twenty and nine. I avow the king shall host a party in your honor, seeing how you are such a brave and important knight."

"I seriously doubt that, although he will be pleased to see me—finally. My news on the renegades will be well accepted. Do not fret, your land shall be returned. I know the king well."

"I hope so." She couldn't help but worry about her standing and was putting great faith in Matthew's influence with the king.

They rode hard all day, making excellent time, thanks to the strong horses. A small wooded area off the road proved to be the best choice for a place to bed down for the night. Matthew could not have been more pleased with his new horse, which he racked his brain all day to come up with a name for. That night, the animal remained nameless, to which Pet found very amusing. She watched as he fussed over the great horse, brushing him down numerous times after removing the saddle and armament.

"The poor beast shall be put out to pasture in his old age with no name," she teased.

"I am quite sure I will think of one before that. It just has to be perfect." He looked the horse over inch by inch, lamenting a small scratch on the hindquarters, as Pet gathered wood for a fire with satisfaction racing through her. She hoped giving him the horse would divert his overzealous attentions away from her, and so far it seemed to be working. He had not once tried to kiss her on their rest breaks, instead focusing on the new darling of his life: his horse. If his attentions could be diverted long enough, she might be able to slip his grasp and head back to Elton when this ridiculous meeting with the king was over with. At least, that was the plan. She wanted to be Matthew's friend, and his amorous attentions confused and unnerved her, making her feel things she didn't want to feel, indeed, could not allow herself to feel.

In a short time she had a good fire going, and she sat making points while their dinner, a pheasant Matthew shot, was cooking. She felt more relaxed than she had in a great time. Matthew soon joined her after assuring himself his nameless horse was fine for the night, and began making points as they talked. He effectively monopolized the conversation, with endless blather about the horse, how Luke was extremely jealous, and what he was going to name the hapless animal.

"I was thinking 'David" to match your Goliath, but that makes sense only when the horses are together."

"True."

"Otherwise, 'David' is not an effective name for such a strong horse. No, 'David" is out."

Pet raised her head and strained to hear over his babbling.

"He deserves a strong, powerful name, does he not? Something big, something mighty."

Pet cocked her head and listened to the right, then to the left. She glanced over to her great sword, which she had taken off and laid on the ground when gathering firewood.

"Something unforgettable, impressive, Herculean…where are you going?"

Pet reached her sword, and casually picked it up. "Continue, I am listening." She sat back down, and Matthew was oblivious to the fact she had taken off her heavy over-jacket and was strapping the great sword on her back.

"Maybe 'Thunder'. No, that sounds dumb. Howbeit—Pet what are you doing?"

She was standing up, staring at him with an odd expression. "Matthew…stand up."

"What?" He stood up and watched in surprise as she ambled up to him and threw her arms around his neck.

"Kiss me," she said quickly.

"Huh? I thought you said…" He gave a shocked look as she pulled herself up to kiss him. He shrugged, and put his arms around her, delightfully giving in to her orders. Before the kiss reached a peak, she turned her mouth to speak into his ear.

"Matthew, we are surrounded."

His budding passion immediately wilted. "W-what?"

"Shhh. Just keep pretending to kiss me. They will think we are preoccupied with lovemaking."

"That would be a much preferable scenario."

"Matthew!"

"Well, what are we going to do?"

"I know not, just kiss my neck so they do not get suspicious."

He found her closeness reassuring, even under the stressful circumstances. His day-old beard rubbed against her tender skin.

"Matthew, you are pretending too hard."

"Sorry. Howe'er many are there?"

"Six, maybe eight."

"Eight? That is four apiece! I cannot fight four."

"Aye, you can. If I can, you can."

"Have you ever fought that many?"

She chuckled against his chest. "Aye, Matthew, many more than four. Just remember everything I taught you. Concentrate. Focus."

"Please tell me you have a plan."

"I am thinking."

"Think faster."

"Very well. We are facing each other and our great swords are strapped to our backs. I have my hands on the pommel of your sword, do the same to mine. When I say so, lean forward and you grab mine, and I will grab yours."

"But is not mine heavier?"

"I can handle it."

"I have no doubt. Why do these things keep happening to me?"

"Quit whining. They are getting closer. Remember all I showed you. Keep alert. Ready? Now."

They stepped back, leaned forward, and grabbed each other's swords. At the same time the clearing exploded with charging, yelling men.

"Back to back, Matthew!" He instantly complied.

His first thought was there were more than eight.

The men surrounded them, but seemed reluctant to attack two extremely well-armed formidable people who no doubt knew how to use their weapons. Pet did not wait for them to attack, knowing the best defense was a quick offense, especially if you were outnumbered. She charged the closest man, swinging the great sword like it weighed nothing. The blade connected with the man's abdomen, and he fell with a loud cry.

Two attacked Matthew at once. He swung vertically across the middle, clipping one, and sending the other to the ground. He had to quickly spin to stop another attack, knocking the sword from the enemy's hand.

Pet was in her element; she fought as if she had been born with a sword in her hand. Two men went down, giving the others something to ponder. Pet was savage. Her ability to focus and block everything out, combined with her unexcelled speed, forced the over-matched men to panic. They struck out blindly; she countered their blows one by one. Soon four lay dead by her sword; two others retreated. She swung around to help Matthew, to discover he didn't need her help. She lowered her sword and watched him fight two men who were striking out alternately. She smirked with satisfaction; he had become a skilled fighter with confidence and grace. Soon one more was dead, and the other wounded and running.

The workout was exhilarating. The two stood gasping for precious air and stared at each other, smiling with pride. Matthew motioned her to him, and she didn't protest as he took her in his arms and held her. Their sentiments were understood without words. He finally pulled away and looked at her sternly.

"There were more than eight."

"If I told you there were at least ten, what would you have done?"

"Probably panicked."

She gave up a rare and wide smile. "You fought well, Matthew, even with my sword."

He glanced at the carnage around them. "Who do you think they are?"

"They are Gideon's men. They have been following us for some time."

"You knew this?"

"Aye."

"And you did not think to inform me of this small detail?"

"I did not want to worry you."

"Worry me?" He chortled a short laugh, and looked at her in disbelief. "No, you just want to get me killed!"

"It appears to me you are still standing."

"No thanks to you."

She glowered, grabbed her sword, and swaggered briskly away, stepping over dead bodies as she maneuvered her way to the horses. She began saddling up Goliath. Matthew followed her and watched her fume, angry with himself and his big mouth. Could he do nothing right?

"Pet, I am sorry. 'Tis only because of you I *am* still standing. What are you doing?"

She didn't answer him, just kept on packing up Goliath with speed only anger could produce.

"Pet, dear, it is almost dark."

"I am not your *dear*."

"Aye you are, you just will not admit it. And it is still almost dark. What are you doing?"

"I am leaving."

"Without me?"

"Suit yourself. You seem to have no need of me."

"That is not true, and you know it." He spun her around and looked upon her pouting, slightly hurt, beautiful face. "You are lovely when you are angry."

"Then I must be lovely every time I am with you."

"Aye, you are." As they continued to stare at each other, her eyes softened from anger to longing. He didn't miss the change.

"To hell with our deal." He grabbed her and forcefully pulled her to him, wrapping his arms around her as his lips attacked hers. "Dear God, help me, I want you so badly." He ignored her feeble attempt to stop him, pulling her closer as his lips did their magic on her. She closed her eyes and moaned as he ravished her lips, and soon their tongues explored each other's mouths with passionate desire. He relinquished her purely from the need to breathe, and rested his head on her shoulder.

"I will admit I love you if you admit you love me first."

"No!" She pushed back frantically, but he held her tight.

"Admit it Pet, and end this charade."

"Never!" This time she broke free. "I cannot love anyone, Matthew."

"Cannot, or will not?" He stared solemnly at her, and then slowly smiled. "Very well, I will give you a little more time. But I warn you, get accustomed to the idea of having me around, for 'tis your destiny."

"Is that a threat?"

"No. 'Tis a promise."

"Then I shall disregard it, for 'tis obvious knights cannot keep promises. You said you would not kiss me."

His cocky grin returned. "I will give up knighthood if kissing you is my reward." His response was an icy glare. "Very well, wait whilst I ready my horse. We will leave this place, since you are so adamant. Where do you purpose we go?"

"Anywhere, just away from here."

"I admit my appetite is not roused by dead bodies, either. But I am bringing the pheasant; wait for me."

She stood by while he packed up his horse. She brought a finger to her lips, contemplating the desire he was able to bring to the surface. An overwhelming panic rose within her, and she calmed down only by reminding herself that soon he would be at his duties in the castle, and she would be in Elton. Then her life would settle down and she could raise the children, and grow old without some over-amorous man demanding her attentions. She had long ago resolved she would not marry, why did Matthew seem so determined to destroy that resolve?

They rode through darkness until they found a town that boasted a small, boisterous tavern-inn. A band of traveling minstrels were spending the night, and Pet and Matthew had to push their way through the rowdy, drunken men filling the tavern. The innkeeper shouted over the din that he only had one small room left. Pet told Matthew to take it, and started to push her way back through the crowd. He grabbed her arm.

"I think not, Pet. You are coming with me." He didn't give her leeway to argue, as he marched her to the room, pushed her inside, and shut the door.

"I know you are as hungry as I. Stay in here, and I will fetch the pheasant. You are staying here tonight; I will sleep with the horses."

She opened her mouth to argue, but he abruptly left, slamming the door behind him. Too tired to protest, she looked glumly around the small room that harbored a small bed with a straw-stuffed dirty mattress, and little else. A chamber pot sat in the corner, and the shuttered window let in little light. A small candle burned in the corner on a small table. She grimaced. *Cheery.*

She took off her weapons, over-jacket, and doublet, leaving only her linen tunic and pants. Sitting on the bed, she pulled off her boots and lay down. The blaring crowd downstairs did nothing to hinder her weary eyes from growing heavy.

When Matthew came back in the room, her sleeping form caused him to smile. He put the food down on the table, and tore off a piece of the cold pheasant. He chewed hungrily as he stripped off his weapons and coats, and then downed the meat with a gulp of ale. A warm feeling flowed over him as he watched her sleep. He loved her. There was no doubt. He had to make her admit her love for him, so he would not appear weak and stupid when he admitted it. Their marriage would be the pinnacle of his life, and they *would* be married, of that he was certain.

He sat on the edge of the bed. To hell with the barn, and to hell with his deal. He gently rolled her over on her side and cuddled up behind her, holding her close in the small bed. In seconds he fell fast asleep.

# ~Chapter Thirteen~

e awoke to the sounds of swords clanking together. Opening one eye, he groped the empty space beside him, then rolled over to see Pet fully dressed and strapping on her great sword.

He hesitatingly sat up and rubbed his eyes. As he opened his mouth to greet her, she beat him to it.

"I will never believe a promise from another knight. You slept with me last night, after you said you would not."

He thought fast. "I said you did not have to lay with me if you did not want to. Last night I heard no protest."

"But I was asleep!"

"A minor detail."

"You are impossible."

"I know."

She cast him a look that could dull a sword. "I am going to purchase breakfast. Tarry not, if you wish to eat today." She left the room in a huff.

He chuckled as he got dressed, wondering if she had any idea how much he loved it when she was incensed.

After breakfast, they were again on the road. It was an overcast, dreary day, but rain didn't seem imminent. Matthew still contemplated a name for the horse, and reasoned out loud as they rode.

"I was thinking of the ancient gods, and came up with some possibilities, I am partial to 'Thor'. What do you think?"

"'Tis fine."

"Then again, because he is so fast, I also am considering 'Achilles'. But, 'Thor' is a much stronger name. Which do you prefer?"

"Neither."

He flinched at her tone. "Fine, I suppose you have come up with a better one?"

"If he were mine, and I remind you he once was, I would give him a name stirring thoughts of nobility and honor."

"Aye! That is precisely what I want, but I cannot contemplate of one."

"I would name him after the most famous sword in folklore: the sword of King Arthur."

"Excalibur?" Matthew pondered that for a few seconds, liking it better and better the more he thought. "By the saints, Pet, you are a genius! Excalibur, 'tis!"

The horse tossed his head as if to agree. Matthew laughed with delight. "The horse concurs. Your name is now Excalibur, my mighty friend." He patted the horse on its neck.

They reached London by dusk, before the walled town gates were closed. As they rode through the streets, city folk gawked at the two figures in black, riding huge destriers and brandishing numerous weapons. Pet displayed no emotion as she rode beside Matthew, who seemed entirely at home in the city. Craftsmen worked at windows opening onto the street, giving them the opportunity to show off their skills to passersby. Finished goods were displayed on a hinged shelf at the front of their workshops. Houses were built very close together, and the upper stories of buildings were "jettied" out to maximize space. In some places, the houses on either side almost touched each other, making the streets gloomy and airless. Pigs and other animals ran free. Pet was apprehensive of the noise, stench, and activity of London, and wanted just to get the land matter taken care of so she could get back home, where she belonged.

As they approached the Tower of London, Matthew explained a little about the castle so she would know what to expect.

"The castle was built in 1080, 90 feet high to the battlements, and originally three stories. 'Tis divided internally by a cross-wall. The topmost story holds the great hall, where you shall meet the king, and the king's solar and chapel. 'Tis quite impressive; it rises two floors. We will go through a forebuilding to gain entrance. Do not fret, they all know me here."

"No doubt." She was overwhelmed beyond belief, but her calm control hid all signs of apprehension. They passed through the forebuilding with no difficulty, and entered the castle's outer wall. The first thing she noticed was the bright colors of tunics, mantles, hose and shoes, all in blues, yellows, crimsons, purples and greens. The fabric of the garments varied from wool to fine silks, samite, sendal, and damask. Tunics and mantles were decorated with embroidery, tassels, feathers, or pearls. Both men and women wore head coverings indoor and out. Pet and Matthew looked especially formidable as they rode up to the stable where grooms instantly attended to their steeds. If Matthew noticed her discomfort, he didn't acknowledge it. Before they walked two feet, they were approached by a man about Matthew's age wearing a suit of chain mail covered by a colorful mantle.

"Matthew? Is that truly you? There were rumors you were dead, as no word was forthcoming." They clasped hands in friendly camaraderie. Matthew gave him a sheepish grin as he greeted his fellow knight.

"I got a little sidetracked, but I am here now. 'Tis good to see you, John!"

"The king has been most anxious of your whereabouts. Make sure to send notice of your arrival immediately, or he shall have your head!" John laughed, and slapped Matthew on the back, then suddenly noticed Pet. His eyes narrowed in contemplation as Pet averted her eyes in an attempt to be inconspicuous. "So, what is this? Have you taken on a squire?"

Matthew flinched at Pet once again being mistaken for a man. "Actually…"

"Aye."

Matthew looked at Pet and raised his eyebrows in surprise as she stared back at him with a stone face. "Very well, yes. This is my squire, Pet…er, Peter."

John gave Pet a perplexed look. "He is a whit on the small side, would you not say?"

"The lad has possibilities. He is already quite adept with the sword."

John folded his arms and cast an amusing look at Pet. "Is that so? Perhaps the, ah, *Lad*, will spar with me sometime. I have a feeling I might enjoy myself." He looked Pet over with appreciative eyes.

Matthew clenched his jaw, and grabbed Pet's arm. "The hour is late, I must report my presence. Come, *Squire*." He hustled her away from his humored friend, who hadn't been fooled for a minute by the beautiful warrior.

John called after them. "Are you also going to teach the lad your way with the ladies?" He then broke out with hilarious laughter.

Matthew didn't answer, just took long, fast strides she had trouble keeping up with. He held her arm even tighter, practically dragging her along as he gazed straight ahead.

"John is incorrigible; he knew you were a woman. Did you see the way he ogled? You are too damned pretty, Pet, to pass for a boy."

"You did not think so."

"I was stupid." He whisked her along so fast that people became a colorful blur with eyes. She was a bit taken back by his jealousy; no one had ever been jealous of her before.

"So *are* you?"

"Am I what?"

"Going to teach me your ways with ladies?"

"I plan on showing you first hand, when you finally admit you love me."

"That is not going to happen."

"We will see." He led her into the castle door, still holding on to her arm protectively. Pet decided to be complacent, as she was intimidated by the bustle of people, the noise, and the strangeness of the king's castle. Matthew saw a young page heading their way, and stopped him.

"Here, boy—I have a message for the king."

The boy drew himself up tall. "Aye, Sir!"

"Tell him Sir Matthew Cameron of Cambridgeshire is back, and brings news of the renegade gang. I seek an audience with the king at his earliest convenience."

The boy bowed, and traipsed down the long hall to deliver his important message. Two young knights in chain mail happened by, looked Pet in the face, and smiled. They kept their eyes on her as they strutted past. Matthew uttered a curse, then resumed dragging Pet down a hall, up some stairs, down another hall, up some more stairs, and finally opened a door and tossed her inside.

"Stay here!" he demanded, and left her alone.

She was only too happy to comply; the huge castle made her nervous. The room she had been left in was big, much nicer than her own rooms in Elton. A great bed with a heavy wooden frame with springs made of interlocked ropes occupied almost half the space. It was overlaid with a feather mattress, sheets, quilts, a fur coverlet and numerous pillows. A trundle bed was visible underneath for personal servants, or in the case of knights, their squires. A large chest sat at the end of the bed, and several stools dotted the room. A table with a basin of water and the ever-important chamber pot were in one corner. The walls were draped with rich tapestries.

Pet took off her weapons and over-jacket, and then sat on the bed. Time passed, and out of pure boredom, she opened the chest and shuffled through the contents. To her delight she found a copy of *The Canterbury Tales*, and sat up against the headboard and began reading.

In a short time, the door flew open, and in came Matthew, holding a large tray loaded with food. He put it down on the bed, and stripped off all his clothes above his waist. He then lay sideways across the bed propped up on one elbow, to observe her reading and effectively ignoring him.

"Are you angry with me again?"

She looked up. "Why would I be angry? You jerk me around by my arm, which is still sore, shove me into a room, holler at me, and leave me alone in a strange castle. 'Tis normal behavior for you."

He flinched at her cold tone. "Pet, I am sorry." His jealousy had died down a bit when he left her to fetch food, but he was totally taken by surprise by his feelings. Other men looking at her drove him mad with jealousy, an emotion he had never felt before with other women.

She went back to reading. He picked up a piece of cheese, and began chewing. "You should eat. Raymond told me you have a problem maintaining weight and your appetite is too small. Here." He handed her a piece of chicken. She just looked at it disgustingly.

"I am not hungry." She went back to reading the book.

"Pet, eat. You will appear before the king tomorrow, and you must have strength. Here—try some cheese."

She held out her hand to accept the cheese. "Very well, I will eat. For the king, not for you." She nibbled on the white, pungent, goat cheese. "Whose room is this?"

"'Tis mine. Why?"

She paused with incredulity. "You have your own room at the king's castle?"

"'Tis my family's room. My father visits often, as does Luke, on business. When I am here, the room is mine. My father is a personal friend of the king." He shrugged, as if it all meant nothing.

She shook her head in disbelief. "Does nothing come hard for you? Do you never have to fight for anything?"

"I would not say that. Right now I am having the greatest fight of my life."

"And what would that be?"

He just chuckled, when they were interrupted by a knock on the door. When he opened it, the young page bowed deeply and straightened up brandishing a large smile.

"Sir Cameron? The king requests your presence in his solar— immediately."

"Right now? Good Lord." He patted the boy on the shoulder. "Go tell the king I will be right there." He closed the door and faced Pet with a look of trepidation. "I have to go see the king."

"I heard."

He sat down and started to pull on his boots. "He is probably angry with me for not reporting sooner. I should have sent a messenger. He is furious, and is going to tell my father I am a fool. Or worse."

Pet watched him fume and fret, and didn't try to hide her mirth. She was finally seeing him caught off guard, and loved every second. He opened the trunk and took out a shirt and blue doublet, and hastily got dressed right in front of her.

"I am going to order you a bath. When I get back from the king, 'tis mine. If you are not out of it, I will join you."

She swallowed and her eyes grew wide. "It shall be the shortest bath I ever take."

"Help yourself to any clothes in the trunk, they are mine but you might find something to sleep in. I will try to hurry back." He finished dressing, and smiled. "It will be fine. I shall talk to the king in your behalf, after he is done yelling at me." He left the room in a hurry.

Pet read the book and waited for the bath. In a few minutes, the door opened, and several servants came in, carrying a large tub. They were followed by at least a dozen servant girls each holding a large bucket of steaming, hot water, who then proceeded to dump it in the tub. In a few minutes, the tub was half full, and Pet was left alone. She had never left the bed during the whole procedure, and the servants had totally ignored her. *Strange.*

Not one to look a gift bath in the mouth, she quickly stripped and eased herself into the wonderful, hot, relaxing water. She silently wished Matthew to be gone all night.

On the floor above, Matthew entered the king's solar to find him sitting at his writing desk. The humble knight kneeled before his king, and Henry waved him to stand.

"It relieves me to see you well, Matthew. I feared for your welfare."

"I am sorry your majesty, I should have reported sooner. I pray your forgiveness."

The king stood up, a tall man with gaunt features, and smiled at his friend's son. "Your father and I worry about you, Matthew. Is there a reason for your long absence?"

"I was able to encounter the renegades, Sire, and I am pleased to announce the gang has been overcome. There will be no more raids. We were also able to…"

"We?"

"Sire?"

"You said 'we'. Who else was with you? I must reward the other men."

"Er, there were no other men, Sire. Just me...and a woman."

Henry laughed. "You managed to eliminate the renegade band with a woman hanging around your neck? Oh, Matthew, I have heard stories, but I never thought them to be true."

Matthew felt his ears flush, and he cleared his throat. "No, sire, I do not think I conveyed my meaning clearly. This woman of who I speak...she is actually the one who eliminated the enemy."

Henry frowned, and looked at Matthew in disbelief. "A woman, you say? May I beseech, where is this woman?"

"She is...ah, in my room Sire—taking a bath."

"Your mother shall have your hide. Does she know of your activities?"

"Sire, truly, I tell you my intentions are honorable. I have not as yet done more than steal a kiss—or two."

"Your intentions?"

"Aye sire, that is what I need to talk with you about. I am bringing her before you tomorrow to state her case."

"Just who is this woman?"

"The lady Rose Boulton of Elton, Sire. Her lands were ordered reduced upon the death of all her brothers and father. They died at the hands of the renegades, your majesty. She went after them, and killed almost all of them. I but had a small part. She deserves her land, Sire."

The king nodded with satisfaction. "Of course, Matthew. Her land would be returned on your word alone. Why do you make her appear before me?"

"You know not of this young girl, Sire. She is extremely independent, stubborn, and commanding. She runs Elton with much efficiency, and fights to defend it as well as most men. She beat me at swordplay when we first met."

Henry drew back in dismay. "Merciful God, she sounds horrid!"

"Oh, no, Sire...I wish to marry her."

"Marry? You? Has my hearing failed me?"

Matthew laughed sincerely. "Aye Sire, I want to marry her, very badly. She is incredible, Sire. But she resists me. That is where I need your help."

"Me? How...Matthew, you do not want me to order her? Why is not this young woman willing? By stories I hear, no woman can resist you."

"This one is different, Sire. I have a plan."

"A plan?"

"Aye, and she will have no choice but to take my hand."

Pet stayed in the hot water as long as she dared, then got out and dried herself off, and found a tunic of Matthew's in the trunk. She was relaxed from the bath, and exhausted. Matthew was not back yet from his late meeting with the king. What could be so important they would be talking for so long? *Just a small nap won't hurt*, she thought, and lay down on the bed. When Matthew entered minutes later, she was curled up on top of the bed like a little kitten, fast asleep. He gazed upon her lovingly.

"Sleep well, my precious Pet. Tomorrow you become mine." He brushed a wisp of hair from her face, and gently kissed her forehead. Then he stripped down, took a short bath in the lukewarm water, and slipped on a tunic. He folded back the covers, gently picked her up, and placed her between the sheets. Then he curled up next to her and went to sleep, holding her close.

The next morning he roused her from a deep sleep.

"Pet, darling, time to rise."

She opened her eyes and blinked, then sat up and looked upon Matthew's fully clothed figure. He was dressed like the other knights in the castle, wearing a colorful mantle adorned with his family crest, the dragon. She yawned, and rubbed her eyes. "I am not your darling. What time is it? Why did you not wake me up?"

"I believe I just did."

She suddenly realized she was under the covers, and narrowed her eyebrows suspiciously. "I fell asleep on top of the bed."

"I know, I covered you. Now, we have a busy day ahead. I found you some clothes in your size." He held up a fine deep-red doublet. "There is also some hose, but you will have to wear your own boots."

"Where did you sleep?"

He looked at her and frowned; she hadn't heard a word he said. "What does it matter? Now get dressed. I will be back in a short while." He smiled oddly, and left.

She got out of the bed, and grimaced at the clothes. She hated bright colors. The clothes were finely made, however, and of good material. She pulled on the hose, which had stirrups for a fashionable slender look, then put on the red linen-lined jacket. It had at least a dozen brass buttons running up the front and came down to her mid-thigh. The sleeves puffed wide at the shoulders, and were tight at the wrists. She buckled the slender belt, and then slipped on her boots. As if able to read her mind, Matthew entered at that precise moment carrying a felt hat.

"Ah, good...try this on." He plopped the hat on her head, and rearranged it three or four times in annoyance. "Damn, you still look like a girl. If there was only some way to ugly your face a whit." She glowered at him, and he quickly smiled. "No? Well, I suppose not. I have told everybody you are my squire, so stick close to me and try not to show that pretty face." He took her by the arm and led her out to the hallway.

"Where are we going?"

"To breakfast first. Then I shall show you around the White Tower. This afternoon you have an audience with the king." He shifted her through people in the busy hallway, protectively holding on to her arm.

"The king! I forgot you conversed with him. Did you happen to divulge my plight?"

He brought her into a huge room where at least a hundred people were seated, chattering away merrily. "I believe your name was mentioned. He is amenable to listen to your case." He hid his smile as he watched her worried expression. "The king is righteous, Pet, do not be troubled. Now, act like my squire, and try not to look at any men. That face will give you away."

They found a space at a low table, and Pet kept her eyes lowered all during the meal. Matthew pretended to ignore her, while being keenly aware of her every move. He almost could not hide his thrill. Tonight she would be his, and she had no inkling.

After breakfast, he took her on a tour of the castle. He was pleasantly surprised she stuck so closely to him, not aware she was actually terrified. Her outward appearance had the same intense control she always exhibited. He dragged her from place to place, explaining details to make the tour more entertaining.

Several times fellow knights stopped Matthew, asking his whereabouts and status. Pet kept her eyes averted, and Matthew ignored her, failing to introduce her as if she were unimportant. He was pleased there was no more ogling.

They finally ended up in the stable to check on their horses. He was dismayed to find Excalibur had not been given a prime stall, and left Pet for a few minutes to seek a groom and speak his mind. Pet felt greatly more at ease in the stable than the castle, and started to relax slightly. Goliath was glad to see her, and she patted the great horse's nose affectionately. Then something white caught her eye.

She carefully moved toward the stall, glancing around nervously to be sure not to be seen. The white horse pawed the stall's floor as she peeked through the boards. Her blood ran cold at the sight of the animal. It was Gideon's.

A noise made her jump, and she quickly went back to Goliath's stall. In a few seconds Matthew appeared with a hapless groom in tow, who was apologizing profusely about the inadequate stall. Excalibur was moved as Pet stood by quietly, glancing every few minutes to the white horse.

He was here, in the castle. Robert's murderer.

Matthew finally was satisfied with Excalibur's surroundings, and he took Pet's arm as they left the stable. Her silence made him pause.

"Is there something wrong?"

"No."

"I know that look, and I know that tone. Tell me."

"He is here, Matthew."

"Who?"

"Gideon."

He stopped and gave her one of his incredulous are-you-crazy looks. "What? Howe'er do you know that?"

"I saw his horse."

"Pet, there are hundreds of white horses in England. 'Tis highly unlikely just because you saw a white horse that..."

"'Tis his, I know it."

He frowned, not liking this development in his carefully laid plans. He didn't want her mind distracted. Not tonight. "Pet, you must be mistaken. Only invited guests, or well-known knights and noblemen can get inside the castle gates. You remember we had to pass through a forebuilding?"

"Matthew, look at me."

He looked down at her serious, determined, stunningly beautiful face.

"Have I ever been wrong?"

"Damn it, no." Despite the softer side he had experienced lately, he was forced back into remembering who she was: the warrior who fought with an unmatched expertise, the fighter with hawk-like instincts, the girl who molded him into a skilled swordsman. His plans began crumbling before his eyes.

"He must be known, or have inside connections. This could make it complicated."

"We have to find him."

"I know." He wanted to curse, scream, throw something, but he sought restraint. "Let us start looking. We have some time before court."

They strolled slowly through the crowd, both inspecting each person closely as they passed by. No one even remotely resembled Gideon. The time drew near for her audience with the king, and they needed to change clothes. He wanted to appear in front of the king dressed alike, wearing their swords, showing unity. They had to abandon the search temporarily to change back at their room. He let Pet get dressed while he waited outside the door. It didn't hurt to let her have some modesty, seeing how in a few hours she would never have to worry about being modest again. Then he went in as she stood guard, although he assured her he didn't mind her watching him dress.

They swaggered purposely down the hall, two matched figures in black, a great sword strapped to their backs, a war sword sheathed to their sides. The crowd parted and jaws dropped in consternation as they walked by. They came before the door into the Great Hall, where the king held court, and announced their arrival to the speaker. Matthew knew Henry was seeing only them today, as a special favor to him. The king had a soft spot for Matthew, seeing how his battle was won because of Matthew's bravery. Matthew wasn't about to let him think any different.

They were announced, and entered the great hall. Court musicians were finishing a song as they entered. The shawm was trilling out loud piercing notes to the beat of the nakers with the background supplied by a psaltery with its harp-like sound. Matthew was totally at ease in the huge room, where knights in full armor stood guarding the king on each side, and numerous other knights stood around the walls, dressed in chain mail and mantles, holding colorful flags. Today the queen sat beside the king, prompting Matthew to realize she had been told of the plan and wanted to be there to watch. Henry Tudor could not keep a secret. That's why Matthew never told him the truth about his little misadventure with the Yorkist spy; in a while all of England would have known, and he would have been a laughing stock. No, better this way, with his family vowed to silence and no one else knowing. Except Pet, damn his brothers' big mouths.

Pet's senses were razor sharp with the knowledge Gideon was somewhere in the castle. She scanned the crowd of knights, noblemen, and noblewomen with cat-like persistence. She didn't even hear Matthew tell her to step forward.

A man caught her notice. All she could see were his eyes, as he was head-to-toe in chain mail. But they were *his* eyes. They had been burned

into her consciousness since the day he struck down Robert. He had a
war sword by his side, and so far hadn't seen her. He moved unnoticed
through the large room, through nobleman gathered for court to watch
or give their comments.

"Pet? Did you hear me? The king will see you now."

Pet looked at Matthew quickly, and then back to the mailed figure
moving closer to the front. Matthew finally took her arm, and led her in
front of the king, figuring she had a case of stage fright.

"Your majesty, I present the Lady Rose Boulton, of the Elton Township."

Gideon stood off to the side where Elizabeth sat. Pet watched him
stand to attention by another guard.

"Her family, namely her father and all brothers, were murdered by
the outlaw renegades who until recently were rampaging our lands."

She saw Gideon draw his sword, and move behind the other guard,
staying close to the curtains hanging against the wall. Pet's eyes
darted to the front. He wasn't after the king, he was after the queen!
Of course, the Yorkists were livid that Elizabeth, the Yorkist heiress,
married the Tudor king, uniting the houses of Lancaster and ending
the War of the Roses. Many considered her a traitor. Pet slowly
reached inside her jacket to bring out a dagger. Then she realized he
was dressed in chain mail that a dagger, no matter how expertly
thrown, wouldn't penetrate. She put the dagger back, and readied her
hand on the pummel of her war sword. The acute point could burst
apart the links of a piece of mail.

"Her lands have been ordered to be reduced, Sire, to one-third of her
current holdings."

Gideon moved closer to the queen. Pet eyed the room; nobody was
really paying attention. It was as if they were all there for the show,
pomp and circumstance of it all, and not really to safeguard. She barely
stopped to think as instincts took over and she began running, raising
her sword and yelling to Matthew.

"Matthew—it is the queen! He is after the queen!"

Matthew drew his sword, and ran after her. She expertly dodged the
crowd, but Matthew was not so fortunate. A confused guard confronted

him, thinking Matthew was threatening the queen, and Matthew had to knock him out of the way. Henry stood up, and was immediately surrounded by three fully armored knights whose only thoughts were to protect him. Gideon saw Pet coming, and threw the heavy mail hood off his head. He moved behind the queen, and raised his sword to run her through. Chaos reined in the court; nobody knew what was going on except one smart black-haired warrior.

"Death to the Yorkist traitor, the queen!" Gideon began his downward thrust behind the frozen, terrified Elizabeth.

Pet rammed her sword between the queen and Gideon's downward stroke, deflecting it away, and allowing the queen to flee. Two guards grabbed her and escorted her away.

Matthew had to fight his own men, who thought he meant harm to the king. "Not me, you fools!" he yelled at them. "The man up there!"

Pet turned to Gideon, who leered at her with rage and hate. "I thought I had you killed."

"Sorry to disappoint you." She thrust her sword across the middle, breaking the chain mail for a future strike. Gideon struck out at her, and she parried the blow. "You cannot beat me, Gideon."

"Oh, so you know my name?" He stepped sideways, and swung his sword in an attempt to gash her arm. She ducked, and struck him in the leg. Although the mail stopped the full impact of the blow, it nevertheless caused him pain.

Matthew finally convinced his fellow knights to stop fighting him, and put up his hands to order them to cease. "She will take care of him. Trust me."

The king had been observing all this action, and interjected at this point. "Listen to Matthew—I trust his judgment. Let the Lady fight!"

They all lowered their swords and watched Pet and Gideon exchange thrust for thrust, blow for blow, with Pet clearly getting the most hits. Matthew glanced up to the king, and saw he was watching in awe. Matthew was almost glad for this development. Pet had just saved the queen's life, and now fought the would-be assassin right in front of the king. Once he saw how good, brave, and courageous she was, he would see why Matthew wanted to marry her so badly.

"You have caused me a great deal of grief, you dreadful trollop." Gideon was now backed up against the wall.

"I am just starting." She thrashed at him with powerful blows, breaking through the mail and leaving great, bloody gashes. Everyone stood by and watched the sword fight with great interest. It wasn't every day they were treated to entertainment like this.

The overwhelmed Gideon was forced backwards as Pet relentlessly pursued him. Her onslaught was merciless; blows came so fast Gideon could not do much except merely defend himself.

"She deserves to die!" Gideon was yelling. "She is a traitor!"

Pet gave a strong lunge, and broke open the mail suit covering his abdomen. He feebly tried to stop her next blow, but she expertly knocked his sword out of his hand. Gideon stood there and sneered at her. "You cannot just strike down an unarmed man. You have not the courage."

Pet didn't hesitate. She raised her sword, and with one powerful strike ran him through, impaling him against the wall. She looked him straight in the face. "That is for my brother, you murdering bastard. Rot in hell."

She withdrew her sword, and stepped back. Gideon fell to his knees, holding the gushing hole in his belly. His eyes rolled to the top of his head and he fell to the floor, writhing in pain as he began his slow descent into death.

There was no sound. Each guest held his or her breath, until the sound of one person clapping came lifting over the hall. All eyes turned to the sound. It was the king.

Soon Matthew joined the king; others joined in, then others, and soon the entire hall was cheering and clapping for the brave girl who had just saved the queen.

Personally, Pet couldn't care less about the queen. All that mattered was she had just killed Robert's murderer. She was not really aware the cheering was for her. She turned and sought out Matthew, who by now was beside the king, clapping enthusiastically with a huge smile. He leaned into Henry's ear.

"Did I not say she was spectacular?"

The king nodded, and put up his hand. The noise started to die down, until it was once again quiet. He strolled back to his throne, but remained standing.

"You have all just witnessed the most magnificent example of swordplay I have ever seen."

Matthew smiled. Funny how the word *magnificent* just always came up when referring to Pet.

"This young woman, in a courtroom full of Royal Knights, saved my and your queen from a Yorkist assassin. There was never a thought for her own welfare, she struck out boldly and stopped a terrible disaster. Lady Boulton, come forth."

Pet still stood by Gideon's body against the wall, and suddenly realized all eyes were on her. She glanced over at Matthew, who approached her and held out his hand. She took it, and he led her before the king.

"Lady Boulton, Sir Cameron has told me tales of your bravery, and to be truthful, until a short time ago I did not believe him." He glanced at Matthew, who looked sheepishly back. "Sorry, Matthew." He looked back at Pet. "If even half of what he told me is true, you are a remarkable young woman. Under the circumstances, I feel only one action is warranted. Lady Boulton, kneel before your king."

Pet looked dazed, and Matthew had to whisper in her ear for her to kneel. She did, and the king took out his own sword as Matthew went up to stand by him. "'Tis not every day I personally choose a knight. This is a rare occasion where I bestow knighthood to a worthy candidate." He took his sword and touched Pet's right shoulder, then her left. "Your bravery is unsurpassed, Lady Boulton. You have saved my beloved wife, Elizabeth, from certain death. For that, I can never repay you enough. All I can do is show you my appreciation. Lady Rose Boulton, I command you to devote your sword to good causes, defend the church against its enemies, protect widows, orphans, and the poor, and to pursue evildoers. All of which Matthew tells me you are already doing. I dub thee a royal knight by the powers granted me as your king." He drew a deep, dramatic breath. "Arise, uh, er…" His face went blank. Matthew quickly leaned into the king, and whispered in his ear. Henry's face lit up, and he nodded.

"Arise, Lady Knight Boulton!"

She stood up in a state of stunned disbelief. The crowd began to cheer loudly, seemingly to go on forever as she glanced up at Matthew standing beside the king, beaming with pride for her. Too stunned to react, she just turned around and faced the crowd who cheered fervently. Matthew came down and stood by her.

"I told you that you were my Lady Knight."

She just nodded, too bewildered for words, with her face showing no emotion, just calm, steady control.

# ❧Chapter Fourteen❧

he king put up his hand, and all went quiet again. "Lady Boulton, Matthew told me of your plight, and the tragic death of your entire family. This has been a terrible injustice, and I extend my deepest sympathy." Matthew cleared his throat, and Henry glanced at him. "Er, there is still the matter of your lands. I would like nothing better than to return all holdings, but this shall require some thought. Would you wait for me in my solar?"

Two knights came by her side, and the king waved them out. They escorted her out of the huge room to the gawking eyes of onlookers, and led her down the hallway to the next room. She was placed inside, the door locked, with guards stationed outside.

Pet felt like a caged animal. She paced the room, wondering what Matthew was saying to the king in her behalf. It was taking way too long, and her patience grew edgy.

The king frowned at Matthew. "Do you still want to go through with this, Matthew? She seems a competent young woman, indeed, more than capable. Are you sure she shall accept her fate?"

"Aye sire, she will do anything to save her lands."

At that moment, a man who was obviously a religious figure came forth. The king smiled in recognition.

"Ah, Herbert, Abbot of Ramsey...what say you of this predicament?"

Pet continued to pace impatiently, when finally the door opened, and the two guards motioned for her to come. She was escorted back into the Great Hall, where everything seemed quieter and people appeared more solemn than when she left. Matthew stood to the left of the king, and a man of God stood to the right. Pet frowned; what was all this about? The king smiled down at her.

"Lady knight, we have been discussing your dilemma. I feel we have reached a satisfactory settlement. Not only shall all your lands be restored, but because of your honor and service today to your king, the Abbot of Ramsey is prepared to relinquish 1000 acres to the south of Elton to your care. This should double your holdings, and increase greatly the coffers of Elton Township. Of course, this is all contingent on one condition."

"Condition?" She glanced at Matthew, but he suddenly seemed fascinated with the ceiling.

"The Abbot, and indeed I, feel this much land is too much for a young lady, even a strong, capable one, to handle. Therefore, as your king, I insist you have a lord to help you. Are there any suitors you are agreeable to for marriage?"

"No." She glanced at Matthew again, who was now smiling, but still studying the ceiling.

The king cast her a dubious look. "There is no one?"

"Your highness, I would not make a good wife. Indeed, by your own witness, I am more a man than woman. I am past a decent marriageable age. I will not wear gowns, and sit idle all day whilst a man does the work. I am headstrong and outspoken, and will not make a husband feel worthwhile and important."

The king stroked his chin, and looked up at Matthew, who gave no indication of even hearing her. "I see. Would it surprise you to know Sir Cameron has addressed all these faults, and still has agreed to accept your hand?"

She glowered at Matthew, who now gazed upon her with a wide smile. "No, that would not surprise me at all."

"So you agree?"

"Not in the slightest. There is still the matter of eight orphans I have taken upon myself to raise. A ready-made family is not the ideal setting for a successful marriage."

"Aye, Matthew has also addressed this matter, and has assured me the children are a primary importance of his, also. He has furthermore agreed to let the running of Elton be your total responsibility, of which he shall intervene only at your asking."

She continued to stare at Matthew. "Truly?"

"He has also espoused strong feelings for you, and implies you return these emotions. Are you agreed, Lady Boulton?"

Pet felt panic rising to her throat, and she fought to control it. "Sire, may I talk with *Sir* Matthew—alone?"

"Of course." He waved them to the side. Matthew followed her with a grin so wide he thought his face might crack. When they were alone in a corner, she turned to him with pleading eyes.

"Matthew, please—do not do this."

He pointed to himself and feigned innocence. "Me? 'Tis not me, Pet, the king is practically ordering us to be married."

"At no suggestion from you, I am sure."

"Very well, so I did mention I wanted your hand. But you just obtained twice your land holdings…think of what that will mean to your people."

Her eyes grew desperate as she begged him to reconsider. "Please, Matthew…I cannot marry you. I wish not to marry anyone."

"Pet, I will be a good husband. I know you care for me, and you know how I feel about you. I do not see a problem, here." He put a hand on her chin, and tilted it upward, a deeply serious expression on his usually casual face. "Marry me, Pet. You will not be sorry."

Her pleading eyes turned to terror. "Matthew, if I do not, what happens to my land?"

He decided a little creative lying was in order. "The king has not come out and said so, but I believe you will lose some of it. He is very stubborn about estates having a lord. He does not want to order you, Pet, but he shall if necessary. He would be more pleased if you agreed willingly."

She suddenly knew what a trapped animal felt like, almost preferring death over entrapment.

"The king awaits. What is your answer, Pet?"

She closed her eyes, lowered her head, and nodded slowly.

Matthew's heart soared. "You will not be sorry, my precious Pet." He kissed her quickly on the forehead. "Come, let us tell the king." He took her hand and led her back to Henry, who leaned forward in his throne as they approached.

"Hence, has a decision been made?"

"Your highness, I am pleased to announce the Lady has accepted my hand in marriage."

The king sat back, satisfied their little charade had come to a successful ending. "Good! In the absence of Lord Boulton, God rest his soul, I would be most honored to give the bride away—if she concurs."

Pet nodded complacently. "Thank you, your majesty." Her voice was almost a whisper.

Henry nodded. "So, a date must be set, and…"

"Now." All eyes turned to Matthew, who was suddenly very serious. "I do not want to give the lady a chance to change her mind. I will marry her now, as she is."

Pet's eyes showed white all around. "*Now?*"

Henry nodded, and smiled at Matthew, remembering his own once-youthful exuberance. "That can be arranged. My chapel is on this very floor."

Pet was in a daze as Matthew took her hand and led her into the king's chapel, followed by as many lords, ladies, and barons that could jam into the small chapel to witness this unusual union. Everyone was required to remove their weapons at the entrance; Pet and Matthew's pile dwarfed all the others. They then strolled to the front of the chapel where the King was speaking to his priest. Matthew held her hand protectively and just stared at her. His dream was coming true, but for her it was a nightmare.

The king's own priest agreed to perform the marriage, at the king's request. A message was sent to the queen, who was recuperating in the solar from the attack, to be a witness. Matthew and Pet were told to kneel before the Priest, and the King announced he was giving the bride away to be married. Pet heard everything going on around her, but seemed to be in a world all her own, a protective place where control hid her real inner self. She felt betrayed by Matthew, whom she knew manipulated their marriage for his own gain even after she begged him not to. Everyone else was a stranger, so essentially she had no one. Loneliness engulfed her as she felt tears begin to form, but she closed her eyes and commanded her mind to bury them. Matthew watched with concern as she fought for control. He was the only one there who knew what she was doing. He pursed his lips in uncertainty, and almost stopped the wedding right then. A trace of guilt jarred through him; was it right to coerce her like this?

Pet heard the words, but they were a blur in her disconnected, stunned mind.

"Most worshipful friends, we are come here at this time in the name of the Father, Son, and Holy Ghost, to join, unite, and combine these two persons by the holy sacrament of matrimony, granted to the holy dignity and order of priesthood. Which sacrament of matrimony is of this virtue and strength that these two persons who now are two bodies and two souls, during their lives together shall be one flesh and two souls."

The ceremony continued, but Pet heard nothing. Despair washed through her, as she remained detached from her surroundings.

"Have you the ring?"

Matthew turned white. He had totally forgotten about a ring. He glanced at Pet, who still kneeled beside him with her eyes closed, and suddenly remembered his pinkie ring. He pulled it off and picked up her left hand. She opened her eyes as he slipped it on her third finger.

"I will get you a better one, later. With emeralds."

She looked at the little dragon ring in silence. "Do not bother. This is the only ring I will ever need."

"I, Sir Matthew Cameron of Cambridgeshire, take thee, lady Rose Pet Boulton, to be my lawful wedded wife, to have and to cherish, through sickness and through health, for richer and for poorer, for better and for worse, till death do us part."

The priest turned to Pet. "And now you, Lady Boulton."

She opened her mouth, and nothing came out. She felt herself start to shake, and gripped the railing for support. This had not gone unnoticed by Matthew.

"'Tis fine, Father. Let her just say 'I do.'"

"Lady Rose, do you take this man for your lawfully wedded husband?"

Pet swallowed, and searched for her voice.

"I—I—,"

Matthew squeezed her hand. "Say it Pet, just say I do."

"I—I do." She closed her eyes tightly.

They then had communion, and the priest finally blessed them and said the words Matthew had wanted to hear.

"By the powers vested in me, and by order of his Royal Majesty, the King of all England, I now pronounce you man and wife. What God has joined, let no man cast asunder. You may rise, Sir and Lady Cameron."

Matthew helped Pet stand up, and without a moment's hesitation took her into his arms.

"You will not be sorry, Pet. I shall give you everything you want."

She just looked at him with sorrowful eyes. "You cannot give me what I want most."

He didn't ask what that might be, just smiled, and brought his lips down on hers in a tender kiss. She closed her eyes, and let the kiss comfort her a little, when the realization hit her that she would be expected to fulfill her duty as a wife that evening. When Matthew concluded the kiss, he drew his face away from a panic-stricken Pet, engulfed in hopelessness.

The king ordered a grand party, and the castle folk jammed into the great hall to celebrate the joining of the first Lady Knight with a favored royal king's knight. Pet had no choice but to stay close to Matthew, as she was frightened, bewildered, and overwhelmed. Matthew was quite at home, however, and was having a regal time. Ale, beer and wine flowed freely, and everyone ate and drank to excess, Matthew included. Pet could not eat; her stomach was churning butterflies. Minstrels provided music, and jugglers and jesters entertained the crowd. The

King and his guests never missed the opportunity to celebrate; the castle loved a grand party.

Matthew knew he was drinking too much, but he didn't care. It was his wedding day, and he finally had gotten Pet as his own. There was just the small matter of the wedding night, which was something he was highly looking forward to. He protectively put an arm around her and held her close, causing her to feel like a novelty, a trophy he claimed as his own. The laughing and joviality around her did nothing to lift her own spirits. She was miserable, and did not try to hide it.

The celebration flowed into evening, when a young chambermaid tapped Pet on the shoulder, and announced it was time for her to prepare for the wedding night. Matthew gave his reluctant bride a hug, and let her go, but not before whispering to her as she rose up.

"Tonight I will prove you love me. Wait for me in bed, Pet. I will not tarry long." He kissed her cheek, and released her into the hands of the servants. Four laughing, happy girls led Pet away to bring her to the bridal suite the king ordered ready for the newlywed couple.

Pet was brought into the room, which was one floor down, to a tub full of steaming water with scented bubbles waiting for her. A great bed was ready, overstuffed with feathers and piled with numerous quilts. The bed had a canopy with curtains for privacy, and a white nightgown dressed with lace was laid on top. Pet felt her throat constrict, and knew she could not go through with this. As much as she loved Matthew, and she did admit she loved him, there was no way she could fulfill the marriage act. A dark secret loomed between them, one she wasn't sure he could accept.

The maids bustled around, and Pet finally ordered all but one to leave her. The young maid who stayed was a comely girl, with curly blond hair and full figure, and chattered on about Pet being so lucky to have married Sir Cameron.

"He is the most handsome knight at the castle," she was saying, "and all the maidens wanted him. I admit I even tried to catch his eye."

Pet sat on the bed, not in any hurry to 'prepare' herself for her wedding night.

"And did you?"

"Alas, no. Sir Cameron is very selective with his favors. But there were a few, and they shared their…er, experiences. I should not be telling you this, you are his wife now."

"No, believe me, I am most interested. Do go on."

"Well, 'tis said that he is…ah, well endowed, and knows his way about a woman's body."

Pet stared at the bed, and her eyes grew large. "What did you say your name was?"

"Me, Milady? Alice."

"Alice, would you like to help me play a trick on Sir Matthew?"

Alice giggled. "What kind of trick?"

Not long after that, Matthew made his way down the stairs, a little tipsy but otherwise feeling wonderful. His beautiful Pet waited for him in the bed, their wedding bed. He was already aroused with just the thought of her. He had been rehearsing what he was going to say, and hoped he didn't sound stupid and weak when he professed his love. And he planned on professing his love in many ways.

He tripped into the room, and found the candle burning low and Pet already waiting, evident by the hump in the bed. Her head was even covered. He hurriedly tore off his clothes, and crawled into the bed with anticipation throbbing throughout him. Before he touched her, however, he wanted to talk to her and calm her down. He had not missed her demeanor all through the celebration, and knew she was disconcerted by the day's occurrences.

"Pet, honey, I know you are upset, but maybe after I tell you some things, you will not be." He brought one arm upon the covers and laid it on the hump. She felt bigger, somehow. *There must be a lot of quilts,* he thought.

"Pet, I love you with all my heart. I always have. You probably know this, but I want to say it. You are the most incredible woman I have ever met."

There was a giggle from under the covers, and Matthew stopped, narrowing his eyebrows. Pet, *giggling*? Well, it *was* her wedding night, and she *was* a girl, but still…

"Darling, I will be the most loyal, doting husband and father. I want lots of children, not just the ones we already have, but our own. I plan to keep your belly full of my babes."

This time the lump tittered. Matthew frowned. A giggle, maybe, but never a titter. He jumped out of the bed and threw off the covers. A strange, blond-haired maiden lay in a full white nightgown, smiling up at his naked body appreciatively.

"Who the hell are you?"

"My name is Alice, Milord."

"What are you doing in my bed? Where is my wife?" He felt his anger rise and his face flush as his passion disappeared.

"Your lady thought maybe I could provide you with your needs tonight, Milord. She said to tell you she is not stupid and weak."

"Oh, did she, now! I think not—get out of here!" He pointed to the door, and the scared maid leapt from the bed and ran to the door.

"I am sorry, Milord—she said it was a trick, to pay you back. I did not mean to anger you."

It was too late for that. "Just get out!"

She ran like her life depended on it, and in the mood he was in, it just might have. He threw on some clothes, and went looking for his wayward bride.

Pet stood by Goliath's stall, her feelings mixed. She had killed Robert's murderer, been knighted, and then married within the course of an hour. There had not been time to think, to reason with Matthew or the king. Now she was his wife, as he always said she would be. Now she knew he had always planned this. Using his close relationship with the king, he forced her into the one thing she feared most. His brother Paul had warned her he would relentlessly pursue her, but she had not thought him capable of this. She hoped leaving the chambermaid in their wedding bed would convince him she did not want this marriage, and wondered if he was even at that minute making use of the willing girl's services. A sickly feeling rocked through her at the thought of him holding, kissing, and otherwise loving another girl. But it had to be this way. He didn't know about Geoffrey.

She was only five when her father brought his bastard son to live with them. Her other brothers accepted him well enough, but he was extremely jealous of Robert and her. He would often hit Robert when no one was looking, but mostly verbally abused Pet, chiding her when no one was around to hear. When the twins were eight, her father left on a hunting trip with her other brothers, leaving Geoffrey behind as a punishment for some misdeed. Geoffrey found her alone outside, and, especially irate at being left behind, took his anger out on her. He was a large boy for his age of fourteen, and she was tiny. He dragged her into the nearest building—the barn—and forced her into the hayloft. There he proceeded to strike and molest her. Robert heard her screams, and jumped onto Geoffrey's back, pounding him with small fists until the older boy left her to strike out at Robert. Pet remembered crawling into the corner, bruised and confused with what he had done to her, closing her mind to the pain. She remembered Robert caressing her and crying, his own body bloody and beaten from Geoffrey's rage. She remembered Raymond's fury in wanting to kill Geoffrey, but instead threatening to kill him if he ever touched her again. No one else ever knew. Robert vowed to stay by her side forever, and he had done so, until Gideon struck him down.

Since Robert's death, her only goal in life had been to kill his murderer. Now Gideon was dead, and she could move on to…what? Certainly not a marriage with Matthew; he deserved much more than her. He was the son of a rich and powerful lord, and would be a lord himself one day. He needed the kind of wife who would fulfill him. She could not do that; she was damaged and not worthy. Her only thought now was to leave, to flee, and to forget the headstrong knight who had wormed his way into her heart.

"I thought I would find you here."

She whirled around and took a backward step at the sight of him. His eyes were red and angry; his shirt was open and untucked. His hair was disheveled and he held an almost-empty wine bottle. He was irate.

"Do you know how many rooms are in the White Tower? Let me enlighten you." He staggered back a step, and regained his balance. "A lot. And I think I visited every one tonight, looking for you."

She swallowed and stepped back. "Matthew, you are drunk and angry."

"Really? Thank you for informing me." He stepped toward her, and she matched his every forward step to one backwards. "Damn you, come here! You are my wife!"

She had never seen him this angry, and she suddenly realized she had no weapons. She was utterly defenseless against him. "Matthew, please..."

"Oh, so now 'tis please, is it? What could you be thinking, Pet? Why? What wife would leave another woman in her wedding bed? Do you hate me so much?" He took longer strides toward her, and she bolted to the back of the barn.

"Come here, damn it! You are mine!" He reached out and grabbed her roughly around the arm, but she shook free and ran to the other side of the barn. He followed close behind. Pet was desperate, and looked for anywhere she could escape while he cooled down.

"God be my witness, I will have you, Pet! Do not run! Come here and face your husband!" He threw the wine bottle down, and reached her as she backed up against the wall in terror.

"I—I am sorry, Matthew!"

"Oh, are you?" He grabbed her aggressively and brought his lips down hard on hers. She struggled against him as his day-old beard scrapped across her face, making it red and raw. Her only recourse at this time was to bring her knee up and kick him in the groin. He let out a yelp, and let go just long enough for her to take the only escape—up the ladder to the hayloft. She reached the top just as he started up, and realized she had trapped herself. The ladder was the only way up—or down. She braced herself and waited for him.

He made it to the top, and stood staring at her, inside a broken man, outside an enraged one. "Come here, Pet."

"No, you are angry with me."

"That is the least of your troubles. I said, come here!"

"No." She backed up as he moved toward her. He suddenly leapt forward, and knocked her to the ground, then fell on top of her. She struggled against his superior strength, which was made powerful by his anger, and his greater weight. He brought his hands down on her wrists, and held her down as he lay on top of her and brutally kissed her face. He reeked of ale and wine, and she fought to move her face away.

"Damn you, Pet...you are mine. Did you really think you could escape me?" He began pulling at her doublet buttons, and she began to shake. Things became a blur, and she fought to maintain awareness. He finally tired of the buttons, and ripped the front of the jacket open, exposing her bare flesh. His eyes widened in drunken lust.

"Oh, Lord, you are splendid. I shall take you right here, Pet. You are mine, now." He took one hand off a wrist in order to cup a breast, and she brought her fist down on his face with all the strength she could muster.

"Hell!" He let go for just a second, and she pushed him off and began crawling away. He tackled her effectively, forcing her to the straw on her belly, and held her legs while she fought to reach him with her fists. He began pulling off her pants.

"Please Matthew! You are drunk! Do not do this!"

"Shut up! I will have you, with or without your consent!"

Pet started to shake. Her head was forced down in the straw, and she couldn't move for his weight holding her. Bile started coming up her throat, and she gagged as her body went into violent shudders. Matthew didn't seem to notice, as he rolled her over on her back, and positioned himself on top of her while holding her arms. "Stop fighting me, damn it! This is my right as your husband!"

She somehow managed to look him straight in the eyes, her fear causing her voice to shake. "P-please Matthew...not like this. N-not like this."

He didn't know if it was the tone of her voice, or the extreme terror in her eyes, but he stopped and really looked at her, not with rage or passion, but with the love he held so deep for her. His alcohol-muddled brain sought control of his actions, and he lifted himself off of her. She immediately rolled upon her side, and brought her knees up in a fetal position. Her body shuddered with fright, combined with violent flashbacks he had no way of knowing were occurring.

"Oh God, I am sorry, Pet." He reached out to touch her face, but she recoiled in terror at his touch. His anger returned, and he stood up.

"Hence my touch repulses you. No matter, Pet. You have said yourself there are many women willing to take my bed. Perhaps I should find one." He had no intention of doing so, but he was hurt, and wanted to hurt her back. There was no way for him to know at that point she was incapable of hearing him. Her mind had reverted to a small eight-year-old child who was alone and terrified.

Staggering from the barn, he searched for the nearest place to sleep. He wasn't there to see her crawl into a corner, and curl up as small as she could. He didn't hear her call for a dead brother who could no longer grant her comfort. He didn't see her body racked with tearless shudders as her mind struggled helplessly for control.

# ⊰Chapter Fifteen⊱

he next morning, Matthew didn't know what hurt worse—his headache or his heartache. He barely recalled confronting Pet in the barn, but he remembered enough to know he had hurt her with his blind, drunken wrath. After he sent the hapless chambermaid fleeing, he proceeded to storm through the castle looking for Pet, and ended up in the Great Hall drinking all the wine he could find, which was plentiful. After a while he thought of the barn, and reasoned out she probably had gone there. He was numb with hurt and disappointment to think she did not want him. She loved him; he could feel it. Why would she do such a thing? His confusion wouldn't let him think rationally, and when he found her he went crazy for want of her. When he saw her fright, and heard her voice tremble with fear, he knew he had lost control, and left as soon as he could. Somehow he made it back to his room, and blacked out. Now he didn't even know the time, or where Pet was. He sat up too quickly, and cringed with pain. Pet. He had to find her.

Pet opened her eyes to someone gently shaking her. She didn't know where, or for that matter, who she was, as someone began talking. A blurred form knelt over her. Eventually the form began to take shape, and she recognized it as Matthew's.

"Pet, honey, please wake up!" He watched as her eyes gradually focused, and recognition set in. "Thank God, you are all right. Come on, stand up." He helped her to her feet as he berated himself for leaving her there. Could he be a bigger imbecile? Finding her curled up in the corner of the barn, her clothes half ripped off, made his heart leap to his throat. Maybe she had hurt him, but he had hurt her more. He held her jacket together as he scuffled her into the castle and led her into his room. She still hadn't spoken, seeming incoherent and confused. He threw the covers back in the bed and picked her up. Then he laid her down in the bed, covered her up, and tucked her in.

"Get some sleep, sweetheart. I will be back in a short time."

Pet watched him shut the door, and then closed her eyes.

When he came back in the room, washed, shaved and dressed, she was sitting on the bed fully dressed in her leather. He was surprised to see her up, but feigned all was normal for her benefit. Deep down he was still irritated, but he was determined not to let it surface.

"Well, you are up and dressed."

She turned and looked at him with sad but controlled eyes. "Matthew, I am going home."

He sat on the bed beside her. "Actually, you are correct. We are going home—sort of. Now that you are my wife, my home is yours, and we leave for Cambridgeshire castle in an hour."

Her face whitened with alarm. "No…I want to go home to Elton. Please, Matthew."

It was all he could do not to give in to her, but he knew his family would love her and win her over for him. "I cannot, Pet—the king sent a messenger yesterday to my father, without my knowledge. They are waiting for us."

Pet lowered her gaze to the floor. "I have no choice?"

"I fear not." He pretended a cheerful attitude. "It will be fine. My mother is very, well, she is my mother. You shall like her, and she will love you."

She raised her face to confront his smile. "Matthew, please let me go home. I promise not to be a burden. You do not even have to live in Elton." Her eyes were pleading and desperate.

"What are you talking about? You are my wife now. Very well, so we have gotten off to a rough start. I was drunk, and you were scared. I suggest we both forget the whole thing." He put his arm around her. "We still have tonight." He leaned over and kissed her cheek, trying not to notice her coldness. "The king has given us a gift. Let us gather our weapons and prepare for the trip, and I will show you what 'tis." He stood up and held out his hand, which she ignored. Her self-control was starting to return, seeing how she had spent the last hour trying to regain it. Everything that happened in the barn was a blur: his rage, her fear, his attempted rape, her flashback. It was repressed to the back of her mind, with everything else painful in her short life. It was the only way she could function.

They recovered their weapons, and Matthew took her hand and led her to the front of the castle. An entire escort awaited, along with a fabulous carriage the king had gifted them. It was lavish, gilded in gold, with cushioned seats and a new spring suspension. Pet wrinkled her nose at it, something Matthew did not miss. She was starting to behave like herself again, and he was truly thankful.

"The king wants us to ride in style. The trip to my parent's castle should be a comfortable one."

Pet looked at him in disbelief. "I am not riding in that."

"Pet, you will insult the king!"

"I do not care. I am not riding in that."

He sighed. "Must you always be impossible? Very well, we shall follow behind an empty carriage all the way to Cambridgeshire castle. Will that make you happy?"

"No. I will simply be appeased."

"I shall settle for that. Let us ready the horses."

The party finally left London. Four escorts rode in front of the carriage, and two behind. Two more steered the carriage. Pet and Matthew rode behind everything. The carriage was a fine gift, one Matthew knew they would make use of once they settled down and traveled between his lands in Cambridgeshire and Elton. Pet just needed to warm up to the idea.

They rode all day, and found an inn for shelter. The escorts would stay with the carriage, to prevent theft or vandalism, and Matthew and Pet would book a room. She noticed he only booked one room, and grew even quieter than she had been the whole trip. He was determined to make up for his terrible behavior on their wedding night, even though he still thought she started it. He took her by the arm, and led her to the room.

The inn was a nice one, being so close to London, where nobles would need to stay on journeys to the king. He took off his coat, then boots, and finally started to take off his shirt. Then he noticed she was just sitting on the bed, staring at the floor. His heart sunk at her despondency, and he sat down on the bed next to her.

"Pet, what is wrong? Why do you hate me so?"

She raised her head and looked at him, her eyes narrowed in complacency. "I do not hate you, Matthew. I am simply wondering what you want from me."

"I want you to love me, but I am starting to get impatient."

"Impatient? Matthew, you forced me to marry you!"

He rubbed the back of his neck, and grimaced. "*Forced* is such a strong word, do you not think?"

"'Tis an accurate word. You betrayed me."

"Howe'er did I betray you? I asked for your hand in marriage, but you kept refusing!"

"Did you ever stop to think maybe I did not want to marry you?"

"But why? I am the son of a rich lord; I offer you much. All I ask in return is your love. Why do you fight me so?"

"Forcing someone to marry him is not very honorable."

"Hence now I am without honor? A woman who has no faith in her husband is not much of a wife!"

"A man who has no honor is not much of a husband."

He sprang to his feet in anger. "Damn it, you are impossible! What do you want from me? An apology? Fine, I apologize for marrying you. Are you now happy?"

"No."

"Very well, keep your blessed virginity one more night…I will sleep with the horses!" He pulled on his boots, grabbed his coat, and stormed out of the room.

Pet closed her eyes, and fought the tears. "No, I will not cry," she whispered. "Oh Matthew…why must you hate me so?"

The messenger knocked on the huge door of the Cambridgeshire castle, and a servant announced him. Lady Cameron accepted the message and dismissed the carrier. She read the message as she hustled into the parlor, her eyes wide with total surprise. "This cannot be correct!"

Luke and Paul looked up from their game of chess in curiosity.

"What, mother?" Paul asked.

"This says Matthew got married…at the king's chapel in London, yesterday! To a Lady Rose Boulton, of Elton, wherever that is."

Luke and Paul exchanged knowing looks.

"I wonder how he did it?" asked Luke.

"No doubt held a dagger to her throat." Paul answered dryly.

"Possibly, blackmail?"

"With Matthew, anything is possible."

Lady Cameron looked at her sons with confusion. "What are you talking about? Do you know this girl Matthew married?"

Paul smiled. "Aye, we met her. She is…is…"

"Married, it would appear, so you can wipe that smile from your face." She turned to her other son. "Luke? What do you know of this girl? Is this not sudden? You do not suppose she is…?"

"No, mother, I can almost guarantee she is not with child. Not this one."

"Oh nay," Paul agreed. "Not Pet. She is not the type. She is incredible."

"Can you not talk of your brother's wife without grinning ear to ear? What do you know of her? Howbeit he has not brought her to Cambridgeshire and introduced her to me?"

Paul took a deep breath, and straightened his face. "She is like no girl I have ever seen. A warrior."

"Warrior?" Lady Cameron drew her eyebrows together in consternation. "A warrior, you say? You mean, she actually…*fights*?"

"I watched her throw a dagger clear across a room and plant it in a poor chap's arm," Luke offered. "It was spectacular!"

Their mother put a hand to her chest. "Good Lord, she sounds like a savage!"

Paul sighed. "A beautiful savage."

"Very beautiful," Luke agreed, "and runs her township with the help of a capable man. I enjoyed my stay there immensely."

"All well for you to say, I was forced to come home to relay a message to father."

"You are not good at handiwork. It was the only choice."

Paul frowned. "You beat me at arm-wrestling, that is the only reason you went and I did not."

Lady Cameron looked at her two sons as if they have lost their minds. "Luke, you know of this girl?"

"Aye, mother. I have to say, I am surprised Matthew was able to get her to accept his hand. She seemed most adamant she would not marry."

Paul nodded his head in thought. "I wonder if he got the King to help."

Lady Cameron's eyes widened with incredulity. "Are you telling me you think there was coercion involved?"

"'Tis the only answer."

"I would agree," Luke said.

"But, any woman would be fortunate to get Matthew as her husband! Oh goodness, they will be here tomorrow afternoon! I must ready the household…prepare a grand meal…oh dear, there is just not enough time!" She fretted as she paced before her amused sons.

Luke cleared his throat to get her attention. "Mother, do not worry so…'tis not necessary to put on airs with Pet, in fact, she would be most uncomfortable if you do."

"Absolutely," Paul agreed. "She is not a pampered frail little thing like Matthew always brings home. She is different." He frowned. "She did not deserve to marry Matthew."

His mother drew herself up tall. "Paul, are you telling me you do not think this girl is good enough for Matthew?"

Paul looked aghast. "Oh, No, Mother…Matthew is not good enough for her!"

"Now, Paul, it so happens I was witness to them together whilst I was there," Luke espied. "I pray there were strong feelings between the two, but they were both too stubborn to admit it to each other. It might work. We should wish them well."

"Well, of course we should!" Lady Cameron agreed. "Oh, and with your father away on that ridiculous trip to his new ship! There is just not enough time!" She left the room, fretting about food and seating arrangements, as Luke and Paul looked at each other in amusement.

Paul let out a large sigh. "It will be good to see her again." His face suddenly got serious. "If he has hurt her, I shall kill him."

Luke was taken back. "Paul, you are talking about your own brother...howe'er can you say that?"

"She did not deserve this, Luke. Matthew somehow forced her to marry him, I just know it. I will probably have another broken heart to soothe, and this time, gladly."

Luke laughed. "Paul, I hate to inform you of this, but I think they are in love. It may be rocky at first, but they have a chance."

Paul scowled. "We shall see, brother, we shall see."

Pet and Matthew did not speak the next morning. He had a fitful night sleeping in the carriage, which was extremely comfortable, but missing one thing—his wife. He cursed himself for his stupid temper. If he would just break down and tell her he loved her, he wouldn't be in this predicament, and she would be lying in his arms right now.

The weather was threatening thundershowers, so Matthew wanted to get an early start. Pet ignored him, and he did the best he could at ignoring her when all he wanted to do was apologize. But, she wasn't making it easy.

A few hours from Cambridgeshire castle the carriage hit a large rut, and became immobile. It was already beginning to sprinkle with huge, dark clouds rolling in overhead. The carriage wouldn't budge, and Matthew could see it was going to take some time to loosen the wheel from the muddy hole. He approached Pet, who was sitting on Goliath watching impassively.

"I am going to send you on ahead with four men. The storm will hit soon, and I do not want you caught in it."

She shook her head. "No, I will stay. I am not afraid of rain."

"Damn it Pet—I do not want my mother's first impression of you to be of a drowned rat! You have no choice!"

to have lost a lot of choices, lately."

red her biting sarcasm. "Tell my mother the wedding carriage and I was detained. I will be there shortly!" He motioned the four men over to her. "Take her on ahead to the Cameron castle. 'Tis about an hour's ride, if you hasten. Go!"

The four men surrounded Pet, and they escorted her away. Pet fumed at the rude way Matthew was treating her, and vowed to get even the first chance she got.

As Pet and the escorts approached Cameron castle, her eyes widened in shock. The castle was huge, almost as large as the king's, with a wide moat and high walls surrounding it. The head escort announced their arrival, and the drawbridge was lowered.

They rode inside the castle gates, and were shown directly to the stable. It was already pouring, and they were all quite drenched. Pet dismounted, and looked up to the high walls of the house she had just married into. She approached the huge double doors to the entrance with trepidation, and knocked.

A male servant opened the door and looked her over with distaste. She was soaking wet, and her hair was plastered to her face and neck. She did, indeed, resemble a drowned rat.

"I have a message for the Lady Cameron from her son Matthew."

The servant lifted his chin and looked down his nose at her. "One moment." He shut the door in her face.

Pet waited patiently, rubbing her hands together in an attempt to warm them. In a few minutes, the door opened, and a lovely woman who unmistakably was Matthew's mother greeted her.

"Aye?"

Pet looked Lady Cameron over carefully. She wore fine clothes, was about Pet's height, only plumper, with blond hair the color of Matthew and Luke's. Her sparkling blue eyes were kind and full of spirit. Pet liked her immediately.

Pet cleared her throat. "I have a message from your son Matthew...the wedding carriage got stuck in a rut, and he is detained. He sent us ahead to inform you."

Lady Cameron clasped her hands together in glee. "Oh, they are almost here! Thank you, young man...oh, you are soaked! Send your party to the servant's quarters next to the stable. I shall have hot food brought to you." With that said, she shut the door in Pet's face.

Pet stared at the door for a few seconds, then slowly smiled. She figured she just got even with Matthew.

About two hours later, Matthew arrived with the rest of the escort and the catastrophic carriage. He left the escort to the business of stabling the horses, and headed directly to the castle. Having been caught in the worst of the storm, he was waterlogged, cold, and crabby. He entered the house with a holler.

"Mother! Father! Luke! Somebody!" He took off his soggy boots at the door, not wanting to track water throughout the house. His mother appeared almost immediately, with Luke and Paul directly behind her.

"Oh dear! You are soaked to the bone! Luke...find some drying cloths! Paul, fetch some dry clothes! He will catch his death of cold!" Luke and Paul departed to fulfill their assigned duties. Matthew stripped down to just his pants.

"That damned carriage! I thought we would never loosen it from the mud!"

Luke appeared with a huge drying cloth, and tossed it over Matthew's head in playfulness. Matthew dried himself off as Paul arrived with a dry tunic and shoes. Matthew dressed in the foyer, and reached for the hot tea a servant just brought him.

"'Tis good to be home! Mother...what think you of Pet? Is she not incredible?"

He received a blank stare from his mother, and contemplating looks from his brothers. Finally his mother found her tongue.

"Is she not with you?"

"Certainly not! I sent her on ahead to escape the storm."

Luke suppressed a laugh. "It would appear she did not make her arrival known."

"That is ridiculous! I told her to tell..." His voice tapered off as he pondered the situation. "Mother, who informed you of my delay?"

"Well, a nice young man came to the door and told me."

A sudden dread swept through him. "Mother, what did this *young man* look like?"

"Let me see…he had black hair—very black and wet—and I remember he was dressed all in black leather. Curious, now that I think about it."

Luke chortled.

Paul rolled his eyes.

Matthew turned white.

"Mother! That was my wife!"

She brought her hands to her face. "Great merciful Heavens! She *is* a savage!"

"Do not be ridiculous…she is no more a savage than you are." He opened the door to the still down-pouring rain. "Excuse me—I must find Pet."

He wondered if he was going to spend the rest of his life searching for his disappearing wife. This time he headed straight for the barn, where he found her brushing down Excalibur. Her hair had dried and fell about her face and shoulders in soft spikes. He stood and watched her for a minute before he let his presence known.

"Hello, wife."

She looked up with a fake bright smile. "Matthew! Your horse needed brushing, so I thought…"

"You thought wrong! Why did you not tell my mother who you were?"

She shrugged innocently. "She did not ask."

He firmly took her arm, and led her to the stable door. "'Tis still raining—run for the house!" He pulled her across the courtyard, running as fast as he could, when she stumbled and fell.

"Pet! Are you all right?" He helped her to her feet, and she flinched when she put her weight down on her left foot. Without a moment's hesitation, Matthew picked her up effortlessly and ran to the door.

"Put me down, Matthew! I can walk!"

"Quiet, Pet. You are hurt." He reached the shelter of the covered doorway and stopped, but continued to hold her. She had her arms around his neck, and he was painfully aware of the closeness of her face. Her hair dripped little streams down her forehead, running down her nose and over her lips, and finally off her chin. At that moment, she was the most beautiful thing he had ever seen. Their eyes locked in longing, and for a brief moment all else was forgotten. He gazed upon her slightly parted, full, wet lips, and began to bring his mouth to hers. She closed her eyes as he drew closer.

The door suddenly flew open, and his over-anxious mother ruined the moment.

"There you are! Get in here, you must be freezing!"

"Actually mother, I was quite warm." He carried Pet in, cursing his mother under his breath, as she fussed behind them.

"Oh dear, is she hurt? What happened? Can I help?"

"'Tis just her ankle, mother. She will be fine." He deposited Pet down in a chair, and proceeded to take off her boots. Paul suddenly appeared and smiled widely when he saw the black-haired warrior he had been fantasizing about.

"Pet!" He advanced over to her, and then noticed Matthew rubbing her ankle. "What is wrong with her foot? Matt, what did you do to her?"

"I did not do anything to her. Fetch some warm water."

Luke entered the room at that moment "Did you find her?" He saw her sitting with her foot in Matthew's hand. "Here! What happened?"

Their mother joined the fray. "Perhaps it needs to be wrapped?"

"Is it swollen?" Paul asked. "Cold water is good for swelling."

"She is already cold and wet—get her some dry clothes!" Luke yelled.

Pet's head spun as she listened to the scurry of comments going on around her. It was overwhelming to her, as she had been close to only one member of her family—her twin. She was not used to all this fuss.

"Should she lie down?"

"I still think we should wrap it."

"She needs a blanket; she is freezing."

Pet, Honey…does it hurt?"

"She needs a pillow!"

"Paul, really, 'tis her foot that hurts, not her head."

"Perhaps some nice, hot tea?"

"*Enough!*"

They all stopped and stared at her.

"I am fine. Matthew, help me get up."

"Do you think that wise?" He put out his hand.

Pet stood up, and accepted the drying cloth Paul handed her. Lady Cameron saw the discomfort in Pet's face, and gave her sons a stern look.

"All of you, get out of here…let the poor girl breathe!" She shooed them away with her hands.

"But, she is my wife!" Matthew protested.

"No matter…go entertain yourselves somewhere, I want to talk to my daughter-in-law." The men all obediently left the room, reluctant, but not willing to argue with their mother. When everything was quiet, Lady Cameron sat on a padded seat and watched as Pet dried herself.

"You are lovely. I know not how I thought you were a man."

Pet rubbed the towel over her head, making the shaggy mop fluff out in masses of tangles. "It seems to be a family trait…all but Paul has thought so."

"Oh, well, Paul…he would know a woman a mile away with her back turned."

Pet smiled at that, and Lady Cameron smiled back. "I can see why Matthew married you."

"Why would that be?"

"You are truly unique. Matthew never did like anything common. Come, Pet—please sit and talk with me." She patted the seat next to her.

Pet's self-preservation reflex kicked in. "I will stand." Having dried herself as best she could, she folded her arms and glanced around the huge room for the first time. It was more richly furnished than her manor in Elton, with lavish tapestries hanging on the walls and impressive framed pictures of various relatives. Lady Cameron intently watched the girl her son had married. Pet's defensive body language was evident; what did this young woman have to fear so?

"Luke and Paul tell me you fight."

"Aye."

"I see you prefer men's clothes."

"Aye."

Seeing her line of questioning was going nowhere, Lady Cameron switched tactics. No yes or no question, this time. "So, how long have you known Matthew?"

"It seems forever. I have not been able to rid myself of him."

"I see. Well, Matthew can be tenacious." She received no answer, so continued with her interrogation. "May I inquire as to what the rush was to get married? Matthew's father and I would dearly have loved to come to the wedding."

"Ask Matthew." Pet slowly began walking about the room, looking at swords on display on the wall, among other novelties.

"Are you saying the quick wedding was Matthew's idea?"

"It certainly was not mine." Pet was all the way on the other side of the room now, and Lady Cameron had to raise her voice to be heard.

"Pet, dear, please do come sit down. 'Tis hard to have a conversation with a roving subject."

Pet turned and realized she was being extremely rude, after all, the woman was her mother-in-law. She meandered back across the room and carefully sat on the far end of the seat.

"Very well, I am here. What do you want from me?"

"My, you are forthright, are you not? Call me mother, dear."

"No."

Lady Cameron drew back, bewildered at Pet's refusal.

"Why not?"

"I have called no one mother."

"Not even your own?"

"My mother died when we were born."

"We?"

"I was a twin."

Lady Cameron stared at the beautiful girl sitting before her. Could her son really have been so fortunate to have won her? Or, did he just marry her?

"Very well, how about Ellen? That is much more friendly."

"Fine."

"Good. Now, Pet…is there anything I can do for you?"

Pet was soaked, hungry, uneasy, and hurt. The only thing she could think of was Matthew. "Aye, there is one thing. Would you please see to it that Matthew and I have separate rooms?"

Lady Ellen looked taken back for a moment, and quickly regained her composure. "You have only been married two days, and already sleep in different rooms? Is there something wrong with my son's, er, lovemaking?"

"I would not know."

"Are you telling me, you two have not…?"

"No."

"But, what of your wedding night? Where did you sleep?"

Pet felt her hands begin to shake, and clenched her fists to calm them. "In the barn, mostly."

"The barn! And where was Matthew?"

"Drunk and angry, and most likely with someone else."

"He would not!" Lady Ellen was totally shocked at this point. "Not my Matthew! Tell me child, why did you marry him?"

"I was not given much of a choice."

"What? Child, you are to tell me everything. I need to know what my eldest son has done this time."

So Pet did. She told her of Robert, the orphans, meeting Matthew, killing the renegades, going to the king, killing Gideon, being knighted, and being practically ordered to marry Matthew. She left out parts of the nights Matthew held her and or comforted her, thinking Lady Cameron would be bored with silly little details. When she was done, Ellen sat back with a stern grimace on her face.

"My dear, Paul had me believing you were a savage. I can see the only savage around here is Matthew. He has much to answer for." She stood up, and went to the door, summoning a servant. "Of course you may have separate rooms. After all you've been through, I would not allow Matthew to touch you. Oh, Judith…would you show my daughter-in-law to her room?" She held out her hand to Pet, and Pet stood up. "We will talk later. I will have some dry clothes found for you; Paul has some he has grown out of that you shall be able to wear."

Pet nodded, and followed the servant out. Lady Cameron drew herself up tall, lifted her chin, and went to find her eldest son.

# ❧Chapter Sixteen❧

atthew! I need to talk with you!"

The brothers all looked up at their mother, standing at the door with a sour, angry look that would curdle milk. Paul and Luke exchanged looks. Matthew had been telling them how he cleverly obtained Pet's hand in marriage. Paul was fuming, Luke was withholding judgment.

"We will leave, Mother." Luke stood up, but his mother waved him back.

"No, I think you both need to know what your brother has done."

"I know what he has done—he forced Pet to marry him, and they have been fighting ever since," said Paul.

Matthew flinched. "*Forced* is such a strong word, do you not think?"

Lady Cameron glowered. "Well, what do *you* call it?"

"I call it pursuing the woman I love and getting her."

"I call it taking advantage of the situation," Paul ranted.

"Matthew," his mother said, "I am going to ask you a question, and I want a straight answer! Was there another woman in your wedding bed?"

Matthew winced. "Well, if you word it like *that…*"

Paul leapt to his feet, his anger exploding violently. "You bastard! Howe'er could you do that to her!"

"I am innocent! I swear!"

Luke tried to intervene. "Sit down, Paul."

"No! I have stood by and watched him blunder through life with no thoughts of others. So far no one has been hurt—permanently. But this is inexcusable!"

Lady Cameron tried to calm her young, hotheaded son. "Now, Paul…let us hear his explanation."

"There is none he could give that is acceptable! I cannot live in the same house as him. I am leaving." He turned to Matthew. "You are no longer my brother." He stormed out of the room, taking long, purposeful strides.

Luke went after him, leaving Matthew and his mother alone. She stared down at him silently, which was almost worse that being yelled at. When she did speak, her tone was one of total disappointment and disgust.

"Matthew, how could you?"

He gave an exasperated groan and slouched back in his chair. "'Twas not my doing, mother! Pet talked a chambermaid into getting in the bed, and fled from me to the barn. I got angry, and we are in a tiff right now."

"A *tiff*? Matthew, this is more than a tiff! That poor child is miserable!"

"Mother, damn it, I love her!"

"Therefore that gives you the right to control her? To force her to do your bidding?"

Matthew swallowed hard and pondered his mother's disappointed expression. He had never had so many members of his family so irritated at him at the same time. "I am sorry, mother, that I let you down. But the damage, so to speak, is done, and we are married."

"No, Matthew, the damage is not done. Pet tells me this marriage has yet to be consummated."

He moaned and sunk even lower in the chair. "Did she hold nothing back?"

"I doubt it, she needed to talk. Matthew, you have to make things right by her."

"What do you mean?"

Luke trudged back in with a frown on his face. "He will not listen. He is going to father's shipping line and demand passage on the next ship leaving, and says he will not come back until Matthew is dead. I have never seen him so furious."

Their mother nodded. "Aside from Matthew's death, I fear this is one time I have to side with Paul."

"Is my whole family against me?" Matthew leaped up from the chair and paced in front of them. "I bring home my bride, hoping you will win her o'er for me, and…" He stopped, berating his big mouth.

"Is that what this is all about?" his mother shrieked. "Your family doing what you could not—win this girl's heart?"

Matthew grimaced. "Well, sort of."

Luke put a hand on Matthew's shoulder. "You know I love you, Matt. I would stand by your side and fight to the death to save you. But this time you went too far."

"You, also? Does no one see my side in this?" He sat and buried his head in his hands.

His mother's voice softened. "I see a love-sick man who is used to getting his own way, and a strong, heartbroken young girl who was vulnerable when you met her. Matthew, do not do this to her."

"'Tis already done. She is mine."

Luke shook his head. "She is yours in name only, brother."

"Then that will have to do."

"Matthew, dear…I have always told myself I would not be the kind of mother who meddles in her children's affairs, but now I am meddling. You must do right by this girl, and let her get on with her life."

Matthew felt his heart stop beating. "W-what are you saying, mother?"

"She is saying to do the right thing, Matt—go to the king and have him ask the priest to get the marriage annulled."

"Nay!" Matthew couldn't believe his ears. "After all I did to get her? That is not even up for consideration!"

His mother stood up tall next to her over-bearing son. "At least consider your actions, Matthew. For once think of someone but yourself." She shook her head in displeasure, and left her sons alone.

Matthew turned to Luke in desperation. "Luke, what am I to do? I cannot let her go!"

"Cannot, or will not, Matt? I fear the choice is yours."

Matthew felt dejected, bewildered, and frightened. His whole family, save for his father who wasn't even there, had turned against him. Was he such a horrible person? Could his love for this girl have blinded him of all logic?

"Help me, Luke…help me make the right decision."

"Very well, Matt. Let us talk."

Lady Cameron strolled into her kitchen, where a frenzy of activity was going on, and went straight to her head cook.

"Lewis, there will be no banquet tonight, after all. I would, however, like a tray made for a guest. I will have it taken up myself."

Lewis rolled his eyes in despair, and wondered what to do with all the food he had prepared.

Pet relaxed in the tub of hot water Lady Ellen had ordered for her. She felt better after dinner, provided by a tray of delicious food. Ellen had also sent up something very special—a bar of lilac-scented soap. She rubbed the fragrant bar upon her hands, and felt the newness of her wedding ring. Lady Matthew Cameron. It seemed inconceivable.

Matthew had a good family. His brothers adored her, and his mother seemed to like her. She was painfully aware how Matthew felt about her. So many people had never fussed over her before, and for the first time in a long while she felt loved. Perhaps she was too hasty in her reluctance? Maybe—just maybe—there was a chance for her and Matthew.

She stepped out of the cooled water and dried herself off, having resisted any assistance from servants for the privacy needed in order to think. She smiled at the fresh, white nightgown Lady Cameron had brought her. Her talk with Matthew's mother had helped; there had been no one for her to talk to and she didn't realize her need to vent. The tensions of the last few days had diminished with the hot water, and she actually felt hopeful. She made a decision to talk with Matthew, to swallow her pride and admit how she felt about him. She loved him. Somehow he had worked his way into her heart, and she knew now she couldn't live without him. She needed to explain about her childhood. If he loved her at all perhaps he would understand. It was a huge risk— he could reject her and leave her alone, but wouldn't that be better than this? She had resisted enough; it was time to talk. She would wait until tomorrow after a good night's sleep.

A shallow knock came on her door, and she quickly threw on the nightgown over her head. It felt wonderful; made of thick damask trimmed with lace. She couldn't wait to tell Lady Cameron how beautiful it was. For lack of a comb, she ran her fingers through her damp hair and hastened to the door to greet her mother-in-law. Her eyes widened with surprise.

It was Matthew.

He had changed clothes and combed his hair. Her first thought was how incredibly handsome he really was. A boyish lock of wayward hair fell across his forehead, and she fought the urge to brush it up. Something in his face bade hopelessness. Pet immediately knew something was wrong.

"Pet, we need to talk."

She smiled. "Aye, Matthew, I know. I…"

"No, let me go first." He didn't need to hear her tell him what a fool he was, or reject him further. It had taken a long heartfelt talk with Luke and three glasses of wine to work up the courage to confront her. He knew it was going to be the hardest thing he ever did.

He opened his mouth to speak, and noticed the nightgown for the first time. Her black hair flowing over her shoulders contrasted against the white material of the gown. She looked like an angel covered in all that white. His tongue wouldn't move.

"You…look good in white."

She created one of her genuine smiles that made his heart skip. "Your mother loaned it to me."

He stepped forward, and sniffed. "You smell of lilacs."

"I know. Your mother loaned me some soap for my bath."

This was too much. Here stood his bride, whom he truly loved, fresh and clean and smelling of lilacs. How much torture could he endure?

"Pet…" He closed his eyes briefly and prayed for strength. He wasn't proficient at doing things he didn't want to do. "The general opinion is

I have greatly wronged you. My family is rather upset with me. And I am rather upset with myself."

"Matthew, I…"

"No, Pet, just let me finish." He swallowed hard, trying to find moisture in his dry, lumpy throat. "I am sorry I made you marry me. It was a selfish maneuver. As my brothers have no doubt told you, I am impulsive and do not like to lose. I did not consider your feelings, and I hurt you. I never wanted to do that."

Pet felt her defensive mechanism come up, and she folded her arms. "What are you trying to say, Matthew?"

"I am saying I was wrong."

"Wrong?"

He fought back unmanly tears; it would not do for her to see him cry. "I should not have married you. You did not want me, but I did not listen. I can only think of one solution."

"Solution?"

"I will beseech the king to allow an annulment." The words caught in his throat as he spoke them. "I will escort you back to Elton, and go to London immediately. You will finally be rid of me, as you have always wanted."

Pet fought to keep her breathing steady. She couldn't speak. Everything Paul had said was true. Matthew fought until he got her, then tired of the chase, and was ridding himself of her. Her face went blank.

"Of course, under the circumstances, I will return your horse."

"Keep him." Her voice was soft and steady. "He was a birthday present."

"Thank you." He couldn't think of anything else to say, except scream he didn't mean a word, and he loved her, but he had been convinced this was the only fair thing to do for her. "I am sorry, Pet." He turned quickly, to hide the tears that would not hold back, and put his hand on the door handle.

"Matthew?" Her voice had a hint of desperation in it, and he spun around to her hopefully.

"Aye?"

She stood there with her mouth open, wanting to speak, but words would not come.

"Nothing." She lowered her head.

Matthew felt his throat swell, and knew he had to leave before he just forgot the whole thing and grabbed her into his arms. "Goodbye, Pet."

"Goodbye, Matthew."

He left her room and headed for his own. As he entered, he closed his eyes and held back stinging tears. Give her up? He would just as soon run a sword through his heart. He thought of the way she kissed him; the times he held her while they slept; her indignant humor; the way he loved to tease her. He remembered watching her grieve at the death of Mary, her bravery at the king's court, and her face as he assaulted her with his rage. Then tonight, he remembered her eyes as he held her in the rain and bent to kiss her before his mother interrupted. His tears would not be held back as he thought of never holding her again. Dear Lord, he loved her so! How could he set her free? He covered his face with his hands and wept.

Pet stood in the same place for several minutes after Matthew left, rooted to the spot. Her body shook with tremors as she controlled this latest anguish, recessing it to the depths of her mind. Finally she felt in control, and sat on the bed in thought. Matthew did not want her. She had been ready to open her heart, and it would have been even more broken than it felt right now. She vowed never to let herself love again. The risk was too great, and the hurt too enormous.

She fingered the sleeve of the nightgown, placing it in her memory of good things to recall, then stood and pulled it off. Her own clothes were still wet, but Lady Cameron had sent up some old clothes of Paul's. She put on a doublet, hose, boots, and her own long overjacket, and wrapped the rest of her own clothes in a bundle. Then she gave the room one last glance, and slipped out the door.

Of all the miserable nights Matthew had ever spent, that night topped the list. Sleep was impossible; he tossed and turned until his bed was a rumpled, tangled mess. He finally got up at the first sign of light, and went down to the kitchen for some tea. He felt as if he had died but no one had bothered to bury his body. Then, with renewed determination, he decided he couldn't do it. Damn it all, he had to try to make her understand how much he loved her. He would talk to her, first thing that morning; tell her he didn't want an annulment. Maybe she would listen.

He started up the stairs, only to meet his mother coming down. One look at her son told her what kind of a night he had. She was feeling a bit guilty herself for meddling in Matthew's life, and wondered if the high emotions of the moment had forced them to make a critical mistake.

"She is gone, Matthew."

"Gone?" He felt whatever bit of hope he had drop out from under him. "What do you mean, gone?"

"I knocked on her door early to talk to her, and found her bed undisturbed—oh Matthew! She left sometime during the night."

"Left! Mother, we have a drawbridge and a moat! Howe'er could she just…" He suddenly remembered who they were talking about. It wouldn't be a hard task for Pet to knock out the drawbridge keeper and ride out. In denial, he ran down the stairs and outside to the stable to check if Goliath was indeed gone. His heart broke as he saw every trace of her missing—her weapons, her horse, her saddle and other tack—everything was gone. Excalibur whinnied in his stall, and Matthew went over and rubbed his nose.

"'Tis just you and me, boy." He ambled remorsefully back into the house. As far as he was concerned, his life had just ended. He totally forgot today was his twenty-ninth birthday.

Pet rode all night and the entire next day straight, and reached Elton by early evening. No one dared ask her any questions as she shuffled up the stairs to her room. William took care of Goliath, noting the poor horse had been ridden hard and long. That wasn't like Pet, to abuse an animal. Something was horribly wrong.

Pet talked to no one, just collapsed on her bed with exhaustion from being up for three days, and slept for eighteen straight hours. When she got up it was mid-afternoon. Servants avoided her; if the look on her face reflected her mood she was not to be reckoned with.

But now she had the children to care for.

She sought them out, and after hugs and welcomes, marched them directly to her tailor's to have a full set of clothes outfitted for each of them. They were now noble children, and needed clothes to fit their standing. The poor tailor reeled with this order, planning to hire additional help.

While the children were getting measured, Pet went to the kitchen to finally eat. Her empty stomach and lightheadedness would not do for the work she had ahead of her. As she sat alone at the small table, Raymond came in for a break from his duties. Upon seeing her, he grinned widely and leaned over her, giving her a huge hug.

"Pet! Thou art back! No one told me."

"It was not important."

Her apathetic response confused him, and he took the seat across from her, staring into her face for a clue.

"All right, what has happened?" He knew this girl too well to not see she was terribly troubled.

"Nothing."

"Nothing, as in *nothing*, or as in *I do not want to talk about it?*"

"Both."

"Ah. Therefore, thou hast nothing at all to report."

She shrugged. "I got knighted."

"What!" He gazed at her complacent face in shock. "Thee calls that nothing?"

"I killed Robert's murderer—in front of the king."

His eyes narrowed. "What else did not happen?"

She looked down at the ring she still wore when she left Cambridgeshire. "I am married." Then, before he could react she quickly added, "but not for long."

Raymond sat back, scratched his head, and frowned, "Mayhap thou should start at the beginning."

So she did, keeping it short and only stating the facts. When she got to the wedding, Raymond stopped her.

"Whoa, young lady…thou sayest thee were forced to marry him? Pet, I know thee better than that. Not even the king could have talked thee into something thee dids't not want to do."

"I had no choice. They were going to take my lands. Raymond, there is something I have not told you."

"And that would be?"

"I spent some time going o'er my father's ledgers. He owed a great deal in gambling debts, and we are almost out of money. I used almost everything rebuilding Elton."

"Why did thee not tell me this?"

"It was not your problem. My father purposely did not tell you, because the debt he was paying was Geoffrey's. He knew there was a conflict 'twixt you two. You could not hide your feelings."

Raymond's face flushed with rage. "That little bastard! I should have killed him twelve years ago."

"No, Raymond, you did what you had to do. Please, make me a promise. Do not e'er tell Matthew about the debt."

"Does't thou think it really would make a difference to him?"

"I know not. All I know is, it makes a difference to me."

"Thou loves him, dost thou not?"

"Certainly not."

Raymond decided some reverse psychology was in order. "Why not utilize his great wealth, then? Take advantage of him, get what thou mayest while thee can?"

"Raymond, you know perfectly well I could not do that. If I asked him for help, he would think I married him for his riches. I have no intention of taking any money from him."

"Why does it matter?"

"It just does." She paused, then in a bitter tone added, "At least Matthew obtained something from our doomed marriage. A former wife carves a deeper notch than a former lover."

Raymond's heart bled for his brave, beautiful girl. He had seen her in all conditions of life, but had never once seen her bitter. The hurt this time must be massive and raw.

For the next few days, Pet relentlessly pursued her duties. She and Raymond had to meet with Abbey officials for the acquisition of the new acreage. She didn't know if the obtainment would be permanent, but at the moment she was still married and she would forge ahead until she heard different. Keeping busy was all that kept her going and her mind off Matthew.

One afternoon, after a week had passed, a servant notified her that she had a visitor. When she entered the hall, she was mildly surprised to see Paul. He smiled widely as she approached.

"Pet! 'Tis good to see you!" His smile faded as he saw her solemn face. "He has hurt you greatly."

She lifted her head high and set her jaw. "No, I am fine."

"You are not fine. No one is fine after my slimy brother gets through with them."

"Paul, he is your brother. Do not speak thus of him."

"He is my brother no more. I have left the Cameron household and am on my way to the Wash bay. My father's shipping line is in Hunstanton, and he has graciously permitted me a trip on his new ship. I had to stop before I left, to say goodbye, and that I was sorry."

"For what? You have done nothing."

"Nothing but be born into the same family as the rottenest creature in all England."

"Paul, do not hate your brother because of me. He did not hurt me; I will be fine."

He narrowed his eyebrows and looked at her suspiciously. "Why do you defend him so? Oh, Pet—you are not in love with him?"

"Surely not. Do not be ridiculous."

"Aye…you are. I know that look." His voice suddenly got painfully serious. "Pet, he is not worthy of you, no more than I am. I do not flatter myself to think I could comfort you, although I would like nothing better. Causing you pain was inexcusable, no matter how much he hurts, also."

She raised her eyebrows. "He is hurting?"

"Oh, he thinks so. He was moping about the place before I took my leave. Thank God we live in such a large castle hence we could avoid each other. He will move on to his next project, God pity whoever that may be, and he will forget you. I, however, will not."

She forced a brave smile. "Thank you, Paul. You are sweet to care about me, but I am fine, really."

"If you love him, you are not fine. At least he did not ravish you and take your virtue. For that I would have killed him."

Pet was saddened by the animosity in Paul. No matter what had transpired between her and Matthew, she didn't want to be the reason for his hatred.

"Paul, you must forgive him, or it shall eat you from within. I have my lands, and my children, and I will be fine."

He snorted a small laugh. "Forgive him? Have you forgiven him?"

She paused at that question. Had she? The brief hesitation was enough to prove his point.

"I thought not. 'Tis hard to forgive someone so vile."

"Paul,"

"No more defense of him. I must leave. Pet, please remember me kindly. I will think of you often." He paused, then reached out and gave her a short hug. "I wish I could have met you first. I would have cherished you."

Pet was chagrined she had driven such a wedge between two brothers. She watched with sadness as he left.

Three weeks followed, and there was still no word from Matthew. Pet still wore her wedding ring as a reminder of what love can do to a person—make one hurt until you become numb to the suffering. And that was what she was—numb. She kept busy with her manor, the fall harvest, and the children, working relentlessly. No one could match her energy and drive.

One evening after an especially exhausting day, she was in the courtyard with William when she heard the clopping of large hoofs. She whirled around and her heart skipped a beat when she saw Excalibur. All her practiced control she had accomplished in the last month temporarily left her as she watched Matthew dismount and walk toward her. He looked more handsome than ever. His hair had grown longer, and touched his collar; he was clean-shaven and wearing fresh clean clothes. She assumed he must have stayed at a close-by inn before he made the trip to her manor.

William was ecstatic, and yelped while running to greet him. Matthew hugged the boy, commented on how big he'd grown, then slowly turned to Pet.

Seeing her again was the most painful experience he'd had for a month. He had hoped his feelings for her would have diminished after a separation, but all emotions came back a hundred fold. His tongue felt twice its size and he couldn't swallow. She was wearing a form-fitting dark-green tunic, black hose, and soft leather shoes. When she was not wearing her leather, her femininity showed through, right now torturing him. Her long, slender legs were as enticing as ever, as well as her large brown eyes that looked right through him. His first impulse was to pull her close to him; instead he did his best at feigning indifference.

"You look well."

"As do you."

He glanced around the courtyard. "Where are the children? I have brought them all something."

She gave him a complaisant look, then asked William to fetch them. William skipped away, and suddenly they were alone. An uncomfortable silence developed, before Pet broke it. She petted Excalibur and smiled.

"You care for him well."

"He is my finest possession."

A breeze caught her hair, and it fluttered across her face. He instinctively reached out and brushed it out of her eyes. She stiffened

when he touched her, and he quickly withdrew his hand. He struggled
for something to say.

"Howe'er is Raymond?"

"Fine."

"And the children?"

"Fine."

"Pet, damn it! Talk to me! I grow weary of your one-word answers."

"I believe you set a new record. You almost went an entire minute
without cursing at me."

He sighed. "Must we always fight?"

"That is your choice."

"And also my fault?"

"I did not say that."

"You did not have to."

At that moment, the courtyard exploded with children, all wanting
to hug Matthew at the same time. Pet let out a large sigh of relief; she
didn't want to continue fighting with Matthew.

"I have brought you presents. I went shopping in London, at all the
finest stores. Who thinks they deserve one?"

He passed out presents to the excited children, one by one. Pet
observed with awe at the presents he had brought; each one had been
hand picked for each child. For Julie, a doll with a blue dress—her
favorite color. Stuart got toy soldiers. Rosie got a brand-new dress with
lace trimming. Little adventurous Georgie received a hammer—in just
his size. It went on and on, each present thought out carefully for each
child. Pet reluctantly felt her admiration grow as she watched him.

Only one child was left…Andrew. He stood with anxious eyes
waiting for his present. Matthew looked down at him, and frowned
unconvincingly. "Hmmm…what do I have for a future knight?" He
reached into the saddlebag and brought out a sword—made just big
enough for little hands. "Pet can teach you how to use the sword." He
looked across at her. "She is very good."

Pet could not help but smile.

Andrew swiped the sword in the air a few times, but lost his balance on his bad leg, and fell. As he began to cry, Pet started to run to him, but Matthew held up his hand to stop her.

"Here, what is this? Tears from a future knight!"

Andrew sniffed and shook his head. "I cannot be a knight. I am a cripple."

Matthew smiled, and brought an item from his pack. "Hmmm…it looks like I have something left? I wonder what this could be?" He kneeled down in front of Andrew and helped him to his feet. "Andrew, I went to the finest doctors in London. I told them all about you, and they made me this." He held up a curious item, a piece of long, polished, smooth wood with padding and straps attached to it. "This is a brace, Andrew. You wear it on your leg." He began strapping it on Andrew's bad leg. "They think if you wear this for a few years, it will make your leg grow stronger. They also showed me some movements you can do to increase muscles."

Andrew stood on his new brace, and slowly began to walk around the courtyard. He scurried faster, and faster, and didn't fall. He beamed a smile at Pet, then at Matthew.

"I can walk!"

Pet brought her hand across her mouth and watched as tears tried to form. She blinked them back. If she would not cry for pain, she would not cry for joy.

Andrew ran over to the other children to show them how well he walked. Matthew watched for a few minutes, and then turned to Pet with a sheepish grin.

"I hope you do not mind. Children should always anticipate presents from their father."

Pet froze. "Their father?"

Matthew looked away to avoid eye contact. "Come inside, Pet. We have to talk."

"Fine." She turned on her heels and briskly sauntered into the house, with him close behind. When they got inside, Pet stopped in the lesser hall. She turned, and stared at Matthew as he rambled in.

"Very well, Matthew, you have been ignoring the subject ever since you arrived."

"I know." He paced a few times, then let out a large breath. "Pet, the king will not allow our annulment. I argued, I badgered him for days, but he would not listen."

Her expression didn't change. "I see."

"I tried, I really did, but he says I made a decision and I have to stick with it."

"That is all very fine for you, but where does that leave me?"

"Married."

Pet took a deep breath. "Matthew, I have spent the last month regaining my life and trying to forget you. Now you arrive and tell me I am married to you and I have no choice?"

"That is the way it appears."

"Nay—this cannot be happening." Her hands tightened into fists and her stomach began to churn. "Matthew, I cannot go through this again, I have to get on with my life, without you."

"Howbeit, with me?"

"Matthew, all we do is fight."

"That is not my fault…you always agitate me on purpose."

"I do not! You are the one who always gets angry and opens his big mouth!"

"Pet, it would appear we are stuck with each other, so we might as well…"

"Stuck?"

He winced. "Perhaps that was not the appropriate choice of words."

"*Stuck?*"

He swallowed as she marched up to him. "Do not ever feel you are *stuck* with me. I did not ask for this. I did not ask for you, or your king, or anything!"

He backed up as she advanced. He had never seen her so angry. "Pet, honey, "

"Do not *honey* me! I cannot do this again, Matthew. There might have been a chance at one time, but Paul is right…you just toss me aside at your whim, and feel you can just ride in here any time, give out presents, and be the big hero!"

Matthew felt the veins in his neck expand. "I am not the one who keeps running away! Every time you get angry, you bolt!"

"The only person I want to bolt now is you."

"You are so impossible! If you were any other woman, I would throw you o'er my shoulders, carry you up those stairs, and make love to you!"

"And why do you not?"

"Because knowing you, you would probably stick a dagger in my back!"

She brought out the dagger from behind her. "Howe'er well you know me, *husband*."

He looked at the dagger in disbelief, and then let out a moan. "All this fighting is getting us nowhere, Pet! The fact remains, we are married, and we are just going to have to live with it!"

"You live with it, I shall not!"

"Damn it! As long as you wear that ring, you are my wife!"

"Is that all it takes?" She pulled the ring off her finger and threw it across the room. It made a tinkling sound by the fireplace as it hit. "I cannot do this, Matthew. It has taken too long for me to become normal again. I want you to leave...and never come back."

"Pet, you cannot mean that!"

She showed no expression as she faced him. "Matthew, please be gone by morning. I never want to see you again." She strutted calmly out the door without looking back.

Matthew watched her go, and this time let her. He had lost her forever. He ambled across the room, searched the floor, and picked up the ring. He started to put it on his little finger, then put it in his pocket, instead. Then he went back outside. Raymond stood by Excalibur, talking with William. He smiled widely when he saw Matthew.

"Lord Matthew! Young William here was just telling me about thy arrival!"

"That may have been short-lived. I am leaving."

"Leaving?"

"Pet just threw me out."

Raymond drew himself up tall. "Threw thee out? Why?"

"Ask her." He mounted Excalibur. "I am still lord of Elton. I will be expecting quarterly reports. Tell Pet goodbye for me." He reined the horse around, and galloped away. William watched him go with tears in his eyes.

Pet ran down the hall as soon as she turned the corner after she left Matthew. Burning tears stung her eyes, and she willed them to stop. She ran into her father's study, and looked desperately up at the portrait of Robert.

"Oh, Robert! What am I going to do? I love him, but he does not want me." She sat in the closest chair, and put her head in her hands. "I cannot live without him, but he regrets our marriage." Despair engulfed her mind as she felt total emptiness consume her.

# ❧Chapter Seventeen☙

### Cambridgeshire
### Three months later
### December 20

ady Ellen Cameron stood at the doorway looking at her son, who was slumped in a chair at the table staring at nothing. His long, unkempt hair fell across his shoulders and a three-month growth of beard now dominated his face. His eyes were sullen and lifeless from lack of sleep and total apathy toward life. It was a familiar sight to the worried mother, one she was fearful would destroy her son before he came to grips with his estrangement from his wife. Ellen had tried everything to lift his spirits, but finally gave up making suggestions. He refused to talk to her or his father. He was determined to mope and feel sorry for himself, doing little else but getting up late and drinking the rest of the day away. His mood was irritable and cantankerous, and the whole household avoided him if at all possible. But right now Lady Ellen had no choice; he had a visitor.

"Matthew? There's an extremely large man here to see you."

He looked up but didn't answer, just stared at her with apathetic eyes.

"Well, shall I send him in, or are you too involved in your sulking?"

Matthew sighed. "Show him in, mother."

Ellen shook her head, and left her brooding son to his misery.

In a few minutes, Sir Raymond appeared at the door, having been adequately warned about Matthew's mood. He cleared his throat, and when he got no response he entered the room without invitation.

"Lord Matthew?"

Matthew didn't have to look up to know who it was. "Aye, Raymond, come in." He motioned the giant to a chair. Raymond sat down and tossed some papers on the table.

"The quarterly reports thou hast requested."

Matthew snorted a sarcastic laugh. "Ah, yes…my duty as Lord of Elton calls." He picked up the papers and glanced over them. "Everything seems in order." He threw the papers back on the table and took a swig of ale from his stein.

Raymond observed him for a few seconds. "Sire, I must talk to thee about Pet."

Matthew raised his dull, reddened eyes to meet the giant's gaze. "And how is my sweet, demure, little wife these days?"

There was a long pause before Raymond answered. "Not well, I fear."

Matthew sat up quickly. "Is she ill?"

"No, not physically, although she hast lost much weight. She talks only to the children, who are all that give her pleasure. She no longer fights, moreover, she hast not picked up a sword since…"

"Since what?"

"Since thou left, Sire. She sometimes spends all day in her room, not even coming out to eat. She confides in me no more, and I fear for her, Matthew. Thou must do something."

Matthew sloughed back in his chair and grunted. "What the hell do you expect me to do about it?"

"Lord Matthew…'Tis time to claim her, or let her go."

"I tried to claim her…do I have to remind you she threw me out?" He stood up and went to the window, gaping out at nothingness with a defeated jeer. "Howe'er can I claim her when she hates the sight of me?"

Raymond looked at the almost unrecognizable man he had held such high hopes for. He looked even worse than Pet, whom Raymond watched daily sink into a deeper and deeper depression. She wouldn't last much longer if something weren't done.

"Then maybe 'tis time to let her go."

Matthew turned and stared at Raymond for a long time, then finally closed his eyes and hung his head. "I cannot."

The giant man sprung to his feet. "God's teeth man, she is dying a slow death! Dost thou hate her so much to make her suffer?"

"Hate her?" Matthew's head snapped up. "*Hate* her? Is that what she thinks?" He shook his head solemnly. "Good God, I love her more than life itself. Her image is always in my mind; I cannot sleep for thinking of her. Not having her is driving me mad."

Raymond lumbered over and put his hand on Matthew's shoulder. "Then thou needs tell her that."

"I tried to—she told me she never wanted to see me again."

"She is terrified, Matthew."

"Terrified? Her? I think not," Matthew scoffed. "She is not afraid of anything, let alone me."

Raymond paused, then motioned back to the table. "Sit down, lad...I have something to tell thee."

Matthew's look of pain turned to alarm, and he sat down across from Raymond. "Very well. Talk."

Raymond shifted uneasily, and stroked his beard. "Pet never told thee about Geoffrey, did she?"

"Geoffrey? Who is he, some other man whose heart she ripped out?"

The stillness from Raymond filled the room. "He was her brother."

Matthew shook his head. "No, she never mentioned him. The only brother she ever mentioned was her twin." He rubbed his fatigued eyes.

"Matthew," the giant started, "hast thou never pondered the reason Pet is as she is?"

"Not really. It did not matter."

Raymond lowered his head, not able to look into Matthew's eyes. "This is not easy for me, lad. I never wanted to have to talk about this." He raised his head and leaned forward. "When the twins were eight years old, there was a..." His voice broke, and he lowered his head. "An incident. Oh merciful heaven, give me strength, I do not want to remember this."

Matthew sat up when the huge knight broke down before him. "What are you not telling me, Raymond?"

"She was so little…only eight. So tiny." He raised his eyes. "When the twins were five, the master surprised the household with a bastard son, Geoffrey. He was second oldest to William, but was a hateful, spiteful boy. He was treated fairly by the master, but the lad tormented the twins for no reason except pure jealousy. One day, after he had fought with Aaron over a maiden they both fancied, he was ordered to stay home while the master and the others went on a hunting trip. The twins, being only eight, stayed home. He was outraged, and found Pet by herself in the courtyard. He used her to take out his revenge. He dragged her to the barn, and forced her up the hayloft. Then he…" He could not continue, and buried his head in his hands.

Matthew's heart jumped into his throat. "Oh Lord, no…you can not mean to tell me her own brother would…"

Raymond's face hardened. "He would, and did. She was held down and…" He couldn't say the word, but he didn't have to.

Matthew shuddered with bewilderment. "Did you say the…hayloft?"

Raymond nodded, his head lowered.

"Oh, great God in heaven…no wonder." Matthew felt tears welling, and he buried his head in his hands. "Could I have been more a fool?" He remembered the look on her face at the King's castle, when he found her in the barn and practically raped her before his better judgment took over. Why didn't he figure it out then? How could he have just left her there, alone, when she was obviously re-living a terrible experience and needed his love, not his lust and anger? At that moment Matthew felt like the lowest insect on earth.

"What happened next, Raymond?"

It took a minute for Raymond to continue. "Robert found them and tried to stop Geoffrey. Robert was able to stop him only by fighting bravely for his sister, but Geoffrey beat him severely. I found them together, Robert holding her in a corner of the barn, and all she did was stare straight ahead with an empty, blank look. She never cried once." His voice lowered. "She has never cried since." He paused, gaining his composure. "I would have killed Geoffrey myself, but I knew the master would not believe me, and both Robert and Pet were so little. They needed me, Matthew. If I were not around when their father was away, who would watch after them? I told Geoffrey if he ever touched her again I would kill him, and he left her alone after that. It was then I started training the twins to fight." He blinked back tears as he gazed into Matthew's grief-stricken face. "She learned to fight so it would never happen again. She buried it all, Matthew. Her womanhood was forsaken all her life, and when thou came along and reminded her of it, she could not cope."

"Oh my God, what have I done?" Matthew could not express his grief. Pet had her young innocence taken from her, so she evaded all risks of the heart, and loved only the brother who fought for her. All her actions finally made sense; he could now understand how losing Robert really impacted her. No wonder she trembled at his touch, and recoiled in terror at the thought of a wedding night. Why didn't he guess it? Because he was so in love, he couldn't think coherently. And he had hurt her even more, more than he could ever imagine. The thought ripped his soul apart. How could he have been so blind? Unmanly tears flowed down his cheeks, and he let them come.

"She tried to tell me, twice. She just could not do it. Great merciful God, she needed me, and I let her down."

"That is not all, lad…Her father was in deep debt paying off Geoffrey's gambling habit, and Pet used most of her family's money to rebuild Elton. She told me not to tell thee, but I cannot keep still longer."

"Good Lord, how much more can she endure alone?"

"She feels she was just a conquest to thee, Matthew."

"It may have started out that way, but I quickly fell in love with her. Raymond, what can I do?"

"Thou hast to set her free, lad. Go back to the king, get the annulment, so she can forget thee. She cannot go on like this, Matthew, she is dying. The king will surely listen after a second appeal. Say she is a shrew, and has made thy life miserable. Say anything. I shall vouch thou hast never lived as husband and wife. Make the king listen."

Matthew leaned forward and covered his face with his hands. What had he done? His selfish pride had manifested itself and hurt the one person he loved with every fiber of his being. He mustered up the courage to confess a dark secret.

"Raymond, I cannot."

"Why, Matthew, why dost thou deny her this?"

"Because I never went to the king."

"What?" Raymond didn't believe what he was hearing. "Art thou meaning to tell me…"

"I could not do it. I love her too much. There is no way I could ask for our union to be dissolved, when marriage to her is all I ever wanted from the moment I first saw her."

"But she told me…"

"She told you what I told her. I lied."

Raymond sat stunned at Matthew's confession, knowing it was clear Matthew really did love her, while she felt abandoned, alone and hurt. "Lad, thou must come back with me. I believe she loves thee, but cannot bring herself to say so."

Matthew smiled slightly, and shook his head. "No, she would appear stupid and weak, and she would never admit to that." A glimmer of hope crossed his face. "Perhaps if I took presents to the children, then I could talk to her, maybe…"

"Aye!" Raymond agreed. "Make her listen."

Matthew jumped up and yelled for his mother, with Raymond right behind him. An idea was beginning to form. He would get his Pet back.

Pet sat cross-legged on the floor with the children gathered around her. A roaring fire warmed the room, so much that she was barefoot wearing an enormous tunic hanging down to her knees. They were making Christmas angels. She didn't even look up when she heard footsteps come into the room.

Matthew watched as she corrected Georgie's cutting, and showed how the wings were glued on. The brave, strong girl he loved seemed a child herself just then, one who needed him desperately, and whom he couldn't live without. Suddenly one of the children looked up and yelled.

"Matthew! You are back!"

All the children jumped up and ran to the man standing in the doorway. He got down on one knee and hugged as many as possible as they all chattered at once. He closed his misty eyes as they enveloped him; God, he had missed them. He raised his head to see Pet now standing where she had been sitting, looking like a lost waif in a horribly too-large tunic. Raymond was right; she had lost weight and by the looks of her, all hope. Her expression was blank. Not controlled, as he was used to, but empty, as empty as his heart had felt the last three months. His throat constricted as he watched her watching him. How could he have let them come to this? The love he felt for her had not diminished, if anything, he loved her even more.

He was finally able to stand up. "I brought you all presents." He turned around and pointed to a big sack bulging to its breaking point. "Who thinks they deserve one?" They all started yelling and jumping up and down as he passed out their gifts, then he told them to go in the other room and open them so he could talk to their mother. They all took off excitingly.

She stood still, and stared at him. There was a discomforting quietness, and then he finally smiled and pointed to her hair.

"Your hair is longer."

"So is yours."

He nodded with a crooked smile. He shaved the beard, but didn't take time for a haircut. "I need a cut."

"I like it."

"Then it stays."

He picked up a special box, carried it across to Pet and handed it to her.

She simply looked at it, then back to him. "What is it?" Her voice was almost a whisper.

He smiled, even though his heart was busting up into little pieces at the sight of her. "Open it."

She gingerly tugged at the ribbon, and lifted the top. She stared at the creamy white material, then back at him.

"Take it out," he encouraged.

She picked up the white cloth that revealed itself into a nightgown, just like the one Ellen had given her that night at Matthew's house. The night Matthew told her he was getting an annulment. The night her world fell apart. She looked at him with lifeless eyes. "Tell your mother thank you."

"Why do you not tell her yourself?"

She looked confused. "What?"

"Why do not you and the children come to Cambridgeshire and spend Christmas with us? Mother is dying to meet the children, and it might be good for you to get away from here."

She expressed no reaction. Finally she just slowly shook her head. "No, I cannot leave here."

He started to reach out to her, but arduously stopped himself. "Pet, we are married, whether you like it or not. The children need to know their grandparents. Please, cannot we do something for them and not just think of ourselves?" He hoped appealing to the children's welfare would change her mind. She stared down at the floor, then slowly lifted her head and met his gaze.

"Very well, for the children." It was more a reluctant capitulation than an approval. She seemed to have no strength, as if vitality itself had fled her body and left an empty shell behind. Matthew wanted to take her in his arms and hold her; kiss her; love her, but he held himself back. He had made too many mistakes in the past, and he wasn't about to ruin maybe the only chance he had to bring Pet back to him. The first step was getting her away from Elton, where there were too many traumatic memories, to a place where she would be loved and accepted. His mother told him to bring her back even if he had to throw her across his shoulders and carry her. He was glad he didn't have to resort to such drastic tactics. In truth, he was a little surprised she gave in so easily. Raymond was right; her spirit was gone and there seemed to be no fight left in her.

The trip to Cambridgeshire took two days, and the children thought it to be great fun. Matthew used one of Pet's carriages for the children, and Pet and William rode on horseback. She wore plain men's clothes, and donned no weapons. She hardly spoke to Matthew the entire trip, even though he took numerous occasions to try to start a conversation. At the inn where they stayed the night, she chose to sleep in the children's room while Matthew slept in the carriage with William. The boy confessed Pet no longer confided to anyone, not even to him. She didn't practice her weapons or go for rides. She had practically stopped eating. In essence, she had stopped living. Matthew's resolve to win her heart strengthened each second.

When they arrived at Cambridgeshire castle, Lady Cameron had everything ready. Servants waited to whisk the children to their rooms, who were wide-eyed at being in a real castle, so the adults could gather in the small dining room for drinks and pleasantries. Pet refused to leave the children, however, so Lady Ellen's first little scheme didn't go as planned. After a long wait, Pet finally appeared with the children all in tow, all freshly dressed and washed. One by one they were introduced to their grandparents, who ooh'ed and aah'ed at how beautiful and well mannered they were. An informal dinner was served, and Pet seemed there only for the children's purpose. She fussed over their food, correcting them if they talked out of turn, and seemed oblivious to anything not involving the children. She avoided all conversation with adults, especially Matthew. When it was time for the children's bedtime, Lady Ellen practically had to order Pet to let the servants take them. Pet finally relented, and curled up in a large chair in a corner by the fireplace where she could be alone. Luke tried to make polite conversation with her, complimenting her on how well she'd done with the children, and she cordially answered as little as possible. Matthew did not approach her. Lady Cameron was livid by this time. She grabbed her oldest son by the arm and, smiling sweetly, pushed him out of the room. When she was sure to be out of earshot, she gave Matthew an agitated look that could wilt flowers.

"For heaven's sake, Matthew, what have you done to her? I dare say she is not even the same girl!"

"She is not, mother. And I have not done anything to her," he paused, "…at least not lately."

"Well, pay attention to her, you've been totally ignoring her! And can you not get her out of those horrid clothes; she looks like an orphan herself. Has she lost weight?"

Matthew took a deep breath. "I tried to pay attention to her and she does not want me to; no, I cannot get her out of those clothes; and yes, she has lost weight." He leaned against the wall. "I know not what to do, mother."

She smiled knowingly. "Well, I do. You go join the men, I will take care of Pet."

Alarms instantly went off in Matthew's head. "I do not think that wise…"

"Shush. Do not talk back to your mother. Leave everything to me." She shooed him back into the room and approached Pet, who appeared engulfed in the overstuffed chair looking bored and exhausted.

"Hello, Pet darling." Lady Ellen grabbed a chair and sat down by her. "We have not yet had a chance to talk."

"There is naught to talk about, Lady Cameron."

Ellen was slightly shocked at the lack of life in Pet's voice. "Pet, I am your Mother-in-law. Call me Mother, it would please me so much."

Pet shook her head, and looked at Ellen with dead eyes. "Lady Cameron, I am married to your son in name only. You are well aware we do not have a marriage in the true sense."

"And why is that, Pet?" Ellen asked. "Do you not care for my son in any way at all?"

Pet closed her eyes, and Ellen was witness to an amazing display of self-control. "He does not want me, Lady Cameron." She opened her eyes. "He is simply stuck with me."

Ellen suddenly saw the pain, hurt, and anguish in Pet's eyes. Pain that deep had to surface sometime, or it would kill her. "Honey, he loves you…has he not e'er told you that?"

Pet raised her head. "No."

Ellen felt her blood begin to boil, and she secretly planned ways to torture Matthew for his stupidity later. Right now she had Pet to contend with. "Men are sometimes stubborn mules. Tell me my dear, do you *want* Matthew to love you?"

Pet sat up and shifted in the chair. "I am not...the kind of woman that a man can love, Lady Cameron. I am not soft and beguiling, and laugh at silly jokes at parties. I am just me. At first I believe Matthew might have liked me, but he grew weary of me, and now he is stuck, since the king will not allow our annulment."

Ellen ignored that last comment, since Matthew had finally told her the truth, and realized Pet had cleverly avoided answering the question. "My dear, you look tired. Let me show you to your room." Pet quickly looked at Matthew, and Ellen hastily added, "Do not worry, Matthew has already arranged for separate rooms."

Pet nodded gratefully.

"My son would never force himself on you, even if you are married. He was not raised that way." Ellen took Pet's hand and led her away from the men, who were trying hard not to notice them, especially Matthew, who appeared extremely nervous.

Ellen ordered a bath over Pet's objections, and finally left the girl alone after the tub was filled and a fresh bar of lilac soap was brought. Then Ellen headed straight back to the gathering to murder her son.

He was talking with his father about land holdings or some other such topic Ellen found utterly wearisome. Men-stuff, she called it. She curled her arm in Matthew's, and gave her husband a sweet but don't-mess-with-me smile.

"Excuse me, my dear, I need to talk to our son."

Lord Cameron wisely capitulated to his wife. "Of course my dear. Make sure you return him all in one piece."

"I am not sure I can make that promise," she stated, as she ushered him out the door. Once safely in another room, she glowered at Matthew in silence as he winced, preparing for her wrath.

"What is this I hear you have never told that poor girl you love her? Is that why you have moped and grumped around here for the past three months, because you do not love her?"

"Mother," he started.

"And she thinks you wanted the fictitious annulment you never bothered to ask for, and that you are simply 'stuck' with her...did you tell her that?"

Matthew turned his gaze to the floor. "Well, I..."

"And I suppose it has been too much trouble for you to tell her she is the only woman you have e'er wanted? That she is lovable, even though she is not, how did she put it, 'soft and beguiling?' Well, have you?"

"I..."

"Oh, Matthew, you have made quite a mess of this whole thing, do you know that?"

Matthew opened his mouth to answer, and found his mother had actually shut up and was waiting for an answer. "Mother, I cannot tell her I love her. She thinks love is stupid and weak."

"So *be* stupid and weak, you idiot! That poor girl feels lost, alone, ugly and forgotten!"

Matthew sighed, and motioned his mother to a chair. "Sit down mother, I fear there is more." He proceeded to tell her everything Raymond had divulged about Pet's childhood, sometimes with tears interrupting his story. Ellen listened with ever-saddening eyes until he was done. "I love her more than anything, mother. I just know not how to reach her. She will not let me in, and she will not come out."

"This might take more time than I first thought, Matthew. But if you love her, you shall find a way to reach her." She smiled a knowingly mother's smile. "Have you e'er considered just telling her the truth?"

Matthew turned white. "About everything?"

"Everything. You might try earning her trust before you earn her love. You tricked this poor girl into marrying you, and then you lied about seeking an annulment. Howe'er can she believe a word you say?"

He nodded, and stood up. "I will go talk to her." His voice was heavy with dread.

"No, not tonight. I left her with a bath and I avow she is exhausted from the trip. Let her rest, and it would not be a bad idea if you took a bath also. You smell like a horse."

"Aye, mother," he agreed with relief, and flashed her a big smile. "Thank you for listening."

"I have always been here, you just have not wanted to talk."

"I know." He took her arm. "Shall we join the others?"

"Aye, it might be a good idea for your father to see you are still breathing."

He laughed, and they left the room to join the family.

Pet soaked in the wonderful lilac-smelling water. She hadn't indulged herself like this for months; it felt good to be back at Cambridgeshire castle. She liked Lady Cameron, and it seemed Lady Cameron liked her. It was so painful to be around Matthew. When he first appeared at her manor, she hadn't believed it at first. He was so handsome, much more than she had remembered. Maybe it was the longer hair, and the fine clothes, or maybe it wouldn't make any difference what he wore; all she knew is her heart felt like beating again when she saw him. She wished he would just hold her again, touch her, anything, but he made no attempt. He obviously had no feelings for her, so she would withhold all of hers for him. She had lost weight lately because of no appetite; maybe she was too ugly now to please him. Perhaps she had never pleased him. She wasn't like an ordinary girl, and she didn't know how to be.

When she had impulsively thrown him out months ago, asking him not to return, she discovered later how vacant she felt. He left before she could confront him again, and she realized then that he didn't want her anymore. Life seemed so empty without him, so she concentrated on the children. Her fighting skills were no longer important, and she put her sword away next to Robert's. There was no longer anything worth fighting for.

She had never told him about Geoffrey. She tried, but she could never quite get the courage. She alone must live with her shame, with not even Robert to comfort her. To share a marriage bed and fulfill the act terrified her. When he suggested she come to Cambridgeshire, she thought of Lady Ellen, and how she had felt wanted there before. The children needed a father, and they adored Matthew. Perhaps she could leave the children there for a while and she could return home...no, the children were all she had. They needed and loved her, and no one else did, most of all, Matthew. Why couldn't she stop thinking of him?

The bath relaxed her, and she put on her new white nightgown. She fell asleep in the fluffy feather bed within seconds.

Down the hall in his own bed, Matthew tossed and turned, then finally got up and sat on the edge of the bed. He rubbed a hand across his eyes in restless despair. "Oh Pet," he whispered, "what it does to me to have you so close, and not be able to hold you. I have to do whatever it takes to bring you back to me."

# ☙Chapter Eighteen☙

et, wake up dear, 'tis Christmas."

Lady Cameron's voice gently summoned Pet awake. She opened her eyes and tried to blink the sleepiness away.

"Well, there you are…we thought you were going to sleep all day."

Pet blinked. "Are the children…?"

"They are waiting for you downstairs in the courtyard. They cannot wait to show you their Christmas presents."

"Presents?"

"Aye, Matthew had Luke find them all something very special." She paused, and then added, "He loves them too, you know."

"I know." Pet sat up and rubbed her eyes.

Lady Cameron watched as Pet awakened and tried to focus her mind. Lord Cameron had a doctor friend that had once talked about people who had lost the will to live. Over-sleeping was an early indicator; she wondered if Pet had reached that stage. Then again, she obviously wasn't eating well, and the trip was probably exhausting.

"Pray, get dressed child, and join us all outside. The children will burst if you do not hasten."

"I will try." She watched Lady Cameron leave, and slowly dragged herself out of bed. She seemed to be sleeping more than usual lately, her boundless energy appeared to have left with Matthew three months before. Every night she willed him to come back, every day was a disappointment. But then, why should he have come back? She threw him out, saying she never wanted to see him again. How could she have been so foolish?

She washed her face in the fresh warm water that apparently a servant had placed there while she slept, and put on a clean tunic, hose, and shoes. Then she made her way down the long staircase and out the front door to the courtyard. The sight meeting her stopped her cold.

Her children each sat on a pony; each child wore a special-made riding outfit and a large smile. Luke and Matthew were helping give instructions, as well as several grooms accompanying the younger ones. Matthew was holding the reins to the pony Georgie was riding, and ambled up to her leading the little horse. He flashed a large grin.

"'Tis about time, sleepyhead! The children have been up for hours!"

She made a confused sweep of her hand in the direction of all the ponies. "Matthew, what is all this?"

"'Tis Christmas! Do you like them? Luke did an excellent job, do you not think?"

"Matthew, these children are too young for riding...Stuart and Georgie are only four!"

"That is fine, the ponies are only four, also."

"But, they could fall!"

"That is why they will have grooms attend them at all times. They are just now going for a ride." He scanned the darkening clouds. "It appears a storm is setting in, so this might be the only time they can ride. Come, let us go in for breakfast, and leave them be." He took her hand and began to lead her back inside the castle, as she looked over her shoulder with anxiety at the children.

"But do you think they..."

"I think you worry too much. This is Christmas, Pet. Let them enjoy themselves. " He led her inside and directly to the family dining room. He ordered a large breakfast, and then watched in consternation as she ate practically nothing, picking at her food like a bird.

"Pet, you need to eat more. I cannot help but notice you have lost weight."

She stiffened, and stared at her plate. "I do not have an appetite lately."

"You need your strength. Please eat."

She raised her head and gazed at him with large dejected eyes. "Am I so displeasing now to look upon?"

He drew up in amazement, and gave a little chuckle. "Pet, nothing you could do would diminish your beauty."

She dropped her gaze again, and picked at the food some more. He watched the magnificent, brave girl he loved, and cursed himself for reducing her to this level. He had to fire her spirit again; somehow he had to find a way.

"Pet, would you take a walk with me? We have extensive grounds with a labyrinth in back. Inasmuch as a storm is eminent, it shall be the last opportunity for a walk for a few days."

Her stomach fluttered with dread. "Matthew, all we do when we are together is fight. I cannot handle that right now."

"I promise upon my honor as a knight, I will not speak one harsh word."

She observed his serious face, and slowly nodded.

He took her hand, led her outside to the gardens and entered the labyrinth. The hedges were over their heads, and even though Matthew had the pattern by memory, he allowed them to walk the wrong way into dead-ends. Pet began to brighten a bit, and even smiled at one point when they appeared to be hopelessly lost. Matthew carefully avoided any touchy subject, letting them simply enjoy each other's company. He did most the talking, but when the subject of the children came up, she definitely came more alive.

"I have worked hard to make them well-mannered. I fear they had none, being children of villeins. It has not been easy for them."

"You have done an excellent job. Any parent would be proud. My parents love them already." He paused, and then asked gingerly, "Pet, do they e'er talk of me?"

"Aye. They mention you often."

He averted his gaze, closed his eyes briefly in thought, and then looked back at her. "Pet, could we start o'er?"

Her heart jumped to her throat as she froze. "I...I do not know. Too much has happened between us."

"Could we not just make the effort? For the children, if not for us?"

"Can you keep from getting angry with me?"

"I cannot think of anything at this moment you could do to make me angry."

There was a long pause. "Very well."

His smile absorbed his face, and he felt like grabbing her and pulling her to him, but he caught himself. He must go slowly if he was to win her back.

"Pet, may I kiss you?"

She regarded him with surprise. "You never asked before."

"I am asking now."

"If you wish."

"I do."

He reached out and cupped her face with both his hands, and slowly tilted his head and brought his lips down to hers. He kissed her tenderly, lightly, gradually applying pressure as he tried to convey his love with his mouth. She closed her eyes and accepted this new tenderness as he kissed her over and over with increased desire, while keeping it gentle. She returned the kiss with the same intensity. When he finally drew back, her eyes remained closed for a few seconds. She opened them and sought his face.

"That was nice."

He almost couldn't breathe. *Nice?* Good Lord, he was stirred clear down to his toenails. The hardness in his groin protested from lack of relief. If he stayed alone with her any longer, he would not be responsible for his actions, so he took her hand and led her out of the maze. New hope sprang through him; if he could just keep from doing anything stupid, there was a chance for them.

Almost immediately, his mother approached them. "Matt, darling, Luke needs your help in the stable. I will take up your little tour with Pet, if she does not mind."

"Of course, mother." He raised his eyebrows in question to Pet. "Does that meet your approval?"

Pet nodded, and he bowed gallantly, kissing her hand. "Until later, Milady." He grinned and bounded off, feeling more alive than he had for four months.

Lady Cameron smiled at Pet, and pointed to a walkway. "Would you please come with me, dear? I have something I want to show you."

Pet followed her through various gardens as Lady Cameron professed how in the summer the scent of the roses permeated the air. There were several other spectacular gardens, all fallow now, but embellished with great pride by Lady Ellen as she guided Pet toward a small walled area. She opened the gate and invited Pet into what turned out to be a small graveyard.

"I do not come here often; this place holds great pain. But I have something to show you." She proceeded to a small grave, and Pet watched as Lady Cameron knelt and crossed herself. "My precious baby is buried here." She looked up at Pet. "His name was Mark. He died shortly after his birth." She rose while Pet wondered how this pertained to her.

"Pet, he was Matthew's twin."

Pet's jaw dropped in astonishment. "Matthew had a twin?"

"He never told you, did he?"

Pet shook her head. Matthew, a twin? Why didn't he tell her? This was a bond they shared; both had lost a twin. Did it mean nothing to him?

"I lost another child, born too early, between Luke and Paul. He is buried over here. His name was John."

Pet followed her to the other little grave, when suddenly the names struck her. Matthew, Mark, Luke, John, Paul. "All names from the Bible."

"Aye. I was raised with great faith, and tried to pass this on to my children." She reached out, and took Pet's hand. "Pet, Matthew has been miserable without you. Please find it in your heart to give him another chance."

"I have. Although, I fear all we shall do is fight. He seems to lose his temper with me very abruptly."

"Aye, his temper has always been his downfall. But he realizes he has made many mistakes, and he wants to amend for them." She grew serious, giving Pet an intense look that made her uncomfortable. "Pet, I am going to ask you a question, and I expect a truthful answer. Do you love Matthew?"

Pet lowered her head, and slowly, very slowly, nodded.

Lady Cameron let out a large sigh of relief. "Oh, thank God! There might be hope, yet."

"There is no hope unless he loves me."

"Loves you?" Lady Cameron snickered and took Pet's hand. "My dear, he more than loves you, he is obsessed with you."

"He has never told me so."

"I know. Men are strange that way, but we are going to change that. Come, it grows chilly, and I fear rain. Let us walk back to the house, and I will tell you my plan."

As they strolled back slowly to the castle, Lady Cameron dropped her little surprise on Pet. "Did Matthew tell you about the party tonight?"

"Party?"

"Aye, four of my guests have already arrived, and three more are due soon. 'Tis a small gathering, but I avow all are anxious to meet you."

Pet stopped and looked aghast. "Me? Why would they want to meet me?"

"My dear, you are the Lady Knight! By now, all of England knows of you!"

"I was not aware even you did."

"You jest, surely. 'Tis all Matthew talks about, as well as your bravery and wit. When he is talking at all, that is. I fear he has not been good company lately."

"Lady Cameron, I cannot attend a party. I know not how to act."

"I do not want you to act. I want you to just be you."

"But I have nothing to wear for such an occasion. No, I cannot attend. I would be out of place and simply embarrass you—and Matthew."

"I insist. And leave the matter of your clothes to me. I have a little surprise for you. Oh, here comes Matthew! I will let him walk you back to the house." She departed and ambled toward her son, who had concluded his business with Luke, which turned out to be nothing but a planned distraction so his mother could talk to Pet. As she approached, she gave a knowing smile to her handsome, happy son, who seemed to be in a very favorable frame of mind.

"Did I detect a stolen kiss in the garden?"

"It was not stolen...I asked for it."

"A new strategy?"

"I am trying the gentle approach." He sighed. "'Tis about the only thing I have not tried."

"She waits for you...and she is softening. Whatever you are doing, continue." She winked, and left him to his wife.

He joined Pet, and quickly took her hand. Just being near to her, even just holding her hand, felt like heaven.

"So, did my mother pontificate with lectures of her gardens?"

"Matthew, there is a party tonight, and I am expected to go to it."

He moaned as he nodded. "I know, I was supposed to tell you, but I got distracted. You do not have to attend, if you do not want to."

"I do not."

"Then 'tis done. I will simply tell my mother you shall stay in your room." His face brightened. "Would you like me to stay with you? We could...play chess—or something."

"No, you should be there. 'Tis your family's party."

"Pet, you are part of my family." He caressed her chin with a hand. "People we barely know have been trying to wheedle invites from us to meet you. You are quite famous. I fear Henry has a big mouth when it comes to this sort of thing."

"I had no idea. Matthew, I need to know...was being knighted pre-arranged like our marriage?"

His face turned pale, and he grimaced. "Howe'er do you mean?"

"You know perfectly well what I mean."

"Fine, since you brought it up, no. That was Henry's idea alone."

"And our marriage?"

"Pet, if we keep with this line of conversation, we will end up fighting. I believe you wished to avoid unpleasantness."

She sighed. "You are right." She suddenly smiled warmly, which lit up his heart. "I believe we have managed two conversations that did not conclude in anger."

"I told you I could do it." He smiled back, and they strolled hand in hand to the house.

As they came in the back door, they heard the thunder of children running down the hall. They saw Pet and Matthew, and all started talking at once.

"Pet! Matthew! Thank you for my pony!"

"Merry Christmas, Pet!"

"Oh, yes! Merry Christmas!"

"Will you take a ride with us?"

A weary servant began to steer them all away, when Matthew stopped her with a firm voice. "Leave the children be. I should like to spend time with them."

Pet looked at him with widened, astonished eyes. "Are you certain?"

"Of a surety. I have missed them greatly." He turned his gaze to her. "But not nearly as much as I missed you."

Her smile was his reward.

The whole afternoon was spent with the children. Pet observed as Matthew taught sword fighting to the boys, and sat and read stories to the girls. They played games, and laughed, and sang songs, and told stories, and anything else they wanted to do. Pet felt more relaxed and confident as the afternoon wore on. Matthew was making a tremendous effort to show her he could change, and she was starting to believe it.

Too soon it came time for Matthew to get ready for the party. The children were reluctantly shuffled away to be cared for by servants, while Matthew and Pet climbed the stairs to the bedrooms. He stopped at her door, and bowed in mock formality. "Your room, Milady." He swept his hand dramatically as she suppressed a chuckle. He opened her door, but gently took her arm before she entered. "Perchance I could warrant another kiss?"

She cocked her head and gazed longingly into his eyes. "Aye, I will like that."

One hand came up and touched her face; the other was placed behind her head. He tilted her face to meet his own, and slowly, determinedly, brought his lips down on hers. Delicate kisses gently touched her lips again and again until she felt quite out of breath. His kisses descended down her neck, as she arched to allow his touch of fire. He gently nibbled her neck, then rose back up to her face and kissed it all over—her cheeks, forehead, and back to her lips. Pet's mind reeled with this new sensation. Oh, how she had missed him! Perhaps he could be something but angry. Maybe he could love her.

He relinquished her too soon, and she fell backwards against the door. He seemed to be in no better shape than her, and backed away in deliberate, slow steps.

"I should go; the guests shall be expecting me." He lingered for a second. "Pet?"

"Aye?"

"Today was most pleasant. I trust it was the same for you."

She smiled. "It was." She watched him leave, and then entered her room with renewed hope in her heart, looking forward to some solitude and reflection. That thought was short lived.

"Well, at last—I thought you would never get back. Did you enjoy your afternoon with Matthew?"

Pet blinked at Lady Cameron and then gazed at the two servants sitting on her bed as if it were perfectly normal. She had completely forgotten about Lady Cameron's little "plan". "Er, Lady Cameron…what are you doing here?"

"Why, getting you ready for the party, of course. I have something to show you. Myra, the dress, please."

One of the servants stood up, and then exited the room to the wardrobe. She came back holding the most elegant gown Pet had ever seen. It was creamy white, of clingy silk, with dark green ribbons running through the long sleeves and hemline. The neckline was low, promising to surely be noticed. It brushed across the floor as the servant brought it and held it up to Pet.

Pet covered her mouth with her hand to hold back a chortle. "Lady Cameron, I sincerely hope 'tis not your intention for me to wear this."

"And why not? The white shall contrast exquisitely with your dark hair. Besides, I had it made especially for you."

"I would look ridiculous in that. I have never worn a gown."

"Then it is about time you did. We will have Matthew groveling so low he will scoop dirt with his jaw." She waved to the two servants. "Myra, Beth, see to it she looks fabulous. It shall not be toilsome…she is already so."

Pet shook her head and tried to sputter out objections. "Oh, really, I do not think…"

"Nonsense. You let them get you ready, and I shall be back in a short time. Your day with Matthew went well, I gather? You seem to have more color in your cheeks."

"Aye. He has changed. Not once did he lose his temper and curse at me."

"Well, that is certainly a start. When you make your entrance tonight, he will stumble all o'er himself."

"Well, I still think…"

"Good, 'tis settled. Girls, do what you can to make my son fall to his knees with desire. I will be back shortly." With that she took her leave, and Pet watched the two servants smile with anticipation as they approached her.

Lady Cameron got ready herself, and hastened downstairs to meet her guests. Lord and Lady Alwalton, their pretentious son Farlay and homely daughter Gail were already engaged in a spirited conversation with Luke. The Baron and Baroness Keyston and son Clayton stood by conversing with Lord Cameron. Lady Ellen swept through the room in regal fashion, made sure everything was in order, and then excused herself as she left to fetch Pet. Matthew was coming down the stairs as she approached. He looked especially splendid in a long black jacket, white hose, and thigh-high boots.

"I am sorry for my delay, mother. I became engrossed with my company, and found it hard to leave."

"I noticed. Your smile is contagious. Does it go well with Pet?"

"It goes most excellent. I kept from fighting with her all day, and was rewarded two lavish kisses for my efforts."

She patted her son on the back. "Most admirable, son. You shall win her over. Have you told her you love her yet?"

"Not exactly, although I know not how any other impression could be formed. I have made every effort to convey my feelings."

"Except tell her?"

"I shall get to it mother, do not worry so. I had best go to the guests; lord Alwalton and his unbearable offspring await me. Why e'er did you invite them?"

"Your father did. They share some shipping interest, or some other such man thing."

"How old is their homely daughter now, twenty-eight? You would think her father would have found some poor chap to have married her, if only for the dowry." He grimaced with distaste. "I do hope she is no longer infatuated with me."

"Be kind, Matthew. Please be civil for your father's sake."

"I will. Oh, mother, I told Pet she would not have to attend. She felt uncomfortable about it, so I told her to have a quiet evening in her room. I hope you are not too disappointed."

"Not at all." She suppressed a smirk.

He raised an eyebrow at her compliant submission. "Fine. I will join the guests. Where are you going?"

"Oh, I just have to…never mind, you shall know soon enough. Now go, I will be right there."

He gave his mother a kiss on the cheek, and joined his father and brother.

Upstairs, Lady Cameron entered Pet's room, and inhaled an abrupt breath at the sight standing before her. Pet stood wearing the gown, or rather, the gown was wearing Pet. It clung extravagantly to her form, flowing from her small waist and across her hips in gentle folds. An elaborate girdle highlighted her waist. The neckline drew attention to her high, firm breasts, which no man would be able to ignore. Her hair was up off her long neck in graceful cascades, with romantic, errant little stands falling around her forehead, temples, and neckline. Lip color was applied, which was all her face needed. She was breathtaking; it was unbelievable Matthew had been so fortunate to have married her. Lady Cameron was completely lost for words.

Pet folded her arms and scowled, mistaking Lady Cameron's silence for disapproval. "I look stupid."

"Oh, my dear, no…you are devastating. Matthew will surely faint at the sight of you."

"He will think I look stupid too, and laugh at me. I cannot be seen like this. The neckline is way too low." She tugged up on the front of the gown.

Lady Cameron tugged it back down. "Oh yes you can, and shall. Come child, the world awaits your debut." She placed her arm through Pet's and led her down the stairs.

Matthew was standing with his back to the door, attempting to engage in a conversation with Gail. The poor girl was ugly as a post, and almost as dumb. She openly flirted with Matthew, much to his chagrin, as they conversed about his unusual wife. Her brother Farlay joined them in the middle of the conversation as Gail was espousing her ignorance.

"So why does your wife not join us, Sir Matthew? Is she only comfortable with a sword in her hand?"

Matthew's blood was beginning to boil, but he remained polite as possible. "She is not feeling well, and is retired to her room. She sends her regrets."

"I hear she is six feet tall and weighs as much as a man. "Tis a pity the king commanded you to marry her. Of course, marriage does not alter other…*enjoyable* activities." She fluttered her eyelashes beguilingly.

Her implication made Matthew's stomach spew acid, and he fought the urge to gag.

Farley sniffed at his sister. "Oh, really now, Gail, do not deride Matthew's wife so. I would think it would be most handy to have a woman who could defend the castle. It would leave me free for other things, right, old chap?"

Matthew groaned inwardly. Farley was an insufferable bore, whom Matthew dearly loathed. "I fear you both have heard untrue rumors regarding my wife. She is not..."

"Good Lord!" Farley cut Matthew off mid-sentence and his eyes became saucers as he stared across Matthew's shoulder at the door. The room became still as the other men all abruptly discontinued their conversation and also stared behind him. Matthew whirled around and he felt his heart stop beating.

Pet stood in the doorway, and she was wearing a *gown*. An extremely revealing gown. Her hair was swept up off her long, beautiful neck he had kissed only a short time ago. The low neckline revealed her flawless skin and enticing cleavage. He became frozen to the spot and forgot to breathe as he watched her enter the room. Luke, seeing his brother lost for any type of action, stepped forward and took her arm. Lord Cameron took the other arm.

"My esteemed guests," Baron Cameron announced, "May I present the Lady Knight, Lady Rose Cameron, my beautiful daughter-in-law." They escorted her into the room, and up to Matthew, whose jaw was dropped in dumbfounded incredulity. He simply stared at her, unable to utter a sound.

Lady Cameron bustled up to him, having let Pet make her dramatic entrance, and poked him in the arm. "For heaven's sakes, Matthew, say something! Your jaw is hanging so low a bird could build a nest in it."

He finally found his tongue, but his words were still incoherent. "You look—I thought—what are you doing here?"

"Silly boy, she is attending the party as your wife. Well, take her arm, and seat her!"

Matthew could not take his eyes off her as he raised his arm, and she looped her arm in his. He blindly led her to the table, where Clayton Keyston had already pulled her chair out.

"This is the Lady Knight? I applaud you, Matthew, for keeping her hidden. If she were mine, I would lock her in the highest tower."

Pet sat down, and Matthew took his place across from her, where he proceeded to simply stare in disbelief at this soft side of Pet he never thought possible. The other guests were seated and numerous servants brought out the food. Gail sat two chairs down from Pet, her homeliness made even more so by Pet's beauty. Luke sat between the two, hopefully to keep peace. As the servants presented a tender roast on its spit to a young gentleman-carver, Gail decided to take a jab at Pet.

"Well, I must say Matthew, your wife certainly is not what I expected. She is most quiet, does the Lady Knight have a tongue?"

Pet raised her chin and glanced sideways at Gail. "Aye, she does, a more discerning one than yours."

Luke cleared his throat loudly, and passed a goblet of wine to Pet. "Er, wine, Milady?"

Gail sputtered with indignation, as Farley entered the conversation. "'Tis said that you had a part in the destruction of the outlaws."

Pet smiled at Matthew, who still stared with mouth agape. "A small part."

That seemed to awaken Matthew's senses. "My lady is too modest. She single-handedly dispatched them all."

Gail gasped. "Really! It must be horrid to live in a house with an uncivilized savage!"

"No worse than living with a featherbrained dullard." Pet smiled sweetly as Gail turned red with rage.

The servants ladled thick stew onto chunks of bread in bowls, and Farlay plucked out a toothsome morsel with his fingers and offered it to Pet with gallant byplay.

"For you, my beauty." He brought the chunk of meat to her lips, as she took it between her teeth and smiled. "The fingers that touched your lips shall never know such pleasure again."

Pet smiled demurely; she had never been so openly flirted with before.

Matthew felt his ears grow warm as he took a large bite of stew and chewed profusely. Men flirting with his wife was not exactly what he had in mind for tonight.

More meat and fowl were served in great variety. Lady Cameron had stopped at nothing to impress her guests, who seemed at the moment only interested in her daughter-in-law. The Baroness Keyston, an older, plump women with a delightful sense of humor, was most taken with Pet.

"Tell me my dear, howe'er did you learn swordplay?"

Pet proceeded to tell about Robert and her, while everyone listened in deep interest except Gail, who stared at Matthew with dreamy eyes. When Pet relayed the story of Gideon, and how she had killed him at the king's court before she married Matthew, Gail smirked.

"I suppose one must be satisfied with the husband the king orders her to marry."

Pet shrugged. "I suppose 'tis better than having no husband at all."

Gail stood up abruptly. "And just what do you mean by that?"

"Only what you take it to mean."

Gail wailed at her mother, and ran out of the room in tears with her mother close behind. Luke, ever the gentleman, bolted out after them. Baroness Keyston decided to help, and left also. Lady Cameron motioned to Matthew to go help fetch them back. Matthew shook his head, but she nodded with a frown meaning business. He reluctantly stood up and left, with Lady Cameron right behind him.

Pet realized she was suddenly alone with all strange men. Clayton switched chairs to the one by her and gazed upon her with wishful eyes.

"You are wonderful. Is there any chance you might leave Matthew for me?" He giggled to cover up the seriousness of his question.

Farlay would not be outdone. "The lady's wine glass needs filling. Here, let me attend her." He picked up the wine cruet and began to pour her wine. Clayton tried to take the romantic chore away from him.

"I was here first, I shall pour the wine."

"I think not, Clayton. Do be gone, the lady and I are becoming acquainted."

"*You* be gone!" Clayton jerked the cruet away, and the wine went flying all over Farlay's jacket.

"You nitwit! Look what you have done!"

Pet stood up, grabbed a napkin, and began to dab the front of Farlay's jacket. "Hold still, let me help you."

Farlay stared back in dreamy compliance. "I will take an entire bath in wine, to earn your attentions."

Clayton fumed at the attention Farlay was getting. "That can be arranged!" He poured the remaining wine over Farlay's head.

"Farley! Stop this behavior!" Lord Alwalton stomped across to his son, and grabbed his arm.

Pet tried to keep the peace, but could not stop Farlay from pushing past her and striking Clayton in the face.

"Farlay, No!" She grabbed his arm and pulled him back. Clayton, in turn, grabbed her and pulled her away from Farlay, which sent her flying into his chest, practically knocking him down. Clayton grabbed Pet for support and they both bobbled off balance.

Baron Keyston joined in the fray, and pushed his son back. "Quit your fawning over the girl! She is married!" He grabbed Pet and tried to loosen his son's grasp. Farlay, meanwhile, had grabbed Pet's arm, and was pulling her back to him. Everyone was yelling at each other in a confused muddle.

Matthew picked that exact moment to enter. His face grew red at the sight of his wife being pulled in all directions by four strange men. His first thought was she was being attacked.

"Unhand her!" He rushed into the fray and began hitting everyone. Clayton got a fist to the eye, Farley the nose, and the two fathers were stuck wherever their bodies got in his way.

"Matthew, no!" Pet pulled him away from the hapless men, who were rubbing their bruised eyes and bleeding noses. "'Tis all right! 'Tis just a misunderstanding of spilled wine, calm down!"

Matthew stood there panting, his hands rolled into fists, his face red with rage turning into embarrassment. "Misunderstanding?" He looked upon his mother's valued guests, whom he had just struck very unknightly-like about various parts of their bodies. His voice rose in fury. "You are telling me this is all a misunderstanding?"

All the others entered the room—the squalling Gail having been calmed down—to the sight of bloody, beaten men and Matthew yelling at Pet. Baroness Keyston buried a laugh with a gloved hand; the other women looked the scene over in stupefaction.

Matthew grabbed Pet's arm and marched her over to the door. "This would not have happened if you had stayed in your room!"

Pet drew herself up tall, and stared defiantly at him. "I came at your mother's request. I thought it would please you."

"Well, it does not! What do you think you are doing, coming in here dressed like that! Good Lord, Pet...are you not aware of how you look?"

"I told your mother you would laugh at me!"

"Laugh at you? Are you crazy? Do you not know what you do to a man? And coming in here flaunting it in that gown is too much!"

"Flaunting? Who is flaunting?"

"You are! And liking every reaction, from what it seems!"

She backed away and raised her trembling chin. The whole room was quiet as she glanced around the room, then back at the raging Matthew.

"I can do nothing to please you. You do not love me, or trust me. You do not even want me here. I cannot be anything but what I am, Matthew. I am sorry that is not good enough for you."

Matthew's rage turned to panic as she clenched her jaw and fought for control. "Pet, I did not mean..."

"Goodbye, Matthew." She turned to Lady Cameron, whose tears ran down her cheek at her carefully laid plans having just exploded in her face. "I apologize, Lord and Lady Cameron. I did not mean to embarrass you. Next time take care not to invite a savage to your party."

She turned and left the room, her head held high with feigned dignity.

Lady Cameron looked at her son, who just stood there with his head hung low, and let out a large breath. "Well, if you are not going after her, I am!"

Matthew looked at his stunned guests, then at his father and brother, and left the room without saying a word. He ambled down the hall to his study, sat down on a stool, and buried his head in his hands. How could he have lost his temper like that? Just when everything was going excellent between them, he had to ruin it with his jealous rage. Oh God, she was beautiful! How could any man look upon her and not want her?

His mother entered the study, and found him in his familiar pose of despair. She stood and watched him for a moment, then broke the silence.

"She is going back home tomorrow. I made her promise not to sneak away during the night. Matthew, she is leaving the children."

His head snapped up "What?"

"She said you could give them more than she can."

"Mother, she will die without..." His face turned white, and tears began to well up in the centers of his eyes. "Oh my God! I have to do something!"

"Whatever you plan to do, it had better be right now. This time I fear you have gone too far."

He nodded, and his gaze fell upon his sword hanging on the wall. He went over and retrieved it.

"I will either win her, or free her." He left his worried mother standing there.

# ✥Chapter Nineteen✥

he staircase seemed longer, and each step higher as Matthew slowly trudged up to the bedrooms. What the hell was he going to say to her? He had just made a total ass of himself; an ordinary girl would have fled the room in tears. But not his Pet. No, she simply held her head high and exited with dignity and no tears, no emotion, nothing. His Pet, had she ever been such?

He stood at her door for several minutes before he worked up the courage to knock.

"Enter."

He opened it cautiously and peered in. She was standing by the window, wearing her white nightgown, listening to the rain and looking out into blackness as empty as her heart felt. Her combed-out hair hung about her shoulders, still slightly curled around her face. She turned and her eyes widened in astonishment.

"Matthew? I…I thought you were your mother."

"I get that a lot." His attempt at humor didn't work, so he entered the room and shut the door. He noticed the beautiful gown lay crumpled on the floor. He wondered if she would ever wear a gown again, after he had spouted off his big mouth. "Pet, we must talk."

She shook her head. "No, Matthew, I have nothing to say to you."

"I know, but I have plenty to say to you. Please listen to me, Pet, and when I am done you never have to listen to me again. I promise."

She stared at him vacantly, and then slowly nodded. He shifted uneasily, pausing to delay the moment, and pointed to a chair.

"Would you sit down?"

"I will stand."

"Fine." He studied her for a few seconds, trying to gain the courage to just once in his life say the right words, and then shifted his gaze downward.

"My mother says I am stubborn and impulsive, among other things. I am not going to say I disagree with her. I am also selfish. Pet, I am the eldest son of a rich Noble. I have always had everything I wanted; nothing has e'er been denied. I learned early that my wit and social standing, plus some semblance of good looks, could get me anywhere or anything in life. My carelessness was never questioned. Women were easy, and life handed no real challenges or pitfalls." He raised his eyes and looked into her face.

"Until I met you."

He paused and ran his fingers through his long hair. "You literally knocked me over when we met, and I have been desperate to have you e'er since. I did not impress you, in fact you thought me a bumbling fool, rightfully so, who took nothing serious in life. You intrigued me; I did not know anyone like you existed. I was precarious, you were controlled; I was lighthearted, you were serious; I was unstable, you were strong. From the moment I met you, I never wanted to leave your side. I pushed myself into your life, and demanded recognition, even though I had done nothing to earn it. Yet you took my impudence and formed me into someone I was not ashamed to face in the mirror. You taught me to fight, you taught me to think, you taught me to care. I knew I would never be the same.

"But still I pushed for what I wanted. My desire for you rid me of all senses. You turned down my hand in marriage again and again, but that did not stop my ego from demanding I get you, at any cost. It was inconceivable that someone would not want me. I saw a way to make you mine, and not caring how you felt I plunged ahead and devised a scheme to force you to marry me. I did not care about the hurt you carried inside of you, as long as I got what I wanted.

"I watched as you bravely sought to seek justice to avenge your family's deaths. My mind reeled in awe as you took on the care of nine orphans. I stood by as you tearlessly buried a child. I beamed with pride as you kneeled before the king. My heart soared when you took my hand in marriage, albeit, unwillingly. My ego plummeted when you refused me to your bed. I dragged you here thinking my family would win you o'er, but you won them o'er, instead. They lost no time telling me what they thought of me for treating you the way I did. My mother threatened to disown me if I did not make things right."

He brought a hand up and wiped his hair away from his face, a gesture to stall as he sought the right words. Confessing was not easy for him, but she was worth anything he had to do to reach her.

"So I set out to do the right thing just once in my life, to release you from a man who was never good enough to stand by your side in the first place. But then I discovered another one of my little weaknesses. I am a coward." He paused, not knowing how this next piece of information was going to affect her.

"I never went to the king, Pet. I never asked him to allow an annulment. I made up the whole story. I could not give you up; at least I had you in a small way, even if in name only. My foolish pride could not admit I was wrong."

Her eyes widened in bewilderment. He had gone too far now to turn back.

"I went to London, and bought presents for the children. Then I rode around for a month, camping in the forests, staying at inns, feeling like I belonged nowhere, wanting only to belong to you. Not having you nearly drove me mad. I finally decided to face you, and you rightfully threw me out of your life. I said stupid things I did not mean, because once again my pride got in the way. But instead of telling you the truth, I retreated to my house to sulk and feel sorry for myself—I do that very well according to my mother—not thinking what it was doing to you. When Raymond showed up and told me of your suffering, I had to make an effort to get you back, ignoring the fact that I never really had you."

He paused, feeling as if a butterfly's flutter would knock him over. He had never felt so exposed and vulnerable.

"These last four months have been hell. I cared about nothing, sent a brother fleeing from my sight, snarled at my own mother, all because I did not have you. I brought you back in hopes of winning you. I have only succeeded in being jealous, pig-headed, and half-witted. And you must add 'stupid' and 'weak' to my long list of inadequacies, because all my behavior stemmed from one unspoken fact: I love you, Pet. I have loved you from the moment I was pushed in that river."

Her pained look made him hesitate, but also drove him onward. "I did not tell you at first for fear you would think me foolish. Later I did not tell you for fear you would not believe me. You pushed me away; I pushed back. I took what I wanted at your expense, and you got hurt. I am an incredible fool; even I marvel at my own stupidity. Hurting you was the last thing I ever wanted to do.

"I love you from the very depths of my heart, and I always shall. If I could trade my own life in return for one minute of your love, I would do so gladly. It would be a small price to pay."

Tears welled in his eyes. "I am sorry, Pet, so very, very sorry. I hope someday you will find it in your heart to forgive me. Here is my sword, take it." He handed her the sword that had gone unnoticed since he entered the room. She accepted it, as a confused, tormented look consumed her face.

"I cannot release you; I have not the courage. I want to be your husband and the father to your children. I want to live with you, laugh with you, cry with you, love with you. For once in my life, I know what I really want, but I fear it may be too late. If you loath me and want to be free, I understand, but you are just going to have to take my sword and run me through, because 'tis the only way you are ever going to be rid of me. I cannot live without you; I am not even willing to try. I love you Pet, with all that I am; but without you life is meaningless, and I would rather be dead than live it alone. The choice is yours."

He closed his eyes, stood up straight, and braced himself for the fatal blow. Nothing happened. The sound of the sword dropping to the floor made him open one eye. Pet stood silently with her back to him. His spirits sank even lower; would she give him no reaction? Was she so far lost to him that nothing could reach her?

"Pet? Please say something. I cannot bear your silence."

There was no answer, but he thought he detected a small tremor pass over her shoulders. A faint alarm sounded in his head.

"Pet? Turn around and look at me."

She turned slowly, and her tear-streaked face greeted him like a lance to his heart.

His mouth fell open in despair. "Pet, I am sorry...I did not mean to make you..." He stopped short when the revelation of her tears connected with his mind. He could barely utter the words for the lump in his throat. "Pet...you are crying."

She simply looked at him with desperation as an uncontrolled shudder shook through her body. He stared back in disbelief as the large tears ran down her cheeks and fell on her nightgown. She made no effort to wipe them, indeed, it seemed as if she was stunned into numbness.

Just then, a knock came on the door, and Matthew uttered a curse. He looked helplessly at Pet, and put up a hand as if he expected her to bolt. "Do not move...just stay right there!" He ran to the door and opened it to his mother, who peered concerned at him.

"Matthew, darling, I just wanted to..." Her voice trailed off when she saw Pet standing behind him with tears running down her face. "For God's sake, Matthew! What did you say to the poor child? Did you strike her?"

"Not now, mother!" He slammed the door in her face.

Lady Ellen stood there, shocked for about two seconds, and then smiled widely. Maybe her son had reached Pet somehow. She strolled down the hallway, humming happily.

Matthew quickly went back to Pet and stood about a foot in front of her. The tears were flowing faster, and he knew at any second the dam would burst. He held out his hands to her.

"I am here, Pet. Just take one step into my arms, and you will never be alone again."

She paused briefly, then slowly stepped forward, and he caught her as she broke into great, heaving sobs. He nuzzled his head in her hair and held her tightly. As she sobbed uncontrollably, he closed his eyes and blinked back his own tears.

"Let it out, Pet. Let go of all your pain, and give it all to me."

Her cries were killing him, but he helplessly held her and prayed for her relief from her torment.

"Cry for them all, Pet…cry for Robert, for Mary, your family, and for you."

She tried to speak his name between healing sobs, unleashing through her body in irrepressible spasms. "M—mat—thew."

"Shhh…just cry, love. Just cry."

Her sobs of pain racked his heart as he held her close and stroked her back in soothing, circular motions. "You know not how long I have wanted to hold you and tell you how much I love you. You are the most beautiful creature alive, Pet, and I love you more than life itself." Her body started to convulse, and he almost became frightened she would pass out. "Shhh, love, it is all right, I am here and I am never going away." He brought his gaze down to look into her strained, pain-stricken face. It almost tore his heart in two. She was lost in a world of grief, where twelve years of withheld emotions had caught up to her at once.

Fearing she would collapse, he guided her to the bed and softly told her to sit down. She clung to him like a little girl, and reacted mechanically to his orders. She sat down on the edge of the bed, sobbing while staring straight ahead into nothingness. As he sat beside her gently stroking her hair, her sobs began to subside into violent shudders as she desperately fought to gain control.

"Do not fight it, Pet, you are going to make yourself ill. Please…it is all right, I am here. Look at me, love."

She turned slightly to acknowledge the fact he was talking to her, but she didn't seem to understand his words. The shock of her emotional outbreak had reverted her to a small eight-year-old child who had withdrawn from reality. Matthew cupped her face with his hands and kissed her tears, then her nose, then her forehead, as strong trembling racked her body every few seconds.

He beseeched her eyes. "Pet, I know about Geoffrey," He caught her panicked look. "Shhh, love...what happened to you was terribly wrong, and you are innocent. Do you understand? You are innocent. And *I love you*."

She broke into sobs again, and he seized her close to him. He gently persuaded her to lie down on her side facing him, then he lay beside her, holding her, stroking her back. She tried desperately to talk between the sobs.

"You...know...about...?"

"Shhh, love, yes, I know." He drew her closer.

"Y...you...still love me?" Her face held the desperate hope of a beaten child.

He pulled his head back to look in her eyes, and let out a small incredulous laugh. "*Love* you? Pet, if God himself ordered me to stop loving you, I could not do it." He kissed her on the forehead, and hugged her close again. "Pet, the night in the castle, our wedding night...I did not know then. If I had known, I would not have done what I did. Forgive me, Pet, I was a fool."

She produced a small, brave smile, and closed her eyes. He held her close as the shudders again started to subside, and she eventually fell into an exhausted slumber.

He didn't know how long he held her, watching her sleep. The candle was almost burned all the way down, and if he didn't light another one they would be plunged into inky darkness. Very slowly, as to not awaken her, he moved his arm out from under her head and replaced it with a pillow. He lit another candle, and after kicking off his boots, returned to her side to lie facing her. God, she was beautiful. He soothed back a damp strand of hair from her temple as he watched her, and then caressed her face tenderly. How could he have hurt her so much? She suddenly awoke with a start and frantically called his name, while reaching out with a hand.

"I am here, love," he answered softly, and took her hand in his.

She again closed her eyes and slept. He wondered in agony how many times she had done that and he had not been there for her.

The candle was half-burned when he opened his eyes and realized he had been sleeping. Rain still pelted the ground outside the window as the storm continued to unleash its fury. He turned to Pet, and was pleasantly surprised to find her staring at him, her face calm and composed. He smiled lovingly at her, and gently kissed her forehead.

"Are you all right?"

She nodded. "I am sorry I lost control."

"Shush, love, 'tis me who made you cry. I am the one who is sorry."

"I guess we both have a lot to be sorry about."

"You have nothing to be sorry for, except marrying the biggest fool in England."

"For that, I am not sorry."

He caressed her hand as he felt tears welling up again. His emotions were as raw as hers. "For that, I am thankful."

She slowly smiled as she reached up with her free hand and traced his lips. He kissed her fingers all over, then brought her other hand up and did the same. Then he pulled her close and brought his lips down to hers. He kissed her gently, tenderly, with more love than he thought possible. She willingly kissed him back, and they began kissing each other's face everywhere. Not a word was spoken; none was needed. He descended on her lips again, this time with more passion, imploring her mouth to open with his tongue. They explored the kiss deeply until they were out of breath, then he pulled her tightly to him and just held her.

"Tell me you love me, Pet," he whispered. "Say the words that will complete me."

She pulled away to look at him for a long minute, then reached up and touched his cheek. He closed his eyes to her touch, and sucked in a long breath.

"You torture me, Pet. Tell me before I pass out with anticipation."

She brought her face up and gently kissed him on the lips. "I have always loved you, Sir Knight."

His eyes sprang open, and his smile consumed his face. "Always?"

She displayed her familiar droll look he had grown so to love. "Well, maybe not *always*, but almost."

"Tell me which behavior you did not love, and I vow never to do it again."

"There is the small matter of ripping off my clothes."

He drew her closer and laughed deeply. "Pet, you kill me. But 'tis such a sweet death."

"I tried to fight you. I did everything to keep from falling in love with you, but you would not go away."

"And I never shall."

"I shall hold you to that promise."

"There will never be a need."

They lay in each other's arms in silence. He pulled her close, and she buried her face in the soft mat of curly hair on his chest. He impulsively pulled her on top of him and she countered by running her fingers through his thick, shaggy hair and kissing his forehead. Her body pressed against him, and he could not help but respond to her closeness. Another deep, probing kiss followed, and he could no longer bear the throbbing between his legs. He rolled her off him, and sat up.

"You hungry?"

Her shake of the head was accompanied by a confused look. "Are you?"

"Not exactly. Thirsty, then?"

Another shake.

He stood up and pondered his dilemma. "Pet, I must leave you for a little while."

"You wish to eat at a time like this?"

He coughed up a short laugh. "Er, no. I just…have a problem."

"A problem?"

"Aye."

"Can I help?"

"Eh, actually you could, but…let me just say, I need to get away from you."

"You mean, I am causing it?"

He cleared his throat. "Well, yes, in a way you are. But 'tis still my problem."

Her chin began to tremble, and he quickly sat back down and held her. "Ah, my beautiful Rose, you are so innocent."

"Wh…what did you just call me?" She pulled away and gazed at him with wide imploring eyes.

"Sorry. I happen to like the name Rose." He wiped a lone tear from her cheek.

She lowered her gaze and stared at nothing, deep in thought. "Those were the last words Robert said to me. He called me his beautiful Rose."

"That's because Robert knew you for the woman you really are…just as I do."

She was silent, and then spoke in almost a whisper. "But you do not truly know me."

"If you mean in the biblical sense, no. But that can wait until you are ready."

She cast a downward glance. "I am ready, Matthew."

"Wha…what did you say?"

"I said I am ready."

He lifted her chin and looked at her with loving devotion; his heart pounded in the anticipation of fulfilling his love for her. He knew the first time would be painful, not so much physically, but many layers of pain would have to be removed, one by one.

"Then I no longer have a problem." He paused and eyed her carefully. "Are you sure?"

"Aye." She gave him a long, earnest look and traced his lips with a finger. "I know not how, so you are going to have to show me."

"Gladly." He pulled her to him with a groan, and attacked her lips with fierce passion. He gained entrance to her mouth, and explored her sweet cavern with his hungry tongue. This was not going to be easy for her, so he vowed to go slowly.

Releasing her lips, he got up on his knees. "Sit up, Pet. He looked lovingly into her eyes. "I have something for you."

"What?"

"Stay here. I will fetch it."

She groaned with disappointment, but watched him get to his feet and go to his coat. He took something out of the pocket and came back. "Now, hold out your hand."

She did, and he dropped something in it. When she saw what it was, she looked at him with teary eyes. "The ring! I looked for it for days, and concluded it must have fallen in a crack. I feared it lost." Large tears fell down her cheeks.

"I declare, can all I do is make you cry?" He took her left hand and slipped it on her third finger. "Which sacrament of matrimony is of this virtue and strength that these two persons who now are two bodies and two souls, during their lives together will be one flesh and two souls."

She smiled through her tears. "Our marriage vows."

"Take a close look at the ring. 'Tis different."

She held it up close, and a large smile engulfed her face. "The dragon has jewels for eyes; emeralds, like you promised. Oh Matthew…I love you so much." She pulled him to her chest, and they hugged lovingly, not able to get enough of each other.

"I have only one order I will make as your husband and lord. Do not ever again substitute another woman in our marriage bed. There shall be hell to pay."

She snickered against his shoulder. "I promise. Matthew?"

"Aye, love?"

"Why did you not take advantage of the situation? She was willing, and I avow she would have provided you pleasure."

"No one can replace you, did you not know that? I only wanted you, and you managed to enrage me. But that is behind us now. We are together, and nothing will separate us." They silently held each other awhile longer before he drew back. "Now to the task at hand. I need to take off that nightgown."

She got up on her knees slowly, but balked when he began to pull the gown over her head. "Matthew, I am naked underneath."

"That is the idea."

"But what if…"

"What if what?"

"What if my body is not pleasing?"

"There is not the slightest chance of that." He pulled the nightgown over her head, and she appeared naked before him, her eyes lowered in embarrassment. For no reason. He drank in her loveliness; her hard, toned body was as magnificent as he remembered from that first day by the river. Her firm breasts beckoned him; her trim, hard thighs summoned him to explore the sweetness nestled between them. Her small waist flowered into perfect, rounded hips that tortured his senses. He sucked in a breath at her beauty.

"By the saints, you are the most beautiful woman I have ever seen, or have not seen, for that matter." He took her hands in his, and guided them to his shirt. "Unbutton me, and remove my shirt."

She timidly complied as he closed his eyes and enjoyed the sensation of her touch. When his shirt was removed he stood up quickly and removed the rest of his clothing. He kneeled back in front of her.

"Now, look at me, Pet."

She slowly raised her eyes, and looked upon his hard, muscled body. His shoulders were wide, his chest was extraordinary, and the muscles on his arms were well defined. Her gaze lowered to his firm abdomen, where no fat had yet accumulated. Then her eyes fell lower and widened, and she drew backward.

He didn't miss her expression, as his eyes had never left her face since she started her visual inspection of him. If she couldn't get past this first step, they would not be able to continue. He was willing to take all the time it needed, although he wasn't sure if his body could wait much longer. He so wanted to be part of her. It was torture looking upon her glorious, nude body.

"Lay down, Pet." He had to have her, but his traitorous mind advised him to go slow, or she would recoil in fear. She slowly lay down, and he snuggled up next to her warm, naked body with a groan of long anticipation. He kissed her gently at first, and then passionately, encouraging her to seek out his body with her hands. "I am going to die if I do not have you soon," he moaned. "Oh Pet, if you only knew what you do to me."

She gasped between his kisses, trembling with a mixture of fear and newfound lust. She knew she wanted him, but something held her back.

He tried to be gentle, but his lust was too great. He accidentally cupped a breast a little too firmly.

She lashed out at him in pain, striking him with her fists while throwing her body into convulsions. He had not been prepared for that.

He grabbed her wrists much like he did in the woods the day she recognized Gideon and tried to single-handedly go after him. This time she was too strong, and they rolled to the edge of the bed, entangled in the comforter. He had once wondered if she would be a wildcat in bed; this is not what he had in mind. They struggled for a while longer, then dropped off the bed with a thud. She continued to thrash about, with Matthew wondering how on earth he was going to control her.

"Pet! 'Tis me! Stop it!" It was then he realized that she was laughing.

He managed to find the part of the blanket that covered her head, and jerked it off with a flourish. "How on earth can you find this humorous?"

She looked up at him with smiling eyes. "I just realized I have nothing to fear from you."

The trust she expressed made him surge with pride.

His eyebrows rose inquiringly. "Try again?"

She nodded bravely.

He nuzzled her neck for the umpteenth time, and began stroking her body all over while talking softly, encouraging her, loving her. She relaxed under his touch and again he suckled her breasts. As he enjoyed the taste of her, she turned and nibbled his ear. He moaned in agony.

"Matthew?"

"What, my love?"

"We are lying on the floor."

"I know. Is it uncomfortable for you?"

"No, the covers are underneath me."

"Then hush."

The pent-up passion he had kept inside for four months steeped through him like fury. He kissed her face all over and she kissed him back with the same fervor. The rain pounded outside and wind whipped through the trees as the storm matched their intensity.

The feeling was beyond anything she could have anticipated. She clung to him, eyes closed, as their breathing became heavy with their passion.

An hour later, they lay exhausted on the floor, fully sated.

Finally Matthew was able to resume thinking. "You will be the death of me, Pet," he panted. "What have I gotten myself into?"

She simply moaned and snuggled closer.

"I fear I grow heavy." He attempted to roll off; she held him tighter so he could not.

"No. Do not ever move again. I want to stay joined forever."

"Do not tempt me."

He finally pushed away, a small groan grumbled from his chest. "The sun is rising. If we do not get dressed and go down for breakfast, I will take you again right here on the floor."

"You could do that? So soon?"

"You forget, I have four long months to make up, and I fully intend to."

"There is no way you can make up four months."

He stood up and offered his hand to her. "Watch me try."

# ✎Chapter Twenty✎

**L**ady Cameron was sitting at the table in the small dining room drinking tea when her son, who looked like he had been up all night, and his wife, who looked the same, strolled sheepishly into the room. She looked up and smiled a knowing mother's greeting.

"So. Am I to assume there shall be a marriage after all 'twixt you two?"

"I think that would be a safe assumption, Mother," Matthew said, as he held a chair for Pet.

"Matthew dear, go fetch us some fresh tea like a good boy. I just brewed some a minute ago." He was aware a servant could be summoned to bring tea, but knew his mother was just trying to get rid of him for a short time. He bowed and winked at Pet before leaving.

Lady Ellen turned to Pet, who was avoiding eye contact as she sat with a sly smile. "Well, you survived the night. What think you now of my son?"

Pet grimaced as she squirmed to get comfortable. "I think he has made me sore."

Ellen laughed loudly, and then put her hand over her mouth to contain her amusement. "My dear, your frankness is refreshing. A soak in a warm tub will help that little problem." She grew serious. "Are you two going to be fine?"

"Oh, yes. More than fine. We are going to be wonderful."

"That is good to know."

Pet looked askance at her mother-in-law. "I am sorry about your dinner party. I guess I ruined it."

"Do you jest? The Baron and Baroness said they never had so much fun! They long ago have wanted someone to put that impudent Gail in her place. However, I do not believe I will be inviting those two families in the same room together again; Clayton and Farlay are still not speaking. Oh, the grooms have taken the children riding on their new ponies, since we seem to have a sun break and they were most anxious. I hope that is fine with you."

Pet's face whitened, and she brought a hand to her head. "By everything that is holy, I forgot about the children! What kind of mother am I?"

"The kind who has finally had a wedding night. Do not chastise yourself, my dear, you had things on your mind, as well as other places. Pet, I must tell you some things, just to clear my own conscious. Do you mind?"

Pet shook her head. "This appears to be a time for confessions."

Lady Ellen folded her hands in front of her on the table. "Pet, I have already told you my first thoughts of you were not favorable. Naturally, I know better now. But I must say, I thought my son had made a mistake in his choice of wife. No, close your mouth, dear, let me finish. I have to say I am sorry. I fear t'was me who put the idea of obtaining an annulment in Matthew's head. I thought it best at the time, considering he had tricked you into marriage. Now I know what pain that caused you both, and I am so glad that Matthew followed his heart and did not take my advice. 'Tis not to say I shall not still give advice in the future, mind you. Pet, dear, I am trying to say that I am extremely pleased you are part of the family. I have always wanted a daughter, and I cannot think of one more lovely than you. We are all so very fortunate, for you and the children are surely blessings. Oh look, now I have got you all teary eyed when all I was trying to say is we all love you, and are so happy to have you, here child, have a napkin."

Pet took the napkin, and wiped her eyes, just as Matthew entered the room carrying a large silver tray with cups and a teakettle. He put the tray on the table, kneeled by Pet, and put his arm around her. "Here, what is this? More tears? I would think your head would be quite empty of water by now. Mother, what did you say to cause this? Here love, blow."

Pet blew into the napkin as Ellen answered her son.

"I simply said we all loved her, and how pleased we all are to add her to the family."

"Aye, well, I can see how becoming part of this family would make anyone cry." Pet laughed at that, and he gave her a kiss on the cheek. "All better, love? Good."

"I am sorry. I have not cried in so very long, I guess this family is my undoing. Matthew, I forgot about the children!"

"Children? What children?"

She punched him in the arm, as he cringed. "I yield, Lady Knight!"

Lady Ellen stood up. "Well, I am leaving you to your wedding breakfast. Judging by the looks of you two, I suggest you eat heartily so to keep up your strength, especially if you plan to continue certain vigorous activities."

Pet blushed profusely, while Matthew stood up to take a chair. "I will stuff myself until sick in order to keep up with my lady fair."

"Matthew!" Pet warned.

Ellen just laughed, and left the two lovers alone. Before either one could speak, three servants carrying enough food for ten people came into the room and sat the trays on the table. Matthew and Pet gazed at the dishes in awe, then glanced up at each other.

"I guess she was not jesting," Matthew said.

It turned out they were both very hungry, and they loaded their plates with ham, eggs, fried potatoes, biscuits with jelly, and many other dishes neither cared to identify. When they had both had their fill, they settled back with a cup of tea. Pet gave Matthew a strange expression, as she appeared deep in thought. It made him nervous.

"What?"

"Why did you not tell me you were a twin?"

He studied her questioning face, and leaned back in his chair. "My mother told you?"

"Aye."

"Would it have made a difference?"

She paused. "I know not. I am just surprised, with you knowing my feelings for Robert, that you never mentioned it."

"It would have been a useless comparison, as I never knew my brother. He died at birth."

"I know, it just tells me something about you that you did not use your twin-hood to try to gain my favor."

"I wanted you to love *me*, not some idealistic notion I was destined for you because I had also lost a twin."

"But we were, you know."

"Destined for each other? Oh yes, I have always been aware of that, inasmuch as there was no way I was going to let you go."

"You are terrible."

"Really? Just a short while ago you were saying…"

"Matthew!"

He just chuckled, and then noticed another serious thought forming. "You have *got to* cease thinking. What is it now?"

"I was just thinking about Paul…he harbors much bitterness for you."

"I know. Simply because he fell in love with the same girl as I."

"Is there some way we can reach him? Let him know all is well between us?"

"I am not sure, I will beseech father. Do not blame yourself, Pet. 'Tis his doing. He has to find his own way; maybe his voyage shall help him. Merciful God, now what are you thinking?"

"Matthew, whilst we were…separated, was there another…I mean, did you seek the favors of…"

He snorted with disbelief. "My love, I have not even *thought* of another woman since I first lay eyes on you, let alone touch one."

"I hope I was worth the wait."

"If I had to wait for all eternity, you would have been worth the wait."

She smiled with all the love she held for him. "I love you, Matthew."

He laughed, jumped up, and pulled her to her feet. "I love you, my Lady Knight. Now, do I carry you upstairs, or do you walk on your own accord?"

Her eyes widened in disbelief. "Again?"

"Oh yes, again, and again, and again, and..."

Just then the room exploded with the children, all rosy-cheeked and excited, wearing their fancy little riding outfits as they came in from their morning excursion. Matthew sat back down and groaned.

"Mother! I did not fall off, but Andrew did!"

"Did not!" "Did too!"

"He pushed me!"

"Pet, we jumped a creek! My pony got wet, but I did not!"

"I ripped my pants on a berry bush."

"Mine is the best pony."

"Is not!" "Is too!"

"Mine is the prettiest, it has dabbles!"

"I am the best rider; William said so!"

"Am not!" "Am too!"

As the children bombarded the bewildered Pet with stories of their adventure, Matthew's favorite little girl, the one with the large blue eyes, hastened to him. "Father?"

He lifted the little girl on his lap. "What is it, Julie?"

"Are you going to come home and live with us?"

"Aye, Julie, and I am never leaving again."

She gave him a big hug. "I think I shall like that."

"I, also."

Just then Luke appeared at the door, and looked the chaotic sight over with consternation. He motioned to Matthew, who kissed Julie on the cheek, and put her down. He joined Luke, and pointed to the hall where it might be a little quieter. Luke looked Matthew over with concern.

"You and Pet?"

Matthew smiled and nodded.

"Ah, that is good to hear. I knew the first time I saw you two that you loved each other; you both just did not know it."

"You did not drag me out here to discuss my marriage. What is wrong?"

"Oh, nothing's wrong, at least I do not think so. I have been asked by the king to meet a woman for possible matrimony."

Matthew threw back his head and laughed. "So, you are going to join me in wedded bliss?"

"Inasmuch as your bliss took four months to obtain, I do not know if I am in any hurry."

"Ah, but 'tis worth it, let me tell you! What is this woman like?"

"I have no idea. The king himself asked me to meet with her, apparently the decision is to be hers. Henceforth, I probably have nothing to worry about."

"Do not put yourself down, brother. You will make a fine husband for some fortunate girl. She is probably ugly as a stump with the mind of a mule, and will not know a good man when she sees one."

"Perhaps. Anyway, I am to take my leave, and wanted to say goodbye. I would like to address Pet, but with all those tots…"

"Someday you will have your own tots to contend with, but never fear, I shall rescue Pet and send her out to you for your farewells. Good luck, brother, I wish you happiness." He gave Luke a brotherly hug, and went back to the dining room.

"Children, leave Pet be…she is wanted in the hall," Pet looked at him curiously, but he just motioned, and she left him to fend off the endless barrage of babble coming from the children.

Luke grinned when she came into the hallway. "Pet! I hear you and my worthless brother are finally together!" He reached out and gave his sister-in-law a huge hug.

"Aye, we will be fine. You wanted to see me?"

"I am leaving soon, and wanted to say goodbye. I am going to meet a woman."

Pet grinned and gave him a little jab in the belly. "I knew your time would come. Just promise me not to be pig-headed and take four months to let your wife know you love her."

"I am not Matthew, in more ways than one. I fear I do not have his way with women, and there is no guarantee this woman will even like me."

"Then she is stupid and blind. You will make a fine husband."

"I wish I had your and Matthew's confidence."

"If we can ever help, Luke, in any way, do not hesitate to ask. I feel I have a family again, and I love you all." She leaned up and gave him a kiss on the cheek.

"Thank you, my little sister. I hope the next time we meet I will have good news."

"I have no doubt."

He gave her a big bear hug, and left her. She joined Matthew back in the dining room, where the children had him on the floor, pouncing on him and laughing hysterically, as he pretended feebleness.

"Rosie! Stuart! Honestly Cassie, I expected more of you! Matthew, really! You are encouraging them!"

She tried to break them up, but somehow ended up on the floor herself, with one bouncing on her belly and another on her knee. She cast Matthew a sideways, desperate look. "You were not entertaining thoughts of having any more, were you?"

"Absolutely, at least a dozen. Or, at least we shall have fun in the attempt." He wiggled his eyebrows playfully.

"You are incorrigible."

"I know, and you love me for it."

They finally got the children under control, and servants took them to change clothes. Lady Ellen had a whole day planned, from a picnic, if weather permitted, to music lessons, then a carriage ride to a fair close by. Matthew and Pet had a feeling there was an ulterior motive for the children's busy schedule.

"Well, you never answered my question…do I carry you or do you walk?

"I walk." She took his hand and they practically ran up the stairs. They entered their room, when Matthew suddenly smiled impishly.

"The thought has just occurred to me we are not confined to just this room. There are many rooms in this castle, as well as a lake with a fine beach, and vast fields with tall stalks."

"Your mind is overactive, my husband. I am rather partial to the floor."

"Then the floor 'tis." He swept her up in his arms, and kneeled down, depositing her on top of the blankets still wadded on the floor. "Do not tarry removing your clothes." He quickly undressed, as Pet took her sweet time just to tease him. She was still wearing her tunic when he approached her, fully naked. "You are too slow, woman. Now you will suffer for your ineptness." He pulled the tunic up to her neck, and lay on top of her.

"Matthew! I will suffocate with my clothing wrapped around my neck!"

"'Tis simply keeping your neck warm. Now hush."

Some time later, they ordered a bath, and soaked together in the steaming water. They scrubbed each other's backs with the lilac soap, and then their fronts, which Matthew greatly preferred, and ended up discovering making love in water was quite entertaining.

"A bath will never be the same for me," Matthew sighed. "I shall only take one when you share it."

"I do not have a tub this large at Elton. I wish I did."

"Done! We will take one home with us, there are plenty here in this old castle. Alas, I know that look...*now* what are you thinking?"

"Is it common for a newlywed couple to do this four times in a day's span?"

He appeared deep in thought. "Hmmm. I believe the norm is seven times a day, at least for the first few months, whereupon it settles down to four or five. We are falling way behind, also we have those four months to make up."

"I shall not be able to walk. Matthew, you *are* teasing, are you not?"

He laughed, and pulled her to him. "My mother said something about eating to keep up our strength. Let's get dressed and go for some dinner. I avow mother has prepared quite a feast for us."

A short time later they stood at the stable's entrance, watching William fuss over the ponies to a hapless groom who could not do anything right as far as William was concerned. Matthew nudged Pet in the back.

"Well, go on...you tell him."

She nudged back. "It was your idea, and a fine one. You tell him."

"No, no, you are his aunt, you should tell him."

"But he adores you. It would mean more coming from you."

"My dear, I must insist, you tell him."

A loud clearing of the throat made them look up at William standing in front of them, his arms folded, with a stern expression. "Tell who what?"

"Oh! William! Matthew has something to tell you."

"Me? Now wait a minute!"

"Would one of you just tell me what you are talking about?" William waited patiently.

Matthew finally capitulated to his wife. "William, ah, I wanted to tell you Pet and I are together, for always. Our stupid little fight is o'er."

William smiled broadly. "Finally! It took you two long enough. I know not which of you is the more pig-headed."

"That honor shall go to Matthew, but that is not what we have to tell you, is it *darling*?"

"Er, no. William, we got to thinking, my father is having his attorney draw up the legal adoption papers for the children, so that they will have a legal claim to Elton, and we wondered if perhaps, if you want to, mind you, 'tis totally your decision as you are the oldest and an actual son to…"

"What exactly are you trying to say, Matthew?"

Pet rolled her eyes. "Oh for heavens sakes! He is trying to ask you if you would like to be our son…our real legal son, and heir to Elton."

William's face showed total surprise, then delight. "I would no longer be a bastard?"

"I never considered you such, you know that, but aye, that is what it would mean."

"Aye! Oh, yes, Pet! Thank you Matthew! I love you both!" He practically lunged into their bodies as they all hugged enthusiastically. He pulled away, and looked at Matthew with teary eyes. "I knew the first time I saw you, when Pet threw you into the river, and you ripped off her clothes, that you were special!"

Matthew made a face. "I told you, that was an…oh never mind, I might as well admit I did it on purpose for all the support I get around here."

Later, Matthew was summoned to his father's study. Baron Cameron, still a strikingly handsome man for his age, handed some papers to Matthew to look over.

"You are sure 'tis what you want, son? You do not have to do this."

"I am sure, father. Giving up my claim in Cambridgeshire is necessary. Divide my land between Paul and Luke. The generous monetary inheritance you are giving me will build Elton into a rich and profitable township."

"Does your lady know you do this?"

"No, and she will not. Elton is all that is important to her, and I fully intend to give it all my attentions."

"I have been going o'er this report your giant provided. There are perhaps some ways to improve productivity. Perhaps I shall make some recommendations?"

"Thank you father, that would be good of you."

The Baron looked his eldest son over with pride. "Can this be my reckless, selfish son? Taking on nine orphans, and giving up his own land holdings? You love her much, do you not?"

"More than I can express, father."

"I thank the Lord you met her. I hesitate to think of howe'er you would have faired without her."

"And I, also."

They delayed their departure as long as possible, but the day came when they could delay no more. Elton needed their attentions, and the children were anxious to return with their new ponies. Matthew's father loaned them another carriage and a wagon, to carry a large tub Matthew insisted on taking back with him. The ponies would stay in Cambridgeshire until spring, when they would make the journey to retrieve them. They all said their teary good-byes, as Lady Cameron kissed Pet and her son.

"I will be expecting a grandbaby soon!" she sniffed.

"It shall not be for lack of trying, mother." He turned to his blushing wife, and pointed to the king's carriage. "After you, Milady."

Pet looked confused. "We are riding in that? Matthew, you know how I feel about carriages! I am riding Goliath, and that is that!"

"I think not, wife." He led her by the arm, and opened the carriage. "The children are all riding in the other carriage my father so generously loaned us, and we are riding in this. It has padded seats, and curtains o'er the windows." He gave her a seductive smile. "Get in, and be prepared to be naked most of the trip. We are going to talk, then make love, then start over again. When the trip is completed, we will know all there is to know about each other. We have four months to make up."

Her protests fell on deaf ears as he pushed her into the carriage, following close behind.

"Matthew, you are horrid! I have a feeling we are going to be making up those four months for the rest of our lives!"

"You can count on it my dear, you can count on it."

# Epilogue

Nine Months later
Elton

atthew and Luke paced together in the hallway, stopping occasionally to stare at the door in exasperation. Lady Ellen sat patiently waiting, looking at her sons with amusement.

"This is terrible!" Luke wailed. "I will never live through this, and this is not even my child!"

"You are not much comfort, brother," Matthew lamented. "Mother, this is ridiculous! Why can I not be in the birthing room with my wife! After all, 'tis my baby too!"

"You know perfectly well men are not allowed at the birth. You would only be in the way, and besides, you would probably pass out at the first sign of blood."

"Well, what is taking so long?"

"Babies cannot be rushed, Matthew. It will come in its own time. Now hush, and relax! You will drop dead from fretting."

The two men paced some more, when finally the door opened and Luke's pretty blond wife, Elanna, stuck her head out. A babe's cry could be heard behind her.

"Matthew? 'Tis a boy."

Matthew let out a sigh of relief, and sank in a chair with a huge smile on his face.

"…And a boy."

The smile faded ever so slightly, and he slowly stood back up. Ellen clapped her hands together, and rushed in to see her grandbabies. Luke laughed loudly, and slapped him on the back.

"Two at once, brother! Methinks you tried too hard for a child, if poor Pet is taken to having two at the same time!"

"Is…is she all right?" Matthew asked Elanna.

"Mother and babes are fine. Pet is strong, as you well know, and the births were easy."

"I want to see them, and her! Now!"

"In time, Matthew. Luke, control him! I fear he shall bust down the door. The babes must be cleaned and swaddled. We will call you shortly."

'Shortly' turned out to be much too long, and by the time Matthew was finally let in, he had worked himself up into a fit. One sight of Pet and his twin boys calmed him down. He sat on the edge of the bed and gazed into his wife's eyes. She smiled back, then down at her handsome babies. One was dark-haired, the other blond, like Matthew.

"Are they not beautiful?"

"Aye, they are, but you are even more so." He leaned over and gave her a tender kiss.

Together they watched their sleeping babies, neither wanting to break the spell of the moment. Finally Pet gave an impish smile and caught his gaze.

"I have already named them."

He raised an eyebrow. "Really? Without consulting me? Very well, what names have you given my first-born sons?"

She stroked the head on the dark haired one. "This one is Robert Luke." She took a tiny hand of the blond one, and wrapped it around one of Matthew's fingers. "And this is Mark Paul."

Matthew's eyes welled up, and he leaned over to kiss Pet's forehead. "You are more precious than words can express, and I love you with all my heart."

Her smile faded. "I wish Paul were here to share this moment."

"We will find him, I have not given up hope."

"I know." The news that Paul's ship was found foundered and abandoned off the coast of France had hit the family hard. They were quiet for a few seconds, and then Matthew caught her thoughtful expression.

"Alas, now what?"

"I have been thinking. You once said you wanted a dozen of our own. If I have two at once, I will only have to do this five more times."

He laughed heartily, and kissed her again. "I love you, my Lady Knight."

*Author's note: For Luke and Elanna's story, read *LADY SEER*

Printed in the United States
114258LV00001B/138/A